PRAISE FOR CAROL GOODMAN

"A terrific psychological thriller that will keep readers guessing through every twist."

—*Library Journal* (Starred Review)

"*River Road* is a gripping read with emotion-charged twists and turns that you won't see coming. Carol Goodman creates a heroine who'll linger with you long after you close the book."

—Tess Gerritsen, author of *Playing with Fire*

"Add *River Road* to Carol Goodman's growing resume of frighteningly real suspense novels. Mixing an unreliable narrator with a dead creative writing student and a plethora of suspects in a forbidding setting of snow and ice, Goodman crafts a gripping novel impossible to put down until the shocking reveal on its final pages."

—Robert Dugoni, author of *My Sister's Grave*

"*River Road* is a must-read for mystery novel enthusiasts. Author Carol Goodman's vivid winter setting and surreal imagery enhance this mystery filled with hauntings and troubles of the past and present."

—*San Diego Book Review*

"Goodman expertly melds the psychological thriller and academic mystery into a compelling story of revenge and grief. . . . Believable twists drive *River Road* to a thrilling denouement."

—Associated Press

"The story is filled with unexpected twists. Like drivers on River Road, readers won't be able to see what's around the next corner."

—*The Free Lance-Star*

"With romance folded between scenes of deadly danger, this is an engrossing mystery."

—*Booklist*

"A suspense-filled page-turner. . . . This engrossing novel will keep readers guessing unitil the end, which showcases the resilience of human nature and the will to survive."

—*RT Reviews* (top pick)

"Goodman provides an insightful look at revenge, grief, and rebuilding one's life after a horrific loss."

—*Publishers Weekly*

"Sharp and a page-turner."

—BookReporter.com

"Goodman pushes the needle over into the red zone and keeps it there through page after page of suspense, until it bursts open like a firework in a redemptive conclusion. Longtime Goodman fans, here's our red meat; newcomers, prepare to become longtime fans."

—*Chronogram*

"A thriller that feels so real you literally will shiver along with the characters as they battle the harsh winter cold while trying to solve a murder. . . . Upstate New York Noir . . . *River Road* is a great literary thriller that takes a tragic event on an icy, dark, winding country road and spins it out like great Greek drama."

—*The Book Report Network*

THE LAKE OF DEAD LANGUAGES

"A wonderfully eerie sense of place . . . deeply atmospheric."

—*Los Angeles Times Book Review*

"Like Donna Tartt's *The Secret History* or a good film noir . . . [this book will] keep readers hooked."

—*People* (Page-turner of the Week)

THE SEDUCTION OF WATER

"Truly a seductive reading experience . . . grabs the reader on the first page and holds on for the entire journey."

—*The Denver Post*

"Like the best mysteries, *The Seduction of Water* offers puzzles and twists galore but still tells a human story."

—*The Boston Globe*

"An atmospheric thriller, but a smart one with a racing story line."

—*New York* magazine

"Seduction enchants with its fairy-tale motif and sensuous atmospherics."

—*People*

"Gripping. . . . Entrancing. . . . A completely involving mystery cleverly tied in with several fairy tales."

—*Booklist*

"Goodman establishes herself as a writer to watch in the field of literary thrillers."

—*Library Journal* (starred review)

"Mystery, folklore, a thoroughly modern romance, a strong sense of place, and a winning combination of erudition and accessibility make this second novel a treat."

—*Publishers Weekly*

THE DROWNING TREE

"Deftly plotted and certainly intriguing . . . infused with the sinister aura of its setting . . . *The Drowning Tree* has its twists and shudders."

—*New York Daily News*

"[A] captivating literary mystery of secrets old and new."

—*Publishers Weekly*

"Goodman's early promise comes to full flower in this work. . . . A novel full of surprises."

—*The Denver Post*

ARCADIA FALLS

"Addictive. . . . Goodman delivers an engaging, original story."

—*The Boston Globe*

"Gracefully written and engaging . . . Goodman specializes in atmospheric literary thrillers, and her newest book . . . is an especially fine specimen of its type."

— *The Denver Post*

"[Goodman] gives her many fans a new dose of what she does best: good storytelling, with velvet swaths of Gothic mist and fairy-tale eeriness."

—*The Plain Dealer*

"[A] moving story of mothers and daughters and the hard choices women must make. . . . Goodman combines gripping suspense with strong characters and artistic themes. Those who read Anita Shreve or Jodi Picoult are likely to become fans."

—*Library Journal*

ALSO BY CAROL GOODMAN

The Lake of Dead Languages

The Seduction of Water

The Drowning Tree

The Ghost Orchid

The Sonnet Lover

The Night Villa

Arcadia Falls

THE BLYTHEWOOD SERIES

Blythewood

Ravencliffe

Hawthorn

RIVER ROAD

CAROL GOODMAN

Touchstone

New York London Toronto Sydney New Delhi

Touchstone
An Imprint of Simon & Schuster, Inc.
1230 Avenue of the Americas
New York, NY 10020

First Touchstone paperback edition January 2017

TOUCHSTONE and colophon are registered trademarks of Simon & Schuster, Inc.

For information about special discounts for bulk purchases, please contact Simon & Schuster Special Sales at 1-866-506-1949 or business@simonandschuster.com.

The Simon & Schuster Speakers Bureau can bring authors to your live event. For more information or to book an event, contact the Simon & Schuster Speakers Bureau at 1-866-248-3049 or visit our website at www.simonspeakers.com.

Interior design by Jill Putorti

Manufactured in the United States of America

10 9 8 7 6 5 4 3 2 1

Library of Congress Cataloging-in-Publication Data

Goodman, Carol.
  River Road/Carol Goodman.—First Touchstone hardcover edition.
    pages ; cm
  1. Women college teachers—Fiction. 2. Traffic accident victims—Fiction. 3. Hit-and-run drivers—Fiction. 4. Psychological fiction. I. Title.
  PS3607.O566R58 2016
  813'.6—dc23
        2015012488

ISBN 978-1-5011-0990-4
ISBN 978-1-5011-0991-1 (pbk)
ISBN 978-1-5011-0992-8 (ebook)

To my mother

RIVER
ROAD

CHAPTER ONE

She came out of nowhere.

I was driving back from the faculty Christmas party. I'd had a couple glasses of wine but I wasn't drunk. Distracted, sure, what with Cressida dropping that bombshell and the scene with Ross, but not drunk.

I didn't see her. It was dusk, that dangerous hour when day slides into night and deer steal out of the woods. I've lived here long enough to know that. I've braked a hundred times to watch a doe lead her fawns safely across the road. A lot of people hate the deer. They eat their gardens and carry ticks. But I have always thought they were more beautiful than any garden I could grow and loved them for Emmy's sake, who thought they were as magical as unicorns.

It was on that blind curve just before Orchard Drive. Everyone takes it too fast. I, of all people, should have known that too, but I was distracted and my vision had gone blurry for a moment. I'd lifted my hand off the wheel to wipe my eyes and something hit the bumper. A horrible *thump* I felt in my chest. Then something white scrolling upward like a long scarf unraveling, its body weirdly elongated like one of those cave paintings from the South of France, a hunter's dream of a spirit deer flying across the cosmos—

But when it hit the windshield it was meat and blood and broken glass and I was pulling blind to the shoulder and screaming NO NO NO NO as if I could unscroll time and undo what had happened even as I felt sure that I'd been on a collision course with that deer all day long. Maybe for my whole life.

I don't know how long I screamed and cried like that, probably only a minute, but when I stopped—*Get a grip, Nan!*—it was dark. I turned on the headlights and a half-crumbled stone wall reared up like a tombstone. My car was angled into a ditch, the front right tire lower than the left, the stone wall only inches from my bumper. If I'd braked a few seconds later I'd have gone straight into it. If the deer had leapt out a few feet farther—

The deer. Was it dead? It must be after that impact—

I started shaking again. I could still feel that horrible *thump.*

But what if it wasn't dead? What if it was lying hurt by the side of the road while I sat here feeling sorry for myself—

Get a grip, Nan!

I was still clutching the steering wheel. I felt a laugh bubbling behind my lips. *Typical, Nan, thinking you're still driving when you're stuck in a ditch.* Before the tears could come again I opened the door. The cold air was bracing. *It's supposed to go down to twenty degrees tonight.* Someone said that at the party. Dottie, it had been Dottie, department secretary and earth mother, always watching the weather from her office on the top floor of the Jewett Faculty Tower. Dottie always warned the students to be careful driving home. Her kind, dimpled face rose up in my mind. *Sure you're okay to drive home, Nan? I'm giving Leia a lift and you're on the way. You could come back tomorrow for your car.*

If I'd taken her up on her offer I wouldn't have hit the deer. Maybe *she* would have hit it and then at least it wouldn't have been me.

I cringed at the meanness of the thought. Poor Dottie would be heartbroken if she hit a deer. She had an *I brake for leprechauns* bumper sticker on her ancient VW and posted notices of stray cats on her Facebook page.

Then again, Dottie would have braked for the deer sooner. And if she *had* hit it she'd already be out of the car looking for it and calling the animal rescue hotline, which she probably had programmed onto her phone.

I felt for my phone in my pocket. I could call someone—but who? Dottie? She was probably already home in bed in her flannel nightgown watching *Downton Abbey* reruns and sipping chamomile tea. Ross? His house was only ten minutes up the road. He'd still be up, cleaning up from the party, or perhaps sitting by the fireside with a few straggler students, regaling them with stories of his Harvard days and the famous writers he had known. Still, he'd come. I could imagine his deep, gravelly voice. *Of course we think the world of you, Nan. This wasn't personal.*

No, not Ross. Cressida? Cressida's face swam into view, pity etched on her fine Nordic features, her shield-maiden braids bristling with indignation. *I'm so sorry, Nan, I tried everything I could but the committee went against you. If only you'd listened to me*—No, not Cressida. Not now.

I got out and wobbled on the uneven ground. I braced myself against the car. Had I hit my head? No, the air bag hadn't deployed. It hadn't been that hard an impact. Maybe the deer wasn't dead. Maybe it had run into the woods.

Wounded. Fragile legs broken. Crawling off to die.

I turned around slowly, looking north to where the road disappeared around the sharp bend and then south where it ran straight under tall sycamore trees between old dry-laid stone walls. Then I stared at the ditch where my car had come to rest, and the broken stone wall above it—and recognized just exactly where I was. There was the gatepost to the old Blackwell estate and the drive that climbed steeply through the orchard where deer came out at dusk to eat windblown apples. I'd watched them a hundred times from my own living room window and seen cars coming around the bend too fast, driving straight into the wall—

I shivered and stared back at the wall. Where it was broken someone had painted a white cross. In the spring there were daffodils here—

This place. How many lives had it taken? I should have been driving slower. But there was nothing I could do now. I should have been watching, but the deer was probably okay. I should just go home. Get in bed in a flannel nightgown with a cup of chamomile tea like Dottie—only I'd add a shot of bourbon. I imagined telling Dottie tomorrow that I'd hit a deer. Her first question would be if I'd gone to look for it.

I turned away from the orchard and looked to the right into the woods. That's where the deer—*hurt, scared*—would have gone. I'd go into the woods a little ways. Just to make sure. If the deer was wounded it wouldn't have gone far. If I didn't find it that meant it was all right.

I climbed over the crumbling wall, tearing my stockings and scraping my hands on the rough, cold stones. My thin ballet flats sank into the deep leaf litter and my legs felt wobbly as I walked away from the wall and into the woods. Shock from the accident, I told myself, and from finding myself *here.*

Not from drinking too much. I'd only had a few. I certainly felt completely sober now. But it had been a long day. I'd given my last finals and held extended office hours for students handing in assignments. I'd had to listen to a dozen excuses for late papers: everything from failed printers and crashed hard drives to dead grandparents and bad breakups—a litany of chaos and drama presented as though no one had ever suffered as they had. If they had used half the creativity in the stories they handed in as they did in their excuses they'd be writing masterpieces, I'd wanted to say, but instead I had patiently repeated my late-paper policy and then granted them their extensions. They really did have chaotic lives, some of them. This semester's creative writing class in particular was a bit of a ragtag crew. The class almost hadn't run, but then Dottie had channeled a bunch of transfer students into it and recruited a few older students, like Leia, even though she was really too advanced for it. For which I was grateful—it wouldn't look great for the tenure committee if the class hadn't run—but transfer students were often . . . *volatile.*

There were the working-class kids from Newburgh and Fishkill who'd gone to community college first to save their parents the higher tuition at SUNY Acheron or to pull up their grades—and some valiant older students like Aleesha Williams, a single mom in her twenties who'd struggled up from the projects in Poughkeepsie and was trying to get a teaching degree. But there were also spoiled rich girls like Kelsey Manning, a media arts major from Long Island who'd asked if she could be excused from the final because she wanted to leave early for a ski trip to Vail (I told her no and saw Cressida, in her office across the hall, roll her eyes), and stoners like Troy Van Donk Jr., whose father ran Van's Auto over on 9G and who was spending a few semesters at Acheron dealing drugs to the rich kids from Long Island and sleeping with the Westchester girls hungry for some "real life" experience. He'd had the nerve to email for an extension because of "girlfriend trouble." I'd had half a mind to fail him, but the truth was that even though some of the stories he wrote had a disturbing *violent* vein running through them, he was the best writer in the class. He'd been working on a satire of *The Odyssey* set in the dive bars and projects of Poughkeepsie that had been funny and promising. I wanted to see what he'd done with it.

Lady Bountiful, Evan used to call me.

You're too easy on them, Cressida, whose office across the hall from mine gave her a ringside seat to my student conferences, always said. *You let them walk all over you.*

And it did take a lot out of me, listening to all those stories of heartache and calamity. Even the happy stories were draining—all those hopes and dreams for the future. All that faith that no matter what, things would work out. The last time a student had said to me that she knew everything would work out I had wanted to ask, "Why? Why do you think that?"

So when Leia Dawson came to see me at the end of the day I just couldn't take any more, even though she was my favorite student. My *prize* student. The one who reminded me of myself at her age. I'd had her for Intro to Creative Writing her freshman year and Advanced Fiction Workshop her junior. Leia was the full package—bright, beautiful, talented—and kind to boot. She brought Dottie flowers on her birthday and baked madeleines for workshop when I told them about Proust. She'd taught creative writing in Acheron's Prison Initiative Program for the last two years. For some real life experience, she'd told me. I'd written her a recommendation for grad school and she'd gotten a full ride to Washington University's MFA program. She'd already published in a few journals and won the department's writing prize. Ross had gotten her an internship at his publisher for the summer. I fully expected to see her first novel in a couple of years—and knowing Leia she would remember me in the acknowledgments—but when I saw her hovering in the hallway outside my office I just didn't think I could take listening to more of her bright, shiny plans for the future.

"I've got to run home and change for the party!" I'd called over my shoulder as I passed her in the hallway. "Can we catch up there?"

But the only time I'd seen her at the party was in the kitchen, pouring a glass of wine for Ross when I'd tracked him down to ask him if it was true that I'd been denied tenure—

I stumbled over a rock and grabbed a pine trunk to steady myself. *Denied tenure.* The words thudded in my head with the same finality as the thud of the deer against my car. It wasn't just that I had been denied tenure, it was knowing that I'd have to *leave.* No one stayed on after being denied tenure. It was pathetic. I might even be fired. And then where would I go?

I looked around me as if I could find the answer to my question in my current surroundings. I'd come farther than I'd meant to and the woods were turning dark—*lovely, dark and deep,* as Frost was no doubt quoted in half the Intro Lit essays lying on the backseat of my car.

Maybe that's why I was here tonight. I'd been led here by that deer to this place to watch these woods fill up with snow—yes, Dottie had been right, it *was* snowing—on the darkest night of the year. It was the solstice, I remembered with a chill that had only a little to do with the dropping temperature. Dottie had mentioned it at the party. John Abbot, who taught the gothic novel and twentieth-century horror fiction, had made a *woo-woo* noise and reminded us all that the Victorian tradition of reading ghost stories on Christmas Eve came from the belief that the solstice was when the dead were supposed to walk. Joan Denning, an adjunct who taught ghost stories to her ESL students, said that one of her students had just handed in a paper on our own local ghost, Charlotte Blackwell, who always appeared on the winter solstice seeking a blood sacrifice for her daughter who had drowned in the Hudson. Dottie, who hated ghost stories, had covered her ears and Cressida had given Joan a nudge and a meaningful look at me to shut her up and Joan had blushed scarlet. I shivered now, but not with cold or fear. I'd already made my sacrifices. What more could this place take from me? If the dead were walking in this snowy wood I'd wait for them here. I sank down onto the ground, leaned against the tree, the bark rough against my back, and looked up at the snow sifting through pine needles, a half-moon caught in tangled branches, so bright I closed my eyes against it . . .

. . . and drifted off for a few moments. Long enough to have the dream. Someone shouting *Come back!*

Me. I was the one shouting *Come back!* to Emmy as she ran down the hill, the lights of her sneakers flashing red through the grass, her childish laughter cut short by a screech of tires . . . a shrill, heartbreaking cry.

I startled awake, my face wet as it always was when I awoke from the nightmare. The nightmare of Emmy run over on River Road. The worst ones were when I saw her running from the house and I looked up from my desk in time to call her back—

Come back!

—and save her.

But I hadn't saved her in this dream. I'd heard the screech of tires and her startled, surprised cry just as I had on that day. I wiped my face. My tears were ice water. My lap was full of snow. It must have been in the teens. The alcohol in my blood—not that I'd had *that much* to drink—had probably lowered my core temperature. How long had I been asleep? If I stayed here much longer I would freeze to death.

It was supposed to be a gentle way to die. You felt warm at the end, like in that story by Jack London. . . .

I shook myself and looked around at the woods. What a pathetic way to go—half drunk (maybe I really had had a little too much to drink), freezing to death . . . *because I didn't get tenure?* That's what people would say. That I was so upset at not getting tenure that I drove off the road, stumbled into the woods, and froze to death.

Well, screw that. So I hadn't gotten tenure. After all that had happened to me—

Emmy running down the hill, sneaker lights flashing, a voice crying Come back!

—I wasn't going to let a tenure decision be the thing to undo me. I could ask to stay on while I appealed the decision. I was a good teacher. I had great evaluations. And if I didn't get the decision appealed I could apply to other colleges. I still had a chance—maybe that's why I had dreamed about Emmy. The time to save her was gone but there was still time enough to save myself. To get myself back on my feet.

So that's what I did. I got to my feet, shook the snow off my coat, and walked out of the dark woods and back to the road.

It was snowing so hard I might not have found my way back without my headlights shining dimly through the snow. My shoes were soaked and my feet numb by the time I scrambled back over the stone wall. I paused for a moment there to clear the snow from the stone and found the painted cross. Someone had painted it after Emmy died. For a while people had left flowers and candles here but I never had. I didn't want Emmy to be remembered as the little girl who had died at the side of a road in a ditch.

Eventually they had stopped leaving flowers.

I was careful to step over the snow-covered ditch getting into my car, but when I pulled out the left tire got stuck and I had a bad moment thinking I'd have to call Van's and explain to Troy Van Donk Sr. what I was doing out on the river road in a snowstorm, soaking wet, breath smelling of wine, but then with a lurch and a sickening grinding against my poor old car's underbelly I cleared the snow-filled ditch and fishtailed out onto the road.

The snow was coming down heavy now and there was no sign that the plows had been out. I crept down River Road with my high beams on and my hazard lights blinking, white-knuckling the steering wheel and leaning forward to peer through my cracked windshield—*crap, what was that going to cost?*—into dizzying snow eddies. I barely got up Orchard Drive. I knew I'd never make it up my impractically steep driveway. A little farther up the road was a turnaround that the trucks from the old orchard used to use and where Acheron students parked to make out or hike into the woods to explore the old abandoned buildings on the Blackwell estate. No one was there tonight. I pulled in far enough so my car wouldn't get hit by a plow and hiked up my driveway to my house, my feet so numb I couldn't feel them by the time I got to my front door.

Oolong, my ancient Siamese, screamed indignantly and threw her bony body at my feet as soon as I walked in. I apologized profusely as I dumped a can of Fancy Feast into her bowl. I got the bourbon out of the cabinet but then I remembered my resolution in the woods. Maybe I *had* been drinking too much. Not that that had anything to do with hitting the deer—no one could have helped that—but yelling at Ross hadn't been the smartest move.

I made myself a cup of tea instead and added milk and sugar—for shock, as people were always saying in British novels. I'd certainly had my share of shocks today. I sat down on the living room couch to collect myself a little before tackling the rotting farmhouse stairs up to my bedroom. It really had been an awful day.

Is it true? I'd demanded of Ross when I'd burst into the kitchen (startling Leia, who had been pouring wine, so that she spilled it on Ross's wrist and then scurried out). *I'm sorry, Nan.* He'd turned away to unbutton his shirt cuff and run cold water over the wine stain so he wouldn't have to look me in the eye. *I didn't want you to find out like this. Cressida shouldn't have said anything.*

But Cressida had told me because she was my friend—my best friend in the department. Since her office was right across the hall from mine we couldn't help but hear each other's student conferences. *Can you believe they still don't know what a dangling modifier is?* I'd moan after a student left. *Don't believe that story about the dead grandmother,* she'd say after a student had wept for ten minutes in my office, *she told me that last year when she was in my Women's Lit class.* So when I'd asked Cressida what had happened in the committee she had only hesitated a moment before breaking down and telling me.

I'm so sorry, Nan, I tried everything I could but the committee went against you. If only you'd listened to me—

She was right. A year ago, when Cressida was up for tenure, she told me that it had made a big difference that she'd just gotten a contract for a new book. I really needed to at least have something under way. She even offered to make an introduction to her editor, but I hadn't taken her up on her generous offer and now I'd repaid her with getting her in trouble with Ross. I'd have to tell him it hadn't been her fault that she'd told me. If I hadn't completely blown things with Ross. Snatches of things I'd said to him in the kitchen were coming back to me. I'd accused him of sabotaging my chances because I'd broken off with him six and a half years ago. Shit. How many people had heard that? How many people were gossiping about me right now? *Poor Nan, did you hear she threw a fit at the Christmas party because she didn't get tenure? Did you know she had an affair with Ross Ballantine? It must have been right after her daughter . . .*

I reached for my tea and upset a stack of papers that slid down onto the floor like a sheet of snow coming off a steep-pitched roof. My living room was a mess. I was a mediocre housekeeper at best and got worse as the semester went on. Half-full teacups tottered on stacks of books. A fine layer of dust and cat hair floated in the air. I'd clean up tomorrow while grading papers. And then I'd write a letter to the tenure committee. I would demand to know the basis for being denied. I had good student evaluations and had published an award-winning novel . . .

But nothing for over six years. Nothing since Emmy.

. . . but I had an idea for something now. Something about hitting that deer. I'd start on it tomorrow. After a good night's sleep. I stretched out on the couch and closed my eyes. I'd rest up a little before climbing the stairs—*I'd call someone in the morning to fix them*—and fell asleep.

In my dream I was sitting at my desk watching Emmy run down the snow-covered hill toward the road. I knew it was all right because the day Emmy had died had been in spring and the apple trees had been in bloom. She was picking daffodils. The best ones grew down on the edge of the road on the other side of the stone wall. She knew she wasn't allowed to climb over the wall. I'd overheard Evan whisper to her that they would pick flowers for me for Mother's Day when he got home from work. She must have gotten tired of waiting. When I found her she was clutching a handful of daffodils. The smell of daffodils and apple blossoms still makes me sick. But in the dream it was all right because it was winter so this wasn't the day. *I had time.* I lowered my head to my laptop. I was writing my second novel, the one that I would never finish . . .

Come back!

A screech of tires . . . a scream . . . and then . . . *thump.*

I startled awake, the remembered impact of the deer hitting my car reverberating in my chest. It was morning, the living room full of that morning-after-the-first-snow kind of light that for a moment made me feel hopeful—like a child waking up to a world transformed. A new beginning. A clean slate. That's what I had promised myself in the woods. I was going to appeal the tenure decision, clean my house, cut back on my drinking. . . .

Something thumped against the front door. For a moment I had the horrible thought that it was the deer throwing itself at my door in vengeance for hitting it and leaving it for dead in the woods. But then I heard the noise again, and the creak of the loose floorboard on the front porch, and realized it was someone knocking at the door.

"Coming," I shouted, getting groggily to my feet. It was probably Dottie, stopping by on her way to work, come to see if I was all right. Dear Dottie, I should take her out to lunch over break. Or it was Cressida, who could have seen my car parked in the turnaround on her way in to work and wondered if I was okay. Or Ross, come to say it had all been a terrible mistake. He'd already talked to the tenure committee and they'd reversed their decision—

It wasn't Dottie, Cressida, or Ross. It was a police officer, his uniformed bulk looking too big for my doorway, breathing cold into the room. His bland, broad face and dark, thickly lashed eyes looked vaguely familiar. I thought for a second maybe I'd had him as a student but I realized he was too old.

"Hi," I said, pulling my cardigan over my blouse to cover up the fact I wasn't wearing a bra. "Can I help you, Officer?"

"Nancy Lewis?"

"I'm Nan Lewis."

"Is that your car parked on the side of the road? The one with the broken headlight?"

Crap. "Yes, is it in the way, Officer"—I peered at his name badge—"Sergeant McAffrey? I couldn't get it up the driveway in the snow last night so I pulled into the turnaround so it would be out of the way of the snowplows. I was going to take it to Van's when I got dressed." I saw his eyes roving over the disarray of my living room, lingering on the bourbon bottle on the kitchen counter, disapproval in his eyes. Well, fuck that. Who was he to judge me?

"Look, I had a crappy night last night. I hit a deer on my way home from the English faculty party. So if you're going to ticket me for a broken headlight . . ."

He turned his cold, disapproving eyes on me. "I'm not here about a broken headlight, Ms. Lewis. I'm here about a hit and run—a student at the college named Leia Dawson. She was found dead on the river road this morning."

CHAPTER TWO

"No," I said, gripping the edge of the door to steady myself, "you must be mistaken. Dottie drove Leia home last night."

"Dottie?"

"Dorothy Cooper, the English Department secr—administrative assistant. Call her. She'll straighten this out." Dottie could straighten anything out, I started to tell him, but then my stomach flipped over and I realized I was about to be sick.

"Excuse me," I managed. I fled to the downstairs half-bath off the kitchen and emptied my stomach of the red wine and three mini quiches I'd had last night. I rinsed out my mouth and looked at myself in the mirror. Mascara under my eyes, hair a rat's nest. *Do rats have nests?* Emmy had once asked me when I used the expression. I finger-combed it back into a sloppy bun and scrubbed the mascara off with soap and cold water. It couldn't be Leia dead, I told myself, but it must be someone.

When I came back the cop was standing at the kitchen counter looking at the bourbon bottle. I wanted to explain that I hadn't had any when I got home last night but then that would sound like I *usually* had a drink when I got home, so I said nothing. He straightened up when I came into the room. His head almost touched the low farmhouse ceiling. I cleared off the nicest chair for him and sat down on the couch, pulling the afghan over my lap. "Why do you think it's Leia?" I asked. "Because of her ID? You know they all use fake IDs to drink at the Black Swan."

"I'm familiar with the underage drinking problem at the Swan," he said. He was still standing. Looking up at him was making me feel sick again. "But I'm afraid there's no doubt about the identity of the girl. Your department head identified her this morning."

"Ross?" My voice sounded shrill and foreign. "My God, he must be devastated. Leia was his favorite student—mine too. Was he absolutely sure?"

"Dr. Ballantine made a positive ID and verified that Ms. Dawson was at his residence last night for the faculty Christmas party. You were there too."

I looked up at him, not sure if it was a question or a statement. "Would you please sit down? I promise the chair is cleaner than it looks."

He blushed, which made him look younger—maybe he *had* been in one of my classes. There was a criminal justice program at the college that local cops took sometimes, but it clearly wasn't the right time to ask him. "Yes, I was at the party. I saw Leia in the kitchen talking to Ross."

Leia, swiveling her swanlike neck as I burst in, spilling red wine onto Ross's wrist, her big blue eyes wide and startled. Those blue eyes that stood out even more since she'd cut her waist-length black hair short at Thanksgiving. She'd lost weight too, and there were dark rings under her eyes, which I'd assumed came from late-night studying. I covered my mouth at the image of those eyes frozen in a death stare. Could it really be true? Was Leia really dead? I found a tissue in my cardigan pocket and wiped my eyes. "But Dottie said she was driving her home."

"Ms. Cooper apparently was unable to locate her and assumed she'd gotten a lift from someone else. She suggested you as a possibility since you left shortly after Ms. Cooper saw Leia leaving the kitchen. Do you remember what time that was?"

"When I saw Leia in the kitchen?" I was shaking my head, but then I recalled the view out Ross's kitchen window. You couldn't see the river from his house but there was a beautiful view of the Catskills on the other side. A couple of students had been sitting on the stone wall next to the old barn Ross used as a garage, black silhouettes against the setting sun, except one who stood out because her red leather jacket caught the sun and glowed like a burning ember.

"The sun was going down over the mountains," I said, "so what time is sunset these days? Four thirty? I left soon after and it was dusk when I was driving home. You know how it's hard to see at dusk. A deer ran right in front of my car on the bend before Orchard Drive—"

"You didn't see Ms. Dawson walking on River Road when you left Dr. Ballantine's residence?"

"No. If I had I would have offered her a lift. She's one of my favorite students—" I gasped, all of Leia's bright future rising up in front of me—the prizes, the MFA, the novels she would never write now—how was it possible that all of that could be extinguished overnight? "I'm sorry," I said when I could talk again. "This is a lot to take in. You say she was hit on River Road? But she wasn't found until this morning? Who . . . ?"

"A plow driver. He saw her boots sticking up out of the snow—"

I pictured bright yellow rain boots, but no, Leia had worn red cowboy boots. And a red leather jacket. A tough-girl look she'd affected since she had started teaching at the prison.

"She was lying in three inches of snow and covered with a foot more so we think she was hit after it started snowing—around five p.m."

"It wasn't snowing when I left the party," I said, "or when I hit the deer. It started snowing later, when I was in the woods."

"In the woods?"

"Yes, I went to look for the deer."

He smiled for the first time since I'd opened my door to him. Two curved lines, like parentheses, framed his wide mouth when he smiled, making his whole face look softer. "Why?" he asked.

"Sorry . . . ?"

"Why'd you go look for the deer?"

"In case it was hurt."

"And what would you have done if you'd found it?"

"Um . . . I'm not sure . . . I just had to see. . . ."

"And did you find it?"

"No," I admitted. "So I suppose it was okay."

"Uh-huh," he said, flipping open a notepad. "So you say it started snowing when you were in the woods and then you went back to your car when you didn't find the deer?"

First I sat down in the snow and had myself a little cry and a nap. "I hiked around a bit."

"In those?" He bent his eyes down to the floor where I'd kicked off the velvet ballet slippers I'd worn to the party last night. I picked them up. They were still damp. Ruined.

"I guess it wasn't very practical of me but I felt bad."

"About the deer?"

"Yeah, I didn't even see her—"

"You didn't *see* the deer?" He looked up from his notebook, eyes narrowing, jaw hardening. "Then how do you know it *was* a deer?"

He held my gaze. His eyes, which I'd taken for black at first, were actually a deep brown with flecks of gold in them. Looking into them was like staring into those eddies of snow through my windshield last night. Dizzying and cold. I drew the afghan up over my chest.

"I meant, I didn't see it until it was right in front of my car and then it was too late to stop. It's dark on the river road. The town ought to put up lights on it. I always tell my students not to walk on it at night. Poor Leia—"

"And you came right home after looking for the deer?"

"Yes. I couldn't get up my driveway so I parked in the turnaround. I went to sleep early." *I didn't even have a drink.* "I'd had a long day—teaching, holding office hours, then the party. . . ."

"And how much did you have to drink at the party?"

He slipped the question in so stealthily that I was already saying

"Not much, a glass or two" before I could stop myself. "Why? Why are you asking me that?"

He looked up, his face carefully blank. "We've had a hit and run, Ms. Lewis. Hit and *run*. That means the driver didn't stop, didn't report it, left Ms. Dawson to die on the side of the road. We're looking for the driver. You were driving home around the time Leia Dawson was hit. Your car was left on the side of the road with visible damage to the front left bumper. You were drinking—"

"Only a glass!"

"Or two."

"I hit a deer."

"That you didn't see and couldn't find."

I stared at him. He wasn't smiling now. His mouth was hard, his eyes unreadable. "Should I call a lawyer?"

He shrugged, his shoulders rolling under his jacket with a smoothness that suggested a hidden reserve of strength. "That depends"—he put his notepad away, braced his hands on his knees, and leaned forward to get up—"on what we find on your car."

I pulled on rubber boots over my bare feet and followed him down my unplowed driveway and across the road to the turnaround through shin-deep snow. We'd gotten over a foot. The snow lay on the top and trunk of my car, but had been cleared off the hood. A narrow strip had been shoveled around the front tires, where a police officer knelt taking pictures. In the bright sunlight the damage looked worse than it had last night, the left side of the hood crumpled. A flatbed tow truck was idling on Orchard Drive, its exhaust pluming blue in the cold, still air.

"You're going to take my car?"

"After the initial forensics, yes—"

"Don't you need a warrant to confiscate my property?"

"A damaged car in the vicinity of a hit and run constitutes probable cause." The cop smiled at me. "I learned that at your college in Intro to Criminal Justice."

"I'm calling my lawyer," I said, taking my cell phone out of my pocket.

"That's probably wise, Ms. Lewis," he said more kindly, which scared me worse than when he'd been mean. "And look, if we find deer fur and blood and no trace of Leia Dawson on your car you'll be in the clear."

My stomach turned at the words *trace of Leia Dawson*. He must have seen it on my face.

"We just want to find the person who hit that girl and left her for dead in the road. You of all people must understand that." His face softened and he looked like he was going to say something else, but then the other police officer called his name—*Joe*—and as he turned I suddenly remembered him. He was the officer who'd responded when Emmy was hit.

He said excuse me—he'd been polite that morning too—and walked toward the cop who was crouched in front of my left front tire. As he knelt down next to the cop, I remembered him kneeling beside me on the road all those years ago. The paramedics wanted to take Emmy but I was still holding her hand. The police officer—*Joe*—had knelt down beside me in the mud and laid his hand over mine. I remembered that the warmth of his flesh had shocked me and that when I turned to him his face had been as white as Emmy's. *Why, he's so young*, I'd thought, *only a boy himself*.

He was leaning forward now, looking at something in a plastic bag that the other cop was holding up for him. When he got up all of the softness in his face was gone and he looked like he'd aged way more than six years since that morning when he'd knelt down beside me in the mud.

"You're going to have to come down to the station now, ma'am."

"But why? I told you, I hit a deer."

"We've found blood and white wool fibers in your tire. The fibers look like a match for the scarf Leia Dawson was wearing last night."

CHAPTER THREE

McAffrey let me get my coat and make a phone call but when I asked if I could shower and change he said he'd prefer I didn't, his face hard, no trace of the young officer who'd comforted a bereaved mother.

"Can I at least go to the bathroom?" I asked, feeling like a child. A scared child.

He nodded, embarrassed, and blushed when I plucked my bra out of the sofa cushions. I did too, but I didn't want to sit in a police station without a bra.

I called my college roommate, Anat Greenberg, who was a lawyer with a practice in Poughkeepsie, from the bathroom. She made me repeat everything twice. I could hear McAffrey shifting his weight over a creaky floorboard on the other side of the door.

"So he hasn't arrested you?" Anat asked.

"No. No one's read me my rights or anything."

"Okay, so they must not have enough evidence. Listen, Nan, there's a lot of pressure in these cases to make an arrest. Don't answer any questions until I get there."

I told her I wouldn't and flushed the toilet even though I'd been too nervous to pee. Then I ran cold water over my hands until they stopped shaking. I wished I could brush my teeth but the brush was in the upstairs bathroom.

When I stepped out I saw McAffrey had retreated to the living room. He was standing at the desk underneath the window that looked out over the front lawn. It was piled high with books and folders. I hadn't sat at that desk since the day Emmy died. He looked up from a copy of *The Odyssey* I'd used in the Great Books class I'd taught this semester and it was on the tip of my tongue to make a comment—like, *do you like Greek literature?*—but when I saw his face I closed my mouth. The time for idle pleasantries had passed when he saw that blood on my tires.

He motioned for me to walk in front of him and I followed him down my unplowed driveway to his patrol car. He opened the back door for me and I got in, feeling like a suspect in a cop show. I stared through the thick bulletproof glass barrier between the front and back seats and felt like I was underwater looking up through a glaze of ice. When I looked out the side window I saw that my car was already gone. He made a U-turn in the turnaround, drove down the steep hill, and made a right on River Road, heading toward town. A flash of yellow caught my eye as we turned. I looked back through the rear window and saw another police car and yellow tape flapping from the old stone wall. I stared at it until the road curved and I couldn't see it anymore. When I turned back in my seat I caught McAffrey's eyes watching me in the rearview mirror.

"Is that where you found Leia?" I asked.

"Uh-huh." His voice was flat. He was still looking at me in the mirror, studying me as if expecting me to break down at the scene of the crime.

"That's where Emmy died," I said.

"I remember," he said. "It's a bad curve. Poor visibility. People take it too fast. Maybe you came around it too fast and didn't see Ms. Dawson—"

"It was a deer!" I said, shutting my eyes so I didn't have to see the cold look in his eyes. I felt that horrible *thump* and saw the white underbelly of the deer flying toward me. It had looked like a long white scarf—like the one Leia had been wearing. *Could it have been Leia I hit?*

But no, I'd looked up and down the road for the deer. *Hadn't I?* I remembered that I'd been a little unsteady on my feet. But I hadn't been drunk. I'd have seen Leia lying on the road. And when I came back—

When I came back the ground was covered with snow, so much snow that I'd barely gotten out of the ditch—

The patrol car came to a sudden stop and I remembered the lurch of my car last night and the grinding noise it had made when I backed out of the ditch. Bile rose in my throat. I opened my eyes and met McAffrey's gaze in the mirror.

"I think I know what happened," I said.

Although Anat had warned me not to talk until she got there I could barely wait until we were in the interview room to tell my story to Sergeant McAffrey and his colleague Detective Stan Haight, a heavy man with a thick mustache who *did* look young enough to be one of my students. I wanted to clear everything up. I wanted to erase that flat, cold look in McAffrey's eyes.

"When I pulled off the road after hitting the deer I went into the ditch. My left tire cleared the ditch but my right tire was stuck in it." I demonstrated with my hands how the car had come to rest unevenly. "When I came back from looking for the deer the ground was covered with snow. I could barely get my car out—the left tire went into the ditch. . . ." I swallowed hard to keep down the bile that rose every time I thought about that sickening lurch and horrible grinding sound. "Don't you see, Leia was *in* the ditch. I ran over her backing out."

I wiped my eyes with the back of my hand and looked around for a box of tissues. There was none. There was nothing useful or comforting in this room. The fever-yellow paint was water-stained and peeling. There was an old poster about AIDS prevention. The air smelled like sweat and burnt coffee. The two men across the scarred table stared blankly at me for a moment and then exchanged a quick look—some kind of prearranged signal that indicated who should talk. Detective Haight won.

"Let me get this straight," he said, spreading his hands out, palms up. "You're saying that after you hit"—he made air quotes with his fingers—"'the deer' you pulled over into a ditch. Then you went into the woods to look for the deer, which you didn't find, and while you were in the woods someone *else* hit Leia Dawson in the same exact location. She landed *under* your front left tire. When you came back you didn't see her because so much snow had fallen and you backed up over her?"

He leaned a little closer to me with each emphasized word until his face was only inches from mine and I could smell stale coffee and something sweet, like maple syrup, on his breath. I had to force myself not to push my chair back to get away from the smell, which was making me feel even sicker.

"Yes," I said, "I know it sounds . . . unlikely." The right side of Detective Haight's mouth twitched in a poorly suppressed sneer. "But that's what must have happened. I hit a deer, not Leia. I *looked* for the deer. If Leia had been lying there I'd have seen her."

"Because there wasn't any snow on the ground when you went into the woods," Sergeant McAffrey said almost gently.

"Right."

"But there was so much snow on the ground when you came back that Leia Dawson's body was covered by it?" Detective Haight asked.

"Yes. It started snowing when I went into the woods."

"And how long were you in the woods?" Haight asked.

"I-I'm not sure. I sat down for a bit."

"You sat down?" Haight asked, his eyes sliding toward his colleague. But McAffrey didn't meet his amused glance. He was staring straight at me, a look of sorrow on his face, as if I'd personally disappointed him. The look I'd wanted to banish from his face had only set harder, like quick-drying cement. I remembered now that when he'd looked up from Emmy's body and met my eyes he'd told me he was going to find the bastard who had done this.

"I was tired," I said. "It had been a long day. Finals, conferencing with students, the faculty party . . ."

"Where you'd had how much to drink?"

"Just a glass."

"Or two," McAffrey added. I was beginning to think maybe I shouldn't have spoken until Anat got here.

"I don't think I should answer any more questions until my lawyer gets here."

Detective Haight made a sound in the back of his throat—something between a snort and a guffaw. "Your call, Ms. Lewis. Interview terminated . . ." He said the time into the tape recorder and pushed his chair back from the table. The metal legs dragging over the linoleum floor sounded like the underbelly of my car scraping against the ground last night and this time I could almost see Leia's blood smearing over the snow.

McAffrey led me back through the waiting room. I looked to see if Anat had arrived but instead I saw Kelsey Manning shifting her two-hundred-dollar-a-pair True Religion jeans–clad behind in a cheap plastic chair, chewing the ends of her waist-length ironed hair.

"Professor Lewis, what are you doing here?"

I could have asked her the same thing. Earlier today she had made it sound like she had to get off campus before the final so she could leave for Vail. "I'm just—"

"Aiding the police in our inquiries," McAffrey smoothly supplied. I stared at him, surprised he was trying to spare me the embarrassment of telling my student I was a suspect.

"Really? Did you see it happen? Can you give me a quote?" She turned to McAffrey. "I work for *Vox Pop*, that's our campus paper, it means—"

"Voice of the People," McAffrey said. "I took eight years of Latin. And I'm familiar with the campus paper. I read the piece on 'police brutality' when we detained one of your classmates for trying to buy liquor with a fake ID."

"Oops," Kelsey said with an engaging smile and a tilt of her slim hips. "Our bad. But I didn't write that. I know that boy—he's an ass. Can you give me a quote, Officer"—she stood on tiptoe to read McAffrey's brass name tag—"McCafferty. I'll make sure I spell your name right and make you look good."

"Sergeant *McAffrey* doesn't need you to make him look good," I told Kelsey. "When my daughter was killed in a hit and run six years ago he found who did it. He'll find who did this too."

Kelsey's eyes widened and she licked her shiny gelled lips. "Is that why you're here, Professor Lewis, because you have a personal connection to the tragedy? Do you think it could be the same person who did it? Like a serial drunk driver?"

"That's enough," McAffrey barked. "Ms. Lewis is here to answer our questions, not yours."

He placed his hand on my elbow and propelled me forward. I saw Kelsey's eyes, which I thought were as wide as three coats of Maybelline could get them, widen to the size of manga princess proportions. When I looked back I saw her bent over her phone, furiously double-thumb typing.

"For a college professor you're pretty stupid," McAffrey said when he brought me to a windowless room that looked like it was once a supply closet.

"I beg your pardon!"

"You gave that girl all the ammunition she needed to write a damning story about you."

"I was just trying to speak up for you."

"As you said, I don't need anyone to make me look good. You're the one in deep shit here, Ms. Lewis. That story about going into the woods and falling asleep while Leia was hit by someone else—" He shook his head, his jaw clenched so tight I could see the muscle throb. Then he turned on his heel and walked out the door, slamming it behind him.

*　　　*　　　*

Anat came half an hour later. "I told you not to talk until I got here," she said firmly after giving me a hug. Anat had spent her summers in Israel and her winters in the Bronx. Her curly brown hair had started going gray at thirty and she refused to color it on principle. The white streaks, flaring out from her temples, made her look like an avenging comic-book action figure. She'd spent most of our time together in college telling me I thought too well of people. She'd stopped that after Emmy died.

"When I realized what must have happened I thought I could clear everything up," I said. She rolled her eyes. "I see now that was a mistake."

Her lip quirked, she tried to rein it in, but lost the battle and snorted. *I see now that was a mistake* was what we'd say to each other after misspent nights mixing tequila and rum.

"Okay," she said more gently. "Tell me this story."

I told her what I'd told McAffrey and Haight. She made me repeat it twice, then she repeated it back to me. She didn't use air quotes or ironic emphasis but I could tell she wasn't happy. "It's a big coincidence," she pointed out, "and I don't like the time lapse in the woods. It sounds like you passed out drunk—" Her eyes slid away from me and I remembered that the last time we'd gotten together I'd had a few too many glasses of wine over dinner. *Hey, we're not in college anymore!* she'd joked, but the next time she'd called she had asked if maybe I shouldn't *rein it in* a bit. I'd told her that it was just being with her that had made me have those few extra . . . memories of our misspent youth and she'd laughed. But now I saw a flicker of doubt in her eyes as she looked back at me. "How much *did* you have to drink?"

"One, maybe two glasses of wine. I wasn't drunk; I was tired and angry." I told her about not getting tenure.

"That sucks, Nan. I know how much you love teaching. But they'll make out you drank more because you were pissed."

"Who will make out?" I asked, my skin feeling icy. "Do you think they're going to arrest me? Won't they leave me alone when they find out who really hit Leia?"

"*If* they find the real perpetrator. Right now they think they've got her. Look," she added, seeing the tears in my eyes, "I'm going to go talk to the boys in charge. Stay put"—her eyes roved around the room, lighting on a stack of toner cartons—"and try to stay out of trouble."

She was gone forty minutes. I wished I'd brought papers to grade or a book to read. I tried getting internet on my phone but there was no cell phone service and the police Wi-Fi was password protected. I scrolled through old phone messages. I'd gotten five calls this morn-ing—one from Ross, one from Cressida, three from Dottie.

When Anat came back her face looked grim but she put on a smile for me. "I've got good news and bad news," she said. She didn't ask me which I wanted to hear first. "The good news is they're releasing you. As I pointed out to the hunky Sergeant McAffrey, the evidence is circumstantial. The forensic evidence isn't in yet. They haven't gotten back the DNA report on the blood or analysis of Leia's clothing. The fi-bers they found in the tires could have gotten there anywhere, anytime. They don't have a witness to the hit and run, you have no previous offenses, and you're an upstanding member of the college community who suffered her own tragedy in this very town."

I nodded at each point feeling a small glimmer of hope prickling my skin. I noticed that she hadn't said anything about my story or the like-lihood that the blood on my tires *would* match Leia Dawson's. "What's the bad news?" I asked.

The smile disappeared from Anat's face. "The bad news is they have a witness from the faculty party who says you were drunk and belliger-ent and that you were heard coming out of the kitchen yelling at your department chair that if you couldn't teach anymore you might as well go drive to the Kingston Bridge and throw yourself in the river."

CHAPTER FOUR

"I didn't mean it," I said for the fourth or fifth time on the drive back to my house.

"I should hope not," Anat said, her eyes fixed to the road as she took each icy curve like a personal affront. "Because it would be a shitty thing to do to the people who love you. It would be a shitty thing to do to *me*. It's not like I didn't worry after Emmy . . . and then when Evan left and then the last time I saw you I noticed that you were drinking more . . ."

"I haven't. I swear I didn't have that much to drink. Two glasses tops." It was true I'd only filled my glass two times, but hadn't Cressida topped off my glass when she was telling me about the tenure decision? I'd been so upset I hadn't been paying attention.

Anat didn't reply. I thought because she didn't believe me, but then I noticed she was leaning forward in her seat and slowing down. "Is that it?" she asked. "Is that where it happened?"

A scrap of yellow still fluttered from the stone wall but the police car was gone. "Yes, it's where Emmy was hit too."

"Damn, the town should lower the speed limit, put up a sign."

I didn't point out that she'd been driving ten miles over the limit. She pulled over to the shoulder, put on her flashers, and got out. "Come on," she called when I didn't get out right away. "Walk me through it."

The last thing I wanted to do was stand in that spot that had claimed Emmy and now Leia. Maybe it was cursed. Maybe all the traffic signs and blinking lights in the world couldn't stop people from dying here. But I followed Anat because I knew she would stand there, hands on hips, shivering in her thin suit jacket, until I did.

"Show me what happened," she ordered.

I started walking around the curve but a car came around going too fast and I stepped into the ditch, hugging the stone wall. I noticed a SUNY Acheron sticker on the sports car as it sped up River Road. Students blowing out of town for the winter break.

"Shit," Anat swore, "this is a death trap."

I shivered at the expression but agreed. "You can't see anything until you come around the wall there. The deer leapt out from the opposite side of the road. I didn't see it until I hit it. Then I pulled over to the side . . . here . . . I almost hit the wall." I showed her how my tires had angled in the ditch, trying not to look *in* the ditch. Would there still be blood? The thought of Leia lying there made my knees weak. I looked instead at the stone wall and saw that someone had swept away the snow and placed a candle there. It was one of those saint candles they sold in the Mexican grocery in town. Something yellow fluttered next to it—an offering at the shrine—but it wasn't police tape as I'd first thought. I took a step closer, my boots sinking into the snow, and saw that it was a bouquet of yellow daffodils.

Anat took me home, bulldozing up my driveway in her four-wheel drive Subaru as if the snow was beneath her notice. "Get some rest," she told me, "you look awful."

I didn't try to explain why the daffodils made me feel sick. She'd tell me that half the supermarkets and convenience stores in a twenty-mile radius sold daffodils. That they didn't have anything to do with Emmy.

"I was supposed to go into school to pick up papers," I said instead.

"No!" she barked. "Get someone to drop those papers off, that secretary you're friendly with—"

"Dottie," I said. "Oh, poor Dottie! She must be devastated. She loved Leia."

"Let her think you're staying home because you're devastated."

"I *am* devastated!" I cried.

"You're also a suspect in her death. I don't want you talking to anyone. Stay home, get some rest, shower. You stink."

"You stink too," I countered. Another endearment we'd trade in college. I thanked her again for coming to my rescue and she hugged me fiercely and told me it was going to be all right.

"When they test Leia's clothing they'll find some other car's paint on it and they'll find debris from another car on the road. Then they'll catch the asshole who did this. You'll be off the hook. Just stay low and for God's sake keep your mouth shut."

I stood on my doorstep until her red car vanished around the southbound curve of River Road, then I turned reluctantly to go into my house. When I opened the door I saw that the living room must have looked to McAffrey like the squalid digs of a broken-down drunk—had he noticed that some of the empty teacups smelled like bourbon?—the kind of woman who would mow a young girl down and leave her to die in a ditch. How had I gotten to this place where I could be mistaken for that woman?

I wasn't that woman, I told myself as I fed Oolong and picked up the bottle of bourbon. *That kind of woman* would have a drink right now after the ordeal of that interrogation in the police station, but I *never* drank in the daytime and *never* before class. I put the bottle away in the kitchen cupboard next to the sink, where I kept my vitamins and Tylenol, and went upstairs to shower. I hadn't hit Leia Dawson; someone else had and the police would find her—or him—just as they'd found Hannah Mulder, one of Emmy's pink barrettes lodged in the grille of her Chevy Corsica, three empty fifths of Four Roses bourbon rattling around in her backseat.

I leaned my head against the shower tiles and closed my eyes until the hot water ran out. Then I toweled dry, rubbing my skin until it was pink, and got dressed.

The bedroom was neater than the living room but even more forlorn-looking. Only half the bed was mussed from the last time I'd slept in it. A half-empty coffee cup sat on the night table next to a splayed mystery novel I'd abandoned when finals started. Dead stinkbugs, their dust-brown bodies like tiny heraldic shields of a lost battle, littered the windowsill. I started dressing in tights, skirt, and blouse until I remembered I wasn't going in to work.

Work. I fished my cell phone out of my discarded cardigan pocket and saw I had three more calls from Dottie and one from Ross. Anat might be right about staying home but it would look weird if I didn't call in.

Dottie answered on the third ring, her voice a fluty warble like a mourning dove's call. "Where have you been? I've been calling all morning. There's been a horr-rr-ible, horr-rr-ible tragedy—"

"I know about Leia," I cut off her rising keen. "The police were here."

"The police? Why did they come to you?"

"I-I can't really talk about it—"

"Did you see something? I told the police officer who came here that you left before me. Do you know who did this?" Before I could answer she gasped. "Oh, Nan! I wasn't even thinking about how terrible this is for you. Are you all right? Are you okay to drive?"

"Actually," I began, planning to ask her if she could bring me the rest of my students' papers on her way home, "if you could—"

"Oh, of course! I should have thought of it before. I'll come get you right now. I have to go out anyway to pick up candles for the vigil tonight. I'll be there in a jiffy."

Before I could object she'd rung off. I thought I should call her back and explain, but then I looked at the message from Ross on my phone. I had to tell him the police considered me a suspect before he heard it from someone else. And I had to do that in person. I'd go in, talk to Ross, pick up my students' papers, and come right back here.

I waited at the bottom of my driveway because I didn't think Dottie's ancient VW would handle the snow as ruthlessly as Anat's Subaru. When she pulled up I started to get into the passenger side, but she put the car in park, hopped out, and came around to wrap me in her arms. I resisted for a moment, then melted into her soft motherly hug. Not that my own mother's angular and guarded embraces ever felt like that. *I'm not one for shows of emotion, darling, it doesn't mean I don't love you.*

But then why did I feel so loved wrapped in Dottie's arms—a woman I'd known for only seven years and with whom I had barely anything in common besides a love of Jane Austen and good tea?

When I shifted my weight back she let go of me, holding me at arm's length to look at me. Her cheeks and eyes were as pink as her flowered cardigan.

"Oh, Nan! I still can't believe it. It's all my fault!"

"Your fault? What are you talking about?"

"I *told* Leia she shouldn't walk home—I'm always telling the students that it's too dangerous to walk on River Road—but then I got distracted straightening up. Ross had disappeared somewhere and I didn't want to leave the house a mess—you know men, he'd have left it all for the morning—and when I went to look for her I couldn't find her anywhere. One of the boys said she'd left, but now . . . well, Ross said the police told him she was run over *after* the snow started and I got home before the snow began so she must have still been at the party when I left." She took a deep, mucousy breath that dissolved into a sob and fished out a crumpled tissue from the cuff of her cardigan.

"I didn't see her when I left either," I told Dottie, squeezing her arm. "Maybe she was outside. A bunch of students were out by the old barn

on the edge of Ross's property watching the sun set and smoking cigarettes." I pictured them, black slouching silhouettes against the red glow
of the sunset. Troy had been one of them, laughing, apparently over his
"girlfriend trouble." Had Leia been the girl in the red leather jacket he'd
been laughing with?

"I told them not to do that," Dottie said, bustling to the driver's side
and getting in. "I told them they shouldn't litter Professor Ballantine's
lawn with cigarettes . . ."

I missed whatever she said next as she ducked inside the car and I
opened my door. She was talking about the arrangements being made
to counsel students when I got in, the emails that had been sent to faculty, students, and parents, the plans for a candlelight vigil tonight and
a memorial service after Christmas in the chapel. I was glad she was as
wrapped up in the details as she was. I hated to think of her blaming
herself for Leia's death. I knew how corrosive guilt was, how it ate into
everything like road salt through the floor of an old car. Kind, generous
Dottie—she'd baked four dozen cookies when she got the call from
Ross this morning so that the students who came to the counseling
center would have something sweet—didn't deserve to feel guilty because Leia hadn't taken a lift home with her. I was almost certain now
that it had been Leia talking to Troy out by the old barn.

By the time we got to the road she was on to an idea for a memorial
quilt for Leia. Dottie was an expert quilter. She made baby quilts for
all the new babies in the department and kept photographs of them on
a bulletin board over her desk. She kept a picture of Emmy up there
too—Emmy in braids with the pink barrettes she loved.

"Leia was working on a quilt with the women at the prison. We
could ask them to contribute. They all loved Leia, all the faculty too,
even the women in the cafeteria—"

A gasp cut off the list of all the people who loved Leia. Dottie braked
so sharply I was thrown against the dash. I braced myself—half expecting that we'd hit something. Dottie was pulling to the side of the road.

"Look," she said pointing across the road, "that must be where it happened. Someone's already started a memorial."

I looked toward the stone wall. Where there had only been the daffodils and candle before there were now a few tall candles, their weak flames flickering in the watery sunlight. How did people know so soon? I wondered. Was grief a flame drawing moths to it?

"Oh! I wish I had something to put on it!" Dottie said. "Wait, I know…" Dottie reached into the backseat of her car and plucked something out of a large quilted tote bag. Then she jumped out of the car and crossed the road without looking in either direction. I watched her cross, my heart thumping, and then got out and followed her across the road. I'd look at those daffodils again later to see if I could tell where they'd been bought. I found Dottie reading a note that had been left under one of the candles.

"Love you forever, Ladybug," she read aloud.

Dottie held up the bit of red cloth with ladybugs printed on it that she'd taken from her quilting bag. "She said that's what her mother called her when she was little— Oh, that poor woman! She'll never be the same—" Dottie stopped and looked guiltily at me. I shook my head, unable to talk, which Dottie took as acknowledgment of the grief I shared with Leia's mother, but it wasn't that. Lying beside the candle among the daffodils was a pink barrette—the mate to the one they'd found in Hannah Mulder's radiator grille.

It was just an awful coincidence, I told myself as we drove north on River Road, like the daffodils. Those pink barrettes were literally a dime a dozen. Well, not *literally*, I would have corrected my students. They were a dollar a dozen at the dollar store in Kingston. I'd bought three packs of them for Emmy, discarding the other colors because she'd only wear the pink ones. "She'll grow out of that," a mother at Emmy's day care had said. But she never had. Never would.

I tried to remember if I'd ever seen Leia wearing pink barrettes. Her style had been edgier, especially since she'd started working at the prison, but she might have worn them *ironically*, the way the punk girls wore torn Hello Kitty T-shirts. I tried to picture her at the party yesterday, standing outside Ross's barn, red leather jacket, long white scarf tied around her thin neck, laughing at something Troy Van Donk had said . . .

"Did you see Troy Van Donk at the party yesterday?" I asked Dottie.

We'd reached the campus, which had the hushed feeling it got between terms. Classes were over—most of the finals too—many students had already gone home, and those who were still on campus were probably sleeping in. They hadn't woken up yet to the notice on their college email about Leia.

"Troy Van Donk? I'm not sure. . . . I wouldn't think he'd come to the department party, though. He's failing two of his classes, you know, and he's already on academic probation. Cressida told me he was in danger of being suspended. It's a shame. I hate to see a local boy like Troy lose his opportunity at the college. I went to high school with Troy Senior, you know."

"No, I didn't." One of the perks of being friends with Dottie was getting to hear all the local gossip, but I wasn't sure I was up to it this morning. "I'm worried about how he'll react because I think he might have been close to Leia. They always sat together in class."

"Leia and Troy?" Dottie said, wrinkling her brow. "I can't see the two of them together—but then, Leia was kind to everyone. Do you know she brought me fabric scraps from a store near her home in Buffalo?" Dottie's voice wobbled at the memory. "Oh, why is it that it's always the best that get taken?"

"Bad people die too," I said without much conviction.

"I hope *this* doesn't make me a bad person," Dottie said, her voice suddenly fierce, "but I hope the person who hit Leia dies. Prison's too good for anyone who'd hit a child and leave her in the road to die."

"If you're a bad person," I said, rubbing the pink barrette in my pocket, "then I am too." I had thought the same thing about Hannah Mulder a thousand times.

CHAPTER FIVE

Dottie had a handicapped sticker because of her bad hip so we were able to park behind the Jewett Faculty Tower. It was an ugly brick monstrosity built in the fifties, but it had beautiful western-facing views of the river and the Catskill Mountains. From Dottie's desk, positioned in the middle of the English Department office, she could see the whole river valley from the window on her left and the hallway with faculty offices to her right. I'd once joked with her and Ross that she was like the Lady of Shalott sitting in her tower and watching over all of us. At the next faculty party Ross had presented her with a plaque that read "Lady Dorothea of Shall Not."

"Because she tells all the students—and faculty—what we shall and shall not do."

Today all the doors to the offices in the hallway were closed. When we passed Cressida's office, though, I heard voices. It wasn't like her to close her door. "The last thing you need is a student accusing you of sexual harassment," she told me when I started working at Acheron. "Even if they're weeping about their dead dog, keep your door open."

So why had she closed it now? Maybe it was someone upset about Leia.

In the main office Ross's door was also closed but that wasn't unusual. I knocked at it, and then Dottie said, "Oh, he's not in. He's driving to the train station to pick up Leia's parents. Poor man. He looked like death when he came back from identifying Leia at the morgue. He adored her . . ." Dottie dabbed her eyes and shook her head, making her gray curls bounce. "He made the call to Leia's parents himself."

"That must have been hard," I said, "but I do have to talk to him. Could you tell him I'm in my office and that it's very important?"

"Is it about what you were talking to the police about?"

I nodded, hating that I couldn't tell Dottie everything. What a relief it would be to pour out the whole story to her! But then I thought about all the stories Dottie had told me over the years about people in town and teachers who had been at the college before me. She knew everyone. I couldn't be sure she wouldn't "share" my situation with someone else. Even if Dottie thought I was innocent—*she would, wouldn't she?*—the story could be all over campus by the end of the day.

"It's just really important I talk to Ross as soon as possible."

"I'll let him know," Dottie said.

I went to my mailbox, pulled out a stack of late papers, and was heading out the door when I heard angry voices coming down the hall from Cressida's office.

"I don't like the sound of that," Dottie said. "I'm going to buzz her to see if she's all right—"

Before Dottie could use the intercom, Cressida's door burst open and Troy Van Donk stormed out and headed down the hall straight toward us. He looked terrible. Curly black hair writhing around his head like Medusa's snakes, face unshaven, blue eyes bloodshot and swollen. He brushed past me, bumping into my shoulder, without any sign that he even recognized me and pounded on Ross's door.

"He's not in—" Dottie began, but Troy silenced her by lifting his middle finger and backing out of the room. Dottie's hand flew to her chest as if she'd been struck. I was as shocked as I had been by anything else today. No one gave Dottie the finger!

"Are you okay?" I asked, afraid that the outrageous rudeness might actually give Dottie a heart attack.

She nodded, speechless, and sank into her desk chair.

Cressida came down the hall, braids swinging, two red splotches on her pale face, and looked at Dottie. "Call campus security now and tell them that boy should be escorted off campus and not allowed back on."

"Did he threaten you, Cressida?" Dottie asked.

"He had the nerve to say it was my fault that Leia was dead because I upset her at the party."

"Why did he think that?" I asked in as neutral a tone as I could. Cressida was my friend but I knew she sometimes intimidated students. Nearly six feet tall, her white-blond hair twisted into a bewildering array of braids threaded with beads, she resembled a Viking shield maiden.

"Leia was upset about something at the party, but it had nothing to do with me." She blinked at me and her face softened. "She came out of the kitchen upset after you went in there to talk to Ross. Did you tell her about the tenure decision?"

"Of course not," I said. "That would be unprofessional."

"Yes it would . . . sorry." She shook her head and her braids rattled like wooden battle spears. "It's been a rough morning. Actually, I wanted to talk to you, Nan."

"Can it wait?" I asked, holding up my armful of papers. "I want to get my grades in as soon as possible." Although I usually enjoyed talking to Cressida she could be a little . . . *judgmental* and I didn't feel up to her brand of tough-love advice this morning.

"It's about Leia," she said simply, a trump card I couldn't dispute.

"Oh," I said, feeling the blood rise to my face. Did she know that the police had brought me in for questioning? I couldn't imagine how, but Cressida often found out things before anyone else. *It pays to stay in the loop*, she was always telling me. "Of course."

I followed her down the hall and into her office, giving Dottie a backward glance and mouthing Ross's name to remind her I needed to speak with him. If Cressida already knew it was only a matter of time before Ross heard. I sat down in the hard, straight-backed chair, which

I suspected Cressida had picked out to discourage students from lin-gering, preparing to explain to her why the police had it all wrong. But instead of demanding an explanation, Cressida perched on the edge of her desk, leaned forward, and put her hand on my shoulder. "Poor Nan," she said, "this must be terrible for you. It must make you relive what happened to Emmy."

Sympathy from Cressida undid me in a way that it hadn't from Dot-tie. A sob escaped from my mouth. Cressida leaned back and plucked a Kleenex from a box on her desk and handed it to me. She waited a moment for me to control myself, lifting her eyes up—a trick that she'd once told me kept her from crying. "Men will judge you if you cry," she'd told me. "They'll think you're a hysterical female and you won't get tenure." Is that why I hadn't gotten tenure, I wondered, because Ross thought I was hysterical and weak? When I'd blown my nose Cressida clasped her hands and looked down at me.

"I think I understand you better now," she said. "Losing Leia—well, she was like a daughter to me."

I looked up, not sure what surprised me more, that Cressida felt that way about Leia, or that she thought losing a student, even a beloved one, was the same as losing your own child. But then I realized how judgmen-tal that was. I hated when parents—like my stepsisters—acted like single women without children were somehow less worthy than those who had wedded and procreated. Cressida had endured her own hardships. Al-though she'd grown up in a wealthy Long Island family (her grandfather was a Polish immigrant who had founded a successful diamond business and appeared on local TV as Dave the Duke of Diamonds), her mother had suffered from undiagnosed bipolar disorder and subjected Cressida to alcoholic rages, and harried her into a grueling career in ballet. I knew all this because Cressida had written a memoir about her struggles with anorexia and bulimia and her time in the ballet world called *Raising the Barre*. She taught classes on body image and gender roles that were es-pecially popular with the female students. I'd often seen Leia talking to her, and I remembered now that she'd been coming out of Cressida's office before she'd come to my door yesterday. Maybe Leia had some body image issue (she *had* lost weight recently) she felt more comfortable talking to Cressida about. I felt an absurd pang of jealousy at the thought that Leia might have been closer to Cressida than to me.

"You must have been close to Leia," I said.

"Ironic, isn't it?" she asked. "I'm the one who always says not to get too close to the students. But Leia—" There was a catch in her voice, a tiny hiccup that I realized was a sob. "Leia was special. We worked together on the prison initiative, you know."

I nodded. The prison initiative was Cressida's pet project. She recruited only the best students for it. Leia had been thrilled when she was selected.

"And when you share an experience like that you can't help but grow close. I wish you had agreed to teach there."

Cressida had often tried to get me to teach a class at the prison, but the last thing I had wanted to do was step foot in the very place where Hannah Mulder was serving out her sentence. *Only, Hannah wasn't there anymore*, I reminded myself, rubbing the pink barrette in my pocket.

"Why?" I asked suddenly. "Would I have gotten tenure if I had?"

Cressida blanched and I instantly felt ashamed of myself. "I'm sorry," I began.

"No," Cressida said, "you're right. I think it would have made a difference. Not just for the tenure decision. I think it would have helped you to get outside of yourself to see what these women deal with. Maybe you would have been able to channel your grief into something productive and creative."

I bit my cheek. As if my grief for Emmy was so slight it could fit into something as narrow as a channel when it was as wide as an ocean. Try to channel an ocean, I could have told Cressida, and you wind up with a deluge. This is why I hadn't felt like talking to Cressida this morning, but I realized she was only trying to help in the best way she knew.

Writing my memoir, she often said, *gave a voice to my silenced pain.* Writing, especially confessional writing, was like a religion to her.

"You're right," I said, and then, looking for a way to make up for snapping at her, my eyes lit on the stack of glossy books on her desk. "It's worked for you. Is this the new book?" I picked up a slim volume. The title *The Sentences* was printed on a graphic design meant, I guessed, to represent prison bars. I remembered that when Cressida was up for tenure last year, she'd gotten this book contract just in the nick of time to present to the committee.

"This is the advanced reader's edition. I've dedicated it to the women I worked with in the prison, but I think there's time to add a dedication to Leia. I had also planned to do a reading series incorporating some of the inmates' writing and I was thinking now that I could use some of Leia's work as well. That's why I called you in here. I was wondering if you had any work of Leia's you think would fit."

"She wrote a fantasy story for my fiction workshop."

Cressida wrinkled her nose. I knew she didn't like fantasy. "I was looking for something more realistic, perhaps about her time working at the prison?"

"No, she wasn't writing anything like that," I said. "But I can look through old papers she gave me in previous classes if you like. Do you need help with the reading series?" I was so relieved that Cressida didn't know about the police yet that I was willing to agree to anything. "I'd really like to be a part of it."

"I'm glad to hear that, Nan," she said, leaning forward and taking my hand. She squeezed it so tightly I could feel her rings cutting into my skin. "Maybe the tenure thing will be a wake-up call for you. Maybe you'll use this opportunity to take some time off for your writing—and yourself. You know . . . do a detox maybe?" She raised one perfectly shaped eyebrow and I felt the blood rush to my face. Was she suggesting I needed to stop drinking? Before I could protest she added, "Even my prison students say that their time there has been a gift!"

*   *   *

I checked back in the main office but Dottie wasn't at her desk and Ross's door was still closed. I hoped he came back soon. I didn't know if I could bear talking to anyone else today. I walked down the hall to my office feeling dazed by Cressida's suggestion about detox and that I look at not getting tenure as a gift. *Crap.* Did that mean I was supposed to quit and skulk away? Would the department fire me? I knew that the protocol was to leave when you didn't get tenure—but leave to go where? It was all well and good for Cressida Janowicz, heir to Dave the Duke of Diamonds, to look at losing a job as a gift of time, but I was barely making do on my salary as it was. State schools did not pay what private colleges paid and the house—the quaint, adorable farmhouse that Evan and I had bought when I got the job here—was a money pit. I'd had to take out a loan last year to have the roof fixed. Of course the smart thing would have been to sell it—

"Nancy? Isn't it awful?"

I looked around, embarrassed to have been caught worrying about money on such a day, and found Joan Denning standing behind me at the door to the adjunct offices. She had a stack of papers pressed to her chest and a rolling suitcase in tow.

"Yes," I said. "It is."

"I had Leia in Composition her freshman year. What a bright girl! And I've heard her at the faculty-student readings." Joan always came to the readings and read a poem. They were good poems. At one of the Christmas parties she'd told me that she had won a PEN award in her twenties. But she was in her fifties now and had left it too long to get a full-time academic job. She loved teaching, she told me, but she had to teach at three colleges to make ends meet. Looking at her—graying blond hair scraped back in an unflattering ponytail, twenty pounds overweight because she didn't have time to exercise, hunched over from dragging reams of composition essays from school to school—I realized that this would be me in ten years if I didn't get tenure.

"Leia told me she liked one of your poems," I said. "The one about the moth."

"She did?" Joan's heavy face was transformed into beatific bliss. "Maybe I'll read it at the candlelight vigil tonight."

"I think that's a lovely idea," I said. I gave her an awkward hug, the papers in her arms crinkling against the ones in mine like dry tinder catching fire, and hurried on to my office, wiping my face, not wanting anyone to see me cry. I just wanted to close the door and wait for Ross—but when I got to my office I found three students sitting cross-legged on the floor outside my door, hugging each other and weeping.

"Come on in," I told them.

I spent the next few hours handing Kleenexes to students and listening to their memories of Leia. Leia had been their lab partner, in their study group, in the same play. She had stayed up all night with one boy when he'd broken up with his boyfriend and had always let in another girl when she'd forgotten her ID at the cafeteria (apparently Leia had worked three jobs while managing to keep up a 4.0 average). I was surprised at how many students were still on campus, but several told me they had delayed leaving to attend the candlelight vigil tonight. I also wondered why they were all coming to me and not the counseling center until Aleesha Williams, who'd come by to check I'd gotten the paper she'd left in my box late yesterday, said to me, "It's like that thing you always told us in writing class, you know? About how writing helps you climb out of the dump?"

"'Writing is a very sturdy ladder out of the pit,'" I quoted. "Alice Walker said that."

"Yeah," Aleesha said. "You always made me feel like I could talk about anything—" Her lip trembled. I plucked the last Kleenex out of the box and handed it to her.

"I guess this class was closer than I realized," I said.

Aleesha blew her nose and looked up. Her eyes were bloodshot, her light brown skin sallow in the bright sunlight pouring through the window. She was wearing a SUNY Acheron sweatshirt and torn jeans. All semester she'd come to class in bright, swingy skirts and soft blouses—styles I often recognized from the Target in Poughkeepsie—and always alert, excited to talk about the story I'd assigned even when she thought it was "messed up." Today, though, she looked dazed. I felt a pang that Aleesha Williams, who had enough on her plate already raising a child on her own, was so upset about Leia.

"I didn't just know Leia from class. You know she spoke up for my cousin Shawna at her parole board."

"I didn't know that."

"Yeah, they met in that class the college runs down at the prison in Fishkill. At first I was kind of mad, Shawna getting to take classes for free after she got arrested for dealing while I'm working two jobs to pay for my classes . . ." Aleesha's lip trembled again. "But then Shawna only got in trouble because of that no-account boyfriend of hers, so I guess it all evens out in the end and I don't begrudge anyone a chance to make something better of themselves, right?"

"Right," I said. "So Leia went to Shawna's parole board?"

"Uh-huh. She even read aloud from some paper Shawna wrote. I think it impressed them—a nice college girl like Leia speaking up for Shawna like that—it was a really decent thing Leia did. I wrote about it in that paper I left for you."

"Really? Professor Janowicz is putting together a reading series about Leia's work at the prison. I could pass it on to her."

"Oh, I don't know about that," she said, looking uncomfortable. "There's a lot in there about the drugs Shawna's done—"

"But she's clean now, right?" I asked, remembering a poem Aleesha had handed in a few weeks ago about seeing her cousin for the first time after she got out of prison.

"As far as I know . . . tell you the truth, I haven't seen Shawna in a few days. . . . Anyway, I wouldn't want to jinx her, you know?" She'd twisted the Kleenex in her hand into a knot. I tried to think of something reassuring to say.

"Maybe if she saw how proud you were of her recovery it would help."

Aleesha bit her lip, which was chapped and peeling. "Yeah, maybe, only—" She stopped at the sound of a deep, booming male voice in the hallway.

"Oh, there's Professor Ballantine," I said, getting to my feet. "I really do need to talk to him . . . about something to do with Leia . . . do you mind?"

"No problem," she said, quickly grabbing her backpack off the floor and getting to her feet. "I'll see you at the vigil thing?"

"Sure," I said, although I had no intention of going to it.

Ross was just passing my door when Aleesha opened it. "Thank God!" I said, more dramatically than I'd meant to. "I need to talk to you." At the sight of him—the strong, clean line of his jaw, the touch of gray at his temples that only made him look more professorial, the hooded eyes that seemed to convey an intimate knowledge of grief even on good days and that now looked haunted—I wanted to rest my head on his broad, oxford cloth–covered chest and weep. All the anger I'd felt last night had fallen away.

"Nan," he said, managing to inject a wealth of sympathy into the single syllable. "I know how awful this must be for you. I've been looking all over for you."

He had? I was about to tell him that I'd been right here waiting for him, but he took my elbow and angled his body so I could see the two people behind him. Although the man was large, he was hunched over in a way that made him seem small, his broad, pale face ghostly in the fluorescent hall lights. He was leaning protectively over a tiny brunette.

"I'd like you to meet Marie and Chad Dawson," Ross said. "Leia's parents."

CHAPTER SIX

I could only hope that the Dawsons thought the horror on my face was at what had happened to them—not that I was being introduced to the parents of the girl the police suspected I had killed.

"I'm so sorry for your loss," I said woodenly, recalling how empty those words had sounded when people had said them to me. As if I'd misplaced Emmy. Carelessly. "Leia was a remarkable young woman and a talented writer."

Marie dabbed her eyes, which were red but still lovely. "You must be the writing teacher she was always talking about . . . Ms. Lewis?"

"Nan," I said. "It's been a great privilege to teach Leia, Mr. and Mrs. Dawson. She was an extraordinary young woman. I can't imagine—"

"Leia said you lost your little girl when she was only four," Marie said, clasping my hand. "So you *do* know. You know that we have to be grateful for the time we had them." She drew in a shaky breath and I suddenly realized how little was holding this woman together. Chad put his arm around her and murmured her name. "I bet you see your little girl's face every day of your life, don't you?"

I nodded, unable to speak, and clutched the barrette in my pocket until it dug into my skin.

"Well, Leia's with her now," Marie said. "I just know my girl will be looking out for her."

Whenever well-meaning sympathizers had reassured me that Emmy was in heaven I'd wanted to scream at them that even if I believed in heaven it was no comfort to think of Emmy there. Now, however, I thought of Emmy and Leia both killed on the same spot and thought maybe there was something to it. Maybe that's why I had found the barrette. Maybe it was a sign that Emmy was with Leia.

"That's a lovely thought, Mrs. Dawson," I said. "I can see where Leia got her generosity."

Marie squeezed my hand and looked up at her husband, whose bland, washed-out face lit up with love for his wife. For an awful moment I almost envied them. There would be no recriminations between them, no accusations that Marie hadn't been watching when her daughter had strayed down the hill and wandered onto the road—

"Will you walk with us to the candlelight vigil?" Marie asked. "We can say a prayer for Emmy too."

The candlelight vigil was the last place I wanted to go. I could almost hear Anat's voice yelling in my ear, *No! Tell her no! You shouldn't even be here!* But how could I tell this lovely grieving woman that I wouldn't go to her daughter's vigil? "Of course," I told her. "It would be an honor."

As we walked from the faculty tower toward the Peace Garden, the Dawsons relived their terrible morning. I had the feeling they had been telling this story all day and that they would be telling it for the rest of their lives.

"When the call came this morning," Marie said, "I thought it was about Tad. He's our eldest and he's serving in Afghanistan. I'd been up since four. I knew something was wrong."

"Marie gets these feelings," Chad said. "She knew when Leia had appendicitis before the doctors did. And when Lucy tore her ACL in soccer Marie called me on the cell before I'd even crossed the field and gotten to her."

"Chad coaches the girls' soccer team," Marie said.

"I suppose that Tad and Travis won't be able to come for the service," Ross said, smoothly segueing from soccer practice to funerals and just as smoothly recalling the name of their other son. "Leia told me that Travis was in the Peace Corps. What about your . . . Lucy . . . ?" He'd been about to say *your younger daughter* and caught himself. They only had one daughter now. It was a tiny slip, but one I was surprised that Ross would make.

"We left her with Chad's sister. She's making the arrangements at our church and the boys are coming stateside for the funeral," Marie answered. "I made the calls from the train."

"Marie runs a tight ship," Chad said with a look of pride. "We were stationed overseas for twelve years—switched countries every three years."

"Leia mentioned that you lived abroad," I said. "She said it was one of the things that made her a writer."

"She said you'd made her a writer," Marie said simply.

I was unable to speak for a moment. Marie, seeming to understand, remarked on the candles set alongside the path in paper gift bags printed with ladybugs. Dottie's idea, I imagined. "Why, they look just like the goody bags for Leia's Sweet Sixteen!" she exclaimed. "I can tell how much Leia was loved here." Chad took his wife's hand and together they walked forward on the path, leaving Ross and me alone together. I realized that this might be my best opportunity to talk to Ross before the vigil.

"Look, Ross, there's something I really need to tell you. The police brought me in today—"

"The police," he said, looking disgusted, "are clueless. They asked me a bunch of questions, too, about Leia's and my 'relationship' as they called it, implying that there was something untoward about it. As if that would have anything to do with some drunk mowing Leia down on the river road."

I stared at him, shocked at his venom; he so rarely allowed himself to get rattled. He was always the strong, reliable one who stayed calm when all around him were losing their heads. Being accused of having improper relations with a student, though, would be the one thing that would unhinge him.

"I'm sorry, Ross, that's preposterous. I'm sure they're just casting about. Still, I think you should know—"

"Later, okay, Nan? I can't take on one more thing today. I just need to get through *this*." He flung his hand toward the crowd that waited at the end of the path in the Peace Garden and I noticed that he was shaking. It took a lot of strength to look as strong as he always did. He had once told me that he was exhausted after his classes. I'd been surprised because he always made teaching look easy. He was known for his relaxed, affable style in the classroom. When I had said that to him he laughed. "It's a performance. That's the only way to engage these students. You have to *emote*. Sometimes it just drains the life out of me."

He looked now as if he'd been drained. I couldn't burden him with my own situation—at least not until after the vigil.

We walked the rest of the way in silence on the candlelit path that meandered through a snow-covered field and a pine copse toward the Peace Garden. Before Acheron was a teaching college it had been part of the Blackwell estate. When the Blackwells lost their only child to a tragic drowning accident—and Charlotte Blackwell killed herself— the estate had lapsed into disrepair and was eventually sold to the state to become a teacher's college and then a state college. The mansion had been turned into a classroom building, linoleum laid over hard- wood floors, and acoustic tiles dropped under ornate plaster. Utilitar- ian brick buildings had sprung up around it in the 1930s and then even uglier cinder block constructions in the fifties.

The one place on campus that retained the feel of the old estate was in the gardens. Most of the statuary was gone except for a few chipped goddesses and satyrs, which students dressed up in graduation robes at commencement and sometimes moved around as pranks. The rose beds and perennial borders had grown wild and unkempt for years. "It was a popular make-out spot where everyone went to get high in the sixties," Dottie had told me. "In the eighties a group formed to save the garden." Although it hadn't been restored to its Italianate splendor at least you didn't find cigarette butts and condoms in it anymore. (The Blackwells' old boathouse on the river had replaced it as a favorite make-out and pot den since then.) And under a coat of snow, with the sun setting over the mountains across the river and candles glowing, it looked like it belonged at a fancy private school, not a state school.

There must have been a hundred people gathered already. As the Dawsons came into the garden Dottie gave them each a candle protected by a white paper shell. She was wearing a heavy purple cape that made her look like a Druid priestess, the candlelight turning her face pink. As if by prearranged signal, the group parted in half for the Dawsons and then formed a loose circle around them. A lectern had been set up at the center of a colonnaded apse that stood at the end of the garden overlooking the river. Abigail Martin, the college president, came forward to shake the Dawsons' hands and give them each a chilly embrace. Abigail was an able administrator, but not the warmest woman. I'd noticed over the last year that she often called on Ross for support at public events. Ross was so much better at making people feel important. I could understand why she'd sent him to collect the Dawsons but I hoped that they didn't see it as a slight. She said a few words now—bland words of condolence—and then turned the lectern over to those who knew Leia better.

Ross took the lectern first and spoke movingly of his impressions of Leia. He told a story about how Leia had taken over reading aloud a memoir piece for a girl who was crying too hard to read it herself. "Leia was always willing to speak up for others, to give voice to the silenced. I cannot believe that Leia's voice has been silenced with death. I must believe her voice will live on in all of those she would have spoken for."

One by one, Leia's classmates and teachers came forward and read poems and told stories about Leia. Joan Denning told a long rambling story about how Leia said she believed in ghosts because she'd seen one when she was twelve and so Joan knew Leia's spirit would always haunt Acheron. John Abbot read Leia's favorite passage from *Wuthering Heights*. Cressida talked about how Leia had been so dedicated to her students at the prison that she'd gone to some of their parole hearings. Listening to the moving tributes, it was easy to forget that the police had questioned me, but when Ross motioned me to the dais, I hesitated. How could I stand up there and talk about Leia while a forensics team labored in a police lab scraping Leia's blood off my tire? But everyone was looking at me, waiting. It would look worse, I realized, if I refused to speak.

I got up and faced the circle of candlelit faces. I saw my colleagues, students, friends—and at the back of the crowd, his police hat in his hands, Sergeant McAffrey, staring at me.

"Every once in a while a student comes along who reminds you why you teach," I said, returning McAffrey's gaze. "Leia did more than that. She reminded me why I live."

A murmur rose up as I left the lectern and I knew that people were telling each other that I was that teacher whose daughter had died. Dottie hugged me. Cressida squeezed my arm. Joan Denning patted me on the shoulder. I looked around for Sergeant McAffrey, but instead I ran into Sue Bennet, a tiny wire-haired woman who ran the local chapter of Mothers Against Drunk Driving. "Well, here we are again," she said by way of greeting. Sue's eighteen-year-old daughter had been killed driving home from her high school prom by a man with a previous DUI driving in the wrong lane on Route 9.

"Yes, it brings up terrible memories," I said, guiltily remembering that I'd dodged Sue's last few calls. "You must be thinking about Allison."

"I'm thinking about the monster who did this," Sue replied in a loud voice.

"I'm sure they'll catch him. The police talked to me—" I broke off, not wanting to tell Sue about hitting the deer. Or about the two glasses of wine I'd drunk at the faculty party. If it were up to Sue all alcohol would be made illegal. Possibly cars as well.

"Who they should be talking to are the DUIs in our town. Hannah Mulder and Peter Ray Osterberg . . ." Her eyes were roving over the crowd as if she expected to find our children's killers here. Instead her gaze fixed on Sergeant McAffrey, who was standing next to the Dawsons.

"You, Officer!" Sue demanded, heading toward the group. "Why aren't you out looking for the monster who did this? Why aren't you hauling in Hannah Mulder and Peter Ray Osterberg? Do you know that one third of all drivers arrested for DUIs are repeat offenders?"

McAffrey turned toward Sue. "Those individuals no longer have driver's licenses, ma'am," McAffrey said.

"So? Fifty to seventy-five percent of drunk drivers continue to drive on suspended licenses. They should be registered like sex offenders."

I saw Marie Dawson flinch at the words *sex offender*. A small crowd had been drawn by Sue's rising voice. Ross leaned over and whispered something into Dottie's ear and then Dottie approached Sue, put a hand on her arm, and whispered in her ear. Sue seemed to deflate, sinking into herself. Without anger pinking her cheeks, her skin was sallow and I could see dark rings under her eyes.

I felt a surge of pity for Sue Bennet. She might seem like a crank right now, yelling at strangers, making a scene, but that was only because she'd thrown all her grief into this cause. Maybe I'd have been better off if I had done the same—if I'd *channeled* my grief, as Cressida had suggested, into writing a memoir or teaching at the prison. Only, I hadn't wanted to make Emmy into a cause or memoir. I didn't want Emmy's face on the MADD website or the cover of a book. I just wanted her home. I started walking toward Sue but before I reached her I saw Kelsey Manning leaning in, whispering something in Sue's ear. Sue listened, the color returning to her cheeks and the fire to her eyes. When she looked up she was staring right at me, all that grief and anger channeled at *me*.

"Is this true, Nancy? Did *you* run over Leia Dawson and leave her for dead?"

I heard Dottie gasp and saw Chad Dawson put a protective arm around his wife as if she was the one Sue was attacking.

"No!" I cried. I looked around the crowd—past Cressida's astonished look—until I found Ross and spoke directly to him. "I hit a deer last night. The police brought me in because of the damage to my car. That's what I was trying to tell you before."

Ross held my gaze for a moment and I saw the same look of sadness and disappointment in his eyes that I'd seen last night when I accused him of denying me tenure because of a broken affair. But now as I looked at him I saw something else—the performer playing the role of able administrator. He turned from me and addressed Marie and Chad Dawson. "I'm very sorry," he said, "if I had known I would have suggested that Professor Lewis refrain from attending the vigil to spare you this scene."

I felt the words like an icy blow to my stomach. I looked at the crowd, warm in the glow of the candlelight. Only I was standing outside in the cold. The only one who would meet my gaze was Dottie and she only mouthed the words: "Oh, Nan!"

I turned away and walked out of the garden, the candlelit path a blur of runny lights like broken eggs. It was all I could do to keep from breaking into a run. I had the absurd notion that if I did the crowd would run after me like a pack of wild dogs smelling fear.

I walked to the edge of campus, toward the river road and home. As I passed Ross's house, I stared at it, shocked at how much had happened since I'd left the party yesterday, when I'd thought my biggest problem was not getting tenure. The old brick colonial looked peaceful with icicles hanging from its black trimmed eaves, the red barn garage positively pastoral against the unplowed snow. Ross hadn't had time to dig out his driveway either, I noticed, although the barn door was partly ajar, wedged open by a drift of snow. The vintage Peugeot Citroën he kept in the barn wasn't meant for driving in the snow anyway; he must have taken his Volvo, which he kept in a covered spot on campus, to the train station to pick up the Dawsons. The Volvo was his *professorial* car, he'd once said to me, the Peugeot the car of his *salad days*. The summer after Emmy died, and after Evan had moved out, it was the Peugeot we took west into the mountains, racing down dark, winding country roads as if we were plunging into a bottomless pool. I had been the one to end it at the end of the summer, because, I told him, I didn't want to risk losing my job. He'd expressed disappointment, but now I thought that he'd have done it if I hadn't. Our affair was part of those *salad days* he liked to relive with students around the fireside, like his days as an undergraduate at Harvard, or working at *The New Yorker*, or driving cross-country with *On the Road* in his back pocket. Our affair would have been partitioned off, just as he'd now sectioned me off into the "undesirable" category.

I turned onto the river road, tears streaming down my face. Although there was still light filtering through the trees the road was dark, a tunnel between the snow-covered stone walls beneath a canopy of bare branches. The sun lit up the topmost branches, turning them into skeletal fingers. Dead fingers on a ghost road. I could no longer tell myself that it would be all right when they found the person who killed Leia. Not after I'd seen the looks on all those faces, all those eyes branding me a murderer. The thing was, I didn't feel they were wrong. Wasn't I a murderer? If not of Leia, then of Emmy, whom I'd let run down the hill and out onto the road while I was too busy—*writing!*—to watch her? The looks of sympathy all these years had always felt false. The damning looks I'd just gotten in the Peace Garden felt *true*.

I walked on the side of the road, not caring if someone came and drove into me. Only when I reached Leia's memorial did I stop. It had grown over the day, filling with candles and flowers and stuffed animals all but covering the daffodils that had turned brown in the cold.

"I'm sorry," I said, reaching past a candle to touch the dead flowers, not sure if I was talking to Leia or Emmy.

As my hand brushed the cold glass I saw it wasn't a candle but a bottle. A fifth of bourbon.

I picked it up, shocked at the *wrongness* of it. The late-afternoon light caught the two inches at the bottom and the red roses painted on the glass. Four Roses bourbon. Hannah Mulder's brand. I slipped it in my coat pocket, where it fit as if that's where it had always belonged, and walked home.

CHAPTER SEVEN

Walking into my house did nothing to alleviate my sense of wrongness. In fact, the emptiness I felt inside seemed to swell at the sight of the stacks of papers and dirty glasses. I picked up a couple of glasses and brought them to the sink. Then I opened the cabinet to the right of the sink and took out the bottle of bourbon. As I took it down I remembered my resolution in the woods and the look on Anat's face when she asked me how much I'd had to drink at the party. But I'd made that resolution before I knew that I had more to worry about than not getting tenure, and Anat hadn't just had to face the entire town looking at her as if she were a murderer. I was pretty sure that if she had she would need a drink too.

I rinsed one of the glasses, poured an inch of bourbon into it, and drank it in two gulps standing at the sink. There. That wasn't so bad. I had no desire to drink more. I'd feed Oolong and then clean up—only, Oolong hadn't come down to greet me. That was weird. Had even my old cat abandoned me? I called her name and went looking for her in the linen closet where she sometimes hid and then Emmy's room on the off chance she'd gotten in there the last time I'd opened the door.

She was curled up on Emmy's bed, which was still made up with the Disney Princess sheets and comforter Emmy had demanded for her fourth birthday. I stood for a moment looking up at the Day-Glo stars

Evan had painted on Emmy's ceiling. They glowed in the dim light of the night-light, but more faintly than they had seven years ago, making me think of something Evan had liked to say when we met in college—how a star you saw in the night sky might have exploded a million years ago and you wouldn't know it yet because of how long it took for light to travel from distant galaxies. Even then it had given me a chill. It was like knowing that the worst thing could have happened already but you didn't know it yet. Like me sitting at my desk and hearing the screech of tires on the river road and not knowing that my life had just been blown to bits. It was that moment I always returned to in my dreams—that second of oblivion that had made me mistrust every moment of my life since.

I went downstairs and started cleaning, tossing out folders, old handouts, blue books from last semester, then pizza boxes and Chinese take-out containers. I stacked the sink with glasses and teacups and the recycle bins with plastic water bottles and newspapers. I put away the bourbon bottle after pouring myself another modest inch and sipped it slower than the first drink. A drunk would have just knocked it back. I was pretty sure that Hannah Mulder wasn't sipping her Four Roses.

As I worked I kept repeating three words—*daffodil, barrette, bottle*—as if they made up a haiku I was memorizing for class. Who had left them there and why? The idea that the barrette was a sign from Emmy had pretty much been ruined by the Four Roses bottle.

I left the desk under the window for last. I shelved the books and threw out old mail. I dusted the oak surface until it shined. Evan had bought this desk at a local antiques store when we moved into the house. "For your second novel," he'd said, "and your third and your fourth."

We'd had such big plans for the future when we moved here. Evan and I had bought the house on the strength of my appointment at Acheron and because we both thought it was the perfect place to raise Emmy. A pretty farmhouse in the country surrounded by apple trees, it was like something out of a storybook. We would get a dog when

Emmy was big enough and maybe even goats when Evan could move up full-time. The only drawback had been that Evan had to commute to the city for his job as a graphic designer at a PR firm, but we hoped that he could go freelance eventually and then he'd have time to illustrate the children's books he wanted to write.

The picture of the three of us living that life was so vivid in my mind—Evan at his slanted artist's desk in the studio we'd build in the old barn, Emmy feeding the goats, me writing my novels at the desk with the view of the orchard—that I sometimes had to remind myself that our first winter had been nothing like that. It had been a struggle to keep up with my heavy teaching load, the new preps, and the sometimes less than cooperative students. Evan was always tired from commuting. The house itself was more work than either of us—both suburban kids—had anticipated. The roof leaked, there were mice in the basement and bats in the attic, the propane heater worked only sporadically, and the woodstove smoked. It didn't help that it was one of the snowiest winters in decades. Evan pulled his back shoveling the driveway and Emmy slipped on the ice and broke her arm, which made her cranky and difficult. I certainly hadn't had any time to write.

It was only when the snow melted and the apple blossom trees bloomed and the end of the semester was in sight that I'd begun to feel that we would make it through. I'd been outside digging in the garden with Emmy when I'd gotten an idea. I'd gone inside just to jot down a note but then I'd sat down at my desk. Emmy was playing right outside the window. I could hear her singing a little made-up song while she dug in the dirt. . . .

Evan believed the house had killed Emmy. I didn't agree with that but I knew it had killed our marriage when Evan couldn't stay in the house and I couldn't leave it.

I took out the stack of papers I'd picked up today and put them on the desk. Then I poured myself another inch of bourbon and sat down. The sky outside was a deep violet, the snow-covered lawn a sea of lavender and mauve with tidal pools of indigo. Down below I could make out the road, winding like a dark river between stone banks, a twin to the Hudson that flowed behind me on the west side of the house.

"A perfect view for a writer," the realtor had said when she showed us the house.

I wouldn't be writing tonight, though. I'd spend the night grading the last of my papers. Tomorrow I'd hand in my resignation. And then? Who knew? My future loomed as mysterious as the ghost river unspooling down there in the dark. Maybe that was why I had to sit here at the window tonight. I had the feeling I had to keep watch. Last night may have been the night that ghosts walked, but tonight felt like something—or someone—else was out there waiting.

The chill from the window made me cold but rather than close the curtains I put on my coat. I started reading with a red pen in my hand to mark spelling and grammar errors but after a while I put it down and just read. I always told my students to dig deep. There was a quote from Margaret Atwood that I liked to read to them: "All writing is motivated deep down by a desire to make the risky trip to the Underworld, and to bring someone or something back from the dead." Many of them *had* made their journeys to their own personal hells in their stories. It felt callous to point out that a student had misspelled OxyContin in a story about how her father's addiction had wrecked her family and left her homeless at fifteen. Even the structural comments that came to mind—did we need to read about every night the author's father had come home drunk? Could he pick out one night to stand for them all?—felt beside the point.

When I'd made comments like that in class the student would usually say, "But that's how it happened!" I would try to explain, as my teachers had explained to me in my MFA workshops, that reality was not the final arbiter. The story had to work on the page. I was beginning to wonder, though, if my students didn't have it right. What did story structure have over the truth?

So I read their stories, crying at details I would have once marked as clichéd or overly sentimental. A ghost story about the local campus legend, Charlotte Blackwell, that I'd seen a dozen times before was made oddly poignant when the writer confessed that the ghost reminded her of her baby sister who had died of SIDS. A story about a family dog dying that I began with trepidation reduced me to tears when my student wrote that his dog was the first one he told he was gay. Maybe it was because standing in front of all those people at the vigil had flayed a layer of skin from my bones and I felt raw and exposed. Maybe it was the bourbon—which I had almost finished—or maybe it was that sitting here watching the dark rise from the road below I felt as if all the sadness, in my life and in the lives of my students, was flowing through my house tonight.

The last story I read was Aleesha's story about her cousin Shawna's heroin addiction. " 'The first time I shot up I felt like I swallowed the sky,' Shawna told me. But the last time I saw her the bruises on her arms looked like clouds before a storm." I read the story gripping my own elbows, my fingers digging into the crooks of my arms as if hiding my own track marks.

When I picked up my pen—a black Flair, not the red one—it was to tell them that I admired their bravery and thank them for sharing their stories.

I gave them all As. *Why the hell not?* I thought. It would be my parting gift to them.

When I got to the end of Aleesha's story I saw that another paper was stuck to it, the staples of each paper clinging together. I pried the bottom paper off, hoping it was Troy's (he still hadn't emailed me his late paper), but it wasn't. The name handwritten in the top right corner was *Leia Dawson*.

I felt suddenly cold, as if someone had opened a window and let in the winter wind. I stared at the paper—at Leia's name—trying to understand how a dead girl's paper had wound up in my house. She didn't owe me a late paper. She'd handed all her work in on time and this wasn't the fantasy story she had written for the class.

Then I remembered. She had come by to see me before the faculty party but I'd been too busy to see her. No, I'd only pretended to be too busy. I hadn't wanted to listen to her bright, happy chatter. But she hadn't come for that. She'd come to show me something she'd written.

Prof, she'd written across the top of the paper, *I know you're beyond busy but would you take a quick look at this? It's something I wrote last year that I have a question about. Could we talk about it before break? Thanks! Leia.*

She'd left it in my mailbox—and then Aleesha had left her paper on top of it. A simple explanation for a missive from the dead. Not a mystery like the daffodils, barrette, and bottle left on Leia's shrine.

I poured myself the last of the bourbon and stared at the paper ten to fifteen pages of double-spaced typescript stapled together staring back at me reproachfully. Then I picked up Leia's paper and began reading her story.

It's quiet in here but not quiet enough to hear a pin drop, which is too bad because if a pin does drop we all have to stay until it is found and accounted for. Such are the perils of running a quilting circle in a prison.

I laughed out loud and reached for my pen, about to scrawl *What a great opening line!* across the page until I remembered that it was too late to tell Leia what a good opening it was. I read the rest of the story through tear-blurred eyes. It was clearly based on her experiences teaching at the prison, running a writing class and a quilting circle.

I find that the women are more likely to tell their stories during the quilting circle when their hands are busy and their eyes are bent down to the scraps of cloth we are piecing together.

The stories of the women emerged with the patches of cloth— *joined together with the sashing as if by a river running through all our lives. Some of the things they've done are bad, but here those bad things are only more torn patches stitched together to make something beautiful. When*

I look up from my sewing I don't see a criminal, an addict, a killer—I see myself.

My eyes blurred on this last line. I looked up from the page—into my own reflection in the window. I stared back at a wasted, spectral version of myself, hair tangled and lank, face white, eyes shadowed—a revenant come back from the land of the dead. Then the figure moved. It wasn't my reflection. It was a person standing outside my house staring at me. A person I recognized from my nightmares. It was Hannah Mulder.

I'm not sure how long we stayed like that, our eyes locked across the barrier of glass. The first thought I had was that she wasn't real, that I'd drunk so much that I'd begun to have hallucinations. But then I thought about the things I had found on the wall—the daffodils, the barrette, the bottle—and it suddenly made sense that Hannah was here. She was sending me messages, trying to tell me something—but what? I had to let her know I understood, that I was willing to talk to her, that I wouldn't chase her away like I had in the past. The only way I could think of doing that was to show her the bottle of Four Roses she had left. It was still in the pocket of the coat I was wearing. I started to reach for it, but the moment unlocked a spring in her. She bolted—faster than I would have thought she could move. I sprung to my feet without thinking and ran to the door, flinging it open and shouting for her to stop.

I could see her lurching through the snow heading toward the road. I followed, a shadow of her, stumbling through the deep snow in my slippers. It wasn't the first time Hannah had left things for me. When she first got out of prison I'd started finding daffodils on my doorstep, tied together with twine and notes scrawled in a childlike script. "I'm sorry" and "I want to make ammends."

Fuck amends, I'd thought. I'd been about to get a restraining order against her when the daffodils and notes had suddenly stopped. Why had they started up now? Was it because she had something new to make amends for? Had Sue Bennet been right that the police should be looking at her? Had *she* run over Leia?

You can make amends by clearing my name, I thought, as I got closer to her at the bottom of the hill. She was having trouble getting over the stone wall. She had the distended belly and twiggy legs of a drunk— plus she was probably loaded. How many fifths of Four Roses had she had to drink to steel herself to face me? Certainly more than I'd had tonight. I only hoped she stayed conscious long enough to make a statement to the police when I dragged her sorry ass there.

I caught up with her just as she was clearing the wall. I lunged and grabbed for her, but my hands were clumsy from the cold and I only got a handful of her denim and fake-sheepskin jacket. Her spindly arms slipped free of the sleeves and she toppled backward into the snow on the other side of the wall. I shook the jacket at her.

"Did you think leaving flowers would make up for what you did?"

Her face crumpled as she struggled to her feet. "I'm sorry," she said.

"Sorry?" I screamed. "Is that why you left this?"

I reached inside my coat pocket and took out the fifth of Four Roses. She threw up her hands to cover her face as if she thought I would throw the bottle at her and stepped backward, shaking her head, her eyes wide and startled in the sudden wash of light as a car came around the corner. I had only time to see her expression turn from confused to terrified before the car, going too fast to stop, hit her.

CHAPTER EIGHT

"She was standing in the middle of the road! I didn't have time to stop!"

I looked up from Hannah's inert body to the man who had gotten out of the car. Silhouetted against the headlights he loomed like the black cutout shape of a monster, but when he crouched down beside me I recognized him.

"Ross! What are you doing here?"

"I was coming to see you—to tell you I was sorry for what happened at the vigil—and then she ran out in front of me! Is she . . . ?"

"I don't know." My hand was on Hannah's neck. How had it gotten there? I couldn't remember the seconds between the car hitting her and my crossing the road, just as I never remembered running down the hill to Emmy. I felt a faint tick under my hand—Hannah Mulder's blood running through her veins.

"She's alive," I said, surprised at the sound of relief in my voice. I should be angry. Why should *she* live when Emmy and Leia hadn't? "We need to call an ambulance."

Ross fumbled in his pocket for his phone, cursed, and turned, mumbling that it was in his car. He left me alone, crouching beside Hannah. She was turned away from me, her face covered by loose, stringy hair, her knees drawn up to her chest as if she'd tried to roll into a ball to protect herself from the impact. *Or from me*, I thought, remembering the way she'd cowered from me. How she'd stared at the bottle in my hand as if I'd meant to throw it at her. Her ankles above her thin canvas sneakers were bare and scabbed, obscene-looking in the yellow glare of Ross's headlights. The same yellow headlights I'd watched light up those lonely mountain roads with Ross six years ago—he'd been driving the little Peugeot, not the Volvo, which was probably why Hannah was still alive. But what was he doing here? What had he just said? To tell me he was sorry for how he acted at the vigil? He hadn't looked sorry. There was something strange about his being here—as strange as Hannah's showing up outside my window—but when I tried to sort it out my mind balked. I brushed back Hannah's hair from her face and caught the scent of cheap bourbon and menthol cigarettes.

"The ambulance is on the way," Ross said, crouching down beside me. "Is she still—"

"Yes," I said, "although I'm not sure why. She must have enough alcohol in her bloodstream to kill a person."

"Is that why she ran into the road—Jesus! She came out of nowhere!—because she was drunk? But what were you doing with her?"

"I saw her standing outside my house. I called to her and she ran. I followed her—I thought she'd come to tell me that she was the one who hit Leia."

"But then why would she run?" He shook his head. "Oh, Nan, I can see how it might have happened. That curve—if Leia ran out in front of you . . . that's something Leia might do. She was impulsive—brilliant, yes, beautiful, talented—but there was something in her that sometimes just had to *burst* out and she didn't always care who was in her way or who got hurt. If she ran in front of you like that . . . well, it wouldn't really be your fault."

I stared at Ross. In the glare of the headlights his eyes looked like gouges carved into his face. Unreadable. Why was he talking about Leia now? Was he trying to excuse himself for hitting Hannah? Did he think that if I admitted hitting Leia it would somehow excuse him for hitting Hannah? But it wasn't the same.

"Whoever hit Leia left her for dead in the road," I said, "and I would never do that." I tried to hold his gaze but it was like trying to grab hold of something in the dark. His eyes slid away from mine.

"I believe you. That's what I was coming to tell you—that and something Leia told me that night before you came into the kitchen—"

The wail of sirens drowned out whatever Leia had told Ross in the kitchen. Then we were surrounded by flashing lights, pinned down by them, as if Ross and I were criminals tracked down by the police. The lights blanched his face and I saw it was wet with tears. *From hitting Hannah?* I wondered. *Or from remembering Leia?* There wasn't time to find out. We were separated by the rush of paramedics and then a police officer was asking whose car it was that had hit Hannah. I heard Ross telling him that he'd been driving—no, Ms. Lewis hadn't been in the car. She'd heard the accident and come down from her house.

"Was that right?" someone asked me.

Dimly I realized that Ross was giving me the chance to recast the events of the night. I didn't have to be the crazy lady who chased Hannah Mulder onto the road straight into the path of an oncoming car. I felt a pang of gratitude toward him, but I couldn't let him take the blame for hitting Hannah by himself.

"Not exactly," I said. "I saw Hannah outside my house and I followed her down to the road." *Chased her* would have been more accurate. "She was standing in the road when the car came around the curve. . . ." *Backing away from me because she thought I was going to throw a bottle at her.* I wasn't being all that honest after all. "Ross couldn't have seen her."

"So you witnessed the incident. You'll have to come down to the station to make a statement."

"Of course," I said, trying hard not to show how much I dreaded going back to the police station. Would they give me a Breathalyzer test? But no—I hadn't been driving. Still, what would McAffrey think if he smelled bourbon on my breath? *Always take the offensive*, Anat would tell me. "Is Sergeant McAffrey on duty? I have some information to give him about Leia Dawson's death. I think Hannah Mulder might have been involved."

After Hannah was loaded into the ambulance the young police officer drove me to the police station. We left Ross talking to a state trooper, describing how the accident happened. I wondered if we weren't being separated deliberately so that we couldn't coordinate our stories. But that didn't matter. As long as we both told the truth our stories would be the same. They'd realize Ross wasn't responsible for hitting Hannah and I would explain to Sergeant McAffrey my theory about why Hannah had been lurking outside my house. When she woke up in the hospital he could question her and she'd admit to running over Leia and then everyone would know it wasn't me. It didn't matter if my breath smelled like bourbon. I'd been drinking in the privacy of my own home. I hadn't been driving. Besides, I hadn't had that much . . . *had I?*

I was taken to the same dreary yellow interview room as before— did the Acheron police station even have more than one?—and left on my own to wait for Sergeant McAffrey. *Because he's busy*, I told myself, *not because he wants to make you more nervous than you already are.*

"Back so soon?" Sergeant McAffrey said by way of greeting. He was carrying two Styrofoam cups of coffee. "You must've missed us."

He handed me one of the cups. The coffee smelled burnt but the warm cup felt good. I wrapped my hands around it, thinking it was a good sign that he'd brought me a cup of coffee.

"I'm sorry Hannah got hurt, but yes, I did want to talk to you. Is she going to be all right?" I asked.

"Too soon to say," he replied, taking a sip of his coffee and wincing at the taste. "Why don't you tell me what happened."

I often told my students that starting in medias res gave the writer the advantage of choosing the most interesting bit to begin with. So although I wanted to tell Sergeant McAffrey about the things Hannah had left on the shrine, I began instead with that moment I looked up from my desk and saw her standing on my front lawn. *Like a ghost*, I wanted to say, *like Cathy's ghost appearing to Heathcliff in* Wuthering Heights, but I didn't. Literary allusions were not going to help my case. "As soon as I moved she bolted and so I ran after her."

"Why?" he asked. "Why didn't you call the police?"

"I knew she had something to say to me and that she might not say it in front of the police. I only wanted to talk to her but she panicked. I smelled liquor on her breath when I caught up to her at the wall. She was drunk. She stumbled over the wall and then she said she was sorry."

"Sorry for what?"

"I think for running over Leia. She left this at Leia's shrine."

I pulled the pink barrette out of my pocket and laid it on the table between us. Sergeant McAffrey's face turned pale.

"You recognize it, don't you? You're the one who found it wedged into Hannah's radiator grille after she hit Emmy."

"Lots of little girls wear these. My niece did when she was going through that pink stage all girls go through. Now she wants to be a cowgirl and will only wear stuff with horses on it. What makes you think it was Hannah who left this on Leia's shrine?"

"Because she left this too." I took the bottle of Four Roses out of my pocket and saw his eyes widen. Too late I realized what it looked like: a drunk carrying around booze in her coat.

"I found this on the shrine tonight. It's Hannah's brand. There were daffodils too, like the ones Hannah's been leaving for me since she got out of prison. She's been hanging around my house, leaving me notes, saying she wants to make amends. Don't you see? She must have been driving to my house the night Leia died—drunk as usual. *She's* the one who hit Leia."

I finished in a rush, gulping for air. Sergeant McAffrey was staring at me, not with the flash of epiphany I'd hoped for but not with disbelief either. Instead he looked sad, as if I'd let him down. But all he said was "Interview concluded" and the time and flicked off the tape recorder. I'd forgotten I was being recorded. Then he spoke into an intercom.

"Louisa, would you please have Ms. Lewis's statement typed up for her to sign. I'll drive her home when she's done."

He left without looking at me. Half an hour later a woman in a red and green Christmas sweater, Santa earrings, and glasses dangling from a chain around her neck came in with my statement. She told me to read it carefully and sign if it was all correct. I reread the story I'd just told McAffrey and saw how outlandish it sounded. *But that's what really happened,* I wanted to say, just as my students did when I critiqued their writing.

A minute after I signed it Sergeant McAffrey came in, as if he'd been watching me. He looked preoccupied. When I handed him the statement he looked up from the page to my face, his eyes narrowed.

"Professor Ballantine says that he was on his way to see you when he hit Hannah on the road. Were you expecting him?"

"No," I said truthfully. "But he said he was coming to say he was sorry that he didn't defend me at the vigil."

"I was there and saw what happened. He didn't look sorry."

It was what I had thought but hearing Sergeant McAffrey say it made me realize all over again how strange it all was—Ross coming to see me, just happening to come around the curve when Hannah ran out. But what other explanation could there be?

"I guess he had a change of heart," I said.

"Uh-huh," he said, not sounding convinced. "And you said you last saw Leia in the kitchen at the holiday party talking to Ross Ballantine? Did you hear what they were talking about?"

"No, I . . ." The sudden change of topic from tonight to the night of the party had taken me by surprise. "I was upset myself."

"Was Leia upset?"

I recalled Leia swiveling around when I came into the kitchen, spilling the wine she'd been pouring, her eyes wide and startled. *Like a deer in the headlights*. I'd thought she was surprised by my abrupt entrance but now I recalled that her eyes had been red around the rims and her cheeks were splotchy.

"Yes, I think she was upset about something. Cressida Janowicz said she was upset when she came out of the kitchen. She thought I had told her about the tenure decision."

"Did you?"

"No!" I cried, offended. "That would have been unprofessional."

The corner of Sergeant McAffrey's mouth twitched, amused, I imagined, that I would be offended at the suggestion I'd complained to a student about not getting tenure when I stood accused of killing that same student. "So she must have been upset about something Professor Ballantine said to her. Was that usual? Had you ever seen them arguing before?"

"Leia could be impassioned about her beliefs," I began. "Ross was just saying, before the ambulance came for Hannah, that Leia could be impulsive." I didn't add that he'd suggested that was why she might have run in front of my car. I was afraid Sergeant McAffrey would guess what Ross had said but he seemed preoccupied. He left the room for another ten minutes and then came to the door and waved for me to follow him out to the parking lot. I was surprised when he opened the passenger door of the police SUV for me.

"I guess you don't consider me a dangerous criminal anymore," I said, climbing into the SUV and looking with interest at the police radio.

"You can ride in the back if that makes you more comfortable," he replied coldly.

I shook my head, cowed by his tone, and remained silent for the rest of the drive. He turned the heater up and it felt good. I closed my eyes and must have drifted off for a few minutes—not surprising after all I'd been through—because when the car jolted me awake we were on an unfamiliar road passing a dilapidated old farmhouse. Was this a short-cut I didn't know? But then we turned in to a trailer park. I shook my head to clear the fog that seemed to have settled into my brain. Where was he taking me and why? I peered out the window for a clue.

Happy Acres Park read the sign in the SUV's headlights, but the park didn't look like a very happy place. The trailers huddled together like sheep trying to keep warm in the snow, their sidings dingy and dented, windows patched with cardboard and duct tape, screen doors torn and hanging crookedly on their frames. A few of the trailers were neater, their front paths shoveled, Christmas lights outlining their plain rect-angular shapes, wreaths hanging on the doors, but some looked as if the residents hadn't bothered even to shovel out from the snow. The one we pulled up to on the edge of the park sat crookedly on cracked cinder blocks; the snow drifted over the stoop was pocked by uneven footprints that led to a covered carport. McAffrey got out, leaving the engine and the headlights on. I sat for a moment, unsure what to do. I looked out the back window and saw a crooked blind move in the win-dow of a neighboring trailer.

I looked back at McAffrey. He was standing under the carport aw-ning staring at the car parked there, hands on hips. Light from the trail-er's windows fell on his face, carving shadows under his eyes and in grooves along the sides of his mouth. He looked tired and sad.

I got out of the SUV and waded across the snow to the carport. McAffrey's head nearly touched the top of the plastic awning, which was so heavy with snow it looked like it might collapse any minute. I stepped cautiously beside him and looked at the car. It was a com-pact sedan painted a dark color that was indiscernible in the dark. The front bumper was dented and listed to the right. That was because its flat tires had sunk unevenly into the asphalt. I looked closer and saw that there were deep ruts under the wheels. The chassis of the car was nearly flush with the ground. When I took another step something rus-tled in the car and a dark shape scurried out of the undercarriage into the dead weeds growing up out of the wheelbases. The car was home to mice and rot. It looked like a skeleton of an animal decomposing into a primordial swamp. I looked back through the driver's-side window and met the wide staring eyes of something covered with mangy fur.

I gasped and covered my mouth, unable to look away, my horror un-diminished when I realized it was only a stuffed animal suction-cupped to the window.

She thought she hit a cat, the caption had read above a photo of the surprised face and the splayed limbs of a stuffed animal suction-cupped to the window of the car that had killed my daughter.

"This is Hannah Mulder's car," I said, then turned to look at the trailer. Through the lit, uncurtained window I saw a cluttered room filled with tables piled high with newspapers and empty beer cans, a sagging couch bearing the impress of its owner, and a lump of mangy fur that might have been the litter mate of the stuffed animal in the car. "I see," I said. "This is to show me that Hannah Mulder didn't have a car to hit Leia with. But what does that prove? She could have bought another car or borrowed one from a friend."

He smiled at me but it was a sad smile. "Look around you. Does it look like Hannah Mulder can afford to buy another car? Does it look like she has any friends to borrow one from?"

I looked back through the window for anything to prove him wrong—pictures on the refrigerator, Christmas cards on the ledge above the television set—any sign that anyone else but Hannah had been inside her house but her since she'd gotten back from prison.

"Okay," I said, "I get your point."

"Do you?" He took a step closer to me and I backed up. Had he brought me here to threaten me? I wondered wildly. Would any of the residents of Happy Acres Park come to my rescue if I screamed? I had a feeling that no one here wanted trouble from the police.

But all he did was sniff. "You smell like bourbon," he said. "You smell just exactly like Hannah Mulder did when I pulled her in after she ran down your daughter."

I flinched. It would have been better if he had hit me. "I'm not Hannah Mulder," I cried, my voice sounding weak and pathetic in my own ears. "I'm not a drunk."

"Maybe not yet," he said, looking at me steadily, "but keep going the way you're going and"—he jerked his chin toward the sad tableau of Hannah's living room—"this is what your life is going to look like in a few years."

CHAPTER NINE

We didn't talk on the rest of the drive back to my house. I was too furious to trust myself to speak. How dare he? I fumed to myself. He didn't know me. He didn't know anything about me.

I expected McAffrey to leave me at the foot of my still unplowed driveway but he drove easily over the rutted tracks Anat had left. It was on the tip of my tongue to say my next car should be an SUV when I remembered that I might not have a car again. Instead, when he pulled up to my door, I turned to him and said, "I understand why you don't believe Hannah hit Leia, but why then do you think she was lurking outside my house—or do you think I was so drunk I made up that part too?"

"I don't think you made up *that* part," he said, staring straight ahead, his emphasis making it clear he thought I'd made up other parts. "I've followed Hannah half a dozen times from the Swan to your home. I know she's been hanging around here since she got out of prison."

"Oh," I said, not sure if I found it reassuring or creepy that McAffrey had been watching my house. Maybe he *did* know more about my life than I thought. Had he watched me buying bourbon at the local liquor store? Did he monitor my recycling for empty bottles? But instead of asking if he'd been watching me I asked, "Why were you watching her?"

"I wanted to make sure she wasn't bothering you. I had a word with her . . . I thought she'd stopped."

"She had . . . until yesterday. Did she say why she was doing it?"

"She didn't have to," he said, turning to me at last, his eyes full of sympathy but whether for Hannah or me I didn't know. "She was obviously looking for forgiveness. A person takes a child's life, they've destroyed their own life. They'll never be free of that."

Joe McAffrey's words rang in my head as I entered the house and the image of Hannah's desolate living room rose before my eyes. My half-hearted efforts to clean up last night hadn't made a dent in the mess that was my life. The clutter might have been made up of books and teacups instead of tabloid newspapers and beer cans, but at least half those teacups had held bourbon and in the gray light of dawn it was clear that the inhabitant of this mess was as broken as Hannah Mulder. The idea that I'd hoped to get out of my own mess by blaming Leia's death on Hannah seemed now as pathetic a delusion as Hannah's quest to gain my forgiveness.

I walked over to the desk below the window and looked down at the paper I'd been reading—Leia's paper—and read where I'd left off.

When I look up from my sewing I don't see a criminal, an addict, a killer—I see myself.

I turned the page and saw there was one more line to the story—

And I know that by forgiving them I have forgiven myself.

I took a shower and changed into sweatpants and a T-shirt. When I lay down in my bed, though, I kept thinking about Leia's paper. What had she done that needed forgiving? Unable to sleep I got up and went back to cleaning the house, working until the sun came up, trying to solve the puzzle of what Leia had to forgive herself for. What could Leia

Dawson—honors student, vegetarian, prison volunteer—have done that made her compare herself to the inmates of the Fishkill Correctional Facility? Handed in a library book late? Cheated on a test? Eaten factory-farmed chicken? But then I remembered what Ross had said about Leia—that she was volatile, liable to outbursts, that she didn't care who got in her way—

Then I thought about Ross and wondered how he was doing. He must feel terrible about Hannah—

Hannah. With a guilty start I realized I hadn't given a thought to her condition. Could I call the hospital and find out? But they were unlikely to tell me anything over the phone. Dottie knew all the nurses there, though, one was even a cousin. She'd be able to find out. I could call her—

But then I remembered how Dottie had looked at me yesterday and I knew I couldn't face her. I sat down on the couch, feeling like I'd just spun around in a circle. Whatever path my thoughts took I ended up someplace bad. Even sitting here on the couch next to Oolong reminded me of the cat lying on Hannah's couch. Was there anyone to feed it?

If I sat here on the couch doing nothing I would think about McAffrey's prophecy that I was turning into Hannah Mulder. He was wrong, of course. I was an English professor who had a few drinks in the evening while grading papers. That didn't make me the town drunk. Only, as I sat there I remembered the bottle of Four Roses in my coat pocket. I didn't think about drinking it. *That* would be pathetic. But I thought about it. And that was enough to get me off the couch and moving. I'd go to the hospital and check on Hannah, then I'd go to Ross's to let him know how she was. I got up, fed Oolong, and took the bottle of Four Roses out of my pocket. I poured its contents down the drain and put two cans of Fancy Feast in my pocket instead. The next time I saw McAffrey I could tell him I'd graduated from drunk to crazy cat lady.

*   *   *

I was outside before I remembered I didn't have a car. But I could hear the squealing brakes of the Loop bus coming from River Road. I ran down the hill, following the sunken footsteps from last night's pursuit, noticing that my own footprints were as wild and erratic as Hannah's, and reached the road just as the bus lumbered around the curve.

The Loop bus was free for SUNY Acheron students and faculty but local residents rode it too. This early, with classes over, most of the passengers looked like townspeople who worked at the college—I recognized Nilda, who cleaned the classrooms in the Humanities building, and a security guard—and some locals. One young man in a leather jacket, scruffy goatee, Ray-Bans, and porkpie hat looked like he'd partied at the college last night and was only now heading back home. He appeared to be college age, only when he took off his glasses to clean them I saw that his eyes were surrounded by a net of fine lines and when the morning sun hit his hair it lit up flecks of gray. An older student, maybe, or an aging hipster who preyed on college girls. I glared at him but he only smirked back and I realized that in my jeans and down coat I probably looked less like a college professor than one of the custodial workers—who, I remembered, had a better right to be protective of the college. At least they still had futures there.

I got off in town, stepping ankle deep into a puddle of icy slush. The temperature had risen above freezing and the sun was out. The owner of the village diner was pushing slush from the sidewalk with a broom. The local Boy Scout troop was selling wreaths in the town square. I was startled to realize that Christmas was only two days away. I had planned to go down to my mother's house in Tarrytown but the thought of spending the holiday with her husband—and his grown children and their children—was unimaginable. I'd call my mother later and tell her about Leia's death and explain that I had to stay at the college over the holiday. I didn't have to tell her that the police thought

I was the one who hit Leia or that I hadn't gotten tenure. Why ruin her holiday? She would act annoyed but I knew she would be secretly relieved. My stepsisters were uncomfortable around me. Without me there they would be free to bemoan my inability to move on—I could have married and had more children, I'd heard my stepsister Amy saying at Thanksgiving—and revel in the soccer trophies and good grades of their own children.

I stopped in the hospital gift shop to buy flowers—a plastic sheaf of red carnations and holiday ivy that looked too festive for Hannah. Remembering her bleak trailer I was betting she didn't celebrate the holidays much either. It didn't matter, though, because the volunteer at the front desk told me that Hannah Mulder wasn't available for visitors. I walked back to the gift shop, only a few steps away, to buy a card so I could leave the flowers. As she was ringing me up the gift shop clerk said, "I couldn't help overhearing that you were here to see Hannah Mulder. Are you a relative? I didn't think Hannah Mulder had any relations."

"No," I admitted, although it felt like a lie. We *were* related, by Emmy's blood and now Leia's. "I saw the accident and I just wanted to know how she was doing."

The salesclerk looked around to make sure no one else was in the store and leaned over the counter to whisper. "I heard the nurses talking . . . they say it doesn't look like she'll recover. But between you and me don't you think it would be a blessing if she didn't? You know what she did, right? Killed a little girl while driving drunk. How does anybody live with that?"

I shook my head, speechless. I'd often thought the same thing and even wondered why Hannah didn't kill herself, but to hear it put so nakedly made me go cold all over, as if I'd stepped back into that puddle of ice water.

"I suppose I should hold my tongue," the salesclerk said, seeing the shock on my face. "But this girl getting killed over by the college has brought it all up again." She held up a computer tablet and I recognized a Facebook page called "Overheard at Acheron," which I'd seen my students reading. "Even if they catch who did it they'll only put them away for a couple of years. I think there should be the death penalty for taking a child's life and I'm not ashamed to say it!" She thumped the tablet down against the counter and I recognized Hannah's face alongside another photo. I stared at it, the blood rushing to my face. When I looked up I saw that the salesclerk was staring at me.

"Why, she looks just like—"

I turned away before she could finish and blundered through the revolving door, which spit me out onto the sidewalk where I stood for a moment blinking in the sunlight. The photograph next to Hannah's was of me. *It's because Hannah ran over Emmy*, I told myself. *It can't be because of Leia.* I hadn't been arrested—

But then I remembered Kelsey Manning whispering to Sue Bennet at the vigil last night. Had Kelsey posted a story about me on the college site? I pulled out my phone, tucking the flowers I'd forgotten to leave for Hannah under my arm, and keyed *Overheard at Acheron* into the search engine. A spoked wheel revolved lazily on my phone's screen. My server got lousy service in the village. I had to get home to check my computer. I walked back to the bus stop and sat down on a bench next to a girl who was wearing earbuds and looking at her phone—as most of my students spent their lives doing, I reminded myself. It didn't mean she was reading about me. I glanced at her screen and saw orange and blue text bubbles. She moved an inch away from me. *Great*, I'd become a creepy stalker, no better than the aging hipster in Ray-Bans partying with college girls.

I looked at my phone. The page had loaded but I had to join a group to read it. I hesitated a moment, wondering what the page's administrator would make of my request, but then decided I had to chance it. I keyed in my request and looked nervously around while I waited for a response. A group of students came out of the diner clutching paper coffee cups and shuffled to the bus stop in a zombie-like trance. Why hadn't they gone home already? I wanted to demand, but I recognized one of the girls, Young Kim, from Intro Lit, an exchange student from Korea, who had written a smart, sensitive paper on James Baldwin's story "Sonny's Blues." "I understand the narrator's frustration with his brother because my family sacrificed so I could come to America to study and I feel I must live up to their expectations," she had written. She probably couldn't afford to fly home for the holidays. I thought of her and the other exchange students staying in the dorms over the holiday, heating up ramen noodles and ordering in pizza, and thought of asking Dottie if some of the professors couldn't get together and have them over—

Young Kim looked up, met my gaze, started to smile, and then looked nervously away. She ducked her head and whispered something to the girl she was with and they both moved a few feet away. Maybe they were just shy around professors, I thought, or embarrassed to see me out in casual clothes, a ridiculous bouquet of crushed carnations under my arm—

—or maybe they'd read that I was a suspect in Leia Dawson's death.

When the bus came I got on and moved quickly to the back. I sat down in the last row behind a familiar-looking porkpie hat. It was the aging hipster. What was he doing riding back toward the college? Maybe he'd forgotten something in some girl's dorm room.

I checked my phone to see if I'd been given access to the site, but my request hadn't been granted yet. Maybe I wasn't being allowed on the site because of the story about me.

Just before the bus started another student got on. I recognized Troy Van Donk despite his sunglasses and hoodie pulled low over his head. He headed toward the back of the bus but when he saw me changed his mind and took a seat in the middle, next to Young Kim, who moved over to make room for him. Was even Troy avoiding me? Well, I'd had enough of being a social pariah. I got up and took a seat on the other side of Troy.

"How are you doing, Troy?" I asked. "I was worried about you after I saw you coming out of Professor Janowicz's office. And then I didn't see you at Leia's vigil."

"I'd had enough of people singing praises to Saint Leia."

"I thought you were friends with Leia. I saw you with her at the faculty party."

He turned to me but I couldn't see his expression behind his dark sunglasses. "Sure, Leia was all right, but people are making her out to be a saint and she wasn't that. She was . . ."

His gaze drifted over my shoulder. I turned and saw that the aging hipster had gotten up and taken a seat closer to us.

"Human?" I asked, looking back at Troy.

He stared at me as if he'd lost track of what we'd been talking about. I wondered if he was stoned, but when I breathed in, trying to sniff for pot without being too obvious, all I smelled was woodsmoke and motor oil.

"It's not just that she had flaws," he said, "it's that she put on a different face for different people. She told me once that every time her folks moved she'd try out being a different person. She said it was like practicing to be a writer, making herself into a new character to fit her surroundings."

I remembered Ross saying that Leia was volatile. "Don't we all do that to some extent?" I asked.

"Maybe," Troy said, "but that doesn't make it hurt any less when you realize you've been lied to."

I was taken aback by his bitterness but when I started to ask what Leia had lied to him about the bus came to a stop and I saw we were at Orchard Drive.

"I think this is where you get off, Prof," Troy said, his voice thick with sarcasm.

"Yes," I said, getting up, "but if you want to talk more . . . I know what it's like to lose someone."

For a second the hardness in Troy's face seemed to soften. There was a quiver in his chin that I thought might be a prelude to tears, but then he swiped angrily at his face and leaned back, his arms spread over the back of the seat, his ankle crossed indolently over his knee. "Sure, Prof, I'll come by. I know where you live."

I thought I heard Young Kim titter behind her hand. I turned and got off the bus, angry that I'd let Troy Van Donk get to me. When the doors closed behind me I turned to cross the road and saw Troy through the bus window. He'd gotten up and moved to sit next to the aging hipster, probably to share ribald jokes at my expense.

I trudged up the hill and through the melting snow in my driveway. The clink of metal in my pockets reminded me I'd forgotten about Hannah's poor cat. It could be starving to death. Another soul on my conscience. By the time I got inside my feet were soaked and cold and I just wanted to crawl under the afghan on the couch with a bottle of bourbon—only there wasn't any more, I reminded myself, regretting now that I'd poured out the rest of the Four Roses—but I sat down at my desk instead and opened my laptop. "Overheard at Acheron" had accepted my request to join their group. I followed the link to their page—and found my photo next to Hannah Mulder's. The subject line read "She thought it was a cat."

CHAPTER TEN

I awoke the next morning to the thump of a newspaper hitting the front door—which was startling because I didn't *get* a newspaper. Sometimes I got local circulars and free editions of the *Acheron Gazette*, but mostly no one wanted to bother driving up my steep driveway, especially not in the snow. But we used to get a newspaper—Evan read the *Times*—and I remembered the sound of compressed paper hitting the front door.

I sat up, dislodging Oolong from my chest and my computer from my lap. I'd fallen asleep watching the comments accruing on "Overheard at Acheron," and public opinion seesawing from cautious censure (*If she hit her own student and left her to die on the road that would be really awful*) to the frenzied cries of a lynch mob (*Nancy Lewis should burn in hell for what she did to Laya Dawson!*). By two in the morning there'd been over a hundred comments. I refreshed the page now and found that the thread had been closed down. "In respect for the memory of Leia Dawson" it read in flowery script across a photo of a muted seascape. I should have felt relieved but the idea that hatred for me had run so deep that someone—Ross, I suspected—had had to step in and shut down the thread was somehow more unsettling. All that animosity was still out there—it would find another outlet.

I untangled myself from the afghan and warily opened my front door, half expecting a crowd of angry students and reporters in my driveway, but there was only a copy of the *Acheron Gazette*. I picked it up, scanning the front yard for anyone hiding behind an apple tree, but the only sign of life I saw was a pair of deer picking their way through the old orchard, foraging for windfall apples under the snow.

I went back inside, locked the door, and retreated into the kitchen before opening the paper. Leia's wide blue eyes, solemn and accusing, stared out at me from above the fold. I guessed from the short haircut and the angular line of her cheekbones that it was a recent picture. I wished they had chosen an older picture with her smiling and the lines of her face softened.

"Leia Dawson, 21, SUNY Acheron student, killed in hit and run. Police are still looking for the driver. . . ."

At least the *Acheron Gazette* wasn't trading in unsubstantiated rumors. I scanned the article, skimming through all Leia's accomplishments, and was relieved to see I wasn't mentioned on the first page. I flipped impatiently through the paper, past ads for Christmas turkeys at the local Hannaford's and a two-inch piece on a Poughkeepsie woman found floating in the Hudson and a story about a Pine Plains resident who used over two thousand Christmas lights to decorate his house, and found my name on the bottom of page 11. "Nancy Lewis, one of Leia's teachers, has been assisting the police in their inquiries. Ms. Lewis was at the party where Leia was last seen alive. . . ."

So were half a dozen other teachers, I wanted to scream. Why had the *Acheron Gazette* singled me out? But at least I wasn't accused of the crime here and it was only a local paper. No one I knew outside of Acheron would see it. Ten minutes later while I was making coffee my phone rang. As soon as I saw my mother's name on the screen I knew that wasn't true.

"Why are you helping the police with their inquiries?" my mother said by way of hello, her anxiety practically making my phone vibrate. "Isn't that code for being a suspect?"

"Not necessarily," I said cautiously. But not cautiously enough.

"Oh my God, Roberta Matheson was right—you *are* a suspect!"

"Roberta—"

"A woman in my yoga class. Her son goes to Acheron and he read on the internet that a Professor Lewis got drunk at a party and ran over that poor girl. Oh, Nan! I offered to send you to Betty Ford last year!"

"I'm not an alcoholic," I told my mother, thinking that there was no way to say that sentence without sounding like one. I didn't even have a drink last night, I wanted to add, but I didn't think that would help my case any.

"You had a lot of wine at Thanksgiving—"

"I spent the day listening to my stepsisters lauding their children's triumphs and pointing out that I was still young enough to have another child and *start over*. As if Emmy were replaceable. I could be excused an extra glass of wine."

"An excuse is worse than a lie—" she began.

"For an excuse is a lie, guarded," I finished the quote for her. "I wasn't making an excuse, Mom, I was speaking *figuratively*."

"As we do when we want to cloak the truth," she said.

I sighed. My mother distrusted fiction, believing it was a thinly veiled excuse for lying. "I wasn't drunk at the faculty party. And I didn't hit Leia Dawson. I hit a deer. The police questioned me because my car was damaged." I paused, but she remained silent, a technique I knew she used with her patients to elicit deeper confidences. She would have made a good detective. "And because they found blood on the tires. I-I may have backed over Leia when I left the scene, but she was already dead—"

"Oh my God, Nancy, do you have a lawyer?"

"Yes, Anat Greenberg."

"Anat's a lovely girl," she said, "but you need someone with more clout. Philip will know someone. We can talk about it when you get here this afternoon."

Crap. I'd completely forgotten that tonight was Christmas Eve. *And* I'd forgotten to call and say I couldn't come. My mother and stepfather always hosted Christmas Eve so that *the children*—meaning my two stepsisters—could spend Christmas Day at home with their children. And I suspect because the furor of kids opening presents was too much for my mother's nerves.

"About that, Mom, the police still have my car—"

"You can take the train. You shouldn't be driving anyway. Text me when you know what train you're on and I'll send one of the girls to pick you up."

I tried to protest, to come up with an excuse for not being able to go, but she had already rung off. It was just as well. She would have only quoted to me another aphorism on the futility of making excuses. Right now I was remembering the one that went "Excuses are the nails used to build the coffin for lost dreams."

The last thing I wanted was to get back on the Loop bus but it was the only way I had to get to the Poughkeepsie train station. I wore a hooded parka and dark sunglasses but the bus was mercifully empty save for a student so immersed in a video game on his phone he didn't look up when I got on. I stared out the window at the road as we passed the entrance to the Kingston-Rhinecliff Bridge. *Life Is Worth Living,* a sign proclaimed. The signs had gone up after a student jumped from the bridge. I sometimes wondered, though, if the signs didn't give people the idea that it was a place where you could kill yourself.

The train was crowded with holiday revelers on their way into the city for Christmas Eve—families on their way to Rockefeller Center and Radio City Music Hall, which meant dozens of little girls in their best wool coats, white tights, and black patent leather Mary Janes. Dozens of shining blond heads with neat braids and red and green ribbons. The whole car smelled like candy canes. "She's too young," I'd told

Evan when he suggested we take Emmy to *The Nutcracker*. "We'll take her next year."

By the time the train pulled into Tarrytown I was sorry I had gotten rid of Hannah's bottle of Four Roses. Maybe if my ride was late I could nip into the liquor store across from the station. I could buy my own fifth and not have to depend on my mother's parsimonious allotment of alcohol. *If you think that means I'm a drunk,* I explained to an imaginary Sergeant McAffrey, *then you haven't met my family.*

But my stepsister Amy was waiting outside in her Ford Escalade with its *My child is an honors student at The Hackley School* bumper sticker and the stick-figure-family decal on the back window that showed she had three kids and a dog. Whenever I saw one of those decals I thought of the story of Niobe, who bragged that she had more children than the goddess Leto and paid by having all fourteen of her children shot down by Apollo and Diana. In her grief she became a stone that wept.

"Hi, Amy," I said, climbing into the car. "Thanks for picking me up."

"I was glad for an excuse to get out of the house for ten minutes. The kids are riding my last nerve—" She looked nervously away and turned red. Amy treated my bereavement as an embarrassment, whereas her sister, Charlotte, saw it as a failing.

"The twins are nine now, right? Is Casey still into soccer?" I peppered her with questions about her children on the ride to the house to overcome her embarrassment—and to keep myself busy as we drove through my old neighborhood. Two years after my father died, during my sophomore year of college, my mother had married our family dentist, Philip, and moved into his (bigger) house just down the street from our old house. I was happy for her—and maybe a little bit relieved that I wouldn't have to worry about her as I embarked on my postcollege life—and Philip had always been scrupulously welcoming of me, but I had never felt comfortable in that house. My father and I had been "the dreamers," as my mother called us. He'd been an artist who ended up working at an ad agency. Without him I felt like I'd lost my ally in the family, the one who understood me. My mother thought that was why I'd married an artist, but I was pretty sure that Evan's draw had been how much he wanted children. I had wanted to start my own family as soon as possible.

The white colonial, with its glossy black shutters and red door, looked like it belonged in a Martha Stewart shoot for holiday decorating, complete with a modest dusting of snow (it had snowed less down here), tasteful white fairy lights trimming the eaves, and a fat evergreen wreath on the door. As I followed Amy up the meticulously shoveled brick path I glanced at my watch. Two hours, I told myself, I just have to get through two hours and then I'll say I have to catch the 4:34 train or I'll miss the last bus home. I can get through two hours.

My mother and stepfather were standing in the foyer when we came in, shoulder to shoulder, in matching plaid sweaters, which I suspected were part of some family photograph scheme. They looked like they were standing on the reception line after a wedding—or a funeral. They must have heard Amy's car and rushed to the front door to greet us. I felt a pang of unexpected gratitude at the gesture and heard my father's voice in my head telling me, "Of course your mother loves you, Nan, she just has her own way of showing it."

Right now she showed it by holding out her forearms, her elbows pressed to her waist, in a sort of truncated welcome. I stepped in between her stiff arms and leaned down to kiss her cool, powdery cheek. Her hands patting my back felt like moths battering against my down coat. When I straightened up she grasped my elbows and looked me in the eye. "Philip has found you the best lawyer in Westchester. You have an appointment with him on Wednesday."

"Mom, I've got Anat—and I probably won't even need a lawyer. They'll find traces of the deer I hit on my car and then they'll find out who really hit poor Leia."

Philip made a dismissive sound. "Those small-town cops couldn't find their asses with their elbows."

"Phil!" my mother *ts*ked.

"Well, it's the truth!" Philip's pale balding head turned bright pink. "Saul Bledsoe said as much when I told him about the case."

"I don't think we should discuss it now," my mother said in a hushed whisper. "We'll upset everyone for nothing."

There was an edge to my mother's voice that I remembered well from childhood—when I spilled my milk at the dinner table, when my father lost his job at the ad agency, when anything threatened the careful order of the household. People often thought that because my mother was a therapist I had grown up in an atmosphere of openness, but I had realized a long time ago that my mother had become a therapist to cope with her own crippling anxiety.

"I agree," I said quickly. "Where are the kids? I have presents."

At the word a small face ringed with black curls appeared between the banister spindles on the stairs. It was my stepniece Amanda, Charlotte's youngest. She was eleven, born the same year as Emmy. She came running down the stairs, sneakers squeaking on the hardwood, black curls bouncing. She was wearing a green velvet tunic over red leggings and looked like a Christmas elf.

"Do you have something for me, Aunt Nan?"

"Yes, but you'll have to wait for Christmas morning to open it."

"But then you won't get to see how much I like it," she replied, poking at the large canvas bag I carried. "And that would hardly be fair to you."

I laughed—and realized it was the first time since hearing I hadn't gotten tenure at the faculty party. "That's a good argument. I'll have to give out everybody's presents, then. Could you take me to where they're all hiding?"

Amanda led me through the kitchen where her mother, Charlotte, was putting the finishing touches on the Christmas buffet. She kissed me primly on the cheek and told Amanda not to pester me. When I explained I was going to find the other kids to give out presents she shook her head.

"No presents before Christmas morning. If you start giving out presents they'll only whine for the rest of them and Christmas Eve will be ruined."

Amanda insisted that wasn't true, then contradicted her argument by starting to whine. Charlotte held her ground, glaring at me as if to say *See what you've started*, and Amanda ran off in a huff.

"You can't let them run all over you," she said, doling out the advice as if I still needed parenting skills when clearly it had been my lack of them that had led to Emmy's death. Who lets their four-year-old play in the yard without adult supervision? That I agreed with her didn't make it any less pleasant to be reminded.

"I'm sorry," I said. "It's just that I won't be here to see her open it."

"I'll make sure she writes a thank-you note. You haven't gotten her anything too . . . elaborate, have you?"

Last year there'd been a ruckus over a pair of velvet ballet slippers I'd given to her. "No, it's a book. About fairies. I hope she's still into them."

Charlotte rolled her eyes. "That's all she wants to read about. I've been trying to interest her in historical fiction. At least she'd get something useful out of it."

"Well, this book was given an award by the American Library Association, so *they* must think it's useful." I hoped that the award and the pretty butterfly on the cover would keep Charlotte from realizing that the book—*Tithe: A Modern Faerie Tale*, by Holly Black—was a deliciously dark tale, but knowing Charlotte, she probably read everything her children read to make sure it met her high standards.

"As long as it doesn't give her nightmares like that last book you gave her—and speaking of nightmares"—she lowered her voice and leaned over a tray of mini quiches—"Cooper and I discussed it and I have to tell you that we can no longer allow you to take Amanda anywhere unsupervised. Given . . . everything that's happened. So while it was kind of you to get those tickets for *Beauty and the Beast* for her birthday—"

"But I already promised her—"

Charlotte held up her hand. "That's our final decision. I'll be happy to take her if you give me the tickets."

I stared at Charlotte. Her face was rigid and set. She had never liked my spending time with Amanda. I think she thought my interest in her was ghoulish and that I was one of those childless spinsters who kidnaps other people's babies.

"I'll mail them to you," I said and then, swiping a mini quiche, turned and left the kitchen and wandered into the family room where Doug and Cooper, Amy's and Charlotte's husbands, were lounging on the couch talking about the stock market and drinking single-malt scotches. I sat with them and helped myself to a glass.

"I hear you've had a spot of bother," Cooper said in the pompous accent he seemed to have acquired from attending Choate and Yale. "A DUI, Char said."

"Not at all. I hit a deer. . . ." I told the story for what felt like the hundredth time. It was beginning to ring false in my own ears, but Cooper seemed satisfied with it. "You've got nothing to worry about. They can't tie the car to you if the cop didn't catch you in it—chain of evidence and all that. A buddy of mine at Goldman got out of a DUI by dodging the idiot cops, ditching the car, and diving into his own EZ-Boy with a glass of Stoli before the cops were at the door. They couldn't prove he didn't do his drinking *after* he got home." Cooper clinked his glass against mine.

"These cops aren't idiots," I said, sipping from my glass. Cooper might be an ass but he had great taste in scotch. "I'll get off because I didn't do it."

I left the family room and wandered into the "entertainment room," where the kids were all parked in front of a huge flat-screen TV watching *Frozen*. At least, Amanda and her two sisters were watching— Casey and Carter were playing games on their Game Boys and their three-year-old brother was building a tower of blocks. I squeezed onto the couch between Amanda and Tracy and watched the movie, which

I'd heard my students talking about but hadn't seen. I knew it was a version of "The Snow Queen" but I found it hard at first to connect the Hans Christian Andersen tale to this story of Princess Elsa, who accidentally hurts her sister, Anna, with her cryokinetic powers and runs off, leaving the kingdom snowbound. But the music was good and the animation was pretty. I sipped my drink with Amanda's and Tracy's warm bodies beside me, laughing at the antics of the reindeer and snowman and crying when Elsa accidentally freezes Anna's heart.

"Don't worry, Aunt Nan," Amanda said, squeezing my hand, "she can be saved by an act of true love."

I sniffed and squeezed her hand back. Then peeled myself off the couch and headed back into the family room for a refill.

"—we don't know she *hit* the girl," Amy was saying. I stopped in the threshold, holding my breath so they wouldn't hear me. They were all facing away from me so they hadn't seen me.

"Sure. She hit a 'deer.'" Doug made air quotes with his fingers. "Have you seen how much she drinks?" *Hypocrite!* I thought. *He drinks twice what I do.*

"Phil's found a good lawyer," my mother said.

"And what's that going to cost?" Cooper asked. "And who's going to pay the legal fees? That second-rate state college she works at sure as hell doesn't pay enough."

"I have enough to take care of it," Phil said.

"No you don't, Phil," Cooper said. "Not without eating into your retirement or the grandkids' college funds."

"I will not sacrifice my children's futures to her," Charlotte said.

"Char's right," Cooper said, swirling the ice in his glass. "If we're not careful she'll drag this family down."

I backed out before anyone could see me, into the TV room, where Kristoff and Anna were wandering on the screen through a blizzard unable to find each other. Even Casey and Carter had put down their Game Boys to watch. I slipped back into the front hall, where I made a call on my cell phone for a taxi, and waited in the powder room until I heard it pull up. My mother was standing in the foyer when I came out.

"You're going," she said, wringing her hands. It wasn't a question.

"I think it's best—before I *drag* down the family."

"Oh, Nancy, you always were too sensitive."

I started to laugh but then I saw how she was hugging her arms around her waist as if she were afraid she'd fly apart if she didn't hold on to herself. *Your mother works so hard to control you because she's scared to death of losing you,* my father once told me. I looked at her now and thought that the only cure for a fear that deep was to finally lose the thing you were so afraid of losing. I think she saw that too— that it would be a relief to let me go and not have to worry about me anymore.

"You're right," I said, touching her arm. Her muscles felt like steel rods beneath the soft cashmere. "I just want to get home early and get some sleep. Anat's calling me tomorrow. I won't need Phil's lawyer, Mom. Don't worry."

"If you're sure. . . ." I could see her relief that she wouldn't have to argue with her stepchildren over the money. There was nothing my mother hated more than conflict.

"I'm sure," I said, leaning forward to kiss her cheek. I turned and left before she could see the tears filling my eyes and managed to get in the taxi before they fell.

I got a window seat on the train on the way back and spent the ride staring out at the river so no one would see the tears slipping under my dark glasses. *Stupid,* I told myself, of all the things to get to me, Cooper's comment about my dragging down the family. It's what I felt like, though, a rusty anchor plummeting down through water as lead-gray and cold as the river outside the train window. Ice was forming along the banks, moving down the river in great dirty-white chunks. I thought of that body found in the river and shuddered, imagining what it would feel like to fall into that icy water—

"Professor Lewis?"

I startled at the sound of my name, afraid I'd been tracked down by the press or, worse, the police, but when I turned from the window I saw it was Aleesha Williams hovering in the aisle. I swiped at my face, embarrassed to be caught crying by a student—and then noticed I wasn't the only one crying.

"Aleesha, what is it? What's happened?"

"It's my cousin Shawna." She sank into the seat next to me. "She was found dead in the river."

"No! I just read about a body being found this morning."

"That was Shawna," she said, blowing her nose, her heavy down coat making a sighing sound as it settled around her. "My uncle Theodore ID'd her this morning. I'm just coming back from my auntie's house in Peekskill—imagine finding out a thing like that on Christmas Eve!"

"Oh, Aleesha, I'm so sorry! Do they know what happened?"

"They're saying she OD'd and fell in the river down by that old abandoned factory where the crackheads hang out, but the thing is, Shawna was clean since she come out of jail. Why's she going to go shoot up in some nasty old factory down by the river?"

I shook my head, not sure how I was supposed to answer when I'd just been imagining sinking into the river myself. "Christmas can be a bad time," I said. "Maybe she wasn't able to handle coming back from prison."

"I guess." Aleesha wiped her eyes. "If I'd've known . . . I should of spent more time with her, but I've been busy with finals—"

"Don't do that to yourself," I said, taking Aleesha's hand in both of mine. "You're working hard to make a life for yourself and your little girl. I'm sure Shawna wouldn't begrudge you that."

"Yeah, but when I think that I was writing papers and taking tests while Shawna was shooting up somewhere . . . and the hell of it is I was writing about *her*. Maybe I jinxed her. Have you ever felt like that, Professor Lewis? That your writing made something bad happen?"

I saw myself writing at my desk, Emmy playing outside the window—

"Nothing you did hurt your cousin," I told Aleesha firmly. "The dealer who sold her the drugs is the one who hurt her and I bet the police are looking for him right now."

Aleesha managed a small smile at that. "For a black girl from the projects when they've got a white college girl's killer to find? I don't think so, Prof. The only one the police are looking for right now is the sorry asshole who killed Leia Dawson."

CHAPTER ELEVEN

It was full-on dark when the Loop bus let me off on River Road. The only light came from Leia's shrine. There were over a dozen candles there now, and the wall was crowded with stuffed animals, flowers, and pictures of Leia. My mind flashed to Shawna Williams. Would anyone build a shrine for her at that abandoned factory on the river amidst the broken needles and empty beer cans?

I looked carefully for anything out of place, like the barrette or the Four Roses bottle, but there was nothing now and nothing more to come now that Hannah was in the hospital.

I trudged up the hill feeling like I'd been gone for a week. With no porch light on, no car outside, and the snow still unplowed, the house looked like it had been abandoned. It might have been one of the deserted outbuildings on the Blackwell estate, like the old boathouse that students partied in and told stories about. A haunted house. That's what my house had become, only Emmy wasn't the ghost—I was.

Oolong was waiting at the door and made a break for it. I scooped her up and tossed her inside, explaining that she was far too old to go out anymore. Didn't she know it was freezing outside? I kept up a steady stream of admonishments as I fed her, trying to dispel the silence that sat over the house like a caul. I microwaved a frozen dinner, looked through my cabinets telling myself I wasn't looking for something to drink, and made a cup of tea instead.

"I am not an alcoholic," I told Oolong, who gave me a skeptical look and went to sleep on the couch.

I sat down at my desk and searched the Web for references to Leia. I found a student site with a discussion even more vicious than the one on "Overheard at Acheron." After reading a dozen nasty comments I went upstairs to Emmy's room and fell asleep watching the painted stars winking in the sandpapery glow. I awoke to a blade of light slicing through the room and the sound of a car engine. My first thought was that the police had come to arrest me; my second that it was a vigilante group come to lynch me. The engine turned off and I heard the heavy metal *chunk* of a door opening. I listened for voices but heard only a single set of footsteps heading for my door.

I got up, scanning the room for something I could use as a weapon. A Fisher-Price dollhouse? A Minnie Mouse night-light? I remembered that Evan had kept a baseball bat under our bed and I wished it was still there—wished *he* was still here. Why had I stayed here all alone in a remote farmhouse where I could be killed in my bed—

The front door clicked open. I was sure I'd locked it—*hadn't I?*—but it was a flimsy lock. Evan was always saying we should replace it.

I reached for my phone but it wasn't on the night table. It must be downstairs in my bag. I'd stopped paying for a landline years ago. I opened the night table drawer quietly and celebrated silently when I found a heavy Maglite inside. Evan had put one in every room because we lost power so often. The batteries were long dead but the metal casing was reassuringly heavy in my hands. I crept out onto the landing and saw that someone had turned a light on in the living room—not standard operating procedure for a thief or vigilante, I thought. There was no point creeping down the rickety old stairs, so I walked down firmly, holding the Maglite over my head, shouting, "Who's there?" When I reached the bottom I saw the silhouette of a man sitting in my desk chair and looking at my computer screen, which I'd left on at a student Tumblr site that had taken up the discussion closed on "Overheard at Acheron."

"These students should be expelled for spreading this tripe on the Web—it's libel."

"Ross?" I asked, lowering my arm. "What are you doing here? How did you get in?"

He held up a key in his right hand. "You gave me a key—remember?"

"Over six years ago!" I said, moving closer. The sudden relief I'd felt when I recognized him was dissipating. Even from across the room I could smell liquor. It was coming from an open bottle of Glenlivet. His usually impeccably coiffed hair stood up in unruly tufts. His beautiful cashmere coat bunched up around his stooped shoulders like a damp pelt.

"You never asked for it back," he said with a sly smile that sent a chill from my bare feet up to the nape of my neck.

"Are you returning it now?" I asked, trying to keep my voice level. "You could have come by in the . . . oh, I don't know . . . daytime?"

"And give the scandalmongers more fuel for their bonfire?" He picked up the empty bottle of Four Roses I'd left on the kitchen counter and shook it at me. "Do we really pay you so little this is the best you can afford even on Christmas Eve?"

I sank down onto the arm of the couch, feeling drained after the rush of adrenaline. "I found that on Leia's shrine," I said. "I think Hannah left it. I see you've brought your own. Do you really think driving drunk is such a good idea after what happened to Leia—and Hannah? If you were pulled over—"

"It doesn't matter now," he said. "By tomorrow this site will be plastered with my picture, not yours. That's why I came by—to give you the good news. The police have a new suspect." He threw open his arms and bowed his head. "Yours truly."

"For Leia's death?" I asked, appalled but also, to my shame, with a queasy twinge of relief. "But you were at home, cleaning up after the party."

"Yes, I *was* at home—not actually cleaning, though, Dottie saw to that—but apparently my car had ideas of its own. Your friend Sergeant McAffrey has informed me that a little bit of Leia's red leather jacket found its way into the radiator grille of the Peugeot."

My mind flashed on an image of Leia standing outside the barn in her red leather jacket, looking brave and jaunty in the cold, and then, horribly, I saw that jacket shredded and bloody, scraps twisted in metal. "There must be some mistake," I said. "You couldn't have run Leia over."

"Because you did?" He suddenly sounded dead sober. A warning shot of adrenaline pulsed through my blood. I remembered how that night over Hannah's inert body he'd tried to coax me into admitting that I'd run over Leia. Was that why he'd been coming here that night— and why he was here tonight? With a bottle of expensive scotch to ply me with? So I would take the blame for something he did?

"No, because I believe that you were home. Dottie will say you were there—"

"She left before the time Leia was run over."

"Was there anyone else with you after Dottie left?" I asked. "I know that the students love to listen to you—"

"You make it sound like I'm the Pied Piper, some lecherous old fart preying on vulnerable young girls."

"I didn't mean that at all," I protested.

"No? Isn't it what you said to me when you broke off with me? That I'd taken advantage of you as much as if you were a student?"

What I'd said, I now painfully recalled, was that a department head who slept with a newly hired teacher was as bad as a professor sleeping with a student. "I didn't know what I was saying. Of course it's not the same thing . . . I was hurt. . . ." I suddenly remembered *why* I'd been hurt. Cressida had taken me out to lunch and explained to me that Ross Ballantine was infamous for seducing graduate students at his last job at Cornell. Why did I think someone of his stature had ended up at a state school? If people learned of the affair—as she had by seeing us coming out of a B&B in Hudson—I wouldn't be taken seriously either and I'd never get tenure. "Ross," I said now, "you weren't . . . you and Leia . . ."

He threw the Four Roses bottle against the wall. The sound of it shattering made me jump. I felt for the Maglite, which I'd let slip into the couch cushions. "There! There it is!" Ross shouted. "That's what everyone will be saying. You take an interest in a student, mentor her—because she's *remarkable*, because she reminds you of yourself when you started writing, when you had that fire in your belly—and everyone wants to make it into something *ugly*. Hell, Cressida Fucking Janowicz spent far more time with Leia than I did. She had Leia to her house for cozy dinners by her fireside. Why not suspect *her* of having an affair with Leia? Does anyone even know what Cressida's orientation is?"

"I'm not sure she has one," I said. I hadn't meant to be funny—Cressida had once admitted to me that she simply didn't have that much interest in sex—but Ross was suddenly laughing and so was I, as much from tension as anything else. And then I noticed that Ross's laughter had turned to sobs.

"Hey," I said, taking a tentative step forward and squeezing Ross's arm. "I don't think you were sleeping with Leia. I know you wouldn't do that. And even if you were, you wouldn't run her down and leave her for dead. Someone else must have taken your car—you leave the keys in an ashtray by your kitchen door, for Pete's sake."

He nodded and wiped his face with his cashmere scarf. "That's right. Anyone at the party could have taken it. But how will I *prove* that? You see how quickly the vultures circle." He pointed at the computer and I saw that the new forum discussing appropriate punishments for me had 263 comments. Even if the police were looking at a new suspect no one would know—*unless someone leaked it.* Ross must have guessed what I was thinking.

"You could have your friend McAffrey whisper a word in Kelsey Manning's ear. I hear she's gotten an internship at *Gawker* out of this—a girl who could barely string two sentences together without dangling a modifier! She hardly passed my British Lit class."

"He's not my friend," I said. "You are. I'd never do that to you." *But he's asking you to*, a little voice said in my head. I shook it away and leaned over the desk, scrolling through the comments. *Nancy Lewis is a washed-up has-been who killed Leia Dawson because she was jealous of her* was one of the kinder ones. "Besides, I think it might be too late for me."

Ross's hand stole over mine. "Don't say that, Nan. It's not too late for you—and maybe it's not too late for us either."

He pulled me down into his lap, one arm circling my waist, the other cupping my face. He felt so warm after the chill of the floor that I wanted to lay my head against his chest and go to sleep, but then he drew my head down to his and found my mouth and I woke up. The taste of the expensive scotch he'd been drinking made me feel instantly drunk. I remembered that this is what it felt like to be with him—drunk, whether we were drinking or not, although usually we were. He deftly repositioned my legs so that I slid into the curve of his lap like a clasp sliding shut. I remembered how well our bodies had fit together in all those corny Catskill hotels—the Dew Drop Inn, the Ko-Z Kabins—and how he'd moved me into positions I hadn't imagined. I remembered that I liked being moved because it meant I didn't have to think and thinking was the last thing I wanted to do after Emmy. And with Ross, after a couple of drinks, I didn't have to think. What I was having trouble remembering was why I had called things off. Because of my job? Well, hell, that wasn't a problem anymore.

I slid one leg up and over and straddled him. His hands were under my T-shirt, stroking my breasts, and mine were pulling at his belt.

The chair creaked beneath us, juddering an inch over the wood floor, the way it had that day I'd looked up from my desk when I heard the screech of tires on River Road—

Come back!

My hands froze on his belt buckle. I could hear the voice calling—as I had in my dream when I'd fallen asleep in the woods—only it didn't sound like my voice—

"What's wrong? Do you want to go upstairs?"

I looked into his eyes—why did they always seem so sad? I remembered the way he would plunge us down those dark roads, the way we lost ourselves at those divey Catskill hotels. I'd thought he was helping me to lose myself but I soon realized he was trying to get lost too. All that posing in front of his classes and sitting around the fireside charming his students with stories of his early successes, the famous writers he'd gone to Iowa with, the need to feel himself reflected in his students' successes. *Sometimes I think that if I'd had the balls to tough it out on my own without the safety net of an academic job I could have been a great writer*, he once told me at one of those hotels. *Now all I can hope for is that one of my protégés will be one.*

"No," I said, easing back. "I don't think this is a good idea . . . we're both not thinking."

"I remember when you liked not thinking," he said, stroking my face and drawing his thumb down my throat until it rested in the curve of my collarbone. As if he were taking my pulse. It made me feel exposed, even more than his hands on my breasts had. I saw Leia turning in the kitchen, her long white neck elegant and fragile. . . .

"I don't think I can afford that kind of oblivion anymore." I swung my leg over his and stood up. The floor felt cold against my bare feet. The draft from the window on the small of my back where his hand had warmed it was like ice. "If I hadn't passed out in the woods that night—"

"Passed out?"

Too late I realized this wasn't part of the story I'd told him. Perhaps because it made me sound like a drunk.

"Fell asleep. When I went looking for the deer I started thinking about Emmy. I sat down on a log and . . . it was so peaceful. Lovely, dark, and deep." I smiled, knowing how much he liked Frost.

But he didn't return my smile. "Do you know how long you were out?"

"No, why?"

"Wouldn't you have heard the car that hit Leia? If someone *did* steal my car and hit her, that is."

A screech of tires. A voice screaming, "Come back!"

"I think I did hear it, but it mingled with my dream and I kept sleeping. When I got to the road there wasn't any car and I didn't see Leia in the ditch so enough time had passed for the snow to cover her."

"Are you sure?" he asked, looking skeptical. "If you saw the car you'd know who was driving it. Maybe you saw it driving away and you didn't think anything of it."

"There were no cars on the road. And the snow had covered Leia."

"Maybe you'll remember something," he said, straightening the seam of his trousers and crossing his legs. "It would be helpful if you did—for you as well as me. My guess is that a student stole the car. Didn't you tell Dottie that you saw some students hanging out by the barn?"

Of course Dottie had passed that on. "Yes, but—"

"Wasn't one of them Troy Van Donk? Damn, I bet Troy knows how to hot-wire a car. He wouldn't even need to steal the keys. And he was fighting with Leia—"

"Actually they were laughing when I saw them."

"*I* saw them arguing earlier. In fact, I think that's what Leia was about to tell me in the kitchen before you interrupted us. She was telling me about some 'bar crawl' in Poughkeepsie she'd gone on with Troy—an odyssey, she called it, nothing romantic. Then you burst in. But we can imagine the rest. Troy had misunderstood her and thought the 'bar crawl' was something more. He started getting possessive, following her. Maybe he decided to follow her home in my car and when she wouldn't get in he drove her off the road in a fit of drug-induced rage."

I stared at him. Sitting back in my desk chair, legs crossed, he looked as he did when he sat by his fireside regaling students with stories. That's what he was doing now. I already couldn't recall where the odyssey part Leia had told him ended and the part about Troy stalking her began. The story he was spinning about Troy had the compelling ring of truth, which, as I always told my students, had nothing to do with whether or not it really happened. All Ross needed were a few corroborating stories. Dottie and Cressida could contribute the scene of Troy bursting out of Cressida's office and giving Dottie the finger. If I just added my suddenly recovered memory of Troy driving Ross's car, the story would gain heft and credence. I wouldn't be a suspect anymore— I'd be a witness. I remembered the bitterness in Troy's voice when he'd spoken about Leia yesterday.

"I saw Troy on the bus yesterday and he did sound very bitter about Leia. He said she played a role with him—that she lied to him."

"You see!" Ross leaned forward eagerly. "Troy is the logical suspect. He even has a record. I *do* blame myself for not seeing it and for not paying more attention to what Leia was trying to tell me but then you came into the kitchen and you were so upset about the tenure decision."

I winced. "That seems so petty now."

"No, Nan, I shouldn't have let *that* happen either. I told you I'd recommend a review and I meant it. Once this is all behind us—if I'm still chair, that is."

"Why wouldn't you be?"

He tilted his chin toward my computer. I glanced back at the screen and saw that the tally of comments had gone up. "While we're sitting here the cyber-scavengers are pecking over your reputation. That's what they'll be doing to me if it gets out that my car was involved . . . un-

less the police focus on another suspect first. Then all this will go away."
He leaned forward and shut my computer. His arm brushed against
my leg but I no longer felt any desire for him. Instead I felt a wariness
creeping up from the cold floorboards. Had Ross just suggested that if
I incriminated Troy he'd see to it that I'd get tenure?

"I can't say that I saw Troy in the car if I didn't."

"Of course not," Ross said, getting to his feet and standing over me.
"I'd never ask you to. But you may remember more as you think about
that night. You were upset, you'd had a few drinks, then you had the police grilling you. Details might come back to you now that you're not so
afraid." He stroked the side of my face with the back of his hand. "That's
the main reason I came here tonight. So you wouldn't feel afraid anymore. So you would feel safe." He looked down at me, his eyes full of
regret. For what? I wondered. Because I'd rejected his advance? But I
already had the feeling that his attempted seduction had been as much
an act as the one he put on in the classroom. That he was more inter-
ested in my getting him off the hook than in my getting into bed with
him. And that if I didn't—

"Be careful driving home," I said, trying not to show him how afraid
I suddenly felt.

He leaned down and brushed his lips against my cheek. "I will," he
said, his breath warm on my face. "You be careful too."

CHAPTER TWELVE

After Ross left I noticed that he'd left the bottle of Glenlivet behind. It glowed in the light of my laptop like those Catskill sunsets Ross and I had driven toward that summer. The smoky taste of the scotch was on my lips from Ross's kiss. It was the taste of forgetting, of oblivion.

I don't think I can afford that kind of oblivion anymore, I'd just told Ross. But sitting here alone in my cold, empty house I wondered if I had the courage to do without it. What if the truth was that while I lay asleep—*passed out*—in the woods someone had killed Leia? *Come back!* I'd heard in my dream. Only, what if it hadn't been a dream? What if someone had been shouting for Leia to come back and when she didn't he—or she—ran her down and killed her? If I hadn't been asleep—*passed out drunk*—I could have helped her. Would I be able to live with that?

Without realizing it I noticed that I'd moved closer to the bottle and was hovering over it as if it were a flame I was huddling over for warmth. Or as if instead of oblivion it promised memory—like Proust's madeleine—one taste and the whole episode in the woods would come clear. *You were drunk then so maybe being drunk now—*

I opened the bottle and poured an inch into Ross's glass before another voice, sounding suspiciously like Sergeant McAffrey's, added: *I thought you said you weren't drunk that night. I thought you said you'd only had two glasses—*

Shut up, I told the McAffrey voice, taking a sip of the scotch. It burned my tongue as if the bottle really did contain liquid flame. *I'm trying to remember.*

I took the glass upstairs. I tried lying down in my room but just as I was falling asleep I heard the train whistle coming from the tracks near the river. It was a lonesome sound that seemed romantic when we first moved here but over the years had come to sound like the keening of a child. I got up and moved to Emmy's room, on the side of the house farthest from the tracks, where the whistle didn't carry, and lay down in her bed. I looked up at the painted stars on the ceiling, trying to remember looking up at the night sky through the tangle of branches. I remembered there'd been a glimpse of moon despite the snow, so bright I'd closed my eyes against it—

Come back!

I heard it now, as clear as if someone had spoken it out loud. I opened my eyes to the stars on Emmy's ceiling, only they weren't Emmy's stars, they were snowflakes, each one lit up like one of the candles at Leia's vigil. They were drifting down from the sky and gathering on the blond hair and blue dress of a little girl.

Emmy. She was standing in front of me, dressed in the Blue Fairy costume she'd worn for Halloween the year she was four—her last Halloween—and the pink leggings and long-sleeved shirt I'd made her wear under the costume because it had been cold that night and she had refused to wear a coat—because fairies didn't wear coats. On her feet were the light-up Skechers that Evan had bought her so she'd stand out trick-or-treating in the village. So she wouldn't be run over. She had a smudge of chocolate on her mouth from the Reese's Pieces she'd sneaked from her goody bag. Each detail was so vivid that even though I knew she was dead I believed she was standing there in front of me.

I held my arms open wide, but she shook her head, blond braids swinging. "No, Mama, you come on. We have to go!" She turned on her heel and ran into the woods.

"Emmy!" I cried. "Come back!"

But she only laughed and kept running. I ran after her, following the flashing lights of her sneakers. She was running up the hill, through the old orchard, dancing behind the gnarled old trees, playing hide-and-seek. My heart stuttered every time she vanished behind a tree.

"Come back!" I cried.

"I'll catch up with you at the party!" she screamed and then ducked behind a thick trunk. When she came out she wasn't Emmy anymore; she was Leia.

"No!" I cried.

Leia looked back at me over her shoulder. She was wearing her red jacket, the old cracked leather peeling like bark, and her red cowboy boots, but they still lit up like Emmy's sneakers when she turned and ran. "Come on, Prof, you said you would catch up, so *catch up*!"

She ran through the snow, flakes of her jacket peeling off in the wind like red leaves, and leapt over the crest of the hill—

When she hit the ground she had become a deer. I followed her, sure that the deer was still somehow Emmy and Leia and that it would lead me to what they had wanted to show me. Even when the deer leapt into the river I leapt after her, into the icy water—

I woke up, gasping for breath, slick with sweat that had chilled in the draft from the open window. My head felt as heavy and clouded as the sky outside, as if I had fallen into the river and gotten sealed under the ice. For a moment I wished I had. If that was where Emmy had been leading me that's where I ought to be. Maybe the dream meant that I was supposed to throw myself in the river and drown myself. Then I'd be with Emmy again—and Leia and Shawna Williams. I felt the weight of the dead tipping me toward them, as if I were standing on one end of an ice floe and they were standing on the other, weighting the balance so I would slide down into the icy water—

Or I'd had the dream because Ross had asked me to remember what happened in the woods the night Leia died.

I walked downstairs. My laptop was still open on my desk, the bottle of Glenlivet standing next to it, a sad tableau that reminded me of a happier one of a plate of half-eaten reindeer cookies, a half-finished glass of milk, and a thank-you note in Evan's spiky handwriting from Santa to Emmy. As I stood on the stairs I imagined the tree we had cut down at the Christmas tree farm on the old Stanfordville Road, trimmed with the ornaments of farm animals and deer and tiny gray mice tucked inside walnut shells that Evan had made. I remembered Emmy running downstairs in her fleecy red pajamas to see if Santa Claus had eaten the cookies we'd left for him. I could feel the weight of her warm, eager body tilting the balance of that ice floe—

I'd go out. Not to town or the college or anywhere I'd meet anyone. I'd go back to the woods where it all started and then I'd follow the path Emmy had shown me last night in my dream. I'd see where it led me. After all, it was Christmas morning, when the past came back to haunt us. Besides, what else did I have to do with the day?

I made myself tea and instant oatmeal, which I had to eat plain because the milk had gone bad, and dressed myself warmly in long underwear and fleece and down. I felt like I was feeding and dressing a child, coaxing myself to complete these burdensome tasks in anticipation of some future treat—

Just one more bite of your peas and then you can have dessert!

You can play in the snow if you put on your mittens!

When I was dressed I washed my mug and bowl and left them to dry in the drain rack by the sink. I put the Glenlivet away in the cupboard next to the vitamins and Tylenol. I straightened out the pillows on the couch, cleared all recent searches on the computer, and closed it. I stuck the *Acheron Gazette* in the recycle bin. I put the *Beauty and the Beast* tickets in an envelope, stamped and addressed it to Amanda, and put the envelope in the mailbox.

When I opened the door Oolong tried to run out and I had to push her back in with my foot. I had the feeling she was trying to flee a sinking ship. Or that she was trying to *get* to something. I looked around the yard, then toward the orchard, searching the trees for something stirring, but there was only the sift of ice spray over the snowdrifts. Still, I couldn't get rid of the feeling that I was being watched as I waded through the untouched snow to the barn.

I slid open the heavy wooden door with trepidation because, I told myself, animals might be hiding—foxes, possums, mice, bats. I hadn't been inside the barn since summer, when I'd stored my bicycle there. Something might fly out at me or something might be dead on the floor. But there was only the flutter of wings, the coo of nesting mourning doves, and slanted beams of light inside. The barn was empty even of the plans Evan had made for it. In a couple of years it would collapse into itself like the old barns on the Blackwell estate and begin the slow decay back into the earth.

For now, though, it held my bicycle, a few boxes of old books, and the cross-country skis Evan had given me for Christmas our first year here. We'd used them Christmas Day, skiing onto the estate, pulling Emmy on a sled. A magical day right out of a children's book. We'd gone out a few more times during the break but then once the semester had started I hadn't had time. I'd never used the skis again. Now they were peeling and warped, the boots that went with them full of spiders. I cleaned them out with an old rag, slid my feet into them, and carried the skis and poles to the edge of the woods. I snapped the boots into the skis and pushed off down the hill, heading toward the road.

The pines here were spaced far apart, making it easy to ski between them. The powdery snow gave way smoothly under me. I was out of practice, out of shape, and my head was still foggy from the Glenlivet I'd drunk last night, but it was easy going down the gentle slope. My leg muscles quickly warmed up and the day, which had started gray and overcast, brightened. The sun felt good on my face; the air smelled like pine and woodsmoke. There was a clarity and stillness in the day that felt like Christmas. Maybe it was being so close to the solstice. It felt as if the earth had paused in its spinning at that moment when it tilted farthest from the sun and had taken a breath before turning back. The day felt poised. Balanced in between. A hawk sailing overhead, its high-pitched keen riding the cold air, seemed to move in slow motion, suspended in ether. I wouldn't have minded staying in this in-between place, coasting over the surface of things, forever.

Then I reached the wall with Leia's shrine. Someone had come early and laid pine boughs and holly amid the candles and stuffed animals. *Merry Christmas, Leia, love you forever!* someone had written on a Christmas card. Again I looked for anything unusual left among the offerings, but nothing stood out. Of course not, I told myself, Hannah had been the one to leave them and Hannah was lying unconscious in the hospital. Then I looked out toward the road. I pictured myself coming around the curve, seeing the deer, and swerving to avoid it, my car coming to rest inches from the wall. I looked down into the ditch between the wall and the road, forcing myself to think about Leia lying there. Could she have been there when I got out of the car?

But no, I'd searched the road, looking for the deer. I'd have seen her.

I turned from the wall and skied into the woods, following the path I'd taken that night to the clearing. I recognized the log I'd sat on, the tree I'd leaned against. I took off my skis and sat there now. I leaned back and closed my eyes, the sun on my face feeling better than it should have. I was here to remember, not sunbathe. I focused on what I'd heard that night—

A squeal of tires. A scream. *Come back!*

A man's voice calling *Come back!*

I heard it now. Startled, I opened my eyes and saw a figure in jeans and hooded jacket striding through the snow. He was only a few yards away from me but he was moving so fast he hadn't seen me. I tucked myself in closer to the tree, not wanting to be seen. There was something in the man's angry stride that instantly made me wary.

"Goddamnit, man, come back! Where the fuck do you think you're going? I can't keep up in this fucking snow."

The voice came from behind me, back toward the road. The hooded man came to a halt and turned around. I was sure he'd see me but he was looking to my right and I was in the shadow of the tree. He shouted at the man behind him.

"Who told you to wear those faggot shoes? I told you we'd have to hike."

I saw now that the first man was wearing a hooded sweatshirt underneath an open leather jacket. The sweatshirt was dark purple with gold lettering—Acheron colors. I'd already guessed from their prolific cursing they were students. Now I saw that I was right. The man in the Acheron sweatshirt was Troy Van Donk.

"I didn't know we were hiking through the fucking snow."

The second man came into view. He was indeed poorly outfitted for hiking in the woods. He was picking his way through the snow like a long-legged crow in skinny black jeans and thin, pointy oxfords, flapping the arms of a loose vintage trench coat as he tried to keep his balance. But it was the porkpie hat that made me recognize him as the aging hipster from the Loop bus.

"Jesus, man, did you think the college was gonna snow-blow us a path?"

"Shit, man, I wish you'd keep it down. The police are bound to be on the lookout."

Troy sniggered. "Right, they're out here with sniffer dogs and infrared night vision goggles while Leia Dawson's killer goes scot-free."

"I thought they had the hot professor for that."

"Nah, Prof Lewis wouldn't do Leia like that, even if she was lit from the party. That's just what the cops want people to think so the real killer lets down his guard." Troy rubbed his hand over his eyes as if trying to erase some painful memory, then punched the other man in the arm. "So do you want to stand out here bird-watching or do you want to see if the stash is still there?"

So they were looking for hidden drugs. It was the only logical reason for them to be out here in the snow but I felt a sinking sense of disappointment in Troy.

"Fuck, man, it better be or my friends in P'town'll have our balls."

"Then let's go." Troy turned around and started up the hill. "Try to keep up."

The second man took off after Troy, flailing his arms more like the scarecrow in *The Wizard of Oz* now. I waited a few minutes, then followed them. Troy's faith that I hadn't killed Leia had been momentarily heartening, but it might have another explanation. Ross might have been right: he knew I hadn't killed Leia because he had.

It was harder going uphill in skis. My leg muscles burned and I fell twice. Each time I was afraid that Troy and his companion would turn around and see me flailing around on my skis. But they were too busy arguing with each other, their voices carrying on the still, cold air, to notice me.

"Couldn't you have found someplace easier to get to?" I heard the other man complain.

"What part about secret hideout do you not get? It wouldn't be secret if it was on Main Street."

"Yeah, but these woods give me the creeps. Who owns all this?"

"There's an old farmhouse up there"—he pointed toward my house—"that's where Professor Lewis lives."

"Sweet. Maybe we should pay her a visit later— Fuck! That hurt."

"Just shut up about her."

"Oh, I get it. You want her all to yourself." He said something too low for me to hear but I guessed it was filthy from his high-pitched, nervous laugh. "Hey, she must be loaded to own all this."

"She doesn't own this land, asshole; it belongs to the school. It was all part of an old estate that some crazy old guy gave away back in the day."

"He just gave it away?"

"Hey, you'd understand what rich people do better than me. He was some lonely old fart who went apeshit when he lost his kid so he gave his place away to become a teaching college. So kids could get a better education—or some bullshit like that."

Troy's voice faded as he and his companion crested the hill. I didn't need to eavesdrop on the history of Amos Blackwell and his lost child— I knew it all too well. Evan had researched all that history when we moved to the edge of the estate, reading in books on the area—*Ghosts Along the Hudson, Haunted Mansions of the Highlands*—and even talking to the local historian at the library. He found out that Amos Blackwell had brought his young bride, Charlotte, from New York City to live at the family estate, River House. They had been happy there for their first year and had a child, a little girl named Flora. But then Flora had died in a boating accident on the river. The wife had drowned herself a year later. Evan had been fascinated with the story and said he might want to write a ghost story about it one day. Later, after Emmy, he said we should have known the place was cursed.

When I reached the top of the hill I paused to catch my breath and take in the view. Even after seven years it took my breath away, especially on a morning like this. The broad sweep of the Hudson glittered in the sun. The Catskills rose blue and purple across the river. The mountains always looked different to me depending on the time of day and year, the distant ridges receding on foggy days and standing startlingly close on clear days like today. As if they were moving when we weren't looking, stealthily shifting the contours of the landscape.

Against this backdrop of frozen river and distant mountain, Troy and his companion looked like two tiny figures from a Brueghel painting—peasants returning home to their village or hunters tracking their prey. They had reached the bottom of the hill and were walking north along the train tracks, heading toward the trestle bridge. I skied across the top of the hill and started down through the woods north of the bridge so they wouldn't see me. These woods were denser, though, full of underbrush and blackberry thickets. I had to inch down the snowy slope, grasping branches and tree trunks to keep from sliding. I fell backward twice, soaking my behind and snagging my clothes in the thorns. Branches snapped at my face. *What was I doing trailing my student and his accomplice in crime into the woods?* I should have called the police.

But I hadn't thought to bring my phone and if I went back to my house now and called Sergeant McAffrey what would I tell him? That I'd seen Troy Van Donk walking through the woods with a suspicious-looking man too old to be a student? That they'd been talking about a "stash"? That my department head was offering me tenure in exchange for my recovered memory of Troy running over Leia? That I thought Troy had run over Leia because he didn't think *I* had done it?

In for a penny, in for a pound, my mother might have said, although I was pretty sure my mother would have discouraged me from following two possible drug dealers to their hideout.

When I reached the train tracks I looked south toward the trestle bridge but I didn't see Troy and the other man. Had they gone over it? But why? What was on the other side of the tracks besides soggy marsh and frozen river and—

The boathouse. I saw it about a hundred feet away, through the trees, on a spit of land that jutted out into the river. The old Blackwell boathouse. Most Hudson River estates had one, to house millionaires' yachts and pleasure skiffs for jaunts on the river. The Blackwell boathouse had once been a grand affair, built in the Adirondack Great Camp style with three pitched eaves trimmed in rustic birch branches over three wide boat berths open to the river. Dottie had told me that there'd been a rowing club in the twenties—there was still a loft with rowing shells and boating gear—but the college didn't have the money to keep the building in repair. Plus it was dangerous to reach it. The trestle bridge was rusted and decrepit and crossing the train tracks on the ground was "strongly discouraged" by the administration.

Of course that made it all the more appealing to college students. I'd heard my students talking about daring each other to cross the tracks, laying pennies on the rails for flattened souvenirs, and the inevitable drama of someone who'd gotten their foot stuck in the track while a train approached. The tracks had featured in so many of my students' stories that I felt dread just looking at them as I stood listening for a train now. Or maybe it was the memory of the keening cry of the train whistle that made me think of the college ghost story.

Every college had them—the dorm room haunted by the freshman girl who got pregnant and hung herself, the twenty-four-hour study room inhabited by the premed who OD'd on speed and lay on the couch for three days before anyone noticed he was dead. Of course an old, abandoned boathouse where a little girl had drowned would have its stories. I'd heard it was a fraternity hazing ritual to make new pledges spend the night there, and it was the most popular spot on campus, according to "Overheard at Acheron," to lose one's virginity. It wasn't surprising that it would also attract drug users. It must be where Troy and the other man had gone.

I took off my skis and hid them behind a bush. Then I listened again for the train, heard only the crunch of ice moving on the river, and stepped cautiously over the tracks. It felt like stepping over a sleeping snake. When I got on the other side I realized I'd been holding my breath. I crossed over the rotting planks that lay over the causeway and crept around the side of the building until I came to a low, open window. I crouched below it, squirming behind a prickly bush that I hoped would conceal me from the two men if they came out, and then listened. At first I heard only the beating of my own heart, then the crack and groan of ice on the river, but then I heard Troy's voice, amplified by the high, peaked ceiling of the boathouse.

"What can I tell you, I thought it was here. The third plank from the third berth."

"Let me guess, you were stoned when you hid it."

"Hell no, I keep a straight head when I'm doing business. These college students will rip you off if you don't."

"You talk like you're not one yourself."

"Not like them I'm not. I can't afford to slack off. I'll lose my financial aid if my average drops below eighty-five."

Then you should have handed in your revision.

"I'm pretty sure you'll lose your financial aid if they catch you dealing."

"It was supposed to be a onetime thing as a favor to a friend. I'm done after this—"

Whatever else Troy was going to say was drowned out by the shriek of a train whistle, so close I nearly jumped out of my skin. Although I was a good ten feet from the tracks, I pressed myself against the wall as it passed and closed my eyes. It felt as if the train was moving just inches from my skin. When I opened my eyes I saw Troy and the other man walking back along the train tracks toward the college. From the dejected slump of their shoulders I figured they hadn't found what they were looking for.

But had I? Was there anything in what I'd seen or heard that made Troy a more likely suspect for running over Leia?

Maybe. But not really.

I'd come so far, though; I might as well see the place. I untangled myself from the shrubbery and picked my way gingerly over the half-sunken planks that led into the boathouse, feeling the cold from the soles of my boots up to the crown of my head. It was the cold of the frozen river, I told myself, it had nothing to do with the ghost stories.

But when I came into the boathouse and saw, dappled by the reflections of river water, a girl's face staring at me I nearly screamed. This wasn't the ghost I was expecting. This was Leia Dawson.

I stepped closer and saw that the face had been painted on the peeling wood of the back wall. There were other marks on the wood—initials, hearts, obscenities, graffiti tags—but this painted face seemed to float over all of them, Leia's wide blue eyes staring through the rippled light like a drowned woman come back to life. I stared at it for several minutes before I noticed the words beneath it—*Winter Solstice Self-Portrait.*

CHAPTER THIRTEEN

It took me a long time to figure out what was wrong about her face. It was in the shading. Leia had somehow created the effect of a shadow over her features, a dark veil that didn't fall from overhead but rose from below. That's why she looked like she was drowning. The light-ripple from the water enhanced the effect, but she'd planned it, working with the painting's setting so that it looked as though a tide of dark water was rising from the river to engulf her. I stepped closer to the painting and saw that underneath her name she'd written *The Dark Is Rising*.

A chill rose up in me. *The Dark Is Rising* was a book we'd read in the Children's Lit class Leia had taken with me two years ago, a British fantasy novel about an eleven-year-old boy who discovers over the course of a Christmas holiday that he is the guardian of the Light charged with fighting the forces of the Dark. Leia had written her term paper on it, exploring the Celtic, Arthurian, and Norse mythology the author had used. I found myself both strangely touched that she had remembered the book and disturbed that she'd painted herself as being engulfed by the dark—especially since if she'd painted it on the solstice she had painted it on the day of her death. As if she'd seen her own death coming for her. What had been going on with her? And what was she doing down here at the boathouse hanging out with the likes of Troy and that sleazy scarecrow?

I looked around and saw signs of recent partying—empty bottles and beer cans, cigarette butts, condoms, even a broken syringe. Stepping back, I looked up at the loft built into the rafters. Old life preservers and boat cushions formed a sort of makeshift bed. I could guess what use the students were making of *that*. I was having a hard time picturing Leia here—unless she was looking for material for her writing or Troy was right and the Leia I knew was only a carefully constructed façade.

I stayed for a little longer, willing Leia's image to answer my questions, but the shadows over her face only deepened as the day grew overcast and colder. I could feel the cold rising off the river as it froze. Finally, I turned from her and left, my feet so numb from standing so long that I tripped on the plank causeway and into the water, soaking one leg up to my knee.

My mind was as clumsy as my limbs, going round and round the question of Leia. Why had she painted herself like that? What dark thing was rising to engulf her? Was it Troy's infatuation for her as Ross had said? Was that what she had come to talk to me about that day? It all came back to that. If I had taken the time to listen to her would I have made a difference? Could I have stopped that tide of dark rising up to engulf her on the river road?

The climb back up the hill was rough. The snow had melted in the sun and then turned to ice as the day grew colder, making the footing slippery. I kept sliding backward on my skis and falling. I fell over and over, my feet and hands clumsy with the cold. By the time I reached the top of the hill I staggered out of the woods like the last survivor of a new ice age—and blundered straight into another skier.

We went down in a tangle of legs and skis and poles. The other skier was wearing a face mask and sleek neoprene leggings and jacket. I couldn't even tell gender until she ripped off her mask, unleashing a Medusa's nest of braids.

"Cressida?"

"Nan? What are you doing here? You ran right into me. I was going too fast to stop."

"I-I-I . . ." My teeth were chattering too hard to talk.

"You're suffering from hypothermia," Cressida said with clinical calm.

I tried to protest but I couldn't form the words. My lips felt swollen and clumsy, my thoughts sluggish and confused.

"Let's get you inside," Cressida said, deftly unsnapping her boots out of her skis and helping me up. "We'll go to my house—it's closer." I tried to tell her that my house was just down the hill but I couldn't find the words. Besides, I wasn't sure I wanted Cressida to see the sad state of my house. Even if I was suffering from hypothermia.

Though we were friends, I'd never been to Cressida's house. I had gotten the feeling over the years that she cherished her privacy. *I could never live with anyone,* she'd once told me. *I think writers are naturally reclusive.* So, even though she lived just up the hill from me in the old Blackwell gatehouse, I'd never "popped in" to borrow sugar or to ask if she wanted to take a walk. We did most of our socializing trading quips across the hall between our offices, at department parties, and over the occasional drink at the Black Swan. Now, approaching the tiny brick house with black-and-cream gables overlooking the river, I felt like I was being admitted to the inner sanctum. I was expecting something like the witch's gingerbread house in "Hansel and Gretel." Instead, she led me inside to a spare but comfortable room with gleaming hardwood floors, a cream-colored sofa and sleek Scandinavian chairs, and uncurtained glass windows with spectacular views facing east over the orchards on one side of the house and west toward the river on the other side. She turned on a gas fire in a circular glass hearth that glowed over crystal shards.

"Take off your clothes and I'll get you something to put on."

Embarrassed, I plucked at my soaked clothing ineffectively. When she came back with fleece leggings and a silk T-shirt I'd barely gotten one sock off. She did the rest, in a businesslike fashion that spared me any further embarrassment. I might have been a Barbie doll she was undressing. The leggings and shirt she put on me felt delicious, like they were made of spun clouds. She put wool socks on my feet and wrapped me in a sheepskin throw, then went to make tea. I sat on the couch and looked around me, feeling like I'd landed in Valhalla. Everything was neat and polished. Even her desk—a gleaming length of pale wood cantilevered beneath a wide window with practically the same view I had from my desk—contained only a neat stack of papers (graded, I was sure) and an open laptop displaying a muted seascape—a familiar-looking seascape.

I got up and shuffled across the floor in stocking feet to get a closer look. Yes, it was the picture posted over the thread on "Overheard at Acheron."

"I think it's unconscionable how social media is spinning your story, Nan." Cressida had come up behind me on silent slippered feet. She led me away from the screen, sat me back down on the couch, and handed me a glass mug of steaming hot liquid. I wrapped both hands around it and took a cautious sip. It tasted sweet and faintly medicinal, some kind of herbal tea with something alcoholic added, brandy perhaps, or some kind of Nordic glogg.

"I tried to add a more reasoned voice to the discussion but things had gone too far. *Fama volat*, as Virgil says, and this is indeed a monster with a hundred eyes and a thousand tongues beneath each wing."

I shuddered at the image and Cressida twitched the sheepskin throw over my shoulders. "It must be awful being the target of such vitriol. I can imagine that you needed to get out. Is that what you were doing in the woods? Or were you coming from the river? Your clothes and shoes were wet . . . you weren't . . . ?"

Her voice trailed off and she lifted her eyebrows expectantly. I stared at her, my mind still so sluggish that it took a moment before I realized that she was asking me if I had tried to drown myself.

"No!" I said, sloshing tea in my eagerness to correct what she was thinking. "I didn't . . . I wouldn't . . ." I could feel my face and hands burning, the blood that had fled from my extremities rushing back in a hot, shameful flood. *Because I had been thinking about it.* The heat at least released my tongue. "I went down to the river because I followed Troy Van Donk to the old boathouse. Apparently it's where our students go to get high."

"I've heard that," Cressida said, steadying my hand and guiding the mug to my lips. The hot liquid was bringing feeling back to my body but my words must have been coming out slurred. "I didn't know you were so concerned about student drug use."

"Of course I am," I said automatically, "but that's not . . . I followed Troy because . . ." I tried to reconstruct the logic of the morning. I'd gone to the woods because of the dream I'd had, but I couldn't tell Cressida that.

"I was trying to remember what happened the night of the accident."

"What do you mean? You said you hit a deer—are you unsure of that now?"

"Not that part. After, when I was in the woods looking for the deer, I sat down . . . and fell asleep for a while . . ."

I waited for Cressida to express the astonishment that others did at this point in the story but she only waited patiently for me to go on. She would have made a good therapist. Or a good cop.

". . . and then I had a dream, someone calling 'Come back.' I thought it was the dream I always have about Emmy but now I wonder if it could have been someone calling Leia back that night . . . someone who . . ."

"Ran her over?" Cressida asked coolly. "Was it a woman's voice?"

"I don't know. I thought so because it always is in my dream, but now I'm not sure."

"You could have superimposed your dream on what you heard. You know my theory about why Jane hears Rochester's voice at the end of *Jane Eyre*?"

"No," I said, smiling. Leave it to Cressida to turn everything back to a literary criticism. "What is it?"

"She's really hearing her own voice, but she superimposes Rochester's voice over her own because she's still in thrall to the male patriarchy. So you did the opposite—you superimposed a female voice over a male's because it's what you expect to hear in your own dream."

"Oh," I said, feeling a little blurry—as I often did when my colleagues discussed recondite literary theory. "I suppose that's possible. At any rate I went to the woods to remember it better."

"And did you?"

"I didn't really get a chance. I saw Troy and this sleazy older guy. They were arguing about something they'd hidden—drugs, I think."

Cressida rolled her eyes. "I'm not surprised. I know you've always thought well of Troy Van Donk but I've always thought he was low-life scum."

"That's a little harsh," I said, "but I am afraid that he may have fallen in with the wrong crowd—Leia too. Troy mentioned her. He said that he didn't think I killed her."

"Well, you *are* his favorite teacher."

"I am?" The pleasure I felt was immediately followed by a surge of embarrassment that I would still feel pleased that a drug-using student liked me. "How do you know?"

"He told me on the day he came in to castigate me for upsetting Leia at the party. He said you were the only teacher he'd had at Acheron who gave a damn about him."

"Oh," I said, thinking guiltily that I hadn't spent much time worrying about him lately. Maybe if I had I would have noticed that he was on a downward path. "He's a good writer. But I'm afraid there might be another explanation for his being so sure I didn't kill Leia."

"You mean if he knew who did?"

"Actually . . . Ross came over last night to tell me that the police have found evidence that his car was involved in the accident." The words were out before I remembered that I wasn't supposed to tell anyone that. Now that I had warmed up I couldn't seem to stop talking.

"Ross's car? You mean his Volvo?"

"No, the Peugeot. He keeps it in his barn and his keys were in a dish in the kitchen. Anyone could have taken them."

Cressida laid her hand on my arm. "Or Ross could have driven the car himself."

Although I'd had my own doubts about Ross's innocence I was horrified to hear Cressida voice them. "I don't believe that. Ross wouldn't have run over Leia and left her for dead."

Cressida looked at me pityingly. "You still have feelings for him, don't you?"

"No—I mean, yes, as a friend. But we haven't . . . not since . . ."

"I know you stopped sleeping with him after we talked. I've always admired you for your resolve. But it must have been hard giving him up . . . and then, for what? You didn't get tenure in the end anyway."

Tears pricked at my eyes. I rubbed at them and my vision blurred. I felt suddenly very, very tired. The hot tea had warmed me up but it had also spread a sluggish lethargy through my veins, an aftereffect of the hypothermia, no doubt. Seeing the exhaustion on my face, Cressida took the cup from my hands and adjusted the throw on my shoulders. I leaned back against the cushions.

"I've even wondered if I was wrong to intervene," she said as she adjusted a pillow under my head. "I did what I thought was good for you, but Ross, well, he would have been better off with you. Maybe he would have stayed away from the students."

"*Students?* You mean there's been more than one?"

"I'm afraid so. There was that girl from Long Island—Emily Auerbach—the one who went on to work at Random House—"

"Ross got her that internship," I said drowsily.

"Yes. Have you ever wondered why it's always the prettiest girls whom he helps to the internships and recommends for MFA programs?"

I searched my brain for a male student who'd been helped by Ross but my head was swimming. When I closed my eyes I saw Leia's face sinking under dark water.

"I'm afraid Leia was just the latest in a long series of conquests. But Leia at least had the good grace to feel bad about it. When she came to see me that day it was clear she was feeling guilty about something."

"When did she come see you?" I asked.

"Just before she went to your office. I thought she might have gone to you for a more sympathetic ear."

I grimaced. "I'm afraid I was no better. I didn't even make time to talk to her."

"Don't beat yourself up about that, Nan. These students act like they own us. Leia wouldn't even come out with what she'd done. She wanted me to sit there and play guessing games. She asked me if I thought confession was good for the soul—if she would feel better about something she'd done wrong if she confessed it or if she made amends some other way."

"You think she was talking about having an affair with Ross?"

Cressida shrugged. "I can't imagine what else she was on about. You can't have helped noticing how much time she spent with him. I think she was asking me if she ought to make it public. Like ruining Ross's career would make up for her actions. I told her that maybe she should worry more about her own sins than exposing anyone else's. I'm afraid I might have been a bit harsh on her."

I pried open my eyes to stare at Cressida, surprised at the bitterness and jealousy in her voice. Cressida was so beautiful—and barely forty. Why envy a girl like Leia? But then I took in the beautiful room we were in—the bare shelves and desk surface, the abstract photographs on the walls. There were no photographs of friends or family, no sign of any human being at all. In her memoir Cressida had described a loveless childhood with a workaholic father and a perfectionist mother who watched over every morsel of food she put in her mouth and hounded her to become a ballerina to fulfill her own unfulfilled dreams. No one in her family had spoken to her since she'd published the memoir. "It's hard to be the one who tells the truth," she'd once said to me. "And lonely." It wasn't Leia's beauty that Cressida would envy, but her likability, the easy way she had of drawing people to her. I knew because I envied it myself.

"Leia could be a bit hard to take sometimes," I said, working carefully to get the words right despite the growing numbness in my lips. "*That's* why I didn't make time for her that day."

Cressida looked at me with such gratitude I thought she was going to hug me. She made do with patting my arm and tucking the throw under my feet. "You mustn't feel guilty about that, Nan. She could be very demanding. They all are, this generation, expecting you to answer their emails within minutes and read their novels, as if you had no work of your own, and to drop everything to listen to their moral quandaries." She shook her head. "I told her that whatever she felt bad about she should examine her own conscience rather than exact retribution from someone else. She didn't like that one little bit. She left in a huff. That's why Troy thought I'd upset her at the party. She must have gone to talk to Ross, perhaps she threatened to make their affair public."

She squeezed my arm, startling me completely awake. Her eyes were wide. "Ross would have offered to drive her home. She might have gotten out of the car—he would have tried to follow her—it could have been an accident. The roads were slippery, the visibility poor. . . ."

Come back! I heard the voice calling, only now it was Ross's voice. I closed my eyes and felt tears sliding down my face.

"She was afraid," I said. "She knew something bad was going to happen to her. The painting she did in the boathouse—"

"She did a painting in the boathouse?"

"A self-portrait—her face shadowed. Beneath it she wrote 'The dark is rising.'"

"How melodramatic," Cressida said, her voice suddenly cool and disinterested. "No wonder it upset you. You need to rest. I bet you haven't had a good night's sleep in days."

Dimly I was aware of her putting another blanket on me and then I heard and saw her turning off a lamp, her steps retreating from the living room.

The last thing I saw before falling asleep was Leia's face, rising out of the dark water, and then I was falling into that icy cold river. . . .

When I awoke the room was dark. Cressida was sitting on the edge of the couch. She leaned over me, her braids clicking together like icicles, and switched on a lamp. The light blinded me. When I opened my eyes again Cressida handed me a mug of coffee.

"Are you feeling better? You were really out."

"I think so." I sat up and inhaled the coffee to clear the fog in my brain. "How long was I asleep?"

"A couple of hours. I didn't want to wake you, but there's someone here to see you."

"To see me? But how . . ." I was going to ask who knew I was here when I looked up and saw a broad figure silhouetted against the dark window and recognized Sergeant McAffrey. My first thought was that the lab had come back with evidence linking my car to Leia and he'd come to arrest me. "How did you know I was here?"

"Dr. Janowicz called me. She told me about what you found in the boathouse."

Cressida squeezed my hand. "I thought the police should know. I knew you'd want to protect Ross, even if it meant not clearing yourself."

"Protect Ross, what—"

"If you don't mind, Dr. Janowicz, I'd like to handle this." He stood over Cressida until she got up and retreated, murmuring that she'd be in the kitchen if I needed her. Then he took her place on the couch. I could feel the cold coming off him, the way I'd felt the cold rising up from the river in the boathouse. "Can you tell me why you went to the boathouse today?" he asked me.

"I was down by Leia's shrine and I saw Troy Van Donk." I told him what I'd overheard and how I'd followed Troy and the other man, whom McAffrey made me describe in detail. He asked me to repeat what I heard them say. Then he asked why I followed them without calling him. I told him I hadn't had a phone and I didn't want to lose them. That I thought I might find out something about what happened to Leia.

"And did you?"

"Only that she was troubled by something on the day she died. Did you see the self-portrait she painted?"

He nodded. "Did you see anything else? Or . . . leave anything there?"

"No, what would I leave—"

"Did you see this?"

He held up a plastic bag with something metal in it—something silver that winked in the lamplight. I had to focus on it to make out what it was. A silver disk with a shield etched on it, lettering inside the shield . . . "A cuff link," I said, "with the Harvard insignia. Ross has a pair just—"

I looked closer. Snagged on the swivel bar were a few dark hairs. "Where did you find that?" I asked, although I already knew.

"You've seen Dr. Ballantine wearing a cuff link like this one?"

"Yes, but I'm sure he's not the only one with a pair of Harvard cuff links—"

"Thank you, Ms. Lewis. That's very helpful. I'll be in touch." He got to his feet. I swung my legs off the couch and started to get up but the sudden movement made me feel nauseated.

"Wait," I said, "it can't be Ross. He wouldn't hurt Leia. He—" I was about to say that he loved Leia, but that suddenly didn't seem like a good idea. "Anyone could have taken his car—"

"Let us worry about who was driving Dr. Ballantine's car. I can't discuss the case any further." He was turning away, but then his face softened. He seemed to be considering something. He leaned down, his hands braced on his knees, the way someone would lean down to talk to a child. "I can tell you that the lab has found deer hair on your car, Ms. Lewis. It looks like you hit a deer after all."

Then he was gone, leaving quickly as if he wanted to put distance between himself and the admission he'd just made. As if he was ashamed of that one act of kindness. He was letting me know I was off the hook—or at least very nearly so. I should have felt relieved. But instead I felt sick to my stomach, just as if I'd blindly come around a curve and struck some poor innocent animal.

CHAPTER FOURTEEN

"It looks like you're no longer the police's main suspect."

Cressida's voice startled me. I hadn't heard her come back into the room. She must have been listening from the kitchen.

"You think he's going to arrest Ross?"

"You said they had traces of Leia's clothing on his car and now they have proof he was in the boathouse with Leia. I don't think it's looking very good for Ross."

I rounded on Cressida. "Did you tell McAffrey that you thought Ross was having an affair with Leia?"

"I had to, Nan." Her voice had turned cold. "Leia came to me in need. If I had taken her more seriously she might be alive. I'll never forgive myself for that. I suppose it must be how you feel about Emmy."

I was so blindsided by the comment that I felt dizzy all over again. "But Leia didn't *tell* you she was having an affair . . . and even if they were it doesn't mean Ross ran her over."

"As your policeman friend said, that's for the police to worry about. I think it's time you started worrying about yourself, Nan, and started taking better care of yourself . . . drinking less, for instance."

"I'm not—" I began to say "I'm not an alcoholic" but then I realized how many times I'd had to say those words in the last few days. *The problem with repetition,* I told my students, *is that words lose meaning with overuse.* "I'm not an alcoholic" was beginning to sound less like a protest and more like an admission.

Cressida gave me a pitying look. "I'm sorry, Nan, I blame myself for not saying something earlier. I've noticed when we go out for dinner and we split a bottle you usually finish it and when you come in to your office in the morning . . . well, you sometimes look hungover. Then at the faculty party—"

"You were the one topping off my wineglass, for God's sake!" I exploded.

Cressida stared at me. "Because you were holding out your glass for more," she said with an icy calm that made me feel chilled. "But I see now that I was enabling you. Now, if you want to stay here tonight we could talk, look up support groups, go to a meeting tomorrow—"

"No, thank you," I said abruptly. "I have to get home to"—I searched my head for a reason. For a terrible moment I had an image of Ross's bottle of Glenlivet in my kitchen cabinet—"to feed my cat."

"If you're sure," she said frostily. "Your clothes are dry." She pointed to a neat pile on a teak bench by the door. "Your boots are still damp but I've got them on a drying rack. You can borrow a pair of mine. I can call a cab if you like. I'd take you myself but I'd have to dig out the car—"

"I can walk," I told her, taking the snow boots she handed to me. They looked too big for me but were lined with something that felt so soft and delicious I didn't mind. "No need to worry I've had too much to drink."

"Oh, Nan." She heaved an exasperated sigh. "I'm sorry if I offended you but someone has to say something."

"Yeah, and you're usually the one to say it." I immediately regretted the words but I was still too angry to apologize. I went into the bathroom to change; it was surprisingly luxurious, with pink tiling and a massive tub lined with expensive bath gels. Cressida took good care of herself. When I came out Cressida was standing in the living room holding my coat. I noticed that she'd already folded the sheepskin throw and straightened the couch cushions, smoothing away all traces of my messy presence.

"I'm sorry I got angry," I said, trying to mean it. "I've just had a lot to take in—the idea that Ross was sleeping with Leia, that he could have been the one to run her over . . ."

"Of course," Cressida said with a conciliatory smile. "It was the wrong time to bring up the drinking. You know that tact isn't my strong suit. But I only did it because I'm worried about you, Nan. You're so trusting . . . so vulnerable." She helped me on with my coat, laid her hands on my shoulders, and looked into my eyes. "You need to be more careful."

I told her I would be and turned to go, thinking it was just what Ross had said to me last night.

It was only a ten-minute walk down Orchard Drive to my house. Really, it was strange we didn't visit each other more. Of course that might be because, as she said, tact wasn't her strong suit. An uncompromising hard-ass, John Abbot had called her. And she'd made Joan Denning cry once by telling her that adjuncts weren't allowed to use the office copy machine. And after her experience with anorexia she had a thing about support groups. Of course she'd see a few too many glasses of wine as a substance abuse problem. But she was right. I did need to cut down. I'd already realized that myself. She was just wrong about going to meetings. She was trying to make me into a cause, like her prison students. Poor Cressida, for all her independence she must be pretty lonely. I should visit her more often, offer to carpool to work—

For the first time Sergeant McAffrey's words sank in. I *would* be getting my car back. The lab had found traces of deer fur on my bumper. They had another suspect. I was, in Cressida's words, not the police's main suspect. I should have felt relieved.

Only I didn't.

The thought that Ross had been carrying on an affair with Leia was bad enough. That they'd had a falling-out and he'd run her over and left her to die on the road made me feel ill. It might have been years ago, but Ross had been my lover—I'd almost slept with him last night!—

Last night. I remembered how he'd asked me if I had run over Leia. Had he been trying to get me to admit to hitting Leia in my confusion so he wouldn't be accused?

By the time I got back to my house I felt like I was coming down with a cold. My feet felt leaden and clumsy in Cressida's luxurious but too big boots. My vision was blurry. As I clumped up my porch steps I tripped on something and went down hard on my knees. The sudden pain brought tears to my eyes as if I were a child who had skinned her knee on the playground. *Get a grip, Nan!* I told myself—only it was my mother's voice in my head. *Quit feeling sorry for yourself and get up.* I planted my hands on the icy steps—and touched something furry. I screamed, thinking some poor animal had crawled to my doorstep to die—*the deer I'd hit maybe*—but then as I drew back my hand it brushed something metal. In the faint light from the fanlight I made out the buckle of a collar. I gingerly stroked the cold, bony animal and recognized her worn, velvety coat and knobby spine. It was Oolong, frozen to death on my front porch.

I brought her inside, wrapped her in the old afghan from the couch that she had liked sleeping on, and then sat with her in my lap by the woodstove, as if I could bring her back to life by warming her up. There were little balls of ice in her matted fur that melted and soaked through the afghan into my lap. *Had I left her outside?*

The thought that I had caused the death of my poor old cat was almost too much to bear. I stroked her fur and wailed, letting loose a keen that didn't sound like it was coming from me. It didn't even sound human. It sounded like the forlorn train whistle I couldn't bear to listen to at night, like the cries of revenants wailing for drowned children, like the deranged lament of old drunks—

Christ! Had I forgotten to bring Oolong inside because I was hungover? But I'd only had a glass of Glenlivet the night before. Right?

I got up, still cradling Oolong, and opened the kitchen cabinet. The bottle of Glenlivet was there but while I remembered it as three-quarters full it was now half empty. Had I gotten up and drunk more last night? I remembered having that strange dream about Emmy. Could I have been sleepwalking during it? It was the dream that had sent me out the next morning searching the woods for a lost memory. What kind of clear thinking was that? I thought of poor Oolong crying at the door to get in as I followed Troy down to the boathouse—

Troy.

He'd known where I lived. His friend had suggested they pay me a visit.

Had he? It would be easy to break into my house. The back door had a lock so flimsy it could be opened by a credit card. Evan had meant to change it, but we lived in the country. What danger could there be? Did Troy break in—looking for money or a way to incriminate me—and let Oolong out—

Or did he deliberately kill Oolong?

I stroked her fur away from her neck to see if there were any signs of strangulation—and saw something snagged on her rabies tag. A purple thread. Troy had been wearing a purple Acheron sweatshirt earlier.

I realized that I should tell Sergeant McAffrey. I got up and carried Oolong into the mudroom and laid her gently in a wicker laundry basket. Then I found my phone to call McAffrey and noticed that there were six voice mails. The first one was from Anat. I guiltily remembered that I'd meant to call her. The second one was from Dottie, the other four were all from Ross. I scrolled to the last message and played it.

"Nan!" Ross's voice was desperate. "Where are you? The police are here to bring me in for questioning. I need to know—"

He was cut off by a man's voice that sounded like Detective Haight's saying they needed to leave now. Then the call ended. I looked at the time. The call had been made forty minutes ago. McAffrey certainly hadn't wasted any time. He must have gone straight from Cressida's to Ross's house. They would be at the station now, sitting in the interview room with the water-stained yellow paint while McAffrey tossed the evidence bag with Ross's cuff link on the table between them.

The cuff link.

Suddenly I recalled where I'd seen it last. In Ross's kitchen. When I burst in Leia had spilled wine on his shirt cuff. He'd unbuttoned it— no, he always wore shirts with cuff links—he'd taken off the cuff link and dropped it into the dish by the sink. The dish with the car keys—

Where anyone who scooped up the keys might take it too.

Which meant that whoever had taken Ross's car and run over Leia could have dropped the cuff link at the boathouse as well.

I realized it was a frail clue. Even if Ross hadn't left the cuff link at the boathouse, it didn't mean he wasn't having an affair with Leia. Leia had gone to Cressida feeling guilty about something—but then, Troy had said that Leia played a role for each new place she moved to and put on a different face for each new person she met. Guilt-ridden mistress might have been the one she was trying out on Cressida.

Or maybe I just didn't want to believe that the Ross I knew would sleep with one of his students.

But it didn't matter what I believed. I had to tell McAffrey that I'd seen Ross taking off his cuff link in the kitchen. And that someone had murdered my cat. I reached for the card he'd given me and started to call . . . but of course he wouldn't answer. He was interviewing Ross. I had to go down to the station to talk to him.

Only I didn't have a car.

But I knew who would come get me.

While I was waiting for Dottie I listened to Anat's voice mail telling me that the police had found deer hair on my car and that they appeared to have a new suspect. "It looks like you're in the clear but you should still lay low. Don't talk to the police without me."

I hit Call Back but got her voice mail. I hesitated, not wanting to tell her I was about to do exactly what she'd told me not to—talk to the police without her and give evidence that might exonerate the police's new suspect. I hesitated so long that the phone beeped signaling the end of my message option and then I heard Dottie's car at the foot of my driveway. I hurried out to meet her before she tried going up and got stuck.

"I'm sorry for bothering you on Christmas night," I said, getting into her car.

"I'm glad you called. I've been worrying about you all day. I know how much you care about your students, Nan. You'd never have left Leia to die on the road. I'm sure the police will figure that out eventually."

"They have," I told her. "Only now they think it was Ross."

Dottie gasped, but then remained silent, gripping the steering wheel, her eyes fixed to the road, as I explained about the traces of Leia's jacket on Ross's car and the cuff link in the boathouse. I didn't tell her about Oolong because I knew how much she loved cats and I thought her sympathy might undo me. When we got to the police station she turned to me, her eyes gleaming in the dark car. "It can't be Ross."

"I don't want to believe it either—"

"No, it *can't* be him. Are you sure he hasn't offered the police an alibi?"

"No," I said, "but what alibi would he give? He said you were the last one to leave the house. And, by the way, you can't tell anyone that he's being questioned. I shouldn't have told you any of this."

"I'd never—" she began, shaking her head so that her tight curls bristled. I interrupted her.

"It's just that . . . I know how much you like having the inside information."

Dottie started at this. "Are you calling me a gossip?" she asked, her voice trembling.

"No—"

"Because I know that's what people think, but no one has any idea how many things I have to keep to myself. All day long my desk faces that row of offices. I *see* things. People think I don't notice, but I do! People treat me like I'm invisible, but I thought you were different. I thought we were friends." Her voice ended on a sob.

"Dottie," I began, shocked and appalled that I had managed to hurt Dottie's feelings. But she was right. I had treated her like she was invisible. I had taken her friendship for granted. "I'm really sorry. I didn't mean to suggest that you were a gossip. I'm the one who should have kept my mouth shut. I should have realized how much it would upset you to hear about Ross. I shouldn't have called you."

"No," she said, her voice hoarse but firm. "I'm glad you did. Only"—she looked away from me and gripped the steering wheel—"I think I'll stay here in the car while you go in. I don't think I could face anyone right now."

"Of course, if you're sure you'll be all right."

"Don't worry about me. You just tell the police what you saw. I'm sure they'll see that it wasn't Ross."

"Okay." I squeezed her shoulder. She still didn't look at me. Perhaps it was because she didn't want me to see her crying. Or maybe she was angry that I'd called her a gossip, and now I'd lost one of the last friends I had at Acheron.

The first person I saw in the waiting room was Kelsey Manning double-thumb typing on her phone.

"Professor Lewis, are you here to give evidence against Professor Ballantine? Is it true he was having an affair with Leia Dawson?"

"Where did you hear that?" I demanded.

"I can't divest my sources," she said smugly.

"*Divulge*," I corrected automatically. "The word you're looking for is *divulge*."

She blinked at me rapidly and licked her glossy lips. "Yeah, whatever. Anyway, it's what everyone is saying. Everyone knows Leia was his special pet and she got all sorts of special treatment from him. He practically drooled over every little thing she said in the Brit Lit class I was in with her. Were you, like, jealous, because he broke up with you and was going out with a younger woman?"

I stared at her, unable to think of a reply that she wouldn't somehow misquote; then I looked over her shoulder and spoke to the clerk at the reception desk. "Can you please tell Sergeant McAffrey that Nan Lewis is here to see him—and that he's got a news leak here in his station tweeting confidential information."

"I'm not tweeting," Kelsey said, holding up her phone. I could make out a post that read *Professor Ross Ballantine taken in for questioning!* "I'm posting to 'Overheard at Acheron.' That's freedom of the press."

"That's interfering with an ongoing investigation."

Sergeant McAffrey was standing in the hallway glaring at Kelsey's phone as if he wanted to snatch it out of her hands. I'd often felt the same when I caught my students texting or playing Candy Crush Saga in class. He took a deep breath and in a firm, controlled voice asked Kelsey to leave.

"This is a public space—"

"You're interfering with an investigation." His voice had dropped two octaves. I could feel it rumbling in my stomach. Kelsey fidgeted with her hair and teared up. I almost felt sorry for her.

"Okay, but I'm putting *this* in my story as an example of police brutality!" She flipped her hair over her shoulder, a defensive gesture that reminded me of how Oolong would nonchalantly lick herself after falling. I felt my lip trembling at the thought of poor Oolong's frozen body. McAffrey, mouth open to say something to Kelsey, must have seen my eyes filling. He grabbed my elbow and steered me away from Kelsey.

"That girl's a menace," he muttered when we were out of earshot. "But you shouldn't let her get to you."

"It's not her," I said, and then to my horror and dismay I broke into loud, mucousy sobs. Looking as embarrassed as I felt, he steered me into the nearest room.

It was a different interview room, a cozier space with cushioned chairs, a coffee machine, and potted plants. This must be where they took traumatized witnesses—the innocent—or at least the ones crying over their dead cats. McAffrey pulled out a chair for me and offered me a cup of coffee. I shook my head but he fixed one anyway. I realized he was giving me time to get myself under control, so I endeavored to do so. By the time he came back to the table with two mugs I wasn't sobbing anymore. I took a sip of the coffee and was surprised at how good it tasted. Even the coffee was better in this interview room.

"Okay," he said, sitting down next to me instead of on the other side of the table. "Tell me what happened."

I told him about finding Oolong on the porch and finding the purple thread on her collar.

"You probably own one of those sweatshirts yourself."

I admitted I did. "Do you think I left her out in the cold to die?"

He looked surprised. "Why would I think that? Did you?"

"I don't think so! I remember tossing her back in the house before I left."

"And did you lock the door?"

"Yes, but the back door is flimsy."

He looked like he was about to give me a lecture on home security but stopped himself. "I don't think your cat died because you left her outside. She would have gone to your barn and burrowed down to keep warm. It looks more like someone sending you a message."

"A message?"

"Yeah, like the things left on Leia's shrine."

"But Hannah left those," I began, suddenly remembering the way Hannah had shook her head when I held up the Four Roses bottle.

"Maybe," he said, "but Hannah's lying unconscious in the hospital now and someone's still messing with you. It could be a crazy vigilante from town. Someone killed Hannah's cat after . . ." His voice trailed off.

"After Emmy? I didn't know that. Shit, Hannah's cat. I meant to go by and feed it."

"I got someone from the shelter to do that," he said. "So is that why you came in? To tell me about the cat?"

"Yes . . . and something else." I told him about Ross taking the cuff link off and putting it in the dish with the keys. "So you see, whoever took the keys could have taken the cuff link too."

"And dropped it in the boathouse after running Leia over?"

"Maybe they went to the boathouse first," I said. "They could have parked in the turnaround on Orchard Drive and hiked to the boathouse. I've seen kids do that. And then they—whoever was with Leia—had a fight. Leia ran back to the road and started walking home on River Road and the driver followed her and ran her down."

For a moment the scene felt so real I could feel the snow falling, hear the crunch of Leia's boots on the snow . . . if only I could see the face behind the wheel. McAffrey might have been reliving the moment too. He was watching me as if waiting for me to reveal that last detail, the face behind the windshield.

"You're close to Professor Ballantine, aren't you?"

"Ross? Yes, I suppose. He's the chair of my department—"

"He could reverse your tenure decision."

"That's not what this—"

"And you had an affair with him?"

"Where did you hear that?"

"Didn't you know that it was trending on 'Overheard at Acheron'?"

"It was a long time ago," I said. "It was the summer after Emmy. I wasn't thinking very clearly back then."

"Neither was he, apparently. I doubt that sleeping with a new hire is professional protocol at your college. And taking advantage of a recently bereaved one is just plain questionable."

The anger in his voice surprised me. It took me a moment to realize it wasn't directed at me. "It wasn't like that," I said. "I was an adult. I knew what I was doing."

"You know, I audited one of your classes that year."

"You did?" Was he changing the subject to keep me unbalanced? If so, it was working. My head was spinning. "I don't remember . . ."

"I sat in the back. You gave these really organized lectures—I still remember one on *Jane Eyre*—but it was like listening to a recording. You weren't *there*."

"That's awful," I said, feeling embarrassed. "I try to relate to my students."

"I know. I've read your student evaluations."

"You what—?"

He smiled. "Dorothy Cooper supplied them to show me what a fine person you are. They all say the same thing—Professor Lewis really cares about her students. But that year after your daughter died, anyone with eyes in their head could tell you were sleepwalking. Anyone who would take advantage of that . . ." He shook his head, his jaw clenched.

He didn't need to finish his sentence. *Would sleep with a student and run her off the road and leave her for dead.* I hadn't helped Ross by coming here; I'd made things worse for him. I could think of only one more thing to say.

"I'm the person who stands to benefit the most if Ross Ballantine is guilty. Don't you think it says something that *I* don't think he did it?"

McAffrey stared at me for a moment and then answered. "Yes. But I think it says more about *you* than it does about Ross Ballantine."

I was still puzzling that out when someone knocked at the door. Detective Haight stuck his head in and jerked his chin without saying anything. McAffrey nodded. "Be right there." Then he turned back to me. "Go home, Ms. Lewis. Get some sleep. Be relieved that you're no longer a suspect. I know I am."

CHAPTER **FIFTEEN**

I sat for another minute, watching the milk congeal on the top of my coffee, fighting against doing what McAffrey suggested. The last time I'd felt like this was when my father died. He'd been diagnosed with bladder cancer three years before. I'd watched him go from a big, hearty man to a shrunken shape under the wrinkled hospice sheets. He was in excruciating pain for the last few months, refusing to take morphine so he'd be lucid up to the last. When he died I knew that I would miss him every day of my life, but I was also relieved that it was over. And ashamed at my relief. I felt that same mix of shame and relief now.

By tomorrow the news that Ross was the new suspect in Leia's death would have spread through the community. By the time winter break was over everyone would have forgotten the few days I'd been a suspect. My colleagues would act sheepish around me. My students would titter over what a lech Professor Ballantine had turned out to be and then they would move on to some new scandal. Whoever had killed Oolong would feel bad about it—

My stomach wrenched at the memory of her poor frozen body.

—and what would I do? I thought about how McAffrey had described me in the year after Emmy's death. *Sleepwalking.* He said I'd eventually woken up, but had I? I remembered the day that I paused in the middle of a lecture and looked out at my class—at twenty fresh (some bored, some polite) faces and thought, *This could have been Emmy in thirteen years. She would have deserved more. They deserve more.* And so I started paying attention. Once I did it was easy to get swept up in their lives, their dramas, their needs. Cressida was right about that— they were a demanding generation. But whereas my colleagues complained about that I welcomed it. Because it was another way of not thinking about Emmy. Just like two or three glasses of wine at dinner and a nightcap of brandy or bourbon had been a way of not thinking about Emmy. Cressida was right about that too. I wasn't a falling-down drunk like Hannah Mulder. I kept my drinking to myself—one reason I kept so much to myself—and managed to teach my classes, but how long would I be able to keep that up without a job to keep me busy and give me a reason to hold it together? Already I was feeling the pull of that bottle of Glenlivet to deaden the pain of Oolong's death.

If I went home now, back to my life, I'd be going back to that, but where else did I have to go?

I got up and opened the door. As I stepped into the hallway I saw someone walking into the other interview room. A woman in a rumpled trench coat, loose grayish blond hair falling over her face. There was something familiar about her but I couldn't place her. Then she disappeared into the interview room. I turned and walked into the waiting room, where I found Dottie sitting in one of the plastic chairs knitting a purple scarf. Her eyes were still red and swollen but she looked like she had regained her composure. When she saw me she tucked her knitting into her quilted handbag. "Are you ready to go?"

Without waiting for a reply she got up and walked ahead of me to the car, humming "Silent Night" under her breath. There was one other car in the parking lot, a bright red Mini Cooper, its engine running, dome light on. Kelsey Manning stared at me defiantly, then bent her head to her phone.

"I wonder what she's writing now," I said.

"Probably—" Dottie began, then she pressed her lips together and said, "I'm sure I have no idea."

Dottie remained taciturn for the ride back. I spent the time thinking of all the things she had done for me over the years—making sure I had a good schedule, reminding me when I'd forgotten some bit of bureaucratic paperwork, baking me little treats and making sure I didn't forget to eat lunch when I was working in my office. She'd watched out for me while I had been sleepwalking. And what had I done to thank her? I'd taken advantage of her friendship to make my life easier. I'd taken her for granted. Even tonight I'd asked her to drive me to the police station without thinking of how devastated she'd be to learn that Ross was a suspect. And then I'd accused her of spreading rumors.

When we got to the bottom of my driveway she stopped the car. "I don't think I can make it up your driveway. You really ought to get someone to plow it. Troy Van Donk Senior will do it for you."

"Dottie," I said, ignoring her plowing advice. "I'm sorry I said you were a gossip. I didn't mean it."

"No, you were right. But that's all going to stop." She drew a line across her lips with thumb and forefinger. "I'm going to keep my mouth shut from now on."

She kept her hands gripped on the steering wheel and her eyes trained ahead, as if she was still driving, as if she'd already dropped me off and was on her way home, as if she'd already left me behind. I couldn't think of anything else to say. I got out of the car and walked up the icy, unplowed driveway to my empty house and to the bottle that was waiting in my cupboard to empty me of the pain.

The wind woke me up the next morning. It sounded like an angry woman shouting at my house and rattling the windowpanes. I turned over in bed, feeling for Oolong's warm body, but then remembered that Oolong was lying cold and dead downstairs in a laundry basket. It felt like part of my body had been scraped out. Not my heart, which is how I felt when Emmy died, but another smaller yet nonetheless vital organ like a kidney or a liver. Unable to go back to sleep I padded downstairs, the house feeling emptier without Oolong twining around my ankles. The first thing I did was to move the laundry basket with Oolong's body into the unheated woodroom, where it was cold but no animals would get to her. The ground was too frozen to bury her.

When I turned to leave the woodroom I felt a pang at leaving her alone in the cold, unheated space. I found one of her toys—a ragged catnip mouse—and brought it back to lay by her body. As I knelt down I remembered the things I'd found on Leia's shrine—the daffodils, the barrette, the bottle. It was like one of those rhymes on *Sesame Street* that Emmy used to sing along to. *One of these things is not like the others.* I could picture Hannah leaving the daffodils and the barrette but not the bottle. Even an old falling-down drunk like Hannah Mulder wouldn't deface a shrine for a young girl with a bourbon bottle. And she'd shaken her head when I held up the bottle. But then who had left it? And who had killed Oolong?

I readjusted the afghan over Oolong's body, then checked that the back door was locked. I looked out the window at the backyard, checking for footprints, but the wind had blown the snow into eddies and drifts that looked like a river at low tide. Any footprints left there yesterday would already have been erased.

Trying to shake off the feeling of being watched, I went back into the kitchen, made myself a cup of coffee, and opened my laptop. If someone was trying to send me a message they might try through "Overheard at Acheron." But I found that the site had been closed, with a message from President Martin requesting students to refrain from speculating about the terrible tragedy of Leia Dawson's death. Then I googled *Leia Dawson.* The first link I got was to an article on *Gawker* titled "Why Acheron President Martin Doesn't Want Her Students Talking about Leia Dawson" by Kelsey Manning. It included a picture of President Martin entering the police station in a wrinkled trench coat and what looked like Ugg slippers. I realized that's who I'd seen entering the other interview room. But why had Abbie Martin been at the police station so late at night? I read the article with a growing sense of unease.

Last night the President of SUNY Acheron made a midnight visit to the police station where the police were questioning Professor Ross Ballantine. The next morning President Martin closed down a student forum discussing Leia Dawson's death. What does she have to hide? Is she afraid that it will get out that Professor Ballantine was having an affair with his student right under her nose? Or had she learned that he had had an affair with Nancy Lewis?

The rest of the article made unfounded allegations against Ross and me. We were having a ménage à trois. The faculty party had been a drunken orgy. I had caught Leia and Ross together and run Leia down in Ross's car. It was a vitriolic rant full of speculation and rumor. I was surprised that even *Gawker* would run it. Unfortunately it had a few crumbs of truth in it—the picture of Abbie Martin entering the police station and the fact that Ross was being questioned there. And that I had had an affair with Ross six years ago. How had Kelsey gotten *that* information? Was it commonly known around campus?

Kelsey went on to accuse the college of sheltering a sexual predator who traded favors (grades, internships, recommendations) for sex. *I can see now why I got a C in Professor Ballantine's British Lit class,* Kelsey concluded, *I didn't put out.*

Ross would be mortified. I thought of him sitting in a circle of rapt students who were listening to his stories. He thrived on that admiration. To have that taken away—

But if he had exploited that admiration—if he had had an affair with Leia, *if he'd run her over*—didn't he deserve this?

Or did I just think that because I was relieved that I wasn't a suspect anymore?

I didn't know what to feel—and I wouldn't until I found out the truth from the one person who could give it to me. Besides, I didn't know how long I could sit in this house, wind shrieking like a banshee, Oolong's body in the woodroom, and that bottle of Glenlivet calling seductively from the cupboard.

I got dressed in warm clothes and walked down to River Road. The wind had blown the candles over on Leia's shrine. Glass shards littered the snow. The woods that had seemed so peaceful yesterday were full of thrashing branches. Like the trees in Dante's third circle of hell that moaned if you broke their branches. I didn't have the patience to stand and listen to them while I waited for the Loop bus, so I wrapped my scarf around my head, pulled up my hood, and started walking toward campus. The wind was so loud that I couldn't hear cars coming until they were passing right by me. Twice they came so close I lurched off the side of the road into the snow to avoid being hit. The second time I heard someone shout "Hey, Prof!" from an open window. In the past I would have thought it was a friendly greeting but now it sounded like an angry jeer. Were they deliberately trying to scare me? Was that what had happened to Leia? Had someone deliberately driven her off the road in a fit of rage?

I tried to imagine Ross doing it. If Leia had threatened to expose their affair he'd have been angry. He would have lost his position at the college. I knew how much teaching meant to him—but would it have been enough to make him kill Leia?

I thought of him racing down those roads in the Catskills the summer we were together. There was a recklessness in him, a self-destructive streak, but I couldn't remember any moment when he'd lashed out at me. Try as I might, I couldn't picture him deliberately running Leia off the road.

But then I remembered what Ross had said about playing a role in his classes. Maybe I didn't know him any better than I'd known Leia Dawson.

When I came to Ross's house at the edge of the campus I was relieved to see how quiet it was. I'd half expected a ring of news trucks around it and angry protesting students. Instead the house looked staid and calm, *solid*, like Ross himself. The paint on the shutters was fresh, the path neatly shoveled, the hedges trimmed for winter. Ross took good care of his home. He had once told me that he chose a house close to campus because he wanted to be able to invite students and faculty over for sherry hours and holiday parties. He always held his last class of the semester at his house. He always hosted the department holiday party and he held a barbecue in his backyard after graduation.

Those days were over, I thought, walking up the path. Even if he was found innocent of Leia's death the accusation of the affair would taint his relationship with his students. Even if he denied having the affair, even if he *hadn't* been sleeping with Leia, even if he had nothing to do with her death, he wouldn't be able to stay here.

The *New York Times*, wrapped in a blue plastic bag, lay in front of his door. I could imagine him not wanting to read the paper first thing this morning, but it was already ten thirty and I knew he always read the paper with his morning coffee. "I barely know how to start the day without doing the *Times* crossword," he'd once told me. "And I can't abide reading the paper online."

He didn't like to read anything online, didn't even own a Kindle. Maybe he hadn't read the *Gawker* article. Maybe he'd slept in after getting back late from the police station. I didn't see the Volvo in the driveway, but he could have parked it in the barn now that the Peugeot wasn't in there.

I picked up the paper and rang the bell. I could hear it ringing in the house, a melodious tune played on antique brass chimes that Ross had restored when he bought the house. They sounded tinny this morning under the shriek and moan of the wind, as if they were echoing in an empty house. I lifted the heavy brass door knocker shaped like a man's head—*Marley's ghost*, Ross would joke to newcomers, *here to remind me of my sins.*

The joke didn't seem so funny this morning. I waited, listening for the sound of footsteps inside. I wouldn't blame Ross for not wanting to answer his door. I might be an irate student or parent. After a few minutes I tried calling his name, but he didn't appear. Maybe he didn't want to talk to me either.

I walked around to the kitchen door. The top half of the door was glass. I could see a wedge of granite countertop and the kitchen sink, both spotlessly clean and bare. He'd had a housecleaner in since the party. The crystal bowl that usually held his car keys and spare change was on the counter beside the sink. I pressed my face to the glass, trying to make out if a cuff link was there, but I couldn't tell through the thick, faceted crystal what were coins and what might have been a cuff link. I knocked again and called and listened to the echo of my voice die in the wind—and to another sound. A low hum. It sounded mechanical. The refrigerator maybe, or some kind of pump or generator. Knowing Ross he'd have an automated system for sucking moisture out of the basement—and it did seem to be coming from *beneath* me. I could feel the vibration in the soles of my feet.

Well, at least his house would be dry and mold free when he came back to it—because clearly he wasn't here. He'd decided to ride out the wave of scandal somewhere else. At a friend's apartment in the city, maybe, or one of those divey hotels in the Catskills he'd taken me to—Ko-Z Kabins or The Stagger Inn.

I suddenly felt foolish for coming. What reassurance did I think he was going to give me? Even if he swore up and down that he hadn't been sleeping with Leia, how would I ever believe a word he said? How would anyone? I turned to go and saw the barn. It stood out in the snow, emblematic and stark, like an old weathered barn in an Andrew Wyeth painting, vibrating with some mysterious emotion.

It *was* vibrating. And the hum was coming from there. Ross must keep a generator in there, I told myself. But I felt a wrongness exuding from the square red façade. I didn't want to go any closer to it. Perhaps because it was where I last saw Leia, standing beside the barn, shivering in her red leather jacket. Laughing with Troy.

She *had* been laughing. But Cressida said Leia had come to her guilt-ridden. And when I saw her in the kitchen she looked like she'd been crying. How could she have been laughing just minutes later? Was she that good an actress?

I started walking toward the barn as if I could bring the memory back into focus by moving closer to where she'd been. As if I could catch an echo of Leia's laugh on the keening wind. Instead the hum from the garage grew louder, like the growl of an angry animal. There was a smell too leaking through the double doors, a sweet, sickly smell—

I started running through the snow toward the door. I pulled at the rusted metal handle, but snow had drifted in front of the door, making it hard to pull open, and I was getting dizzy with the effort—no, dizzy from the fumes leaking out of the barn. I yanked my scarf over my mouth and nose and, using both hands and bracing my feet, pulled the door until it opened a few feet. It was dark inside and thick with exhaust fumes, but I could make out Ross's Volvo, the engine running. I took out my phone to call 911 but then I saw the slumped shape behind the wheel of the Volvo and I ran for the car door. It was locked. I pounded on the partially opened window and shouted Ross's name. I thought I saw his eyelids flicker but it was hard to see in the dim barn through the fumes and my own eyes were stinging. If I didn't get him out soon I would lose consciousness. I should get out of here and call 911—

But Ross could be dead by then.

I tried the handle of the door again, but it was locked. I tried sticking my hand in the cracked window, but I couldn't reach the lock switch. Then I noticed the combination pad below it. Ross had to have the latest, fanciest gadgets. Including a combination lock on his car. If I knew the combination—

I did. Ross had told it to me once so I could get something from his car. It was the pub date of his first book. But what the hell was that? Why couldn't he have used his birthday, like a normal person? All I remembered were the first two digits, 03—March—and then I remembered him laughingly adding, "Published on the Ides of March in the first year of the nineties—I should have known the book was doomed!" I punched in 031590, squinting through tears now streaming down my face, and the door unlocked. When I pulled the door open Ross slumped out. I caught his shoulders before he fell to the ground, nearly falling myself as the weight of his body fell against me. I scrambled to hold my footing, afraid that once I hit the ground I'd stay there. I readjusted my grip under his armpits, the cashmere slippery and cold under my hands, and dragged him backward toward the door—or at least toward what I hoped was the door. The barn seemed to be spinning. Crazy slants of light shot through cracks in the roof like laser beams in one of those video games my students played. I looked behind me for the door and it seemed like it was a mile away—and as if someone was standing in the doorway. A slim, dark figure silhouetted against the light that swelled until the dark blotted it out. It took me a second to understand what I'd seen. Someone had closed the door.

CHAPTER SIXTEEN

With the last of my strength I pulled out my phone and dialed 911. Before I passed out I managed to give Ross's address and tell the operator I was trapped in the barn with a running car.

When I woke up I was outside, throwing up in the snow. I felt an arm around my shoulders and cool hands holding back my hair. I looked up into Joe McAffrey's face, his skin as white as it had been that morning when he knelt beside me on the road with Emmy.

"You're okay," he told me now. "A few minutes later you might not have been. I heard the call come over the radio while I was driving back from the impound lot. If I'd been ten minutes later . . ." He looked like he was going to throw up too.

"Ross?" It came out a croak. My throat felt as if it had been seared. Before I could say anything else a uniformed paramedic was clamping an oxygen mask over my face and ordering me to breathe. I looked past McAffrey to an ambulance where two paramedics were loading a stretcher. A bit of caramel-colored coat flapped in the wind. I looked back at McAffrey.

"He's alive but unconscious," he told me. "They don't know what the damage will be."

I nodded, unable to talk with the mask over my face. One of the paramedics came and said something to McAffrey and he nodded and waved them back to the ambulance. "Get Ballantine to the hospital. I'll follow with Ms. Lewis." He turned to me. "Is that okay?"

The paramedic lowered the mask from my face so I could talk. "Yes. I'm okay—they need to help Ross."

"They're going to do that. We have to get you to the hospital to check you out too." He helped me to my feet and steered me to his car. I felt dizzier when I stood up and I wondered if I really was all right, whether I shouldn't also be in that ambulance that was pulling out onto the river road, lights flashing, sirens shrieking. It sounded the way the wind had this morning, as if the wind had been trying to warn me.

"You're not going to turn on the siren, are you?" I asked as McAffrey helped me into the passenger seat.

"Not if you don't want me to. My niece always begs me to."

"The one who loves horses?" I asked, the question popping out before I'd even realized it.

He looked up from snapping my seat belt, his face so close I could make out the fine lines around his eyes and smell the crisp citrus tang of his aftershave. "You're waking up," he said. "Good. I need you alert."

His hand brushed against my leg as he pulled it away from the buckle and then he moved quickly away, slamming the door and jogging around to the driver's seat. He barked something into his radio—I only caught the part about taking me to the hospital.

"Why?" I asked when he signed off and reversed the car onto River Road. "Why do you need me alert?"

"So you can help me figure out what the hell just happened."

"I thought it was obvious. Ross was so upset that he was under suspicion for Leia's death he tried to kill himself."

"But that's just it. He wasn't under suspicion anymore. Abigail Martin came in last night and gave him an alibi for the time of Leia's death."

"Abbie? But if he was with Abbie why didn't he say so?" And then I knew. "Oh!"

"Exactly. Your friend Dottie saw them together the night of the party."

"She did? When?"

"She went back because she'd forgotten a casserole dish in the sink. She didn't tell anyone because she saw President Martin and Professor Ballantine in the kitchen, but when she found out last night that Ballantine was under suspicion she went and told Dr. Martin, who came down and gave a sworn statement that she was with Ballantine until the early hours of the morning."

"But Abbie is married and"—I was going to say "old" but then I realized that she wasn't much older than Ross—"his boss. If this gets out . . ."

"It will hurt both their careers, which is why I was inclined to believe it. We're dusting the keys and the interior of Ballantine's car for prints and any other evidence that someone else drove his car. What I'm having a hard time understanding is why Ballantine would try to kill himself when he'd just gotten an alibi."

"Because the damage is already done. Kelsey Manning has already spread the rumor of his affair with Leia on the internet. Even if it's not true, Ross's reputation is ruined and the respect of his students meant the world to him—"

I stopped, reliving those nightmarish moments in the garage, the terror of seeing the light in the doorway obliterated—

"The door . . ."

"The wind must have blown it shut," McAffrey said.

"No, there was someone there. I just couldn't make out who it was."

"Are you sure? You had carbon monoxide poisoning. You might have been hallucinating."

I pictured the dark figure in the doorway, the arm lifting and drawing the dark around it. "No, I definitely saw someone there. Whoever it was shut the door. They wanted Ross dead. It wasn't a suicide attempt; it was attempted murder."

I expected him to argue, to say I was hallucinating again, but instead, as we pulled into the hospital parking lot, he said, "If that's true it wasn't just Ballantine they tried to murder. Someone wanted you dead too."

*   *   *

McAffrey left me in the hospital after making sure I had a doctor with me who promised not to let anyone in to see me. "Stay here," he barked at me. "I'm going back to Ballantine's to have another look at the scene. I don't want you going anywhere without me."

As I was hooked up to an oxygen machine and IV—for fluids, I was told—the order seemed superfluous, but I agreed. I was feeling woozier than I'd thought. Maybe it was the idea that someone was trying to kill me. The same person who had killed Oolong and left the bottle on the shrine. Someone who thought I knew something about Leia's death. But what? I felt as if I knew less than ever. I hadn't even known about Ross and Abbie or that Dottie knew—of course! That's why she'd clammed up on me last night. Did that mean she wasn't angry with me—

Awash with questions and lulled by the rhythmic pulse of the oxygen pump I drifted off to sleep. When I awoke the room was dim and gray, the light grainy like an old black-and-white television broadcast. For a moment I thought I was back in the barn, struggling under Ross's weight. I craned my head for a glimpse of the door—for a way out—and found it blocked by a dark figure.

I lurched from the bed but was pulled back by something. *Ross*, I thought, *dragging me back down with him.* But then I realized it was the plastic IV and oxygen tubes. I tried to scream for help but my throat was so sore barely any sound came out. I tore the oxygen tubes off and grabbed the IV stand, grasping the cold metal for support, and tottered out the door, sure that the figure was the same as the one who had closed the barn door. The one who was trying to kill me. The hallway was empty but I heard a door swing shut at the end of it. I pattered down the hall, clutching my hospital gown with one hand, the IV stand with the other. I pushed open the last door on the hall into a double room. The first bed was empty, the second hidden by a drawn curtain. I'd woken up enough to wonder if this wasn't a bad idea. *Someone* had closed the door of the barn; *someone* wanted me dead. But I kept on, as if I were skidding down an icy hill, unable to stop my own forward momentum.

I stepped past the curtain. A woman was huddled in the bed, her knees drawn up to her chin, lank hair hanging over her face.

"Hannah!" I said. "You're conscious."

"I-I just wanted to see that you were all right," she stammered, cowering as if I meant to hit her over the head with my IV stand. "I heard the nurses talking about you. I-I just wanted to make sure you were okay. That's all I ever wanted to do."

"Is that why you left those things on the stone wall—the flowers, the barrette, the bottle?"

"I didn't leave no bottle. I left those other things for your little girl. That's what I was doing when I saw you in the woods."

"What?" I noticed that there was a large bandage on the right side of her head. She'd hit the pavement pretty hard when Ross's car ran into her. She might have brain damage. "What do you mean *in the woods*? You were outside my house—"

"Before that," she said. "I wasn't spying. I was only walking home on the road and I saw you hit the deer. It wasn't your fault. It came outta nowhere!"

A day ago I would have been glad of her eyewitness account. But today, not only was it a bit too late, I remembered that Hannah Mulder had thought Emmy was a cat when she hit her. She wasn't exactly a reliable witness. "I suppose you were walking home from the Swan."

"I'd only had a few." Suspicion flared in her eyes. "I saw the deer, then you got out of your car and went into the woods. I followed. I only wanted to see you were okay. That's all I ever wanted."

"Because if I killed myself you'd have another death on your head?"

She flinched as if I'd struck her. I instantly regretted my words, not because they were cruel but because she might stop talking. But she recovered soon enough.

"I saw you on the bridge that night."

Touché. I could have pretended not to know what night she was talking about but there didn't seem to be much point. It was a few months after Emmy died. Hannah must have been out on bail, not in prison yet. Evan had left that day because he said he couldn't bear to be in the house surrounded by reminders of Emmy. I'd driven him to the train station and then, instead of going home, I'd driven across the Kingston-Rhinecliff Bridge, then halfway back. There weren't any other cars out, which I'd taken as a sign. I'd pulled over on the south side of the bridge on the highest point of the span. Whenever we'd driven over the bridge with Emmy she would strain against her car seat belt crying "Bon Boy-Osh, Scuffy!" Evan had read her a story in which a toy tugboat named Scuffy floats down a little stream to a bigger stream to a river and all the way to the sea. All summer long she and Evan had launched twig boats on the stream that ran behind our house and down to the river. *Bon Voyage, Scuffy!* we'd all shout as the twig crafts bobbed on the current, or *Bon Boy-Osh!* as Emmy would shout as we crossed the bridge, hoping for a glimpse of Scuffy the Tugboat headed down the Hudson to the sea.

Earlier that day I had come into the kitchen and found Evan holding a plastic mug with a picture of Scuffy the Tugboat on it. He was quietly weeping, trying not to let me hear. I knew then that he was going to leave. After I had taken him to the train station I drove to the bridge and stood at the guardrail watching the dark water flowing toward the sea thinking *It will be quick, like flying into a wall of ice and then nothing.* I'd leaned into the wind, yearning for that nothing, but then I heard Emmy's voice shouting *Bon Boy-Osh, Scuffy!* and I couldn't do it. It felt like betraying her somehow.

"How do you know it was just that one night?" I asked. "How do you know I didn't go stand on the Kingston Bridge every night while you were in jail?"

She shrugged. "Because if you were gonna do it you'd've done it that night," she said with the authority of someone who had stared into that dark water herself. "But when I saw you sit down in the snow I thought you'd come up with another way. Freezing to death would be slower but you wouldn't feel so much like you were to blame. It would just sorta *happen*, like it was taken outta your hands."

"You sound like you've given the subject a lot of thought." She shrugged again, a habitual cringing gesture that summed up her preferred mode of suicide—something that was taken out of your hands. "So you watched me in the woods. What would you have done if I hadn't gotten up?"

"Dragged you back to your car, I guess. But then I saw the girl and thought maybe I could get her to help."

"What girl?"

"One of them college girls. Skinny. Short hair. Long neck. Red leather jacket."

"Leia."

"Yeah, that's what her boyfriend called her. They were walking in the woods together, friendly like at first."

"Did you recognize the boy?"

Her eyes slid away from me toward the door. I followed them, but the curtain blocked my view.

"It was dark. He was wearing a hood. They were going fast. I followed for a bit. They went over the hill and down to the boathouse. I don't like it down there . . ." She hugged her knees in and shivered, as if the cold of the night had penetrated into the hospital room. "I went back to check on you. You was still sleeping. I thought I'd have to do something but then that girl came back. She ran right past me, the boy following her, calling her to come back."

A man's voice calling *Come back!* I could almost hear it. "And did she?"

"No, she was scared . . . of *her*."

"Her?"

Again Hannah's eyes slid toward the door. This time I leaned back and saw Joe McAffrey standing in the doorway.

"He don't believe me," Hannah said.

"What don't I believe?" Joe asked, coming into the room.

"What I seen in the woods. I told you once before and you didn't believe me."

"What does she mean?" I asked McAffrey.

"I told Hannah to stop hanging around your house," he said to me. "She gave me a rather remarkable story about something she'd seen in the woods. Are you starting with that again, Hannah? Let's stick to the boy you said was chasing Leia Dawson in the woods."

"Not chasing. Following like."

"Okay, *following*. Did you recognize him?"

"He was wearing a hood—"

"That isn't what I asked you. Did you recognize him?"

Hannah cringed and looked nervously from me to McAffrey. "Might of been the Van Donk boy. They must of had a fight down in the boathouse. She was running when they came back, him following her, yelling come back!"

"And then what?"

"I-I don't know . . . I saw *her*. I got scared then and ran. I heard the car, the tires squealing, the girl screaming . . . and I ran. I didn't want to see . . ."

"So you ran away from the scene," McAffrey said, his voice tight with anger. "You didn't think about helping whoever was hurt?"

"I was scared!" Hannah cried, her voice high and childish, like Emmy's when she woke up from a nightmare. "I was afraid of *her*."

"Who?" I demanded, exasperated. "Who else did you see in the woods?"

"The same one I seen lurking around your house. Her that drowned herself in the river. She's covered with ice from head to toe, icicles hanging from her hair and clothes. That's who I saw watching Leia—just like I seen her watching you: the ice hag."

CHAPTER SEVENTEEN

"Do you think she made up the ghost because she didn't want to tell us about Troy?" I asked.

We'd gone back to my room after a nurse came in to tell us that Ms. Mulder needed her rest. It was clear Hannah wasn't going to tell us anything more anyway. At least anything coherent.

"Maybe, but it's not the first time she's told me about the ghost. She told me she'd seen it in the woods behind your house. She thought it was an omen that you were going to try to hurt yourself."

"Great. That's an image I need on cold, lonely nights—the ghost of a suicide clattering her frozen shroud outside my window."

"Don't tell me you believe in all that nonsense."

"Of course not! What kind of an idiot do you take me for?"

"I know you're no idiot, but your book had ghosts in it. It almost made *me* believe in ghosts."

"You *read* my book?" I tried to keep the pleasure out of my voice. I wasn't even sure why it pleased me. Usually when people told me they'd read my book I immediately assumed they were wondering why I hadn't written another one.

He looked embarrassed. "Yeah, well, I'd never met an author before. When I heard you'd written a book I thought it would be a children's book or one of those romantic things with a bare-chested guy on the cover, like the ones my sister reads, not a *ghost* story."

"It was supposed to be a postmodern homage to the gothic tradition." I nearly laughed at his blank stare. "Yeah, it sounds pretentious to me too now. The fact is, it kind of scared me too and after Emmy . . . well, it no longer seemed like fun to write about the dead, ironically or not."

He shifted in the too narrow hospital chair, looking uncomfortable. "Some women who'd lost a child would go the other way. You know, contacting psychics, going to séances."

I shuddered. "So charlatans could tell me that Emmy's up in heaven and just wants me to be happy? No, thank you. Just because I wrote a ghost story doesn't mean I believe in ghosts. Still, I'm not immune to suggestion. I don't like to think of Hannah seeing the ice hag peering in my windows."

"So you've heard of her?"

"Sure. It's a popular legend at the college. I get a couple of papers on her every semester. I'm sure my students sit around the boathouse, smoking pot, scaring themselves silly by telling the story of the grief-stricken mother who walked out onto the frozen river and fell through the ice."

"And whenever a mist comes up off the river they say it's the ice hag come to drag little children under the ice."

"So you know it too," I said, shivering at the image and drawing the hospital blanket over my legs.

"When I was in sixth grade a boy named Arlen Mott went out onto the frozen river on a dare and fell through the ice. I had nightmares about the ice hag until I was in high school."

"What stopped them?"

"Thinking about girls," he said with a slow smile that took the chill off my skin. I could feel the heat in my face and I felt suddenly conscious that I wasn't wearing anything under the thin hospital gown.

"Hannah must have grown up on the same story," I said. "A couple of pints of Four Roses and she starts seeing the ice hag in the mist. Speaking of Four Roses, Hannah said she didn't leave that bottle on the wall."

"I didn't think it was Hannah, but I do think it was someone who might want to direct our attention to her if Hannah claimed she saw him in the woods."

"Troy?"

McAffrey nodded. "It could have been Troy you saw in the garage with Ross—"

"How *is* Ross?" I asked, feeling a sudden pang of guilt that I hadn't asked after him when he'd almost died today.

"Still unconscious but stable. They moved him to Vassar Brothers in Poughkeepsie to put him in a hyperbaric chamber. The lab results indicate that he had a lot of alcohol in his blood. Do you think he would have tried to kill himself?"

"It's what I was afraid of when I went to his house—that all this scandal about having an affair with Leia would devastate him. He lived off the admiration of his students—but would he kill himself? I don't know. Do you think someone did this to him?"

"I went back to look at the barn. Unfortunately the snow outside the door was completely trampled by paramedics, but I was able to make out only three sets of tracks from the kitchen door to the barn. A women's size nine L.L.Bean snow boot, which I believe belongs to you"—he glanced at my boots, which were sitting on the floor by the closet—"a size twelve men's oxford shoe, which matches what Mr. Ballantine was wearing today, and a size ten construction boot, one of those steel-tipped things a lot of the college kids like to wear, whattaya call them—"

"Doc Martens?" I suggested. I was trying to recall what Troy had been wearing in the woods yesterday. Something sturdier than his friend's pointy-toed oxfords.

"Yeah. Those tracks were right beside Ballantine's. The thing is, Ballantine's tracks were all over the place, like he was drunk. The Doc Martens were steadier but following Ballantine's."

"As if someone was walking beside him trying to keep him from falling?"

"Exactly. You'd make a good detective, Ms. Lewis."

"Thanks. I may be looking for a new job soon . . . but I can't think why anyone would want Ross dead."

"Perhaps he figured out who took his car keys that night."

"And he confronted whoever did it—but how would that person get him in the car?"

"If Ballantine was already drinking he could have slipped sleeping pills in his glass, lured him to the car somehow, waited for him to pass out, and then closed him in there. Then he waited to make sure no one came along to save Ballantine. When he saw you go into the barn he was afraid that if Ballantine lived he'd be caught for Leia's death *and* the attempted murder of Ballantine."

"So he closed the door and left me there to die." I tried to picture that dark figure silhouetted in the doorway, searching my memory for some identifying feature, but I could only see an amorphous cutout shape. "You keep saying 'he' but the figure I saw could have been a man or a woman. It was slim, hooded—"

"Troy was wearing a hood when Hannah saw him in the woods."

"But what about the ice hag?"

He paused as if humoring me. "I think that was a hallucination on her part. But I think Hannah did see Troy Van Donk in the woods. You saw him too—talking to Leia outside the barn the night of the party and later in the woods walking to the boathouse. Unfortunately, it wouldn't be out of the question for it to be Troy. I picked him up for possession of marijuana last year. He got off with community service. I'd hoped he was straightening himself out . . ." He frowned and ran his hands through his hair. He looked tired—and sad. I saw the same look of disappointment that I had when a student I'd been working with failed to show up for a final—or didn't hand in a paper, like Troy had failed to hand in his final story.

"He was doing well in my class this semester," I said. "Handing in work, writing some great stuff—and then a week or two ago he started missing classes and then he didn't hand in his final paper."

"So something went wrong. Maybe he got involved in something over his head. A couple of weeks ago we picked up an Acheron student with heroin."

"*Heroin?* At Acheron? I know the kids smoke pot, but heroin?"

He pursed his lips, suppressing a smile. "You don't think college students do heroin?"

I blushed, remembering Aleesha's paper on her cousin Shawna. "One of my students, Aleesha, did write about her cousin Shawna doing heroin. In fact, Shawna just died of an overdose."

"Shawna Williams. That was a tragedy. I met her in a drug prevention program we ran last summer. But it's not just black kids from Poughkeepsie doing heroin; it's an epidemic. I've got high school kids here in Acheron shooting up. I went on a call last month—a sixteen-year-old boy, star quarterback on the football team, OD'd. We gave him naloxone and revived him but he suffered brain damage. Mom finally came to tell me that he started on painkillers last year after he broke his femur playing football. When he couldn't afford the OxyContin he switched to heroin. It's cheaper." He sighed, truly looking defeated now. "The same thing is happening all over the country. People get addicted to Oxy then switch to heroin when they can't afford it anymore. And we're right in the middle of the traffic pattern here in Acheron. It moves up from the city, through the projects in Poughkeepsie, then up to Albany and on into Canada. Route Nine is a major drug traffic route. I caught a dealer just last month pulling him over for an expired inspection ticket. The smart ones take the Loop bus."

That caught my attention. "The Loop bus? The one the Acheron kids take?"

"Sure. Dealers from Poughkeepsie come up here, sell to high school and college students, and ride the bus back to Poughkeepsie. No worries about getting pulled over for a broken taillight."

"The older guy I saw walking with Troy in the woods—the skinny scarecrow one—I saw him riding into town on the Loop bus and then back again."

"That could be Troy's connection," McAffrey said, pulling out his notebook and writing something in it.

"But what does this all have to do with Leia?" I asked.

"Maybe Leia found out what Troy was doing and threatened to turn him in."

"Hmm. Leia could be righteous, and Troy certainly was angry with her when we spoke on the bus, but I don't see Leia being that concerned about drug use, unless . . ." I remembered Leia's paper. "Unless she knew Shawna Williams had started using again. That might have made Leia look at drug use differently. Then, yeah, she might have threatened to turn Troy in for dealing."

"And he went after her in the car."

"It could have been an accident," I said, hating to think of Troy running over Leia in cold blood.

"Might have been, but leaving you and Ross Ballantine to die in that barn was no accident."

"Are you going to bring him in?"

"Detective Haight's out looking for him now." McAffrey looked at his watch. "I'd better get going back to the station, but I could give you a lift home first. Your doctor said you were good to go."

I remembered the last time he'd driven me home. "Are you going to take me for another glimpse into my dreary future living in a trailer park?"

He gave me a long, assessing look that brought the blood back to my cheeks. "You look like you've seen enough today," he said finally. "No detours this time. I promise."

I met McAffrey downstairs after I'd been discharged and gotten dressed. He was on his phone. He looked unhappy.

"Haight hasn't been able to find Troy," he said. "He didn't show up this morning for his shift at his father's garage. I'm afraid he's done a runner, which doesn't look good for him."

"He was often late for class," I offered.

"You don't want to think it's him, do you?"

"No," I admitted. I could picture Troy accidentally hitting Leia and fleeing the scene in a panic, but when I tried to imagine him leading Ross out to his car and deliberately leaving him to die—or closing the barn door on me—my mind balked. Maybe I just didn't want to imagine any student of mine hating me so much that they would kill me. But that could just have been my vanity.

I rode again in the front passenger's seat. We drove south on Route 9 and turned west on 199, past a farm stand closed for the season and a low-lying orchard, under a dark, overcast sky. The road climbed from there up a steep hill. As we passed Van's Auto I glanced out the window and saw a boy in a familiar purple and gold sweatshirt bent over a truck's engine.

"Hey, I think that's Troy."

McAffrey followed my gaze and then swung the car into Van's, blocking the entrance. "Stay here," he barked, jumping out of the car.

I hadn't really thought he would stop. I felt a qualm that I'd set a policeman onto Troy, but then it was better if McAffrey didn't think that Troy had run away. I still was having trouble imagining Troy as a killer. He was bent over the engine of a red pickup truck, using a wrench to loosen something, his face red in the cold air. When he looked up and saw McAffrey approaching he tensed, looked behind him, then hauled back his arm and threw the wrench at McAffrey.

I screamed as McAffrey ducked and Troy ran past him and past the police car. I could see his face as he streaked by. His eye caught mine and the panic turned to something else. I opened the door and got out, calling Troy's name, but he was already past me, in the road—running directly in front of an eighteen-wheeler barreling down the hill. There was no way the truck would be able to stop in time. McAffrey saw it too. He'd reached the edge of the road, his feet skidding on ice and rutted snow. I saw his muscles bunching, getting ready to sprint into the middle of the road to make a lunge for Troy.

"Joe! Don't!" His arms pinwheeled as if caught in a current. Troy gave one glance over his shoulder and then leapt for the other side of the road. The truck thundered past us, horn blaring, brakes squealing, kicking up so much dirty snow and ice I wasn't sure if Troy had been hit or not. But then when the truck passed I caught a glimpse of a purple sweatshirt vanishing into the woods on the other side of the road. McAffrey sprinted across the road and disappeared into the woods.

I stood by the side of the road staring into the woods as if they were a dark lake that had swallowed both men, and I was waiting for them to come to the surface. Another man came to stand next to me. With his bulging stomach, balding head, and grease-stained hands, Troy Van Donk Sr. had none of his son's good looks, but he did have the same expression of fear on his face that I'd seen on Troy's as he'd run by.

"What's the boy gotten himself into now?" he asked, the angry tone belying the fear on his face.

I couldn't bear to tell him. "Sergeant McAffrey just wanted to ask him some questions . . . maybe he just got spooked."

Troy Sr. shook his head, took out a bandana, and wiped the sweat that despite the cold beaded his forehead. "There's been something these last few weeks eating at him. He's mixed up in something. Goddamnit!" He spit into the dirt. "I knew no good would come of going to that college and mixing with spoiled rich kids, making him want things he couldn't have."

I wanted to object, to tell him that his son was a talented writer, that he had promise, but then I pictured Troy and Leia outside Ross's barn, Leia in her red jacket, Troy in his purple sweatshirt, framed against the fiery backdrop of the sunset—all that youthful promise about to go up in flames—and thought that Troy Sr. had been right. No good had come of Troy's going to Acheron.

CHAPTER EIGHTEEN

McAffrey came back half an hour later, his uniform soaked and covered in pine needles and burrs. "That kid of yours sure can run, Van," he said to Troy Sr.

"What's he done, Joey?"

"I just need to talk to him. Tell him that if you see him. Tell him it'll go better for him if he comes in himself."

"I will if I see him, but knowing my boy he's gone to ground. Back when he was little he'd go hide in those woods when he was angry or scared. Stayed in there a week once when some girlie broke his heart."

"Temperature's going down below zero tonight," McAffrey said, looking up at the darkening sky. "He'll be looking for a warmer place to bed down. You call me if you see him, Van, and I'll make sure he gets a fair hearing."

Troy Sr. squinted at McAffrey as if trying to bring him into focus. Then he looked up at the sky too. "Yep, it's gonna be a cold one," he said as if all they'd been talking about was the weather. Then he nodded at me and walked away, his broad back stooped and round-shouldered. I remembered Dottie telling me she'd gone to high school with him. I tried to picture him as a young man. Then I thought of how Troy must see his father. He'd written in one of his stories about a young man who "saw himself turning into his old man with every grease stain, every backache, every bad choice." I had written in the margin, "Beautiful! But you can write yourself a better future." That's what going to Acheron was supposed to offer him—a different future from his father's—but what if Leia had threatened to turn him in for dealing? That bright future would have gone up in smoke. Would he have killed her to keep that future and keep from turning into his old man?

We didn't talk much on the drive back to my house. McAffrey looked angry, but whether at me or himself I couldn't tell. When we pulled up to the house there were two surprises—the drive was plowed and my car was parked in it.

"My car!" I said, surprised at how glad I was to see the seven-year-old Honda Civic. The front hood was dented, giving it a disreputable air, but it looked drivable.

"My big surprise," he said. "I was over at the impound lot signing release forms when I got the call on the radio. I had a friend bring it over and plow the driveway so you'd have someplace to keep it . . ." His voice trailed off and he looked embarrassed.

"Do you do that for all your suspects when they've been proven innocent, Sergeant McAffrey?"

He smiled. "You called me Joe before."

"Oh," I said, feeling embarrassed myself now. "I thought you were about to fling yourself in front of that truck."

"So it takes a life-threatening situation for me to achieve first-name status?"

"I guess that *is* what it took," I admitted.

"Well, now that you've started there's no going back to Sergeant McAffrey."

"Okay . . . *Joe*. As long as you call me Nan."

"Okay . . . *Nan*." He held out his hand to shake mine. His grip was warm and firm. When I let go and turned to go into my empty house I could still feel the heat of it cradled in my palm, like the live ember ancient Romans carried into their homes to light their hearths on sacred days.

I needed all the warmth I could get. Joe (I said his name to myself like a teenager doodling her crush's name on her school notebooks) had been right. The wind, which had been blowing all day, had brought in colder air with the night. I turned up the heat and closed all the windows tight and made a fire in the woodstove. I sat next to it, bundled in a SUNY Acheron sweatshirt and sweatpants, drinking hot tea. I thought of adding a shot of Glenlivet to it but then I thought of Joe's face when he said he thought I'd seen enough and I didn't want to prove him wrong. Maybe there was still time to change what my future looked like.

In the spirit of starting over I sorted through all the papers from the semester, burning what I didn't need anymore—extra syllabi, campus memos and flyers—and filing students' papers. When I came across one of Troy's, though, I sat back in the rocking chair and read it.

It was the first draft of a story about a young man named Uli wandering around Poughkeepsie one night. Troy had taken my Margaret Atwood quote about making the risky trip to the Underworld to heart and based his story on *The Odyssey*, which he'd read in my Great Books class the year before. Uli was clearly supposed to be a modern Ulysses, and his travels through the streets, bars, twenty-four-hour convenience stores, derelict houses, and projects of Poughkeepsie were supposed to be his odyssey—his ten-year journey home from the wars. The spelling and grammar were abysmal, but the dialogue was great and the scenes were funny updates on the wanderings of Odysseus. Uli is detained by a witchy ex-girlfriend named Calinda Lipschitz. He and his best friend, called Jay Crew for his preppy attire, wander into a bar called Circe's Den. The bar is shaped like a ship and adorned by a wooden figurehead of a buxom woman that the locals call the Sea Witch. There they meet three Siren-like prostitutes who lure them into an alley and steal

Jay Crew's wallet. Uli escapes, but then must navigate his way between a patrol cop's cruiser and an angry dealer named Scully—so named for a skull tattoo on his shaved head but also an obvious nod to the monster Scylla—to whom he owes money. He descends into the "underworld" of the projects, looking for a friend to loan him the money to pay Scully back and take the bus to Ithaca where his girlfriend, Penny Lopez, a freshman at Cornell, has been posting pictures of herself at a frat party with a bunch of drunk frat boys. The story ended with Uli lost in the projects. I'd written Troy a long comment, praising his dialogue, sense of scene-building, and inventiveness, suggesting he clean up his spelling and grammar, and urging him to finish the story for his final assignment. I'd made a copy and given him back the original. At the bottom I'd written, "I want to see Uli make it home!" and added, "I'm assuming that while based on personal experience much of this is fictional. But if there's anything you want to talk about, my door is always open." I'd added a smiley face. It wasn't a winky face, but it might as well have been. The story made it clear that Troy had interactions with dangerous drug dealers, but I'd pretended that the work was strictly fictional. But what was I supposed to do? Turn Troy's story over to the counseling center?

It was one of the quandaries of teaching writing to undergraduates. I often saw things in my students' stories that reflected troubling circumstances—drug use, depression, abusive families. If I turned every one of them in to the counseling center I'd lose the trust of my students. Over the years I'd referred three students there—one who had admitted to being depressed and wrote a story about killing himself, one who had written a story about shooting everyone he knew, and one from a girl who wrote about an abusive sexual relationship. The depressed student had dropped out, the "shooter" had laughed in my face and written on his student evaluation that "for a writer Professor Lewis has a fundamental lack of imagination and sense of humor," and the girl in the abusive relationship had thanked me for making her face her problems.

So when I read Troy's story about drug dealers in Poughkeepsie I thought it was likely based on some real life experience but that it was probably exaggerated. I knew he was a fan of hard-boiled crime writers like George Pelecanos and Richard Price. A lot of my white students affected black street language and clothing. When we workshopped Troy's story, Aleesha had rolled her eyes and asked why "all you white boys try to sound black." But she'd also admitted that Troy sounded like he knew the neighborhood. "Circe's Den is Noah's Ark, right? I live right around the corner." Leia had said—

What had Leia said?

I sat, staring at the fire, trying to remember. I pictured my students sitting in a circle, Troy slumped in his chair, hood up, listening to the comments with a bored look on his face, which I could tell was as much an affectation as the gangsta language in his piece. I could tell by the jitter in his leg that he'd been nervous about being critiqued and from the way his body had slowly relaxed that he was pleased with the way the workshop was going. His peers really liked the story. Then Leia had said something that made everybody laugh. What had she said?

"I'd sure like a tour of the underworld."

And Troy had smiled a slow, seductive smile and said, "Anytime, Leia, I'll be your Virgil."

I remembered at the time being proud that Troy remembered that Virgil had been Dante's guide to the Underworld and thinking that Leia would be a good influence on Troy.

But what kind of influence had he been on her?

And what had Leia seen on her odyssey to Poughkeepsie? Something that Troy didn't want anyone to know about? Something worth killing Leia to keep secret?

I read Troy's story over twice, looking for some clue, while the wind wailed outside like a pack of Furies bent on vengeance. A cold draft snaked in through the curtains. I went to draw them closed and found a horrible, grimacing face staring back at me from the glass. Even when

I saw that it was only a pattern etched in ice my heart still pounded. It looked like the ice hag had pressed her face against the window and left her icy impression on the glass. I thought of what Hannah had told Joe about seeing the ghost wandering the woods behind my house. The reason it had frightened me so much was that it made an awful sort of sense. The ice hag was a bereaved mother who had taken her life in her grief. Why should I survive the death of my child? What was I still doing here, the wild wind demanded of me as I climbed the stairs, which groaned under my feet as if the very house resented my presence. Why was I inside, safe and warm, while Emmy and Leia were dead and Troy was out there in the cold? *Gone to ground*, his father had said, like a hunted animal.

It was that last thought that haunted me through the night. No matter what Troy might have done I still hated the thought of him outside on a night like this. Whenever I drifted off to sleep I dreamed of him wandering through a driving blizzard like Kristoff and Anna in *Frozen* and I would startle awake, shivering in my drafty house.

In the morning I called Joe to ask if he had found Troy or heard anything. He hadn't. I told him about Troy's story and the locations in Poughkeepsie he mentioned. "Maybe he's hiding down there."

"I'll check it out," he said, "but don't you get any ideas of looking for him. That's a pretty dicey neighborhood around Noah's—and there's a snowstorm coming tonight."

"I wouldn't begin to know where to look," I said. "I'll leave that to you."

When I got off the phone I realized I hadn't asked about Ross. Was that because I didn't want to bring up my ex-lover with Joe? Ridiculous, I told myself. As if it would matter to Joe McAffrey. I considered calling him back to ask if he'd heard anything about Ross but then realized that was even more ridiculous. I could call the hospital myself—although they might not tell me anything over the phone—

Or I could go there. Vassar Brothers was only a half-hour drive away. I had my car back. I didn't have anything else to do and I didn't relish the idea of lingering around the house listening to the wind shrieking and imagining the ice hag lurking around my windows.

The ice hag had done a number on my car. There was an inch of ice coating the windows and the lock was frozen. I had to pour hot water over the keyhole and the seams of the door to get into the car and then run the engine with the defrost on high and scrape the windows for twenty minutes. I considered giving up and going back inside, hunkering down by the woodstove. *With a glass of Glenlivet,* the ice hag whispered in my ear.

I'm laying off, I countered.

Then why haven't you poured the rest of it down the drain? she jeered back.

I kept scraping to drown out the voice. When I was finally about to drive the car I took the turn at the bottom of Orchard too fast and skidded onto River Road. Luckily the road was empty.

There wasn't much more traffic on Route 9. People were staying off the roads on this frigid Sunday between Christmas and New Year's. Or maybe it was the gathering storm clouds over the Catskills that were keeping people off the roads. With little or no traffic I got to Vassar Brothers in less than half an hour. I parked in the visitors' lot and hurried into the building. The lobby had the sad look of public places after Christmas, the artificial Christmas tree beginning to droop, the smiles of volunteers, with their holly pins and reindeer sweaters, strained. Who wanted to be in a hospital at Christmastime?

"Mr. Ballantine has been moved out of intensive care but he can only have one visitor at a time and there's someone with him now," a woman with short silver hair in a red sweater set and plaid pants told me.

"It's probably a colleague of ours from work," I said. "Couldn't I go up and wait outside the room?"

"I suppose . . . since it's so quiet." She gave me directions to his room that I immediately forgot when I got off the elevator. Why were hospitals so confusing? I wondered, walking down a hall with a green stripe on the floor—presumably to guide the way—and generic photographs of cheerful landscapes and happy children. I'd gone to visit my father almost every day when he'd been in the hospital and I'd still gotten lost in the hallways. They all looked alike. And they all smelled like death.

What finally led me to Ross's room was a familiar voice—"and you're not to worry about the house. I went by this morning and set the taps to drip and opened the cabinets under the sinks so the pipes won't freeze. And I called Charlie Maynard to come by and clear the ice dams in your gutters. They say the temperature will remain in the single digits through New Year's—the river is almost entirely frozen."

I followed this companionable chatter to a private room, where I found Dottie sitting beside Ross's bed, her hands working busily knitting a colorful afghan square. Ross's eyes were closed and his mouth was covered by plastic tubing. I couldn't tell if he was conscious or not.

"Dottie?" I said softly as I came into the room.

"Nan! Look, Ross, Nan is here. I told you she'd come."

Ross's eyes flickered open. They were an alarming shade of red. I moved quickly to his side and took his hand. "You're awake," I said. "You gave me quite a scare." I felt like I was reading from a script, a stupid smile pasted to my face. He responded with a soft moan.

"Does he have to have that thing over his mouth?" I asked Dottie.

"Until they're sure his lungs are working all right."

I turned back to Ross. "Do you remember what happened?" I asked.

He nodded, then grimaced at the pain the motion must have caused. "You're tiring him," Dottie said, tugging at my sleeve. "The doctor said he shouldn't be stressed."

I pulled Dottie a few feet from the bed and whispered in her ear. "I need to know if he tried to kill himself."

"Why?" she cried. "Why can't you leave it?" I'd never heard Dottie sound so upset.

I took her hand. "If he didn't do it to himself then someone tried to kill him."

"Kill Ross? Why would anyone . . ." Dottie's eyes grew wide. "You mean if he knew who killed Leia?"

"Yes."

"But who?"

I considered telling her what Joe suspected. She saw the doubt in my face. "I see. You still don't trust me because it was my fault it got out about Ross and Abbie—but I *had* to tell Abbie that Ross was a suspect—"

"Of course you did, Dottie. It's not that. It's just that it's a police investigation and I'm not sure what I'm supposed to tell." Then I recalled Troy giving Dottie the finger and realized that if I didn't tell her and something happened to her I would never forgive myself. "Sergeant McAffrey thinks it might have been Troy Van Donk."

Doubt flickered across Dottie's face, her loyalty to Troy's father warring against Troy's insult to her. Loyalty won out. "I don't believe it of Troy," she said firmly.

"Well, then I'd better ask Ross what he remembers because Sergeant McAffrey is out looking for Troy right now."

We went back to Ross's bed. His eyes were closed. I was afraid he'd drifted off while Dottie and I conferred, but his eyes struggled open when I took his hand.

"Ross, I need to know what happened to you. Can you answer some questions?"

Instead of nodding he lifted his other hand, pinched his thumb to his forefinger, and waved it in the air. It took me a second to realize he was miming the motion of writing. I dug in my bag for a piece of paper, but Dottie had already pulled out a small memo pad with a quilt design on the cover. She braced the pad up under Ross's hand and gave him a pen. Ross's face tensed with concentration as he moved the pen across the page. I felt a pang recalling the ease with which he'd signed his name at bookstore signings, but then, as he wrote, I saw his face relax. This was what Ross loved—writing, telling a story.

He might have been penning his memoirs from the exhaustion on his face when he at last dropped the pen and pushed the pad away. I took the pad from Dottie with a shaking hand. Would he confess that guilt over his affair with Leia had driven him to try suicide? Would he name Troy as his attacker? I looked down at the page. For a moment I thought I was so nervous that I'd lost the ability to read. But then I heard Dottie gasp.

"It doesn't make any sense at all," she whispered, her eyes filling with tears. "It's all gibberish!"

CHAPTER NINETEEN

It took me ten minutes of walking around in a blur to find my car in the parking lot. That Ross, a brilliant and eloquent literary man, had been reduced to writing in gibberish struck me cold with horror. It had been one of my worst nightmares—before I learned what nightmares really were—that something would happen to my hands and I would be unable to use a pen or type. But this—writing gibberish—was worse. And it wasn't just the writing. When I asked him point-blank if it had been Troy who had led him to the garage he stared at me with vacant eyes. Would he ever regain his faculties? What would become of him if he didn't? I couldn't imagine Ross without the ability to write.

By the time I found the car I was weeping loudly and openly. I could barely see to navigate my way out of the lot and onto the streets of Poughkeepsie where the falling snow limited my vision even further. I headed north toward Route 9 but after a few blocks realized I must have missed the entrance. I was in a neighborhood of modest two-story houses that had once been beautiful Victorians but now featured discolored aluminum siding and sagging porches. I could make out Route 9 below me to the left and beyond that the frozen river. I kept going, assuming that I'd eventually come to an entrance. I passed an apartment complex named for Harriet Tubman and then a desolate-looking park. I crossed an arterial thoroughfare that had been built in the '70s and, according to an urban planning lecture I'd once attended, gutted downtown Poughkeepsie, hastening the decline of the city from the days when it was a thriving ferry and train destination. Despite its neighborhoods of once beautiful Victorian houses, a major train station, and nearby colleges (Vassar was east of the city, and Marist College and the Culinary Institute of America just north of it), the city had one of the highest crime and welfare rates in the state. It was no place to get lost in—but that's what I was. Every time I tried to head toward the river I was turned back by a one-way street. I passed an abandoned establishment called Spanky's and a church building with crackled paint that reminded me of the rectory in *The Exorcist*. I saw the train station and headed there, figuring I could ask someone how to get back to 9, but then an outlandish figure loomed up ahead out of the snow—a bare-breasted woman with hair blown back and skirts flapping in the wind. I skidded to a stop and stared at her. It was a ship's figurehead, carved out of wood and painted in bright colors. She was mounted to the brick façade of a river-facing building as if to a ship's prow, breasting the snow as she once might have parted the waves. She was a strange sight in these derelict streets, but the reason I stopped was that there was something familiar about her, something I should remember . . .

The Sea Witch. She was the ship's figurehead Troy had described in his story, above the bar he called Circe's Den. This bar was called Noah's Ark, but it had to be the same place. How many antique ships' figureheads could there be in downtown Poughkeepsie? I stared at her through the swirling snow as if she were a landmark pointing the way home.

But what home? The empty, haunted house I'd been rattling around in since Emmy died? What did I have there but a few frail memories of Emmy? I wouldn't have a job much longer—my one real supporter lay in a stupor, unable to string letters into words. My reputation was ruined at Acheron—and even if it weren't, what business did I have there? I'd prided myself on being a good teacher—on being the kind of teacher who cared about her students—and look what had come of that. I'd run Leia off when she came to me for help. I'd ignored the obvious signs that Troy was involved in a dangerous drug world—why, he'd practically drawn me a map of his downward spiral into hell and I'd treated it like a goddamned literary metaphor! I didn't deserve to be a teacher anymore.

I wiped my eyes with my coat sleeve, then swiped at the windshield, which had fogged over during my sobbing. Yes, the Sea Witch was pointing home—I could make out a sign for 9 North just beyond the bar. I put the car in drive and began to pull into the road . . .

When a familiar-looking figure came out of the bar. Skinny legs, pointy shoes, vintage tweed coat, porkpie hat—it was the Aging Hipster I'd seen on the Loop bus and walking in the woods with Troy. He paused in the doorway, pulled his collar up around his scrawny neck, and lit a cigarette. I guess even Noah's Ark obeyed the state no-smoking law. I stared at him, wondering how many drugs he'd sold my students. He was looking up and down the street, his eyes lingering on my headlights for a minute but then returning to the sidewalk. As if he were looking for someone. A drug connection? I had half a mind to get out of the car and tell him what I thought of him—

But then two other men came around the corner, two teenagers in hooded sweatshirts, huddled against the snow. As they approached the doorway of Noah's, Aging Hipster stepped forward to greet them. They exchanged a complicated series of hand gestures that ended in a power fist bump and then the three of them turned and started walking away from Noah's. As he turned, Aging Hipster took off his hat to shake snow from the brim and I saw that the back of his shaved scalp was tattooed with a large, grinning skull, identical to the tattoo described in Troy's story for the drug dealer he'd called Scully. I'd thought it was Troy's invention but I doubted it was a coincidence that the same man whom Troy had met in the woods and who was hanging outside the bar Troy had described in his story had the same tattoo. This was clearly the dealer Troy had written about—the name even fit his skeletal frame and disjointed gait—and this was the neighborhood Troy had promised to take Leia to for "some real life experience." What if Leia had seen something she shouldn't have on that little field trip? What if it hadn't been Troy's secret she'd threatened but Scully's?

Scully and the two men were turning a corner. Before I knew I planned to do it, I pulled out and followed them. When I turned the corner I saw them halfway down the block. I let a taxi pull in front of me to make my pursuit less obvious. The neighborhood was sliding from slightly disreputable to downright derelict as I followed the three men down the hill toward the river, passing buildings that were only burnt-out shells. A group of homeless men stood at a corner warming their hands at a fire burning in a garbage can. The waterfront was cut off by a chain-link fence topped with razor wire. Beyond the fence I could see a brick tower with the words *Blackwell Machine* picked out in grayish ceramic tile that might once have been pastel blue. Below the tower was a tin-roofed building covered with large, colorful graffiti tags. Scully pulled back a loose flap of wire fence as if it were a flimsy curtain and waved the two young men to go ahead. One of them looked around nervously. I slid down in my seat, afraid he'd see me, but my car, with its dented hood, must have looked disreputable enough to blend into the neighborhood. As he turned back and followed his friend and Scully into the abandoned factory, a sharp rap at the window made me jump. A snow-covered figure, face obscured by a fur-trimmed hood, was peering through my window. Recalling the ice hag's face at my window last night my heart raced, but then she pushed down her hood and I recognized Aleesha Williams. I lowered my window.

"Professor Lewis, what in the world are you doing here? This is no place for you!"

I started to point out Scully and the two men but they had vanished into the grafittied building. For a moment I wondered if I had summoned them up out of Troy's story. But then Aleesha said, "Come on before that bastard Scully comes back"—she was looking toward the river. She didn't look afraid, she looked angry—"and I kill him for what he did to Shawna."

Aleesha got in the car and directed me back up the hill to a three-story gingerbread-trimmed Victorian house overlooking the river. "You'd better come on in if you want to hear the full story," she said.

I was happy to get out of the car and follow Aleesha up the peeling, uneven steps onto the front porch. There were six mailboxes lined up beside the front door. The fanlight over the door was painted over and missing several panes of glass and the molding in the front hall was chipped and dingy. Aleesha's apartment was on the first floor. She unlocked three locks and let me into a light, airy room with a desk, a small television, and a playpen full of toys.

"This is the study/playroom," she said with a wry smile. "The only way I can get any work done at night is to put on a *Dora the Explorer* show for Isabel. But I read to her plenty." She gestured to a stack of children's books with library stickers on them. "I don't want you to think I'm a bad mother."

"I once had the flu and my husband had to work, and I let Emmy watch *Pinocchio* six times in a row."

Aleesha laughed and then stopped abruptly. "That's your little girl who died, isn't it?"

I nodded and looked away to a wall with a line of crayon pictures taped to it. "Did Isabel do these? Wow! She's really talented!"

"She loves to draw. This one's of a trip to the park." We followed the trail of Isabel's drawings down a long hallway to the kitchen. Aleesha put on a kettle for tea while I sat by a radiator on which a pair of tiny pink mittens lay drying. The kitchen was freshly painted a bright, cheerful yellow. Yellow checked curtains hung at the window, which had a view of the Blackwell factory and the river. A large calendar with

Izzy's and Mommy's chores written out on it hung on the refrigerator along with magnets that spelled out *cat, hello*, and *Isabelly*. The room smelled like coffee and pancake syrup and I felt safer than I had in any place I'd been in years.

"Am I keeping you from picking up Isabel?" I asked.

"Nope. My sister's taking her and her cousins to the movies. I was just getting off my shift at Dunkin' Donuts when I saw you. At first I thought you must be looking for me—then I saw you watching Scully."

"You know Scully?"

"That scumbag? Yeah. He hangs out at the college trying to blend in with the kids even though he's ten years older and hasn't taken a class in years. Then he hangs out in the neighborhood acting like he's a black dude."

"And rides the Loop bus between the two," I added. "He's dealing drugs, isn't he?"

"Uh-huh." Aleesha put two mugs of steaming tea on the table and sat down across from me. "But he prefers to use a go-between —a college kid to make the deals—calls it his 'work-study' program. He asked me to move some product since 'I was making the trip anyway.'" She snorted and blew on her tea. "Like he was asking me to pick up a loaf of bread while I was at the Kwik-E-Mart. 'Easy money,' he said, 'selling to white kids with their daddy's money burning a hole in their pockets.' As if he wasn't white himself. Wasn't like I didn't need the money but what if I got caught? What would happen to Izzy then? I told him no."

"These college kids he used—was one of them Troy?"

Aleesha took a sip of her tea and tilted her head at me. "Why do you think that?"

"Because I saw Troy in the woods with him and because Leia and he fought the night she died. He was seen in the woods with her later that same night. The police think he had something to do with her death."

She put down her cup and leaned toward me, fixing me with her large amber-colored eyes. "Do you think he did?"

I looked away, out the window at the falling snow coming down as heavily as it had that night. "I think Leia knew something that Troy didn't want anyone to know. If she knew he was dealing drugs to Acheron students and threatened to tell . . ." I thought of the deserted factory that Scully had just disappeared into. Blackwell Machine. I'd heard about it in that urban planning lecture I'd gone to. It was an old iron forge that specialized in dumbwaiters and elevators. The company had started failing after the Blackwells' daughter died. Now the factory sat abandoned on the edge of the river, a haven for drug users, as if the Blackwell family tragedy was still spreading out, catching innocent victims in its web. I had read something about the factory recently—

"Didn't the paper say that the police thought Shawna died at an abandoned factory down by the river? Did Troy sell to Shawna? Did he get her hooked again?"

Aleesha bit her lip and looked down into her mug. "No. That was Scully's doing. Scully's the one who got Shawna hooked in the first place."

"But I thought in your story— Oh." Now I undersood. "Scully was Shawna's boyfriend."

"Uh-huh. They got together when Scully was still taking classes at the college. She thought she'd really stepped up in the world going out with a college boy, but he brought her nothing but trouble. I thought she'd gotten clear of him, thought that was the one good thing to come outta her being in jail. But he was waiting for her when she got out. He told me if I dealt for him he'd leave her alone—" Her voice cracked. "If I'd've done it maybe she'd still be alive."

I scooched my chair closer and put my arm around her. "You don't know that. How could you trust a creep like that? Once he got you dealing for him what would keep him from going after Shawna?"

"I guess . . ." She blew her nose.

"And you couldn't have taken that risk with Isabel."

"Yes, but . . . I can't get rid of the feeling I could've done more. Maybe if I hadn't been so uptight with Shawna—but when she started bringing friends here, like it was a stop on the Magical Mystery Tour, showing off to Troy and Leia—"

"Troy and Leia? Shawna was hanging out with them?"

Aleesha nodded and took a sip of tea. "She dragged me out one night to Noah's while Izzy was with my sister. Said I deserved a night out. Truth be told, I needed one, but I wished I'd never gone with her. We ran into Leia and Troy there. Troy was showing Leia the 'hood as he called it." Aleesha rolled her eyes and I recalled what she had thought of white kids affecting black street language.

"Was that after we workshopped Troy's story in class?"

"Uh-huh. Leia was all jazzed up to see some 'real life,' like what she'd been doing before was all pretend . . ." Aleesha paused, looking around her kitchen, at the pretty curtains, the crayon drawings, the paper Christmas garlands. "I never could get my head around that. A white girl like Leia from a nice family, not rich maybe, but I saw her parents at the vigil and they looked like good people, steady like. I'd kill to be able to give that kind of life to Izzy. That's *real*. I understand why Troy was down here—he was showing off to Leia—but I don't understand why Leia would want to hang out with scum like Scully."

"They were hanging out with Scully?"

"Yep. He came into the bar that first night and invited them all back to his place—'for a taste,' I heard him say."

"You mean Scully was offering them heroin?" I felt like a sixty-year-old schoolmarm, but I couldn't hide the shock in my voice. "Do you think Leia did it?"

"Definitely. I could see it in her after that. That smug look Shawna and my uncle Teddy always got. Like they'd found the key to the VIP lounge in heaven."

I tried to picture Leia in class. There were times that she had a secret smile on her face—a Mona Lisa smile. I'd always thought she was thinking about the story we'd just read. How could I have been so blind?

Because you were spending your nights drinking.

"Do you think she was hooked?" I asked.

Aleesha shrugged. "I don't know. I think she thought she wasn't. I think she thought she could play at smack the way she played at everything else. Maybe she thought only weak-willed people like Shawna got hooked. Maybe she thought she had it under control because she still showed up for class, got As, and had all her shit together— Sorry," she added, seeing the look on my face, "for my language."

I shook my head. It hadn't been Aleesha's language that had shocked me, it was how much Leia sounded like me. The way I thought I didn't have a drinking problem because I showed up for class with a lesson prepared and papers graded—*all my shit together.* "I think you put it exactly right."

Aleesha smiled wryly. "Yeah, well, I wouldn't have cared what Leia did with herself but she drew Shawna back in—and now they're both dead."

The smile twisted into a sob. I squeezed her shoulder and looked away, not sure what to say. It had all happened in my class, under my eyes. I'd told them that Margaret Atwood quote about making the risky trip to the Underworld to bring someone back from the dead but I hadn't meant to give them a ticket for the boat trip to hell. Shawna had died because of my students and now Leia was dead—

"Aleesha, did Leia know that Shawna OD'd?"

Aleesha wrinkled her brow, thinking, then shook her head. "She couldn't have. Shawna was found after Leia died. The only way she could have known—"

"Was if she was with Shawna when she died."

CHAPTER TWENTY

Aleesha said I was welcome to spend the night rather than drive back in the snow. It was coming down pretty hard but I also saw that I would be crowding the small space once her daughter got home.

"Thank you, but I should get home. The plows will be out on Route Nine and it's a straight shot back to my place."

"Are you sure you're not too upset to drive? I know I'm shook. If Leia and Troy were with Shawna when she died—well, I sure as hell would like to have a word with Troy about that."

"Me too," I said. "I promise I'll let you know whatever I find out."

Aleesha walked out on the street to point out the way back to Route 9. "Keep your doors locked and your windows up," she told me. "This is not a safe neighborhood."

I told her I would. I looked over my shoulder when I pulled out and saw her standing on the porch, her hands tucked into her coat sleeves, snow melting from her thick black curls. She looked like a snow angel, the opposite of the ice hag.

The route she'd given me took me back past Blackwell Machine. I kept an eye out for Scully but the site was deserted; the brick tower whipped by the snow could have been the abandoned watchtower of a vanquished people, the bright graffiti their ancient lost language.

Route 9 had been plowed and sanded but it was snowing so hard the road was still slick. I crawled along at twenty miles an hour, hands clenched on the wheel, leaning forward trying to make out the road through the swirling snow and trying just as hard to make out Leia's true face through all the whirling, contradictory pictures of her that had emerged since her death. The perfect daughter, student, promising writer morphed into seductress, shape-shifting trickster, heroin user. Saint Leia, Troy had sneeringly called her, because of the pedestal everyone put her on, but I had truly made of her a graven image—the girl my Emmy might have grown up to be. Had she come to my office that day to tell me about Shawna? She'd left me the story she'd written about working in the prison. Did she want me to understand how she felt about Shawna before admitting that it was because of her that Shawna had started using again? That she'd been with her when she died? Had she come to me to ask my advice on whether she should go to the police?

But I'd turned her away that day, so she went to Ross and then I'd even interrupted *that*. She must have felt that fate was conspiring to keep her from confessing her sins. What was left for her to do?

The next time I saw her she was with Troy. *Laughing*. How could she be laughing if she was thinking about Shawna—

Unless she was playing another part. That's what Troy said she did. So what part had she been playing with him that night? Why feign indifference over Shawna's death? What did she want from Troy?

I was so immersed in speculation that I didn't notice the light changing at the intersection with 9G until it was almost too late to stop. I slammed on the brakes and skidded to a stop, the brakes of the car behind me squealing in protest. I looked in the rearview mirror and saw a hulking tanklike vehicle inches from my bumper. I couldn't make out the driver's face through the snow but I was pretty sure he was scowling at me. I could feel his angry glare on the back of my neck while I waited for the light. When the light changed I inched into the right lane, hoping the tank would pass me, but he tailed me instead, brights glaring in my rearview mirror. Only when I turned onto Orchard did he move on without me, gunning his engine and disappearing around the curve in a spray of snow and blue engine fumes.

I was so busy watching him in my rearview mirror that I missed the turn into my driveway. I yanked the wheel sharply and the car spun 180 degrees and began sliding toward the stone wall on the opposite side of the road. I watched the wall coming, the wheel useless under my hands. *Useless like me*, I thought, *as powerless as I'd been to stop what happened to Leia. Steer into the skid*, they always said. Hadn't that been what I'd been doing this whole time, moving straight toward disaster? Fuck that.

I wrenched the wheel at the last moment. I missed the wall by inches and landed in a ditch, right wheel lower than the left, a gruesome reminder of how I'd landed the night Leia died. For a second I had the feeling that I'd gone back in time, given a chance to stop what happened. I turned off the engine and sat listening to the snow filling up the woods.

The place I'd come to rest was the turnaround that the farm trucks used to use, protected by a canopy of pine trees, the favorite make-out spot for local high school kids and where college kids parked their cars to hike into the woods—

To go to the boathouse. You couldn't drive to the boathouse. You could hike to it from the college along the railroad track but that was a long way. The shorter way was to park in the turnaround on Orchard Drive and hike in. If Leia wanted Troy to take her to the boathouse they could have taken Ross's car and parked here.

But why? Why did she want to go to the boathouse? What was there?

Their stash, of course—that's what Troy and Scully had been looking for the day I saw them walking into the woods. But it wasn't there. Why not? And why had Leia wanted it? As proof that Troy had been dealing to Shawna?

Come back! I heard the anger in that voice now—and something else. Desperation. The desperation of someone who has lost everything, who already knows it's too late.

My boots sank into half a foot of snow. I stared into the woods. I could see the wall where Leia's shrine was from here but all the offerings were covered with snow. Hannah had denied leaving the bottle there. Could it have been Troy who left it? But why? To incriminate Hannah? I pictured Troy following Leia back from the boathouse—only, Leia hadn't gone to where they left the car. *Come back!* Troy had yelled. Angry that she was leaving him, angry at something she had done. He gave up following her and went for the car. Leia would continue walking south on River Road, toward her apartment in town. If he drove fast down Orchard he could head her off—

I heard the screech of brakes, a scream—Troy might have just been trying to stop her from going to the police, he might not have meant to hit her—but once he did he'd seen my car in the ditch, one wheel hovering in the air like an unanswered question. It wouldn't have taken much to drag Leia under my car, leaving me to run over her when I pulled out.

I rubbed at my face, wet from falling snow and tears. Had he known it was my car? The slim hope that he hadn't was extinguished by the memory of him working on my car last spring and of him once saying he had total automobile recall. He never forgot a car. Stupidly, that's what hurt the most. That he'd deliberately tried to frame me for Leia's death. *And* left the bottle of Four Roses on the shrine to incriminate Hannah and killed Oolong.

I crossed the road and walked up my driveway, slipping in the soft, deep snow. I'd need to get the drive plowed again—but I sure as hell wouldn't be asking Troy's father.

When I got inside I kicked snow off my boots and peeled off wet clothes, leaving them in soggy heaps on the floor. I pulled on the sweatpants and sweatshirt I'd left on top of the dryer. I thought about the Glenlivet but instead turned on the electric kettle. Or tried to turn it on. The switch light didn't go on. I checked that it was plugged in, shivering in the cold and dark. *Too cold. Too dark.* I checked the thermostat and saw that it had dropped below fifty. I turned the dial, waiting for the reassuring roar of the furnace but heard only the dry rasp of the snow. Then I tried switching on a lamp. Nothing. The power was out. It had happened half a dozen times the first year we were here. Evan had said we should get a generator but we hadn't been able to afford it and I hadn't bothered since. The power usually came on before too long.

I started a fire in the woodstove and then took out my cell phone to call Joe.

It was dead.

I couldn't remember the last time I'd thought to charge it. There was a charger in the car but the car was down the driveway and across the road in the turnaround. I pulled the curtain back to look outside. It was nearly dark, the world outside a grainy blur of shadows and spinning flakes. There was no guarantee I'd ever find my way back from the car. I could barely see the barn—

A flicker of light flashed through a gap in the boards and then was extinguished in a gust of snow. It was so brief I might have imagined it. I watched for it again, staring so hard into the snow that I began to see shapes moving in it—sea witches breasting surging waves, ice hags screaming in openmouthed horror. My head ached. The flash of light might have been a migraine symptom. What else could it be?

The ghost of Charlotte Blackwell, the snow whispered, *come to take you at last to join Emmy.*

Emmy. In my dream she had led me to the boathouse with her flashing sneakers. If her ghost came for me now I'd gladly go. I felt tired of pretending that it was enough for me just to care about my students, that I didn't need anything more in my life. Look what had come of that. My two favorite students had gone on a heroin spree and then one had killed the other and tried to frame me for her death.

I saw the flash of light again. A red flash like the lights on Emmy's sneakers. A beacon calling me through the storm. Or to my death. Why should I answer it? It could be Troy luring me to the barn just as he'd lured Ross out to his barn to kill him. I should lock the doors and stay huddled by the

woodstove with the bottle of Glenlivet until the morning—which is exactly what I'd do alone in this cold house. I'd drink the whole bottle. Even
after I'd promised myself that I wouldn't. And that would mean that all of
them—Anat, Cressida, my mother, Joe McAffrey—had been right; I was
a washed-up drunk like Hannah Mulder. Or I could go out and face whatever was out there. Right now it seemed like the less frightening choice.

I pulled on coat and boots. As I stepped outside I thought of early
settlers leaving their snowbound cabins drawn by solitude-induced
phantoms and losing their way between house and barn. As soon as I
stepped off the porch I was swept into a blind current like being pulled
out to sea by a riptide. Too late I thought of tying a rope to the porch as
a guideline. But then part of me didn't think I was coming back anyway.

I walked as straight as I could, buffeted by gusts of wind, toward the
only slightly darker and more solid shape in the gray, which was the
barn. As I got closer I saw the light again—an orange glow through a
chink in the old wood. Only when I rested my hands on the door did I
think to be afraid, but then it was too late. I was more afraid to turn my
back on whatever was inside.

I pushed open the door, the metal tracks screeching in protest, giving whatever was inside ample warning.

She was waiting for me, her long cloak trailing on the ground, her face
beneath her deep hood a void waiting to swallow me like a black hole.

Then she pushed back her hood and the ice hag was gone. Troy Van
Donk stared defiantly out at me instead. He clutched Evan's old baseball bat in his hand, braced to swing. Only the tremor in his hands gave
away how scared he was.

"Put that thing down," I said in my firmest teacher's voice, "and
come back to the house before we both freeze to death."

I sat Troy down by the fire and went out onto the porch to get more
wood. And to give myself a moment to think. If Troy had killed Leia and

dragged her under my car to frame me, he was dangerous. He might have been waiting out in my barn to kill me, wait out the storm in my house, then steal my money and car to escape. Everything I had learned in the last twenty-four hours had taught me to doubt my own judgment, but still, when I looked at Troy I saw a scared kid, not a hardened criminal. As I went back inside I realized that a scared kid might be just as dangerous.

He was waiting at the door for me when I came in. He took the wood from me and dumped it in the bin by the stove. When he grabbed the iron fire poker I held my breath, but he only used it to stir up the fire. I looked at my phone lying on the table and noticed that it had been moved.

"It's dead," he said, keeping his eye on the fire, "so I'm guessing you didn't get a chance to call your cop boyfriend."

"He's not my boyfriend," I said, sounding all of twelve.

"Then why were you with him at my dad's garage?"

"He was bringing me back from the hospital. I nearly got asphyxiated dragging Ross Ballantine out of his garage."

I watched Troy's face, lit up by the glow of the fire, for any reaction, but he only sneered. "Don't tell me the asshole tried to off himself."

"Someone tried to kill him." This time he did flinch.

"Really? A jealous husband?"

"I imagine it was Leia's killer, afraid that Ross saw him take his car that night."

Troy turned to look at me. He was still holding the poker. "And you think that was me. Why would I kill Leia?"

It might have been more prudent to pretend I thought he was innocent but I was tired of being careful. "Because she knew you gave Shawna the heroin that killed her and she was going to turn you in."

A muscle on the side of his mouth twitched. "How do you know about the heroin?" I noticed he hadn't denied anything.

"I talked to Aleesha. She told me about your Poughkeepsie odyssey."

"That was all Leia's idea. She wanted a taste of real life—and apparently that meant trying smack."

"So you obliged her."

He shrugged, his face a bronze mask of reflected firelight.

"Leia's—Leia *was* a pretty girl. Why wouldn't I want to spend some time with her? As for the heroin—I thought she'd sprinkle a little snow on her joint and then she'd be able to write about the experience. And for a while that was enough. She smoked some of the stuff a couple of times hanging out with Shawna behind Noah's and then down at the Blackwell factory. I didn't know she was getting hooked—or that Shawna would OD—" His voice broke on the last syllable and the mask slipped. Without it he looked young and afraid.

"Were you with Shawna when she OD'd?"

"We all were. Scully, Leia, me, and Shawna, down at the Blackwell. Leia said she wanted to shoot up and Shawna said she'd show her how to do it . . ." His mouth twisted. "I thought Leia would be squeamish but she made Shawna talk through each step so she could remember and write about it later. I think she would have taken notes if she wasn't afraid of Scully making fun of her. Finally, Shawna got impatient and says, 'Let me just show you.' So she takes the needle, ties off her arm, taps her vein"—Troy tapped the inside of his own elbow with two fingers—"and shoots up. I turned away. I don't care what anyone thinks, I can't watch that, but Leia watched the whole thing. Then I see Leia's face go all white. I thought she was faint from watching the needle but then she screams Shawna's name and grabs for her. Shawna's jittering all over the floor, foam coming out of her mouth, Leia's crying, Scully's cursing at her to get out of the way. Then he was doing CPR, pounding on Shawna's chest so hard I heard a rib break, and he kept saying, 'Shit, what they cut this shit with, what they cut this shit with?'"

"He thought it was something in the heroin?"

"Yeah, strychnine or quinine or some other shit. He was mad. Later I realized it wasn't about Shawna dying—he was mad he'd been sold bad product." Troy took a breath and then went on. "When Scully sat back and stopped Leia says, 'There's something they can give you if you OD—nalo-something.' She said she learned about it in some substance abuse workshop she'd taken. She said cops and EMTs carried it. She takes out her phone like she's going to call nine-one-one and Scully knocks it outta her hand. Calls her a stupid bitch and stomps on the phone, shouts: 'WE AIN'T CALLING NO POLICE.' "

Troy's rendition of Scully's voice sent chills down my spine. I realized, too, that Troy, despite how painful this scene was to him, had gotten into the telling. He was doing all the voices. " 'But they could save her,' Leia cries. I thought Scully was gonna slap her but he only shakes his head and says, 'She gone, baby, gone like the wind. Nalo don't cure no strychnine poisoning.' Leia's eyes got big then. I think that's when she realized it coulda been her. She got hysterical. 'We can't just leave her here,' she starts screaming. So Scully goes, 'We ain't gonna.' He picks Shawna up like she was a bag of mulch—he's a lot stronger than he looks—and carries her outside and dumps her in the river. Leia really freaked out then. Scully says to me, 'You make her shut up or I will.' I thought he was gonna kill us. I grabbed Leia and hustled her out of there, one hand over her mouth. Frog-marched her to the train station to catch the Loop. She cried all the way back to campus. Kept saying it shoulda been her and we had to do something. But what?" He looked at me, as if I had the answer. "What could we have done for Shawna? What good would it do her, at the bottom of the river, to get ourselves involved?"

I shook my head. "You can't live keeping something like that to yourself. It will eat you alive."

"Yeah, that's what Leia said. But then I reminded her about her fancy internship and her scholarship at Wash U. and she seemed to see sense. She said she only wanted to make sure nothing like that happened again—so she asked me if I had any more of the stuff Shawna had taken."

"And did you?"

"Yeah, a couple of bags, hid in the boathouse. She said we had to get rid of it, so no one else would die like Shawna had."

"And did you agree with her?"

"Of course. I didn't want to have anyone else's death on my con-science, only . . ."

"Only what?"

"I told her that Scully either wanted the stuff back or the money for it."

"Do you think Scully would have sold it even after what happened to Shawna?"

"I think a man like Scully doesn't like to see a profit loss. He told me he planned to cut the stuff again with baby powder—said it would be safe enough to give a baby." He saw the face I made and grimaced. "Yeah, I had the same reaction. But what was I going to do? That was ten grand worth of product. Where was I going to get that kind of money? I told Leia that and she said she'd get the money, that if I dumped the product she'd give me the money to give to Scully."

"Where would Leia get ten thousand dollars?"

He shook his head. "I asked her the same thing. She said she had someone who would give it to her. That must be some friend, I said, and she said, no, not exactly a friend but someone who would pay to keep her quiet."

"She was going to blackmail someone?"

"Yeah. I figured it was someone she was sleeping with. When I saw that stuff about Professor Ballantine on 'Overheard' I figured it was him. That Leia tried to blackmail him. But it must have gone wrong. Only she didn't tell me that. When she met me at the barn she said it had all gone fine. She was even laughing—"

"I saw that. But she'd been crying a minute ago in the kitchen."

"Like I told you, she played a part. She wanted me to think she had the money so I'd take her to the stash so we could get rid of it. I told her I had to have the money first and she said she'd give it to me when she saw the stash. She was acting all coy, like we were in *Pulp Fiction* or something. Like it was a game. She'd even lifted Ballantine's keys so we could 'ride in style.'"

"So you *did* take Ross's car."

"*Leia* took the keys and *Leia* drove. We left it in the turnaround on Orchard Drive and hiked to the boathouse. I'd hid the stuff under the floorboards. I showed it to her and asked to see the money, but she started chucking it in the river. I knew right away that she'd lied about the money. I tried to stop her but she was like a crazy woman. She pushed me away and I fell in the water. She threw the rest of the stuff into the river and then ran. I got out of the water and went after her. I'm not even sure why. The stash was gone, she didn't have the money—"

"You must have been furious with her."

"Yeah, but I was more pissed at myself for believing her." He smiled wryly. "I guess I had a thing for her. I—" He stopped and looked toward the door. "Did you hear something?"

I'd been so immersed in Troy's story that I hadn't heard anything but his voice. I listened now but all I heard was the whisper of the snow, like a chorus of Furies calling for the next chapter of Troy's sad tale— the part that would tell how he chased Leia down in the car and ran her over and left her for dead under my car wheels. He'd been angry with Leia, hurt and betrayed, he'd followed her back through the woods and chased her on the road. He hadn't meant to hit her—

A sharp crack broke the silence. It came from the front porch and sounded like someone stepping on the loose floorboard. Troy's eyes opened wide. "Someone's here," he hissed. "Are you expecting McAffrey?"

"No," I said, wishing I were. "But he might have come to see if I'm okay. I didn't hear a car, though—"

Another crack came from the porch. Troy put his hand to my mouth and pushed me down as the door exploded inward in a shower of sawdust and splinters and snow. I looked up and saw that where my door had been stood Scully holding a shotgun.

CHAPTER TWENTY-ONE

"Well, well, my man Troy!" Scully sang in a high-pitched voice. "I'm impressed. I figured Princess Leia was having it on with her professors but I didn't know you were too."

I started to deny it but Troy spoke first. "She's the police chief's girlfriend, Scull, so you'd better not hurt her."

"Screwing the police chief's bitch, well, well, that's even more impressive." He pointed the shotgun at me. "Is that true, bitch, are you the police chief's piece on the side?"

I didn't think it was a good moment to split hairs, either about McAffrey's rank or our relationship status. "Yes, and he's on his way over. You'd better leave now."

Instead of leaving Scully took a step into my living room and looked around. "Ain't this romantic, with a fireplace and candlelight and all. You think I'm an idiot? Why you snuggled up with your boy Troy if you're expecting Mr. Police Man?"

"I showed up unexpected, man," Troy said. "I've been hiding out from the police since yesterday, waiting for a chance to get out of here."

"Waiting for a chance to grab the stash and double-cross me, more like," Scully said, shoving the shotgun into Troy's face.

"I told you, man, Leia dumped it all," Troy said. "I showed you where I'd hid it in the boathouse."

"You showed me an empty hidey-hole." Scully spat on the floor. "Don't mean nothing. You coulda hid it anywhere. Why else you hanging around here? Why else was this bitch down visiting my girl Aleesha? The two of you were planning to take the rest of the stash."

Troy didn't say anything right away, then a slow grin spread across his face and he opened his hands wide. "Okay, man, you got me fair and square. The stash is still there. What, do you think I'd let a little bitch like Leia Dawson ruin my business? I knew she'd want to dump the stuff so I made up some little bags with baby powder and let her throw those in the river. The real stuff is still hidden."

I stared at Troy. His voice was barely recognizable, but then, he'd done voices for his story before. Was this an act? Or was the Troy I thought I knew the act?

"So you *were* still holding out on me." Scully jabbed the barrel of the shotgun into Troy's chest. Troy only shrugged.

"Hey, man, can't blame a guy for trying. I'll split it with you now. It's down in the boathouse. We can go there. I got some money there too. Leia gave it to me so I'd dump the stuff."

Was he making up a story to get Scully out of here? Or was this what really had happened? Had Troy taken money from Leia and tricked her into thinking she had gotten rid of the bad heroin? And then run her down? I didn't know what to believe or what to hope for. If the latter was true, Troy really was an irredeemable sociopath. If not, if it was an invented story to save both of us, then what would happen when Scully found out Troy was lying?

Scully seemed to be considering the options as well. He looked down at Troy's shoes—heavy Doc Martens—and then at his own thin-soled oxfords. "Okay—but first we're gonna trade shoes and then, if you're lying to me . . ." He jabbed the shotgun into Troy's chest.

"Yeah, man, I get it. You'll get your stuff." Then Troy glanced at me. "Better tie up the bitch and leave her here. She'll just slow us down."

Troy's face was still calm but I was close enough to see his leg jiggle—the way it had in workshop when he was nervous. Was he lying about the money and the stash? And why was he trying to get Scully to leave me behind?

"You'll never get there in the dark and the snow," I blurted out. "But if you wait here until dawn—the snow's supposed to stop—you can go then."

Scully looked at both of us and then a slow smile spread across his face. "Well, look at you two, all trying to protect each other. Ain't that sweet?" The smile suddenly slipped off his face, replaced by an expression that made my stomach turn. "Unh-uh. We go now." He took a flashlight out of his pocket and threw it at me. It only missed hitting me because I flung up my hand to catch it. The metal felt cold in my hand. "Come on, Prof, you gonna make like the Statue of Liberty and light the way."

Scully let me put on my down jacket after searching my pockets but he wouldn't let me give one to Troy.

"My boy will do fine the way he is, ain't that right, Troy?"

Troy nodded grimly. Scully smiled and clapped him on the back. "And this way he won't get no ideas about running away. He'd freeze to death on a night like this out in these woods."

I thought it likely we'd all freeze to death before we made it to the boathouse. The temperature must have been in the single digits. The snow was that dry, pellety kind that fell when it was really, really cold, and it drove against my face like needles as we crested the hill and started down toward the river. Scully made me go first, holding the flashlight, but all the beam showed was a narrow blade of swirling snow that was cut short by darkness. Like a light saber. I giggled.

"What the fuck, Professor," Troy, a step behind me, whispered. "Are you losing it?"

"I was thinking that if Leia is Princess Leia you must be Luke and then since I'm your teacher that makes me Obi-Wan Kenobi."

"Fuck no!" Scully roared. "I'm Obi One Kenobi. You're . . . you're maybe Yoda."

"Obi-Wan Kenobi would not be forcing us at gunpoint through a blizzard," I shouted back. "Let's face it, in this scenario you're Darth Vader—"

Troy stumbled into me with a pained cry and I went down to my knees, my face in the snow. The flashlight skittered out of my hands and landed upright in the snow, illuminating an enraged Scully looming over us. "I'm no fucking Darth Vader, bitch. I'm Obi One, got that?"

I nodded, afraid that if I opened my mouth, hysterical laughter would come bubbling out. I was out in the middle of a blizzard arguing with a murderous drug dealer/*Star Wars* fan. It just went to show that what I told my students was true: everyone's the hero of their own story, never the villain.

Scully jabbed the shotgun into my back and I grabbed the flashlight and struggled back to my feet. My pant legs were soaked through now and as we headed down the hill they froze in the sharp wind coming off the river. It felt as though the river had jumped its banks and was rushing over us in frozen waves. How would we even know that we had gotten to the river? The train tracks must be beneath two feet of snow by now. I hadn't heard a train whistle since we'd left the house. We could have passed over them without our knowing and already be on the frozen river. We would just keep going until we broke through the ice and were sucked down the river to the sea. Bon Boy-Osh, Scuffy.

"What's so funny, now?" Scully was at my side. Troy had fallen back, stumbling in the snow. I suspected that without a coat he was already suffering from hypothermia. If he stayed back maybe I could lead Scully onto the ice. We would both drown, but at least Scully wouldn't deal anyone else a lethal dose of heroin. It would be worth it, I thought. All these years since Emmy died, when I'd come close to killing myself I hadn't been able to go through with it because it felt as if I'd be betraying Emmy's memory. But if my death could do some good—if I could take an evil out of the world and save all the lives Scully would destroy—

"We're here." Scully grabbed my wrist and yanked my hand higher so that the flashlight caught the three-gabled outline of the boathouse. It seemed to be floating in the air, a castle in a fairy tale carved out of ice and magic. Or like the evil witch's cottage in the woods, built out of candy and malice.

"We have to be careful," I said. "There's water all around it. We could go into the river."

"That's why you're going first." He pushed me forward and I stumbled and landed in the snow, my knee hitting something hard and metal. The tracks. We were right on top of them. If only a train would come right now, I'd gladly drag Scully down with me. But Amtrak wasn't running in this blizzard, and Scully was already going on ahead toward the boathouse. I felt a hand on my arm helping me up.

Troy said something to me but a gust of icy river wind snatched the words right out of his mouth. I only caught "run for it." Had he been warning me against trying to run for it—or urging me to try it?

"What—"

But before I could finish my question Scully turned around and aimed the shotgun at both of us. "Come on now, you two lovebirds, don't you want to come inside where it's nice and warm?"

"Yeah, Prof," Troy said, his voice trembling, whether from cold or fear I couldn't tell. "Let's give the man what he wants so we can all go home."

Scully waited for us at the door of the boathouse and waved us inside with the butt of his shotgun. I shone the flashlight up into the dark depths of the storage loft—straight into a pair of glittering eyes.

"Shit!" Scully swore as the giant barred owl swooped down from the loft straight toward him. He raised the shotgun in one swift arc and fired it at the owl. The air filled with feathers and the smell of blood and gunpowder and the bird landed on the floor at my feet, its brilliant gold eyes already dimming. I felt a scream itching the back of my throat but I swallowed it down.

"Fucking boondocks!" Scully swore, spitting on the owl. "This is why I hate the country. Get me my product now so I can get the hell outta here." He swung the gun around at me and Troy.

Troy held up his hands. "Sure, man, it's right over there, under a floorboard."

"You tried that on before. You'd better have the right floorboard this time."

Troy attempted to shrug and keep his hands over his head at the same time. "I was just trying to keep it safe, man. And good thing I did. When Leia went on her rampage she only got the fake stuff. She didn't know where I'd hid the real stuff."

"Big man," Scully said, "foolin' a lil' girl. Why'd you go and kill her after, then?"

Troy's jaw tightened and his eyes flicked to me for a moment. We hadn't gotten to this part of the story yet, but I'd figured it out. "You felt betrayed by her, didn't you? She'd lied to you about the money—" I stopped, an awful thought rising in my head. Troy had thought Leia was blackmailing Ross for the money, but what if she'd come to me for the money, what if *that's* why she had wanted to talk to me? Of course I didn't have that kind of money but if she had told me I would have gotten help for her—gone to the police—only, Troy would have been angry about that. He would have lost his scholarship and without that he would have seen no future but ending up in his father's garage, turning into his father—

"You were afraid," I said, looking into Troy's eyes. "Leia threatened to tell the police. You followed her in the car. It was snowing. You could have skidded into her. It could have been an accident . . ."

Troy stared at me. In the glare of the flashlight his eyes glittered as if full of tears but that might have been a trick of the light.

"Sure, Prof," he said, his voice hard. "If that's what you think. I suppose you think it's an accident that Leia's body wound up under your car."

Scully whistled under his breath. "That's cold, man. Getting it on with your teacher and then framing her for murder. I guess you won't mind what we do with her after I get my stash?"

As cold as I was I felt ice water sluice through my bowels at Scully's words. He had no intention of letting me go after he got his drugs and money. He could do what he wanted to me and then dump me in the river. He'd already disposed of one body that way. I clutched the flashlight, wondering if I could use it to defend myself. But what good was it against a gun?

"Keep that light steady, bitch," Scully told me, all the laughter gone from his voice. "Help your boy here find that stuff or you'll both be in the river."

I shone the flashlight on Troy as he walked to the back wall, beneath the loft, and knelt down. As the beam followed him it caught Leia's painted eyes on the wall above him. Where I'd seen sadness in those eyes before now I saw reproach. *If only you'd listened to me*, they seemed to say, *you wouldn't be about to die.*

"Shine the light on Troy," Scully growled. "That painting is fucking creepy."

So I wasn't the only one reading reproach in those eyes.

I lowered the beam down to the floor where Troy was running his hands over the floorboards. "What's the matter?" Scully demanded. "Did you lose track of your hidey-hole?"

"Nah, it's just that the wood's swollen with the cold. I'm having trouble prying it up."

"Lame-ass college boy," Scully muttered, stepping toward Troy. "Lemme at—"

As soon as Scully was near, Troy rose, a length of wood studded with nails in his hands, and swung it at Scully's face. One of the nails went into his eye. A jet of blood gushed up like a geyser, rising with Scully's high, inhuman scream. Troy was yelling too.

"Run!"

For half a second I thought my feet had frozen to the floor, but then I turned and fled, out of the boathouse and into the storm, the shriek of the wind merging with the shouts and screams of the men I'd left behind. I still had the flashlight in my hand but all it showed me was a spinning galaxy of snow. I switched it off and stowed it in my pocket so it wouldn't give away my location and headed toward what I thought was the riverbank. If I could find the train tracks I could follow them back to campus but I couldn't see the tracks. I could just make out the tree line, though, so I ran for the trees, instinctively seeking their shelter.

I remembered the distance between boathouse and woods as short, but wading through thigh-high snow, battling gusts of snow-filled wind, it felt like a mile before I stumbled against a broad-trunked pine. I wrapped my arms around it and pressed my face against the rough bark, inhaling its resinous scent. I felt like I could stay here forever rather than brave the chaos of the storm, that it would be good to become a tree, like Daphne, who prayed to her father the river god to change her into a tree to evade her pursuer, Apollo.

Reminded of *my* pursuer, I inched my way around the back of the tree so I was concealed from anyone coming from the river. There was a depression in the snow here because the wind was blowing off the river. I crouched in it, looked toward the boathouse, and listened. The screams that I'd heard as I ran were gone now. Did that mean Troy had overpowered Scully? He'd had the advantage of surprise—a wave of nausea overtook me recalling the sound of the nail-studded board whacking into Scully's flesh and the sight of his blood gushing into the air—but Troy had said that Scully was stronger than he looked, and he was angry. Even with one eye he might have killed Troy. And then he'd be looking for me. I had to stay hidden.

The snow was mounting on either side of me, blown by the wind around the tree. It made a natural hiding place. I even felt warmer here, the snow acting as insulation. Maybe I could stay here until morning, gone to ground like a small animal in its burrow.

Then again, I might freeze to death by morning.

I had to keep moving. I could follow the line of trees that flanked the tracks, keeping behind them as much as possible so Scully wouldn't see me.

Or Troy. He'd helped me escape but did I really know he meant to let me go? He'd as good as confessed to killing Leia. He had to know I'd tell Joe what I'd heard—if I survived.

I looked again toward the boathouse. It crouched like a large black toad on the edge of the water. No sound or light came from it. Maybe Scully and Troy had killed each other. I felt a twinge of guilt at the relief the thought brought me. No matter what Troy had done he was still a young man I had cared about. I just couldn't trust him anymore. And I couldn't just stay here waiting for one of them to come get me or to freeze to death.

I crept out of the shelter of my tree and flung myself toward the shelter of the next one. I stayed low to the ground, in the lee of the high drifts mounding up at the tree line. I felt like a small animal tunneling through the snow, fleeing the hunting owl, scuttling away from its deadly talons—

The fingers that suddenly closed around my neck felt like talons. They plucked me out of the snow as if I weighed no more than a mouse and shook me. I was staring up into the bloodied pit where Scully's right eye had been.

"Bitch!" Flecks of spit hit my face. "You're gonna join your boy in the river."

He wrapped his hand around my hair and dragged me to the river's edge. He flung me onto the ice like I was a piece of trash. I heard a crack as the ice broke beneath me. I dug my nails into the ice. If he left me here maybe I could cling on to this piece of ice and float away like a polar bear on an ice floe, like—

He kicked me in my side. I heard another crack and from the excruciating pain in my side I was pretty sure it was one of my ribs. The ice was cracking too. If only I could hold on—

Scully's boot came down on my hand, breaking my hold and at least two of my fingers. I screamed and tried to scuttle away from the next kick—into ice water. My ice floe was tilting down into the water. I could drown or face another blow—a real Scylla and Charybdis choice, I thought inanely.

But maybe there was another choice.

When the boot came down again I grabbed it with both hands—the hand with the broken fingers lighting up with pain—and yanked. Unbalanced on the slippery ice, Scully crashed down to one knee. When he tried to get up his other leg went through the ice. He screamed at the shock of the ice water. I crawled across my ice floe, toward another one that had broken loose and was floating on the current. Before I could get to it something yanked me back by my foot. I reached into my pocket and closed my hand around the flashlight. I thumbed on the light as I drew it from my pocket and aimed it in his eyes. I almost wished I hadn't. The view of one-eyed Scully holding a jagged shard of ice over his head and about to bring it down on my skull was not my choice for the last thing I'd ever see. Emmy's face is what I'd have chosen. But then another face reared over Scully's shoulder, one almost as welcome as Emmy's.

"Put it down, asshole, and we might all get out of here alive. Move one inch and I'll put a bullet in your thick skull."

If I couldn't see his face I wouldn't have recognized Joe's voice. Scully heard the same deadly intent in it. He started to lower the ice shard but then he slammed it into Joe's face and lunged to the left into the river. Joe grabbed for him, then Scully vanished under the ice, sucked into a whirlpool as deadly as any Charybdis.

CHAPTER TWENTY-TWO

I almost followed him. Without Scully's counterweight my ice floe tipped. I began to slide into the water. Joe grabbed me around the waist and pulled me out. We fell to the riverbank, both soaked in icy river water.

"Troy," I said when I had breath. "Scully said Troy went in the river. We have to find him."

"We can't help him now and if we don't get someplace warm we'll both freeze to death—damn—" He was patting his clothes, as if trying to pound feeling into his flesh. "I had my radio clipped to my belt but it's gone. Come on, we've got to get moving. Up the hill . . . your house . . . my car . . ." His teeth were chattering so much I could barely understand him. When I tried to stand I couldn't feel my legs.

"Don't think I can," I said. "Go on . . . go get help."

He shook his head and pushed me ahead of him, into the woods. "Use the trees." He grasped a branch and pulled himself forward, pushing me ahead of him. When I tried to grab a branch with my broken fingers the pain nearly made me pass out. Joe caught me and kept his arm around me the rest of the way. I could feel his breath on the back of my neck and smell the sharp tang of his sweat despite the frigid air. All I wanted to do was lie down in the soft, pillowy snow.

"Not far now," he rasped, his breath warming my frozen ear. "Just a little farther."

He was lying, of course. The hill had grown twice as steep and twice as long since the last time I'd climbed it. We had both died and been sentenced to the infernal punishment of eternally climbing this frozen hill. When we read Dante's *Inferno* in the Great Books class, I taught my students that Dante gave his sinners a *contrapasso* punishment that fit their sin so that we could see their suffering as the fulfillment of their destiny. I knew what I was being punished for—my indifference to Leia that day that had led not just to her death but now to Troy's—but what had Joe ever done to deserve an eternity of climbing up a frozen wasteland? Maybe Joe was here to make me feel worse for inflicting this punishment on him. I must have been a selfish sinner, then, because I was still glad to have him by my side. When we finally reached my house, after what seemed like an hour, I would have gladly welcomed the fires of hell with his company.

He sat me down by the woodstove and coaxed a fire from the embers. He disappeared for a few minutes, long enough for me to wonder if he wasn't a mirage I'd summoned to keep me going on the long trek up the hill. But then he was back with a pile of clothing. "You have to get out of these wet things," he said, tugging at my soaked shirt.

"I can do it," I said, his obvious embarrassment rousing me out of my dreamy state.

"Good. Keep yourself dry and warm. I'll be back in just a few minutes."

"Where are you going?" I asked, alarmed.

"Down to my car to radio the station. I have to let them know about Scully and Troy."

"You said there was nothing we could do," I said, hating the whine in my voice. A minute ago I'd thought he was a mirage; now I couldn't bear the thought of him going.

"For Scully, probably not, but we don't know for a fact that Troy went into the river; we only have Scully's word for that. If he didn't he could be out in the storm, freezing or . . ." He didn't finish the sentence.

"Or he could come back here to make sure I don't tell anyone what he did to Leia."

"Yes," he admitted. "I don't like leaving you alone but I have to radio the station. I'll be back in five minutes—ten minutes tops." He looked toward the door. The lock was broken off where Scully had forced his way in. He got up and pulled the couch in front of the door, then angled it so he could get out.

"Push this back when I go," he said, "and hold this." He gave me the iron fire poker. "If Troy does come, hold him off. I'll be back soon." He held me by the shoulders and looked into my eyes.

"How will I know it's you when you come back?"

"I'll knock three times." He smiled. "Try not to fall asleep. If you don't let me back in I may well freeze to death." He squeezed my shoulders and bolted out of the door as if he was afraid of what he might do if he didn't leave quickly enough. I stood at the door a moment watching him go, but he vanished so quickly into the snow I once again thought I'd imagined him. Like one of those pioneer ghost stories in which a dead loved one visits a snowbound cabin.

I shook the thought off, closed the door, and pushed the couch in front of it. I wished I had some heavier piece of furniture, but I could barely move the couch with the pain in my ribs and hand. I had started shivering so I went back to the fire, stripped off my wet clothes, and put on the clothes Joe had brought for me—a strange combination of old, worn-out jeans, a silk shirt, and a Christmas sweater Dottie had knitted for me three years ago—

Dottie. She would be devastated when she learned that Troy, whether he was dead or alive, had killed Leia.

I was too agitated by the thought to rest. I dug in the closet for an old gym bag that Evan had left behind. It had SUNY Acheron sweatpants and a sweatshirt he hadn't wanted to take with him. *As far as I'm concerned the whole place can fall in the river and wash out to sea.*

I draped them in front of the fire, along with a towel that had also been in the bag, so they'd be warm for Joe when he got back. I should have made him change before he left. He could be freezing to death out there.

I filled the kettle with water and put it on the woodstove so there'd be something hot to drink when he returned—which should be soon now. How long had it been? Surely more than ten minutes. I should have checked the time—

A thump at the door made me jump and drop the log I was adding to the fire. I waited for two more thumps, but none came. I picked up the poker and approached the door. The window beside the door was glazed with ice so I couldn't see out of it. I pictured not Troy but Scully, risen from the frozen river, ice dripping from his empty eye socket. An ice Cyclops. But then I pictured Joe McAffrey coming back to my door and finding Scully there ready to knock him over the head—

I pulled the couch back and, holding the poker up with one hand, flung open the door. For a second I thought I had opened my door to the ice Cyclops. A frozen body fell across my threshold. It was covered in snow and icicles hung from its hair. But it was Joe under there. I pulled him to the fire and helped him off with his sodden, frozen coat.

"What happened?" I asked.

His teeth were chattering too hard for him to answer me. I helped him off with his shirt and rubbed the warm towel over his chest and arms. His skin was so white I was afraid he was frozen all the way through. "Are you always this color?" I demanded.

He barked—a sound I realized was a laugh only by looking at his face.

"B-b-bog Irish," he chattered. "G-give me that." He snatched the sweatshirt and sweatpants out of my hands. "And g-give a f-fellow some privacy."

I ran upstairs, the heat in my face quickly evaporating as I moved away from the woodstove, to collect blankets and quilts from the bedroom. When I came downstairs Joe was crouched in front of the stove, Acheron sweatshirt stretched over his chest. He was broader than Evan, and taller. The sweatpants only came to the middle of his calves. I handed him a pair of heavy wool hiking socks and draped a blanket around his shoulders. I dumped the rest of the quilts in front of the stove and poured hot water and packets of hot cocoa into mugs. I held his mug for him to sip from until he was able to hold it himself. Then I sat down across from him, on top of the quilts, and watched him. The color was returning to his skin—a rosy pink in his cheeks and at the tips of his ears, a gold flush along his throat. The firelight made the fine hair on his arms glow red-gold and his hair, as it dried, revealed red sparks I hadn't noticed before. He looked away from the fire and caught me staring at him.

"I thought I told you not to open the door until you heard three knocks."

"Sorry," I said. "I heard a big thump and I thought one-eyed Scully had risen from the river and was waiting on the doorstep for you."

"So you opened the door?"

"I couldn't let you die on my doorstep—which is what it looked like you were fixing to do. What happened? You were gone so long."

"It took me a while to dig into my car. I was able to reach the station but they've got their hands full—the roads are completely impassable and the state has suspended plowing until the snow lets up. I told them we were fine where we were. Then I was barely able to get up here and then, when I got to your door, a sheet of snow slid off your roof and nearly buried me."

"That was the thump I heard? You could have died out there on my doorstep!"

"And you could have died if I had been Scully risen from the dead—or Troy, who might not be dead at all."

"I don't believe Troy would kill me. I've been thinking about the story he told me in the boathouse." I told Joe everything Troy had said.

"Did he actually *say* he'd run over Leia?"

"No, that's just it. That's what *I* said. Don't you call that *leading the witness*?"

"But he didn't deny it."

"No," I admitted. "But then he risked his own life to give me a chance to escape. Why would he do that if he'd killed Leia and then framed me for it? Why not just save himself and let Scully kill me?"

"Maybe his plan was to take out Scully and then come after you and blame your death on Scully. He could come up with a story then that Scully had killed Leia."

"Seems pretty elaborate, and I just find it hard to believe of Troy."

"Do you always think the best of people?" Joe asked, shrugging the blanket off his shoulders. It had gotten quite warm in the nest of blankets we'd built in front of the stove.

"No, not always. I spent six and a half years wishing Hannah Mulder dead. But when I saw her lying unconscious on the road it didn't give me any joy at all."

"No," he said, his smile slipping. "It rarely does—although I would have enjoyed seeing Scully put away for good."

"What about you?" I asked. "Does your line of work lead you to see the worst in people?"

He looked away from me, into the fire, and I was afraid I'd insulted him. Like asking a soldier if he'd killed anyone. "I'm sorry," I began, but he had started talking.

"I see some bad stuff. The worst was seeing your little girl on that road. Maybe because I was still new to the job." He turned to me. "Maybe because it didn't make any sense at all. But then I tracked down Hannah Mulder and arrested her and she went away to jail and I thought, 'I did that poor family some good.' But then I heard your husband had left—"

"You heard that?"

He shrugged, his shoulders tight in the too small sweatshirt. "It's a small town. Small enough that it wasn't hard to keep an eye on you. Sorry. I hope that doesn't sound like I was stalking you. Although I guess that's what I was doing. I had to know if you were okay, if catching Hannah Mulder had made any difference."

"And what did you decide?" I asked, not sure I wanted to hear the answer.

"At first I didn't think I'd done you any good. When I took your class—well, I could see you were only half there. But then, over the years, I'd hear about you from students at the college."

"Really?"

"Small town; even smaller college," he replied. "Okay, I may have helped things along sometimes by asking kids who their favorite teacher was. A lot of the time it was you. I started thinking that you must've made some peace with what happened—or at least turned your grief into something productive."

"You must have been pretty disappointed when you thought I'd run down Leia."

"I was," he admitted. "I looked around here"—he glanced around the living room, which looked marginally better than it had the morning after Leia died but still reeked of the solitary life I'd been leading— "and I thought this woman's life was broken by what happened to her daughter and nothing I did made any difference. That's what a crime like that does—it breaks people—it breaks places. Look at what Leia's death has done to everyone who knew her. The whole town turned on you—someone killed your cat, for God's sake—then Hannah gets run over, then Ballantine gets asphyxiated, and Troy ends up out there in the river—all these lives ruined as if Leia's death was a stone dropped in a pool, and the ripples from it spread out to drown us all."

"But that didn't happen the first time," I said, staring at the fire.

"What?"

"When Emmy died. You found who did it. No one was falsely accused. The ripples stopped. It was just me and Evan and Hannah who got caught up in it and we deserved to be—at least Hannah and I did. Poor Evan—"

"He left."

I pictured Evan standing in the kitchen, weeping over a Scuffy the Tugboat mug. I remembered I'd taken a step toward him—and then stopped, as if there were an invisible wall of ice between us.

"I didn't ask him to stay," I said, looking away from Joe. "I didn't *want* him to stay. I wanted to be alone with my misery. I wanted . . ." *I wanted to drive to the Kingston-Rhinecliff Bridge and throw myself into the Hudson.* And when I couldn't go through with that I wanted to drink by myself every night until I felt numb. I looked around the room as if I'd never seen it before. As if I'd been asleep for years and had just woken up. My skin was tingling from the warmth of the fire, thawing from my dip into the icy river. The two fingers Scully had stepped on were swollen and throbbing, my fingertips still ached from digging my nails into the ice. I had wanted to stay alive. "I built myself a tomb here. But I'm still alive. I'm not even sure why—"

He reached out and wiped a tear from my face. His skin felt hot, warm from the fire, or as if the blood was still surging to bring life back to his frozen skin. It hurt. When the blood rushed back into frozen fingers and toes, it stung. His touch stung now, but I was afraid that if he moved his hand away I wouldn't be able to stand the cold again.

He didn't move his hand away. Instead he cradled my face, his thumb drawing a line from my temple to my mouth. My lips parted and I felt him shiver as my breath touched his skin. The few inches between us suddenly vanished and his mouth moved toward mine. His lips brushed against mine so lightly I thought I must have imagined it. He pulled back and looked at me, his firelit eyes holding a question. I answered it by returning his light butterfly kiss with a swift's lunge. He met me midair, matching my sudden urgency. The heat of the kiss spread waves of warmth through my body and his as we circled our arms around each other. His hands were in my hair, under my shirt and sweater, touching skin that had been frozen an hour ago and now lit at his touch. It lit up the pain in my ribs and fingers too but I didn't care. I could feel my blood racing to meet his. We fell down into the tangle of blankets and quilts and added our tangled clothing to the pile. Outside the wind roared and threw snow against the walls and roof. Inside the firelight moved over our bodies like ripples in water, as if we were moving together on a current, the pull and tug between us the resistance between the lunar tide and the pull of the open ocean. Keeping us in motion. But when he entered me all the motion stopped for a moment and I felt like we'd both come to the still, quiet spot at the center of all the circles.

CHAPTER TWENTY-THREE

When I woke up in the morning I was alone in the nest of quilts in front of the woodstove. *He's left*, I told myself, the sting worse than the stab of pain from my broken rib when I sat up. *He's embarrassed that he gave in to the moment—the narrow escape from death, the excitement of the chase, the enforced closeness of a snowbound farmhouse....* The memory of how we'd come together in the firelight sent a current of desire through me even sharper than pain and sadness. It was the first time I'd felt alive since Emmy died. Would I go back to feeling dead if he was gone?

A sound from the kitchen drew my attention. Joe, in his own jeans and flannel shirt, came in carrying two mugs of coffee. He knelt down beside me and placed both mugs on the edge of the woodstove and looked at me. I'd thought last night that his eyes had that glow from the firelight but I saw it was something he carried around inside of him—now that I finally noticed it.

"Last night . . ." I began.

"Are you going to tell me that it was all a mistake because we were caught up in the moment? That you're grateful I saved your life and all but what's an educated college professor want with a hick policeman?"

"Wow, you're even more paranoid than I am if that's what you're thinking."

"And what were you thinking?"

"That you must regret getting into bed with a worn-out, older—"

"You're only two years older than me."

"—*older*, most likely out-of-a-job, drunk."

"Ouch! You *are* hard on yourself. We're gonna have to work on that." Then he kissed me, his unshaven cheek rough against my face, and all the desire from last night leapt up in my blood. We took our time, last night's urgency tempered by daylight and the aches in both our bodies. When we were finished the coffee was cool and the fire in the stove had burned down to embers. We lay side by side, his hands lingering on my bruised ribs and fingers, mine tracing the bruise from the ice block Scully had rammed into his face. We both looked like we'd been through the wars, but I suspected the wounds we carried inside were going to give us more trouble.

"I wish we could just stay here," I said. "Snowbound."

"You're afraid once we leave and deal with the outside world, this"— he touched my face and made me look at him—"will vanish. But this is real. Just as real as all those people out there. And I, for one, want to give it a chance."

"I do too," I said, meaning it.

"So let's promise not to start this with doubts. We'll have enough to deal with in the next few days. I'd like to have this to come back to. Deal?"

"Deal," I agreed, kissing the bruise on his cheekbone.

He brushed his hands one more time over the length of my body, as if memorizing its curves and valleys, and then turned to find his clothes in the tangle of quilts.

"I'll hike down to the road and flag down a plow, get them to clear Orchard Drive, and dig out my cruiser and your car."

"I'm in the turnaround," I said, extricating my jeans from under the couch. "I skidded into it last night."

"I know. I saw it last night and came up here to make sure you were okay. When I saw that your door had been forced open I knew something bad had happened. I thought it was Troy."

"You'll look for him, right?"

"I'll put out an APB. The snow's stopped." He was standing at my desk looking out the window. I came to stand next to him. He put his arm around my waist without turning around, as if he knew where I was without having to look. "But it looks like we got over three feet. It will be at least a day before the town's dug out. Hard to organize a search operation but we'll get snowmobiles out there to cover the woods and riverbank. Amtrak will have crews digging out the tracks. We'll coordinate with them." I could see the police officer in him coming to life, ticking off the business he had to attend to. "I'll alert the coast guard to watch out for bodies—but I'm afraid it may be until spring before we find Scully—" He turned to me, the businesslike look on his face softening. "And Troy. I know you don't want to think he's dead."

"I keep thinking about his father."

"I'll go talk to Van first thing I'm dug out—or rather, second thing. First thing is to get you to the hospital and get those ribs taped up and your fingers splinted. You'd better stay here while I go down to the road."

"No way. I didn't like waiting for you last night. I can help dig out."

I started moving away but he pressed me closer to him and kissed me. The look in his eyes was so heated I expected a romantic declaration. Instead he asked, "Do you have any Ace bandages?"

I laughed and went to find some. Evan used to keep a roll in the same gym bag I'd taken the sweats out of. Joe used it to splint my fingers and tape my ribs. It made me feel like a mummy, but it hurt less when I moved and I was able to put mittens on over my hands and follow him outside.

The sky was the brilliant cobalt blue you only see after a big snowstorm. Although it was cold—my porch thermometer read 19 degrees—the air was still and dry. The snow was powdery, easily moved aside by the shovels I'd luckily kept on my porch since last year's snows. Still it took us a good hour to shovel a path down to Orchard Drive, where Joe's police cruiser sat under a drift of snow. It was parked at a crazy angle that revealed how rushed he'd been to find me when he saw my car abandoned in the turnaround. It was lucky he had seen it. The turnaround wasn't visible from here at all.

"Hey, Joe," I called to him, "how did you see my car in the turnaround from here? It's completely blocked by the angle of the wall."

"I didn't." He was half in the car, reaching for the radio that squawked when he took it off its holder, so I thought I might have misheard him.

"But you said you saw my car."

"I did, but not from here. I was coming down from the top of Orchard— Hello? Dispatch? This is Sergeant McAffrey." Joe rattled off some numbers and codes as he slid into the car, giving a report of where he was and why. His face had taken on the rapt attentiveness of someone who's good at his job. I found that instead of feeling excluded I liked watching him, but then I thought I should give him some privacy. I walked up the road a bit, through knee-high snow, past where it curved. When I turned around and looked back I saw the back fender of my car sticking up out of the snow. Joe would have easily seen my car there last night before the storm buried it. Which had been lucky.

"Nan?"

I turned around and found Cressida standing behind me. She was on skis, wearing the sleek Nordic outfit she'd had on the other day and a patterned wool headband holding back her blond braids.

"Cressida, you're out early. Did you ski down from your house?"

"It was the only way to get out. I was coming to see that you were all right—and to say I was sorry about the things I said the other night."

I felt a surge of gratitude. Outfitted in her Nordic skiing outfit, Cressida looked like an avenging Valkyrie. "You don't have to apologize. You were right—I have been drinking too much. I'm going to cut back.

It was kind of you to come check on me, but I'm okay. Joe—Sergeant McAffrey—is here." I pointed down the road to where Joe sat in his cruiser, still talking on the radio.

"Did something happen?" Cressida asked. "Are you all right?"

The story came spilling out. Cressida listened without comment, her expression unreadable behind her dark sunglasses. Given the way Troy had yelled at her in her office a few days ago, I thought she would tell me that Troy had gotten what he deserved but she said instead, "That poor boy. No wonder he was acting out when he came to see me. The guilt must have been crippling—so much easier to blame me. You say that Scully person said he was in the river?"

"Yes, but he could have been lying. Joe's organizing a search party with snowmobiles."

Cressida wrinkled her nose. "So loud—and that will take time to organize. I'll go now on my skis. Do you want to go with me? Your skis are still at my house."

"I'd love to, only . . ." I was going to tell her I had a broken rib and broken fingers, but with the bandage Joe had put around my chest I felt fine and I couldn't feel my fingers at all. I looked down the hill and saw that Joe had been joined by a state trooper. "Hold on, let me just tell Joe what I'm doing."

I walked down to Joe's car and told him I was going back with Cressida to look for Troy. "She'll take me to the hospital later to get my rib looked after."

He looked like he wanted to argue, but the state trooper was waiting so he lowered his voice to an authoritative bass and told me, "You'd better make sure you take care of that rib." I could tell he was being mock-serious, but the trooper must have thought he was really scolding me.

"I'll do that, Officer," I said.

"I'll check with you later to make sure you did," he growled.

I turned around before the state trooper could see me burst out laughing. It was the first time Joe and I had navigated the outside world and I was reassured that we'd managed it all with a good sense of humor, even if holding in that laughter made my ribs ache by the time I got back to Cressida.

We skied down from Cressida's house, taking the slope as though we were on downhill skis instead of cross-country. Despite the gravity of the situation I felt a surge of excitement swooping down the slope in the bright morning air. Or maybe it was the memory of how Joe had looked at me that had my blood stirring.

The sight of the boathouse and the memory of what happened there last night sobered me.

"I've talked to Abigail Martin about having that place condemned and torn down," Cressida said as we approached it.

"That would be a shame," I said as I peered into the open doorway. It was the likeliest place that Troy would have come back to. Enough snow had drifted inside that I could ski across the length of the floor. "It's a historical landmark. It could be converted into a rowing club."

"Kids would still get high in it." Cressida had come to stand in front of Leia's self-portrait, staring at it with an unreadable expression. "Is that what this was all about—drugs?"

I began the story of Troy's Poughkeepsie odyssey as we left the boathouse and skied along the riverbank. Cressida was silent throughout and I kept my eyes on the woods and frozen river, looking for Troy. When I finished she still didn't say anything. I looked at her and was surprised to see that her face was wet with tears. It was the first time I'd ever seen her cry.

"Cressida, what is it?"

"Don't you see," she cried, "it's all my fault."

I stared at her. "How in the world is it *your* fault?"

"I recruited Leia for the prison initiative program. That's where she met Shawna—and that must be where she got the idea of trying heroin."

"I don't know," I said. "Leia was perfectly capable of coming up with her own ideas. And it was Troy's story that led her to that bar in Poughkeepsie where she ran into Shawna and Scully. So even if she hadn't been teaching at the prison, she would have ended up asking Troy to score for her. And if Shawna hadn't been there—"

"Leia would have gotten the bad heroin and died," Cressida finished for me.

"I suppose that's possible. And Troy would still have had Leia's death on his conscience."

"They're like one of those doomed couples from Greek tragedy," Cressida said, wiping her face. "No matter how they tried to evade their fate they were still destined to end up dead."

I wanted to argue—to say that we didn't know that Troy was dead—but it was getting harder to believe he had survived the night. We'd come to the edge of the campus without a sign of him or of his drowned body. Another search party was heading toward us from the Peace Garden— three women in long coats wrapped in copious layers of scarves and shawls—plodding across the snow in snowshoes. If we were in a Greek tragedy these would be the chorus of old village women who would keen and tear their hair out in grief for the victims. When they got closer I recognized Dottie, Abigail Martin, and Joan Denning.

"Nan, thank God you're all right!" Dottie cried when she recognized me. "Abbie heard from the police that you were almost killed last night by a drug dealer from Poughkeepsie and that Troy is still missing. We came out to look for him."

"That's good of you," I said, looking dubiously at their cumbersome snowshoes. It was hard to imagine them getting very far on them wrapped in their multiple layers.

"I'm not doing it out of the kindness of my heart," Joan said. "If that boy ran down Leia he needs to be caught. Drowning's too good for him."

"We don't know for sure that Troy killed Leia," Dottie said. I could tell from the edge in her voice and from Abigail Martin's pained expression that the two of them must have been having this argument since they began their trek across the snow. "Do we, Nan?" Dottie asked, turning to me.

I must have looked stricken at the question because Dottie's eyes filled with tears.

"See, Dottie, I told you," Joan said. "That boy's no good. He failed my comp class and was rude to me when I tried to explain what a comma splice is."

I wanted to tell Joan that poor grammar and rudeness did not make Troy a murderer, but I'd heard enough to have good reason to think that Troy had killed Leia. Instead I said, "Whatever Troy did, he doesn't deserve to freeze to death. Have the dorms been checked? He could have made it to campus and hidden in one of the empty buildings."

"I have security going through all the buildings," Abigail replied. "I'll leave it to a court to decide Troy Van Donk's guilt or innocence. I just want to make sure that he and the scum he brought up from Poughkeepsie are off my campus. Thank God it's intersession. Think if we had two criminals at large with a campus full of students! We could have an incident like Virginia Tech on our hands."

I wanted to point out that Scully was probably hanging around the campus long before he met Troy, but I felt Cressida fidgeting beside me, stamping her skis in the snow. "Let's keep looking," she suggested. "My muscles will cramp if I cool down."

"Yes," Joan said, adjusting a fringed scarf, "I'm not sure how long I can be out here in the cold."

"Bunch of vultures," Cressida remarked when we'd skied away.

"What, them? What do you mean?"

"Dottie's all right—and Abbie's only trying to hold on to her job after having her affair with Ross made public—but Joan, did you see how she was *enjoying* this? I've always thought she was jealous of her students."

"Jealous? Why?"

"Because they have a future, while people like Joan . . . look at her—over fifty, adjuncting at three different colleges. She should have buckled down years ago and either gotten a PhD or teacher's certification and taught high school."

"She's a good writer," I said, remembering that a few days ago I'd seen my own dim future in Joan.

"She's a second-rate poet and an even worse prose writer. Did you read the maudlin essay she wrote for the campus magazine? And she always talks about this book she's been working on for years but it's never done. She's a wannabe writer who clings to teaching college classes part-time because it makes her think she's better than a high school teacher, but she's jealous of her students who have more talent than her."

I winced at the description. She could have been talking about me. "I think we should turn around," I said. "Troy wouldn't have come this far and I'm getting tired. My ribs and fingers are beginning to ache." I began the long, laborious process of making a turn, my skis printing a wide fan in the snow. Then I fit my skis in my old tracks and started skiing back. The riverfront was crowded now with searchers: a half-dozen snowmobiles patrolled the woods, a police team led sniffer dogs along the riverbank, and volunteers had set up warming stations with gas stoves and thermoses of hot chocolate. Despite the gravity of the mission, the scene had a festive air. The whole community had come together to look for Troy. I recognized townspeople, faculty, college staff, and students who hadn't gone home for the holiday, many of whom greeted me by name. I was no longer the pariah. By now, a rumor had spread that Troy was responsible for Leia's death, not me. I should have felt glad to be welcomed back into the fold, but when I thought of Troy trapped dead under the ice I could feel no joy.

"You look like you're in pain," Cressida said when we came back to the boathouse.

"I can't help but feel that it's all my fault. That if I'd just paid attention to what was going on around me I could have prevented *all* of it—Shawna's overdose, Leia's death, Ross ending up possibly brain damaged, Troy becoming a hunted criminal—if only when Troy handed in that story I had called him aside."

"And what? Told him it was wrong to do drugs? Like that would have made him stop. You give yourself too much power. But that's not what I was talking about. You look like you're in physical pain. Your color isn't good. You're sweating and you're panting. I think I'd better take you to the ER to have those ribs and fingers looked at. Besides"—Cressida finished taking in the bleak, frozen riverside—"we're not doing any good here. Troy is either dead or long gone."

CHAPTER TWENTY-FOUR

Cressida took me to the ER, where a harried-looking intern retaped my ribs and fingers and gave me a prescription for Vicodin. Seeing what had come from opiates perhaps I should have been more wary of taking the painkiller, but I would have done anything to stop the throbbing in my torso and hand. I swallowed the Vicodin on the drive back from the hospital.

"Do you want to come stay at my house?" Cressida asked as we turned up Orchard Drive. "I would think you wouldn't want to be alone."

Knowing how much she valued her privacy I was grateful for the offer, but determined not to take it in case Joe came by. "Thank you," I said, "but I'll be okay."

"Well, if you need anything, call me. I'm just up the hill."

I thanked her again and gave her an awkward one-armed hug before getting out. To my surprise she leaned in and squeezed me so hard my ribs throbbed. The Vicodin had kicked in, though, spreading an agreeable fuzziness and sense of well-being. "Thank you, Cressida," I said, "you're a good friend."

She looked startled and I decided I'd better get out before I started bawling.

My drive and path had been shoveled and my car moved from the turnaround. When I got to the door I found that the lock had been repaired. *Joe*, I thought, the warmth spreading from my chest all the way out to my fingertips and toes. The elation seemed to spread into the house when I opened the door. The heat and electricity were on, courtesy, I suspected, from the hum I heard coming from the basement, of a new generator. The blankets had been folded next to the woodstove. There was a note on the kitchen counter.

I may have to stay at the station late overseeing the search operation. If you still want me to come over when I'm done leave a light on in the window.

All right, I thought, *I can do that.*

I got down on my hands and knees in front of the cabinet under the kitchen sink and reached past cleaning bottles and cobwebs to a box shoved all the way in the back. It jingled as I dragged it into the light, like bells. I lifted the box onto the counter, registering but barely feeling the twinge in my side as I did. *Vicodin.* No wonder people got hooked on this stuff. I thought foggily that taking Vicodin might not be the best way to quit drinking but I decided to worry about that later.

The first candle I took out was a tall blue glass column with a picture of St. Christopher on it. Protector of travelers and preventer of car accidents. Fitting. I placed it on the desk in front of the window and sat down at the chair with a matchbook in my hand. This is where I had been sitting the last day of Emmy's life. I'd just come in to jot down an idea before it flew away. The window was open and she was playing right outside. The door was open too, so I could run out if she needed me. I could hear her voice as she played in the little patch of dirt that Evan had decreed Emmy's Garden. She had been narrating a story in a singsong voice about a girl named Emmy and her voyage with the little tugboat Scuffy on the river down to the sea—it had given me an idea so I'd gone inside for just a minute to write it down in my notebook and then—

There'd been a moment of silence and I had thought, *I'll just get this down while she's quiet*. And then I'd looked up—it had just been a second, hadn't it?—and saw that it was quiet because Emmy wasn't there anymore.

I opened my eyes and the candle swam in front of them. I lit a match and, tilting the glass column, held it to the wick. It guttered for a moment, struggling to burn through years of dust, but I held it even as my fingers stung. *I'm sorry*, I said as it caught. Then I went back to the box and took out another candle, a Yahrzeit candle with a blue Jewish star on it, and a purple votive candle with a mandala. The people who had brought candles to Emmy's shrine had held a rainbow of beliefs, but I had plucked their candles off the stone wall, extinguished their flames, and carried them away in my pockets. Later I hid them in the box under the sink like a secret drinker hiding her empties. (When I started drinking I didn't bother to hide those.) I couldn't bear to look down the hill and see that shrine and be reminded of the moment of silence in which I could hear my own thoughts.

"I'm sorry," I said aloud, lighting the Yahrzeit candle. I said it as I lit each candle in the box and set it on the desk in front of the window. When there wasn't any more room on the desk I put the candles on the living room table and lined them along the mantel. I wasn't seeking forgiveness. There was no forgiveness. I would forever know that my momentary lapse had led to Emmy's death. That guilt was the flame at the center of my core. It would keep burning as long as I lived.

When Joe came in and saw the dozens of candles burning in the room he smiled. "I guess this means you want me to come over?"

"Yes," I told him, giving him his smile back. "That's exactly what it means."

With the heat on, we could have gone upstairs, but we made love again in front of the fireplace in the flickering light of all those candles. We went slower this time, because of the bandages around my ribs and his fatigue from a day of searching for a boy he suspected was dead, but also because we both wanted the other to know there was no rush. That what was happening between us was real and not just the result of being thrown together by the freakish life-and-death circumstances of last night.

I believed he meant that. And I think he believed I did too.

We made love until the morning, until the last of the candles guttered out and was replaced with the glow of dawn in the window. I fell asleep then, the afterimage of the candles still burning beneath my eyelids turning into the red flashes on Emmy's sneakers.

She was running away from me across the ice.

"Come back!" I screamed.

She stopped. Thank God, I'm on time—

But then a hand broke through the ice and grabbed her ankle to pull her down into the frozen water.

I startled awake to the smell of coffee and toast. Joe was already dressed. He brought me a cup of coffee with milk and a slice of the good sourdough from our local bakery.

"You went shopping," I accused. "When did you have time for that?"

"I didn't, someone left it at your door. I think people in town are feeling bad they gave you a hard time. Like a loaf of bread makes up for treating you like a pariah—"

"It's how I treated Hannah Mulder," I said. "I can understand how people felt."

When I looked up he was watching me. "You're a lot more forgiving of others than you are of yourself."

"You're a good detective," I said, pulling his face down to mine to kiss him.

When he straightened up his eyes had clouded. "Not good enough to find Troy," he said.

"Now who's hard on himself?"

He smiled. "We make quite a pair. Promise to rest today? There's no point going out looking for Troy. I'm afraid we'll find him when the ice on the river breaks up."

Emmy running across the ice. A hand breaking through to drag her down—

"I promise I'll stay away from the river today."

I kept my promise but I didn't stay holed away at home. I had things to do. First on my list was to visit Aleesha. She needed to know that Scully was dead. His death wouldn't bring back Shawna but at least she would know that he wouldn't hurt anyone else. I packed up a box before I went, straining my aching ribs in the process. I wanted very much to take another Vicodin but I couldn't take the risk of driving under the influence so I took two Extra Strength Tylenol instead. Besides, I'd been numbing myself with alcohol for years. It was time I let myself feel.

Aleesha was just getting off her night shift at Dunkin' Donuts when I pulled up in front of her house. She had a wax paper bag and a large thermos, which she handed me when she saw me struggling to remove a large box from my trunk.

"Lemme get that, Prof," she said. "You look like you got a pain. What happened to you?"

I started telling her the story as we carried box, bag, and thermos into her kitchen and I finished telling it at her kitchen table over sticky sweet doughnuts and hazelnut coffee.

"Scully must've followed you from here," she said. "I should've known he had eyes on my house. You say you saw a black-and-gold tank at the stoplight? That's his ride, all right. You could've gotten killed."

"I would have if Troy hadn't attacked him. He did it to save me—and probably died doing it."

She shook her head, her amber eyes shining in the clear yellow light of her spotless, cheery kitchen. "Maybe it was his way of evening things

out for what he did to Shawna and Leia. I can't forgive him for the part
he played in Shawna's death but I don't figure him for a cold-blooded
killer. If he did those things to Leia it was because he was scared and
desperate. He'd have felt sorry. Saving you might've been his way of
saving himself."

I nodded and took a sip of my lukewarm coffee, easing the tightness
in my throat. "I wish there'd been a way I could've saved him."

She reached across the shiny table and squeezed my hand. "Thank
you for coming and telling me about how Shawna died. It might sound
funny but I'm glad to know she wasn't alone with that bastard Scully
and that Leia cared enough about what happened to try and make
it right. And I'm glad Scully's dead." She took a deep breath, looked
around her kitchen, and spied my box on the floor. "So what else did
you bring me?"

"Just some things for Isabel—they're a little out of date. . . ."

Aleesha squealed when she opened the box as if she were the four-
year-old for whom the contents were intended. "Jasmine Barbie!
Isabel loves her—and Mulan, that's her favorite. And Cinderella and
Snow White. You've got all the Disney Princess dolls—and Disney
Princess bedding! Hey, I thought you were too feminist for this kind
of stuff."

I laughed. "Evan said the same thing when I bought it all for Emmy
but she begged for it and I have to admit that I love the stories. This was
her favorite collection of fairy tales." I held up the lavishly illustrated
book to show Aleesha and noticed that there were tears in her eyes.

"Are you sure you want to part with all this?" she asked. "Your little
girl's stuff?"

"Yes," I said, getting to my feet. "It will make me happy knowing
Isabel is enjoying it."

"She'll be over the moon," Aleesha said. She stood up from the box
and threw her arms around me. I hugged her back, gratefully inhaling
the warm scent of powdered sugar and hazelnut in her hair, and then I

got out of there quick, before she found the envelope at the bottom of the box.

I stopped by Vassar Brothers next to visit Ross. He was sitting up in bed, gold-rimmed half-moon glasses perched on his nose, reading the *New York Times*. To my surprise and relief he greeted me with a smile and a coherent sentence.

"Nan! My savior! I've been trying to call you since they took me off that blasted ventilator."

"You can talk," I said, sitting down in the chair by his bed. "And you're making sense."

He laughed. "The doctor says my aphasia was only temporary—although I *am* finding it hard to finish today's crossword, and it's only a Tuesday puzzle! I find it all fascinating. I'm thinking of writing something about it—a writer loses his words. It's actually made me feel . . . *inspired*."

"I'm glad nearly being asphyxiated has cured your writer's block," I said.

"Abbie says it was a wake-up call—quite literally—for both of us."

I tilted my head and raised an eyebrow. Ross blushed. "I know, I should apologize for the other night. I don't know what I was thinking—I thought that things were never going to work out with Abbie—but now she's leaving Dave and we're going to try making a go of it, gossip be damned. And if we lose our jobs . . ." He shrugged. "I've got money put aside. We'll move someplace warm and I'll write again. Abbie has a book idea she's been wanting to get to."

"Everyone's a writer," I said drily. I found I didn't mind the idea of him and Abbie together. They were more suited for each other than we'd ever been. "You sound . . . *happy*."

"Happy to be alive! And I have you to thank. If you hadn't dragged me out of that garage—"

"Do you remember how you got there?"

"No. I'm sure I wouldn't have done it myself. Yes, the rumors being spread about me were heinous, but I knew they weren't true. I *never* slept with Leia—and you know I wasn't driving the Peugeot when it hit her. . . . Dottie says the police think it was Troy."

"Yes, so it seems. . . . Are you sure you don't remember Troy leading you out to your garage?"

He screwed up his eyes in thought. Ross was a good storyteller. I was afraid that if he thought too hard he'd invent a story about Troy luring him out to the garage, but after a moment he shrugged his shoulders. "It's a total blank. It may be the first time I've forgotten something that happened to me. I feel like I'm in an Oliver Sacks essay!"

"The man who forgot his own story," I said, not sure if I was disappointed or not that he couldn't corroborate Troy's part in the garage incident. If Troy locked me in that garage why had he saved me from Scully? Would I ever know—or would that part of the story always remain a mystery?

On my way out I ran into Dottie. She was carrying Ross's briefcase and a bag of grapes. "Oh, good, Nan, I'm glad I ran into you. There's a memorial service being held in the chapel this afternoon. Nothing formal—Abbie says there will be a proper service when the students come back in January, but she wanted to gather a few of Leia's teachers and friends together to share memories of Leia and read something she wrote. Do you think you can come?"

"What time?" I asked.

"Four thirty. Abbie wants to do it at sunset."

"I can make it. I'll have to think about what I'll read."

"I'm going to read a poem Leia wrote for me that she said was inspired by my quilts," Dottie said.

"Oh, that reminds me of something Leia gave me about the quilting circle she led at the prison. I'll read that."

"Perfect," Dottie said. "She was such a lovely girl. I still can't believe Troy . . ." She shuddered and I wrapped my arms around her before the sob could overtake her.

"You're a good friend," I told Dottie. "I don't think I tell you that enough."

"You don't have to," Dottie said, hugging me back. "That's what makes a good friend—not having to be told."

I was exhausted on the ride back and my ribs had started to ache but I had one more stop to make. The Happy Acres Park was only haphazardly dug out from the storm, making it difficult to navigate the narrow, winding road to the last trailer. No path had been shoveled to Hannah's trailer, but there were deep footprints in the snow leading up to her door. I followed them, noting that my feet fit them perfectly. I left the box on her doorstep without knocking and retraced my steps to the car. I didn't think I could take another emotional scene. When I got in the car, though, I saw her open the door. She was wearing a pink sweatshirt with a cat printed on it. Her own cat was twining around her ankles, sniffing the box. Hannah bent down and looked in the box. Then she lifted the carton of Fancy Feast and looked up to see me. She stared at me and then nodded once, raising the carton as if raising a glass. I stretched my fingers up from the steering wheel—a truncated wave— and drove away. Toward home.

CHAPTER TWENTY-FIVE

The first thing I did when I got home was take a Vicodin standing at my kitchen sink, scooping water with my hand. Then I spilled the pills out in my other hand and counted them. Eight. The intern had prescribed ten, the same number that my endodontist had prescribed a few months ago when I had root canal. I'd only used two then; the bottle was still in the cupboard next to my vitamins and, I noticed, as I opened the cabinet door, the half-full bottle of Glenlivet. No wonder people got hooked on this stuff. If I wanted to I could keep taking the pills even after the pain went away. And if I told my doctor my ribs still hurt? Would he cut me off because he suspected I was getting hooked—or would he assume that a respectable college professor wouldn't become an addict? I realized it was why no one had guessed I was an alcoholic these last few years. No one suspected a college professor as long as she showed up for class and got her papers graded and grades turned it. I'd fooled even myself.

I slid the pills back in the bottle, resisting the urge to take another, and put it in the cabinet next to the old bottle and the bottle of Glenlivet. I stared at that tableau for a moment. I should just pour it down the drain, I told myself. If you're serious about quitting, why haven't you? But I didn't. I closed the cabinet door and went upstairs to Emmy's room. Without the Disney Princess comforter and sheets and the row of dolls on the shelves the room looked barer, but I found I didn't mind. The thought of Isabel playing with the dolls made me feel happy.

I went into my room and lay down on my bed. I reached for the mystery novel I'd abandoned halfway through the semester when work got the better of me, but then I noticed the bound galley of Cressida's new book. *I should really read that*, I thought. Cressida had been a good friend these last few days. She hadn't abandoned me when everyone thought I'd run over Leia, and she'd taken me in when I was half frozen. She'd told me the truth about my drinking even though she must have known I'd be angry. She'd come down to check on me after the storm. I'd always thought of her as a bit of a cold fish, but maybe I was the one who had been the cold fish. I'd taken her friendship for granted, just as I had Dottie's. The least I could do was read her book and tell her I liked it.

I turned it over and looked at the back cover. *A searing exploration of the world of women's prisons . . . the new* Orange Is the New Black . . . *luminescent prose . . .* She'd gotten some great blurbs. The marketing and promotional material also looked impressive. *Six-City Author Tour, National Review and Feature Attention, National Radio Campaign, Online Promotions, Online Reader's Guide.* This might really be a breakout book for Cressida. It certainly had cinched the tenure decision for her last year. I felt a sharp twinge in my side that might have been my ribs or the stab of jealousy every author is prone to. I put the bound galley back down on my night table. The Vicodin was making me sleepy. I'd read it later . . . I needed to be rested for the memorial. . . .

I slid into sleep and onto a sheet of ice. Cressida and I were skiing on the frozen river. "You see," she was telling me, "if you'd taught in the prison initiative like I asked you to, *you'd* be the one with the new book."

"I don't think it works like that," I said, trying to keep up. While Cressida was gliding along smoothly, I was slipping and sliding clumsily.

"That's *exactly* how it works. A really newsworthy back story gives you an excellent media platform. Look at how well it turned out for Piper Kerman! But it's not too late—you can still go to prison."

"You mean *teach* at prison?" I asked, stumbling.

"No, I don't, Nan. I don't think that will do it. But a four- to six-year incarceration . . . I can almost guarantee you a book deal. And it will be easy. All you have to do is tell everyone you got in Ross's car—it was right there waiting in the turnaround—and drove over Leia."

"But why would I do that?"

"Jealousy. Just like you're jealous of me." Cressida stopped to let me catch up with her. "But you'll never get anywhere dragging *that* with you." She pointed at my feet. I looked down at my skis and saw why I was so clumsy and slow. Tangled in my skis were black hair, blood, and torn flesh—the mangled remains of Leia Dawson.

I woke up screaming, fighting off the covers as if they were Leia's bloody limbs. The sweat covering my body felt sticky like blood. Even when I got up and ran cold water over my hands I couldn't get rid of the sensation that Leia's blood and hair and torn flesh clung to me.

It's the Vicodin, I told myself, staring at my reflection in the mirror. If that's the kind of dream it gave me I was staying away from it no matter how much pain I felt.

I wanted to shower but I didn't want to risk disturbing the bandages and causing more pain, so I took a sponge bath and dressed for the memorial, all the time reliving the awful dream. Of course it came from looking at Cressida's bound galley and feeling jealous of her success. And then the guilt of not listening to Leia—*that* was what I was dragging around with me. The rest of it—Cressida's suggestion that I could claim that I had driven the Peugeot—must come from looking at my own car in the turnaround yesterday.

I checked my phone and saw there was a voice mail from Joe and a text. They both said that he was following a lead in Poughkeepsie and couldn't come by until very late—did I still want him to come if it was after midnight?

I found an emoji of a candle and sent a dozen to Joe. Then I got Leia's "Pins" story from my desk. I brought Cressida's galley down with me and put it on the desk while I reread Leia's story. I read it from its first disarming line—"It's quiet in here but not quiet enough to hear a pin drop, which is too bad because if a pin does drop we all have to stay until it is found and accounted for."—through to its heartbreaking ending—"Some of the things they've done are bad, but here those bad things are only more torn patches stitched together to make something beautiful. When I look up from my sewing I don't see a criminal, an addict, a killer—I see myself. And I know that by forgiving them I have forgiven myself." Even though I knew that Leia had written this before Shawna's death I couldn't help but feel that she was asking for that forgiveness here.

Yes, I would read this. It captured so much of Leia's voice and it would go well with the quilting poem Dottie planned to read. I'd ask Abbie if I could read right after Dottie.

I folded the pages over and stuffed them in my bag, put on my coat and boots, and hurried out to my car. I was running late, but when I got to the end of my drive I turned right instead of left. I drove up to the turnaround, pulled into it, and got out. Looking down the hill I could only see the top of my roof, but when I looked up I could see Cressida's house perched on top of the hill, her wide glass windows reflecting back the last of the winter sunlight. I remembered noticing that her desk faced in the same direction as mine. I must have noticed, too, that she could look down and see the turnaround.

I got in the car and drove down to River Road, watching for patches of ice on the steep incline. It had been snowing hard the night Leia died. Troy could have skidded coming down Orchard Drive and slid out onto River Road where Leia was walking—

When he admitted to running over Leia he hadn't tried to say it was an accident, but then there hadn't been a lot of time and maybe he didn't want to look weak in front of Scully.

I made the turn and drove north on River Road, past Leia's shrine. Someone had carved niches in the snow to place the candles. They glowed like arctic crevasses in the fading light. I thought of the "of-

ferings" that Hannah had left—daffodils, a barrette—and was almost
sorry I'd taken them away. As for the Four Roses bottle . . . it might have
been Troy—or whoever killed Oolong—but I'd never know for sure
now. When I looked away the road seemed suddenly darker. I drove the
rest of the way at a crawl, searching the shadows at the edge of the road
for anything that might leap out.

By the time I got to the chapel the sun had dipped behind the
mountains across the river. The lingering gold glow spilled across the
frozen river and bathed the stone face of the chapel. I followed the path
of light through the chapel door. Sue Bennet, sitting next to Kelsey
Manning, turned and glared at me. Hadn't she gotten the memo that I
wasn't the one who ran over Leia? I walked past them and met the accusing glare of Troy Van Donk, Senior. Or maybe it was that his eyes
looked so much like Troy's that made me see accusation there. I looked
away. Surely there was someone here to welcome me.

Cressida, in a beautifully tailored winter-white wool dress, was
standing near the dais at the front talking to John Abbot, who was holding out a copy of Cressida's bound galley to her. I noticed that there
was a stack of them on a low table next to a framed portrait of Leia. It
seemed a little questionable for Cressida to use Leia's memorial as an
opportunity to promote her own book, but then I remembered that
she planned to dedicate the book to Leia and figured that's why she
had brought the copies. At any rate, she looked busy, so I decided I
shouldn't bother her. I saw Abbie, but she was sitting next to Joan and I
didn't feel like hearing another rant about Troy's grammatical failings.
Finally I spotted Dottie sitting in the front pew. I hurried over to her,
wishing she hadn't sat up front. I could feel the eyes of the assembled
mourners on the back of my neck as I sat down.

She patted my hand. "I'm glad you made it, Nan. I was worried you
wouldn't feel comfortable."

I almost laughed. When was the last time I'd felt comfortable? *In
Joe's arms*, a voice suggested, making me blush.

Dottie read the color in my face as something else. "I just want to say that I think it's completely unfair and inappropriate."

"What's unfair and inappropriate?" I asked, looking behind me and meeting the accusatory glare of Sue Bennet.

Before Dottie could answer, Cressida came over and sat down next to me. "Did you bring something to read, Nan?"

I took out the "Pins" story. "Leia left this for me the day she died. It's quite lovely and I thought it would go well after the quilting poem Dottie's going to read."

"May I see it?" Cressida asked. "So I can estimate how long it will take to read?"

I handed her the pages. She put on the reading glasses that were dangling from her neck and bent her head to the page. While she looked at it I turned back to Dottie and repeated my question, "What's unfair and inappropriate?"

Dottie looked like she was about to cry. "I shouldn't have said anything!" She got out her phone and tapped on a page open to "Overheard at Acheron." She handed me the phone and I read the comment on the top of the page.

"To be a true writer you must experience everything," Professor Lewis exhorted her students. And so Troy Van Donk and Leia Dawson embarked on a drug spree that ended in both their deaths.—Posted by Kelsey Manning.

"What the hell!" I said too loudly for the quiet chapel. "Where did she get this? Troy's death hasn't even been confirmed . . . and how does she know about Troy and Leia's involvement with drugs?"

"Don't look at me," Dottie said, tears filling her eyes. "It could have been Abbie. The police told her about the drug connection so they could search the campus. Or it might have been Van—he's pretty angry about you and Joe showing up at the garage and scaring Troy off like that. But of course it's ridiculous. You'd never say anything like that to impressionable young students."

But I had. I heard myself saying it. *You have to experience everything, no matter how painful.* "I meant that they shouldn't run from the hard stuff—that they should let themselves experience it—not that they should seek out drug dealers and shoot heroin."

"Of course that's all you meant," Cressida said, handing me back the pages. Her face was pale, her voice strained. "Unfortunately people who aren't writers won't understand that. I'll have a word with Sue Bennet to make sure she doesn't disrupt the reading."

"Maybe it would be better if I left," I said, getting to my feet.

"If you think so—" Cressida said.

"Of course Nan shouldn't leave," Dottie cried, pulling me back down. "Leia loved you. She'd want you to be here."

I turned to Dottie; her kind, dimpled face was the opposite of Cressida's pinched one. Tears threatened to spill from her eyes. She needed me to stay. I squeezed her hand. "Thank you, Dottie, I'll stay." I looked back at Cressida. "I don't have to read if you think it will upset anyone."

"I won't have Sue Bennet drive you out. I'll speak to her." Cressida strode down the center aisle, boot heels clicking on the stone floor, braids swinging. I almost felt sorry for Sue as Cressida swept down on her. I couldn't hear what she was saying but when Cressida was done Sue looked as pale as Cressida had a moment ago. Cressida, on the other hand, was glowing as she walked back up the aisle. Perhaps it was the light of the candles in the tall holders on either side of the dais. Or perhaps it was the righteous fervor of putting Sue Bennet in her place. As she stood at the center of the dais, Cressida looked like one of the glowing saints in the stained-glass windows behind her.

"We have come together this evening to celebrate the life of Leia Dawson," she began, her voice filling the stone chapel. "Although Leia's short life was tragically severed, she lived it to the fullest. Writers come into this world knowing they must experience everything"—Cressida's blue eyes fastened defiantly on the back of the chapel, at Sue Bennet, I suspected—"and Leia was a true writer. Tonight we will let her speak for herself. We'll let her words fill this sacred space and radiate out into the world—for that's the true immortality a writer seeks—*so long lives this, and this gives life to thee.*" Cressida paused a moment for the Shakespeare quote to sink in and then began again in a softer voice. "Here is a poem Leia wrote in my advanced poetry seminar last semester."

She read an elegant sonnet about the shortness of summer that so echoed the brevity of Leia's own life I could feel the indrawn breath of grief sucking all the air out of the chapel. I felt Dottie's hand steal into mine. She knew it would make me think of Emmy. I gave her a reassuring squeeze back to tell her I was all right—and I was. When I closed my eyes I saw Emmy's face, brighter than the candles in the chapel, and heard her voice singing about the little tugboat. How could she be gone if I carried her image and voice inside me?

John Abbot followed with a short ghost story that was unexpectedly chilling. Abbie Martin read a letter Leia had written to her telling her how valuable her time at Acheron had been. Joan Denning read a poem called "Bluebird" that she said Leia had given her because she knew how much she loved birds. In each piece, whether funny or sad, arch or wry, lyrical or bawdy, I heard Leia's voice. Her range was remarkable—changing like a chameleon for the teacher, reader, or audience the piece was intended for. Yes, Troy had been right. Leia had played a part for each of us, trying out new voices, reflecting back what we wanted to hear and see. But didn't we all? she seemed to be asking.

When Dottie got up to read the quilting poem, I was afraid she was crying too hard to read, but she took a deep breath, held up the crumpled sheet of paper in a trembling hand, and read in a surprisingly strong voice.

How to Piece a Quilt

First choose your scraps—

Gingham from the baby blanket
Your parents wrapped you in

Pink for the girl they wanted
Soft for the life they wanted for you.

Blue velvet from the dress
You wore to church
Where you learned to be quiet
Where you prayed for grace.

Denim for the miniskirt
The boys liked you in
That brushed your thighs
Like too eager hands.

White satin for the prom dress
You never wore
Bruised as the flowers
Crushed against your breast.

Red leather for the jacket
You wore like armor
Bright as laughter
Hiding tears.

Piece them all together.
Hope no one sees the stitches.

The last line echoed in the chapel. Dottie lowered the page and looked out for a moment as if she'd forgotten where she was. I got up and met her at the dais, put my arm around her. She stirred to life and gave me a grateful look as she sat down. I turned and faced the pews, at the faces tilted up, like cups of gold in the candlelight. I unfolded the pages and read, thinking as I began the first line that it could have been written for this silent chapel.

"It's quiet in here—"

"Murderer!"

My head jerked up to see Sue Bennet standing in the last row. Everyone had turned around to stare at her.

"You sent Leia to her death!" she cried.

John Abbot stood up and approached Sue, his hands patting the air as if he was trying to put out a fire.

"Sue, please . . ." Abbie's voice was more plaintive than authoritative. "We know it wasn't Nan who ran over Leia."

"She told Leia to try heroin. Leia made her drug connection in *her* class." I could have pointed out that she'd made that connection in the prison, where she taught in Cressida's program. I looked for Cressida now. Hadn't she talked to Sue? Couldn't she do anything to stop her?

But Cressida was standing in the aisle, one hand over her mouth, the other folded across her waist, looking at me. She had the same look on her face that she'd had the night of the Christmas party. Like she was very sorry but really, what could she do? I'd gotten myself into this mess.

And I had. Sue was right—I'd sent Leia to her death. Not as Sue thought, but because I hadn't listened to her. I hadn't seen her. I'd seen a girl with a perfect future who made me too envious to look at when actually she was a girl stitched together from scraps, just trying to hold them all together. Like the rest of us.

I folded Leia's story in half and left the dais. Instead of going back to my seat I walked straight down the aisle, not looking to my left or right, and out the door into the night.

CHAPTER TWENTY-SIX

I drove home, my vision blurred with tears, not caring how fast I took the curves on River Road or what might be fixing to jump out of the shadows. I didn't think there could be any more surprises tonight. *Stupid!* I said to myself, thumping the steering wheel with the heel of my hand. To think I'd be welcomed back into the fold. To think it was all going to be all right.

I'll just have to leave Acheron, I told myself. I was ready, wasn't I? Wasn't that why I'd given away Emmy's things? And gone today to see Ross? And dropped off Oolong's food at Hannah's?

The thought of Oolong brought a jolt of pain. Someone in this god-forsaken town had killed my cat and thought a loaf of bread made up for it. How the hell could I stay in such a place? I'd leave—

And lose Joe. He was rooted here. He couldn't leave—*wouldn't* leave for someone he'd just met—would probably be grateful I was going. He was probably already regretting that he'd hooked up with me—or why else wasn't he here? I thought as I pulled up to my house. *Following a lead* sounded like a generic cop excuse, like *working late at the office, honey.* He was sending me a message, trying to back off tactfully.

Another jolt of pain shot through me as I got out of the car. This time I recognized its source—my ribs. Well, I had something for that.

I went to the kitchen, fished the Vicodin out of the cupboard, and took two with a mouthful of water straight from the faucet. When I lifted my head I was looking straight at the bottle of Glenlivet. I'd wondered earlier why I hadn't poured it down the drain and now I knew. Some part of me had known that the resolution to stop drinking wouldn't last. That the moment things went wrong I would be right back here staring at that bottle. And things certainly had gone wrong.

I took the Glenlivet and both bottles of Vicodin from the cabinet and carried them to my desk. I lined them up under the window just as I'd lined up the candles last night. In the light of my desk lamp the orange plastic bottles and the golden scotch glowed feverishly. I sat back to look at the still life I'd created. It might be one of those Dutch vanitas paintings. All I needed was a rotting piece of meat or a skull. Instead I had a small stack of books left over from the Great Books class—*The Odyssey*, *The Aeneid*, Dante's *Inferno*—a trip to hell in every one! Even Cressida's galley, which lay on the top of the stack, had an appropriately doom-and-gloom title—*The Sentences*.

I took a long swallow of the scotch and stared at the bottles as if they answered a question I'd forgotten.

No, not quite forgotten.

I'd given away Emmy's things.

Said goodbye to Ross.

Made my amends with Hannah.

And not because I was moving.

Would Cressida grieve for me? I wondered. Or Dottie? I imagined them learning of my death. They would be sorry, yes, but it wouldn't be entirely unexpected. Even Anat had said she'd been afraid I'd kill myself those first years. Cressida would probably write something about it—turn the experience into art, as every true writer did. That's what she'd said about Leia tonight, that writers came into this world knowing they must experience everything, echoing the words that Kelsey had quoted me as saying in class. Had she meant to echo my words?

Had she been trying to tell Sue that she shouldn't blame me for Leia's death? Well, it hadn't worked. Nor had whatever she had said to Sue before the reading. In fact, it seemed to have fanned the flames—

Unintentionally, of course. Just as Cressida hadn't meant to make things worse by telling me about the tenure decision at the Christmas party—

I took another long drink from the bottle, then I picked up the galley, turned it over, and looked at the author photo on the back cover. Cressida at her desk, a view of snow-covered fields in the distance—

I looked closer. The view was facing east from her house and it took in the orchards, my house, and the turnaround. Hannah had said she'd seen the ice hag lurking around my house. The hair on the back of my neck rose with the familiar feeling of being watched. Cressida. She could see my house from her desk window—see everything I did—

I opened the book, half expecting to find an account of my days on its pages, but instead on the first page I read: *It's quiet in here. So quiet—*

"I can explain."

The voice sounded so reasonable, conciliatory even, that I wasn't afraid until I looked up and saw the gun in her hand.

"Cressida?" I croaked, so shocked by the sight of her still in her tailored white dress, holding a gun, I thought I must be hallucinating from the Vicodin. "Explain what? What Leia's story is doing in your book?"

"I didn't mean to copy it."

I looked down at the book and flipped through the pages, still feeling too stunned to fully register what was going on. *Cressida was holding a gun* and *Cressida had stolen Leia's story* came through as remote messages from a distant planet. "It's word for word," I said.

"I have an eidetic memory," she replied with a hint of pride in her voice. "And we were both working in the prison. I ran a quilting class too. Those pins, they were a bitch to keep track of. Sometimes I thought the inmates hid them on purpose so they wouldn't have to go back to their cells."

I stared at her—it was hard not to stare at the gun, which had a magnetic pull, but I tried to focus on Cressida. She looked calm, annoyed but not angry. *Keep her talking*, came a voice through the Vicodin haze. The voice sounded like Joe's. Although we'd never had a conversation about what to do if someone was pointing a gun at you, I was pretty sure that's what he would tell me to do.

"Yes, that must have been stressful," I said. "I've always been impressed by how much you do—your classes, the prison program, writing a book—"

"Exactly!" she said, looking grateful that I'd hit on the right answer, as if I were a student in one of her classes. "How do they expect you to teach a full load of classes and have time to produce a book every couple of years? It's easier for fiction writers—you can just make something up—but I'm a memoirist. I told my whole life story in my first book. How am I supposed to repeat that?"

I could have suggested she try writing about *other* people, but I didn't think she'd come here for constructive criticism or writing advice. She'd come because she knew I had Leia's story—the one she'd plagiarized—but surely that wasn't reason enough to kill me, unless—

Icy sweat broke out under my arms and on my brow, fear finally penetrating the Vicodin cloud. Leia had gone to see Cressida before coming to me. She would have seen an advance copy of her book. What had she thought when she saw that her teacher had stolen her writing? What had she *done*?

"You must have been under a lot of stress," I repeated, still trying to keep her calm even though anger was bubbling up along with the fear. I thought of Leia opening Cressida's galley and seeing her own words there. *That* was why she had left me the story. *That* was what she had wanted to talk to me about. "It would be natural to let something you'd read slip into your own writing." *Word for word?* "Anyone could have made that mistake."

"That's what I tried explaining to Leia. We have to read so much of our students' work that our heads fill up with their words. I swear my grammar has gotten worse over the years reading their tripe."

"But Leia's work wasn't tripe." *Not a good idea to interrupt,* Joe's voice said in my head, *not if you want to live through this.*

"No, it wasn't." She waved the gun at me. "You know what's funny?"

"No," I said. "What?"

"I gave her the job at the prison. I suggested she write about it. I made her rewrite that piece until she got it right." She pointed the gun at her own book. Her hand was wobbling—I could make a grab for it—but then she swung the gun back at me. "But was she grateful for my help? Was she grateful for the recommendations I wrote to graduate schools for her or the extra time I spent going over her writing samples? These students—they think we're all *dying* to read their first novels, like we have nothing better to do with our time. I must have read two hundred pages of Leia's work over the last two years. Is it any wonder that some of it *leaked* its way into mine? But instead of being grateful she had the nerve to try and blackmail me."

"Blackmail?"

"She said that if I gave her ten thousand dollars she wouldn't tell anyone that I plagiarized her work. As if I had ten thousand dollars just lying around my house. As if it was nothing to me."

"Did you have it?" I asked, curiosity getting the better of me. "I mean, you'd gotten the advance for the book—"

"A paltry advance. My publisher said my past sales numbers didn't justify a bigger one. Of course, I could have gotten it out of my trust fund but my bitch of a stepmother administers that and she'd have asked annoying questions. Besides, that's not the point. It was the principle of the thing."

I laughed. I couldn't help myself.

Cressida slapped me across the face with the butt of the gun. I fell to the floor, my ears ringing. Worse than the pain—the two Vicodin I'd taken with the scotch mercifully blunted that—was the shock of it. The casual ripping away of the veneer of civilized discourse. We weren't two English professors debating the ethics of literary appropriation. We were a killer and her hostage.

"Do you think it's funny to be blackmailed by your student?" She was bent over me, shouting, shoving the gun in my face.

I shook my head. Something seemed to be loose in it.

"Besides, she was lying that she wouldn't tell anyone. She had already shown you the story."

"She left it in my box," I said, sitting up and leaning my aching head against the desk leg. "Because she wanted my advice. She hadn't decided to blackmail you yet. She must have decided when Troy told her that Scully would need the money back if they dumped the heroin."

Cressida sat down on the edge of my desk and tilted her head at me. One of her braids was sticking straight up, I noticed, giving her the air of a demented Pippi Longstocking. But her face was calm—not at all like a woman who had just pistol-whipped her colleague—and curious. I had a story to tell her as well.

I explained how Shawna had died from tainted heroin and that Troy had hidden the rest of the stash in the boathouse. "She told Troy that she could get the money. Had you told her that you'd give it to her?"

"I said I could have it in a few days. She insisted I give her proof, so I went back to my house for my financial records. I was trying to figure out what I should show her. I didn't want her to get the idea I had so much money she could blackmail me for the rest of my life—don't look at me like that. People think that just because I have a trust fund I have nothing to worry about. But my portfolio took a beating back in two thousand eight and my father made some foolish investments in his later years. I have enough for now, but it has to last me my whole life. This miserable state school salary certainly won't."

"I've always thought it admirable that you work at all," I said, the truth slipping out.

This time she was the one to laugh.

"Ha! The diamond heir slaving away at a state school. The truth is, it's a condition of my trust that I work a *salaried* job. It wasn't good enough for Daddy that I write books. He didn't consider that *real* work."

I winced. "Neither does my mother," I said. "So you were trying to figure out what bank statement to show her when . . ." Her author photo came back to me. "You were at your desk and you saw Troy and Leia park in the turnaround."

"Yes. In Ross's car. At first I thought it was Ross come to see you— yes, that's how I knew about the affair. I used to see him park in the turnaround when he came to visit you. But then I saw it was Troy and Leia. I watched them walk up the hill—practically past my house— and then to the boathouse. I thought they'd just come to make out, smoke some weed, celebrate their victory over Professor Janowicz who had money to burn. But then I saw Leia running back, Troy following her, shouting at her to come back."

Come back! His voice had echoed through the woods and into my dream.

"I went down to see what was going on. I thought"—she laughed at herself—"I actually thought that Leia was in danger from Troy and that if I saved her she would reconsider blackmailing me. But then I saw Troy back off and walk away. Leia was walking to River Road. I saw the car—Ross's Peugeot—parked in the turnaround, the keys in the ignition. Careless kids. I just thought I'd follow her, offer her a lift, tell her that I'd return the car and not tell Ross she'd taken it. I wanted to catch up with her before someone else came along. I may have taken the curve a little fast . . . and she turned and looked right at me, as if she knew it was me, as if she knew I'd come following her to beg her to let me off the hook. I swear, she looked so . . . *smug.*"

I pictured Leia turning her long, swanlike neck to look behind her, seeing the Peugeot—

"She thought it was Troy."

"I couldn't help it. She made me so . . . *angry.* I hit the gas. I think I just wanted to scare her, to wipe that smug expression off her face, but then the car lurched forward and skidded in the snow. The car hit her."

The car. Not her.

"I wasn't going to drive away—I got out to help her but she was already dead. I had my phone out, I had already started calling nine-one-one."

"But then you saw my car."

"Yes! It was such a strange coincidence. It felt almost . . . *fated*. I figured you must have passed out. I checked to see if you were in the car but when I saw you weren't I thought you'd gone home. Then I saw you in the woods unconscious. I thought . . ." She looked down at me and then at the desk. I knew she was looking at the pills.

"You thought I had killed myself."

"Yes. To tell you the truth, Nan, I've always wondered why you didn't do it years ago instead of slowly drinking yourself to death. I don't know how you can live knowing that you caused your own child's death. I don't know how you could bear it."

"How have you found living with Leia's death?" I asked, unable to stop myself.

"That's different!" she snapped. "Leia's not my daughter and she drove me to it."

"Like she drove you to set me up for it?"

"I thought you were dead—or would be by morning. So what did it matter if everyone thought you'd run over Leia first? It made sense."

"So you dragged Leia into the ditch under my wheel. Weren't you concerned that the police wouldn't find her blood on my car?"

"I smeared some of her blood on your tire. I figured that would be good enough for the idiots in our local constabulary—and if it wasn't they'd find Ross's car. I even had Ross's cuff link. It came out of Leia's jacket pocket when I dragged her. Leia must have picked it up when she took the keys out of the dish in Ross's kitchen. I figured if the police didn't believe you killed Leia, I could implicate Ross."

"Is that why you tried to kill Ross?" I asked, taking a chance.

"He called and asked me to come over. I thought he'd seen me bringing the car back to his house that night, but it turned out he only wanted to talk about reversing your tenure decision. He needed me to change my vote."

"Your vote? But I thought—"

"That I'd voted in your favor?" She smiled coldly. "A washed-up novelist who hasn't published anything—not even an article—in years? *Please.* I was offended Ross would even ask."

"So you decided to kill him?"

"I slipped Ambien into his coffee." She seemed to be bragging now. "I figured I could pin everything on him and the police would stop looking. I hadn't expected you to show up or that Officer Joe would be so diligent. Speaking of whom, we ought to get going. He's probably realized by now that the anonymous tip that got him down to Poughkeepsie was a fake."

I felt an absurd surge of relief that Joe hadn't made up the "following a lead" excuse—cut short by realizing what she'd just said.

"Go where?"

"Well, Nan, that's up to you." She picked up one of the pill bottles in her gloved hand and rattled it at me. "It looks like you were planning an exit of your own. You can continue with that—I even have a few extra Ambiens to add to the mix—or you could opt for a more scenic dive into the river. No one will be very surprised after what happened in the chapel. All you've been through—someone killed your cat, for God's sake!"

I stared at her. "You killed Oolong, didn't you?"

She sighed. "The damned cat got out when I came here while you were sleeping at my house. I was only planning to have a look around but when it got out . . . well, I figured you only needed a little more to push you over the edge. That cat should have been put down years ago. She was only skin and bones."

I stared at her, anger now taking the place of fear. "I won't be so easy to get rid of. How are you going to force me to take those pills? If you use the gun your suicide story is ruined."

"True, but this is a very special gun with a very special provenance. I got it from one of my former students in the prison initiative. It's been used in a liquor store robbery and a drive-by shooting in the Pough-keepsie projects. Your boyfriend will deduce that one of Scully's colleagues came looking for the rest of that stash. Sadly for you, drug dealers are none too delicate in their interrogation techniques. He would start with shooting you in the kneecap"—Cressida aimed the gun at my knee—"and proceed up through other nonvital body parts before he dealt the final death blow. I'm afraid that not even the Vicodin you've been taking will dull *that* much pain."

She smiled at me. I would have accused her of bluffing but she so clearly wasn't. She was so clearly out of her mind. I didn't want to get shot in the kneecap—neither did I want to die from pills or drowning. *I didn't want to die.* The revelation was enlightening, even if it did come a little late in the plot. So which option should I choose?

The one that gives you more time, Joe's voice said in my head.

"I choose the river," I said.

CHAPTER TWENTY-SEVEN

Cressida wouldn't let me take a coat. "Suicides don't bundle up and remember their mittens." I suspected it was to discourage me from running. "But remember," she said, in case I was thinking of it, "our putative drug czar would shoot you in your legs first and then make you crawl the rest of the way to the river."

She was enjoying this role of drug czar. It occurred to me, as we began my forced march to the river, that she was as prone to playing roles as Leia had been—the wounded daughter, the ballerina, the professor, the prisoner's advocate, the concerned friend—all deftly concealing the plagiarist, murderer, and now underworld thug. When I glanced back at her, her face was stony and impassive in the moonlight. Trying to appeal to her sympathy wasn't going to save my life—and I did want to save it. That revelation hadn't been fleeting. We crested the hill and the ice-covered river appeared below us. I was stunned by how beautiful it was. An hour earlier I'd been ready to leave this world but now I couldn't imagine closing my eyes on it forever. Even the bite of cold against my skin and ache in my ribs felt good. Was it knowing I was going to die that made life seem so precious all at once? Or the combination of Glenlivet and Vicodin? I didn't care. There had to be some way to change Cressida's mind—if not by appealing to her sympathy then to her pragmatism. I searched my drug-addled brain for a good reason for her to spare me. If nothing else, at least if I kept talking someone might hear us.

"You know, it's bound to come out eventually," I said, turning my head so she could hear me, and hoping my words might carry over the frozen hills. "Leia must have shown her 'Pins' story to someone else. Your plagiarism will be revealed and then someone—Joe, for instance—will start asking questions about your role in Leia's death and mine."

"Leia never showed the piece to anyone else. She told me after she submitted it to me that she didn't want anyone else to read it. She felt that she'd *appropriated* the stories of those women in the prison. I told her she was giving them voice and she said that was an arrogant assumption—what a righteous little prig! To call me arrogant!"

"But she showed it to me. She might have shown it to someone else—Ross, for instance."

"No, I checked on that when I went by for my little chat with him. He said Leia was going on about something to do with plagiarism that night but he thought *she* had possibly stolen someone else's work. Before she could tell him what was really on her mind, though, you burst into the kitchen and interrupted her. Thanks for that, Nan. Your hysteria over not getting tenure has been very useful."

"She might have told Troy."

"Troy's dead," she snapped. "And good riddance. He was a posturing idiot, with all his Hemingwayesque macho prose and overinflated Greek allusions." She went on harshly critiquing Troy's writing and then the literary failings of the rest of her students. I let her. Her voice echoed off the icy hills. It gave me time to think, to find some flaw in her plan. There must be some mistake she'd made that would expose her, but even if I came up with one she would dismiss it. She was the one who was arrogant. She believed that she'd plotted this scenario out perfectly, that all she had to do was dispose of me and she would be free to bask in the success of *The Sentences*, no doubt enjoying the irony that she had evaded her own prison sentence.

We had reached the train tracks, which had been shoveled out by Amtrak crews. I listened for an approaching train, thinking I might be able to attract the attention of a passenger—a thought that made me laugh.

"What's so funny?" Cressida asked.

"I was thinking of that Agatha Christie novel in which an old woman sees a murder from a train window."

"*4.50 from Paddington*. Thanks for reminding me." She looked down at her watch, which had an illuminated dial. "The nine fifty-six will be through in ten minutes. Let's get across the tracks and into the boat-house. You have a suicide note to write."

She gave me a nudge with the gun and I stumbled over the tracks. The narrow path to the boathouse was covered with ice. The river itself had reached an uneasy stasis. It was frozen as far as I could see but this close I could hear the creak and moan of the ice moving, nudged by the current flowing beneath the surface. Even if the temperature stayed this low it would be weeks before the ice was solid enough to venture across safely. If I tried to run across it Cressida would only have to shoot me down and give me a nudge into the water. I would join Troy and Scully and our bodies would stay trapped beneath the ice until the spring thaw.

"Come on," Cressida said, "plenty of time to admire the river later. Time to make your amends. Just think of the boring AA meetings I'm saving you from."

The cold pressure of the gun against my neck propelled me into the boathouse. It was darker in here, with only the glow from the open berths to light the high-ceilinged structure. I could use this darkness, I thought, with Cressida close behind me, if I rammed back into her and knocked the gun loose I could get away and hide in the dark—

But my plans were cut short by a flare of light. Cressida had taken a flashlight out of her coat pocket. She was aiming it at the far wall.

"Over there," she said. "Under Leia's masterpiece."

I walked toward Leia's self-portrait, which was lit up by the flashlight beam. The wavering light—*she must be cold if her hand is shaking*—made it look like there was life in those eyes, as if Leia was following my progress across the slick boathouse floor. They had the same startled look they'd had in the kitchen when I interrupted her talk with Ross. *Why didn't you listen to me?* they seemed to say now. *If you hadn't been so caught up in your own problems, if you had just stopped and listened, neither of us would be here right now.*

She was right, of course, but it was too late. The irony was that I could hear her voice now. There was nothing else to hear but the creak of the ice and the stir of wings in the loft overhead.

I stopped and did what Leia was asking me to do. *Listen.* There *was* something stirring overhead in the loft. The last time there'd been the owl. I remembered looking up when it flew toward Scully. It came from the boat loft built high in the rafters, the place where the Blackwells had stored boating gear—life jackets, blankets . . . a person could hide in there and insulate themselves from the cold—

"Don't tell me you're afraid of facing Princess Leia," Cressida snapped. "Or do you believe those ridiculous ghost stories the students tell?"

I looked back over my shoulder at Cressida. The light from the flashlight cast ugly shadows on her face, making her look like a ghoul from a horror movie. But it wasn't just the light; there was fear in her face. She didn't like looking at Leia's portrait either—and she didn't like the idea of ghosts.

"You mean like the ice hag?" I asked. "You know, Hannah told me she'd seen her lurking around the house, looking in my windows."

"I'm sure Hannah Mulder sees a lot of things after a drink or ten at the Swan."

"I think she saw you that night Leia died. I think she'll tell Joe that if I die."

"And do you think anyone will believe anything Hannah Mulder says? But thank you for the heads-up. I can easily arrange for Hannah to have a little accident on her way home from the Swan. Just as easily as I arranged for her to 'leave' that bottle of Four Roses on Leia's shrine."

A floorboard in the loft creaked. I spoke quickly to cover it up.

"How many people will you have to kill, Cressida?" I asked. "Do you really think you can have all these deaths on your conscience without paying a price? Leia, Troy—"

Another creak came from the loft. There was someone up there. It could be some homeless person taking shelter, but I was hoping it was Troy. That he hadn't drowned in the river, that he'd dragged himself out and found shelter in the loft. He would be half frozen to death. The only way he could help would be if he could pounce right on top of Cressida. I had to get her directly underneath the edge of the loft.

I turned back to the painting of Leia and walked up to it, feeling a prickle at the nape of my neck as I passed under the edge of the loft.

"You can't even look at her, can you?" I said to Cressida. "A girl with her whole life ahead of her cut short because you were afraid of people finding out you plagiarized her story."

Cressida moved forward but stopped a foot or two away from the edge of the loft, her head tilted as if consulting Leia's face.

"It wasn't just that," she said. "When she came to me to ask—no, *demand*—that money she called me a leech. She said I didn't have any more of my own life to write about so I had turned to other people's lives to steal from—as if that's not what all writers do, as if that's not what *she* did when she wrote her precious poems about quilting circles or your boy Troy when he hung out with drug dealers in the projects."

I heard another creak from overhead.

"You're right," I said, hoping the surprise of hearing me agree would distract Cressida from the noise. "We are leeches. That's why I stopped after Emmy died. Because I'd cared more about getting something down on the page than about her and that moment's distraction—"

My voice wobbled. Cressida smiled, which only made her look more ghoulish in the flashlight's glare. "Poor Nan, what a terrible thing to live with. That's why artists should never have children. Well, you won't have to live with it much longer. Here—" She reached into her coat pocket. She had to hold the flashlight and gun in one hand in order to take out a red Sharpie. "You're going to write 'I'm sorry, Leia. I'm sorry, Emmy' beneath the painting. Then I'll let you take the rest of the pills and you can have a nice, quiet nap on the ice."

She was holding the pen out for me. I didn't move. I held my breath, waiting for her to come to me, hoping it *was* Troy up in the loft, hoping he saw his opportunity.

She stepped forward, the boards creaked—

She stepped back, dropping the pen and grasping the gun with two hands, the flashlight crossed over it, both aimed at the loft. "I see you, Troy Van Donk," she shouted. "Come down slowly or I'll blow your brains out."

I took a step forward and she aimed the gun at me. "And your favorite teacher's. Come down and join the party. You, Nan—over here so you can see your pet student." She waved me out from under the loft. I came forward, hoping now that I'd been wrong, that it wasn't Troy.

"Don't come down!" I called. "She's just going to kill us both."

"Yes, but it can be a quick bullet to the head or a slow, agonizing gang war execution. Which do you prefer, Mr. Van Donk?"

A hooded figure appeared at the edge of the loft and lowered himself down to the floor. The young man was so thin and scared-looking that for a second I barely recognized my cocky student, but then his eyes skittered toward me and I did.

"I'm sorry, Professor Lewis, I was gonna try to jump her but I was shaking so bad."

"Have you been hiding here since the fight with Scully?"

"Yeah. He left me for dead in the river but I got out, made a fire, found some clothes up there . . ." He pointed to the loft. "I thought *you*

were dead until I heard you two come into the boathouse yesterday."
He switched his gaze toward Cressida. "Did you really kill Leia, Professor Janowicz, all because she asked you for money?"

"She didn't ask, Van Donk, she was threatening to blackmail me."

"It was so she could give me the money to pay back Scully. So I
didn't get killed." His eyes were glassy in the glare of the flashlight as he
looked back at the painting of Leia.

"I guess Saint Leia wasn't so bad after all," I said.

"Well, you'll all have a chance to be reunited," Cressida said. "In the
great writing workshop in the sky. Troy's eleventh-hour appearance
calls for a change of plan, but I can accommodate this plot shift. Maybe
I could write fiction after all! So, let's see, Nan, what do you think of
this: kindhearted but too trusting Professor Nan Lewis went looking
for her lost student, but when she found him hiding in the boathouse
he shot her and then, in a surge of grief and self-pity, shot himself—all
with a gun he got off the lowlife scum drug dealer who tried to kill him.
How's that for a narrative even your dim-witted cop boyfriend can follow? Do you see any holes in it? Come on, don't be shy, let's workshop
this sucker!"

There was a manic glee in Cressida's voice that made my skin prickle.
The fact was, I couldn't see any flaws in the story she'd outlined. Then
I looked down.

"Your footprints," I said.

"Thanks for the reminder, Nan. I'll clean up in here. As for outside . . ." She looked over her shoulder at the open berths. "Look, it's
snowing again. The weather has been very accommodating, although
I must say that when my book takes off—which I'm sure it will, with
all the publicity it will get after the recent tragic events the author
witnessed at Acheron—I may chuck this job and move to someplace
warmer. So"—she smiled at us—"let's move this party outside. I think
an open-air shooting on the river is so much more poetic, don't you?"

I looked at Troy and nodded. We'd have a better chance of making a run for it outside, which Cressida must have known. So why didn't she shoot us right here? Was she losing her nerve?

As she waved the gun to make us move, I saw her eyes snag back on Leia's self-portrait. Was that it? Did she not want to kill us in front of those accusing eyes? Troy looked at me questioningly. I was the older one, the teacher, I should have a solution. I nodded for him to go first. I followed, Cressida behind me. If I turned on her quickly, maybe I could divert her long enough that Troy could get away. But I saw how weak and faltering Troy's steps were. He'd never be able to run fast enough.

Cressida was right. It was snowing. Light, lofty flakes falling out of a black sky. I turned my face up and felt their feathery kiss on my skin. They seemed to carry their own glow with them, lighting up the frozen river. I could see the Kingston-Rhinecliff Bridge arcing south of us, its lights a string of garland against the looming mountains. The mountains were edged with a greenish glow as if the sun, long gone, still burned somewhere on the edge of the world. If that's where I was going, if Emmy was waiting for me there, I wouldn't mind dying so much . . . but Troy didn't deserve to lose his life.

I turned at the edge of the frozen river to face Cressida. "Let Troy go," I said. "No one will take his word against yours." I turned to him. "You'll take the blame for Leia's death and mine, but at least you'll be alive. You're young. You can survive this."

"No," Cressida said, pointing the gun at Troy. "Actually, he can't."

I think I already knew that she wouldn't spare him before the gun went off, because I was already moving, already putting myself in between Cressida and Troy. Still the impact was shocking—a fireball exploding in my chest. I heard the crack of ice as I landed flat on my back. Cressida was staring down at me, shocked by this development. But Troy wasn't. Good boy, I thought, he'd seen it coming. He lunged at Cressida and knocked the gun from her hand. It skittered across the ice. I followed it with my eyes; it seemed to leave a trail of lights behind it and multiply into two guns that swam and bobbed and then blurred.

I closed my eyes and felt something brush against my face, something soft and feathery as a kiss, silky as a child's hair—

I opened my eyes and she was there, her face lit up from within, blond braids held back by pink barrettes, breath that smelled like cherry Chapstick—

"Emmy." The word came out a wet rasp. There was something blocking my throat and liquid filling my mouth as though I was already beneath the ice, already drowning.

"Wake up, Mommy," Emmy said, shaking me.

I tried to keep my eyes open, taking in every millimeter of her, but that black water was rising—

She shook me. "Wake up, Mommy, and look!"

She was pointing at something. I didn't want to look at anything that wasn't her but her voice was imperious. I looked where she was pointing. The gun lay a few feet away on the ice.

"You have to get it," she said, shaking me again.

Her touch seemed to rouse me. "Okay, honey," I told Emmy, forcing my eyes open and making myself turn over on the ice. "Mommy's getting it."

I crawled across the ice, dragging myself with my arms because I couldn't feel my legs, digging my fingernails into the ice, until I reached the gun. The cold, hard reality of it shocked me awake. *This* was real. I tried to wrap my hand around it but I couldn't grip. Then I felt Emmy's small hand on mine steadying me. I grasped the gun and turned to find Cressida and Troy. They were a few yards away in a patch where the ice was broken. Cressida was on top of Troy, pressing his face down into the water, drowning him. I pointed the gun at Cressida, Emmy's warm hand steadying mine, and fired.

Cressida was knocked back so hard that the ice below her broke off and floated free. Troy struggled to his knees, watched her go, and turned toward me. I felt Emmy's hair brush against my ear, heard her sweet, happy voice.

"Bon Boy-Osh, Scuffy!"

I started to laugh. Blood bubbled from my lips instead. I turned to find Emmy, to see her face once more—

But she was gone. The only trace of her the red lights of her sneakers retreating to the riverbank. "Come back!" I cried.

And she did. The lights stopped and then came toward me, growing larger, joining with the roar of an engine and a familiar voice. It was Joe on a snowmobile, bringing Emmy back to me. She'd be safe now. I closed my eyes, content, and let the black water rise up to take me.

CHAPTER TWENTY-EIGHT

Joe told me later that when he reached me I had no heartbeat and wasn't breathing. He administered CPR there on the frozen river, the ice breaking up around us, Cressida floating down to the sea, Van busy getting his son out of the water, until I drew in breath.

"That ice could have broken underneath us," I scolded him from my hospital bed. "You could have drowned trying to save me."

"And you could have died stepping in front of a bullet meant for Troy Van Donk. We make quite a pair."

He'd given me a smile that told me he meant us to remain a pair. He visited me every day for the next month, bringing flowers, books, and, one day, news from the aftermath of Cressida's death. When her house was searched the police found a glove with Leia's blood on it—presumably the one she used to spread blood on my tires—and a journal that Leia had kept when she was doing the prison class.

"So much for Cressida's eidetic memory," I said, glad of the distraction from the pain in my chest. The bullet had punctured a lung and narrowly missed my heart. "And all that about Leia's words *leaking* into her own work was a load of crap."

Not that I didn't have plenty of visitors to keep me distracted the rest of my hospital stay. Dottie came nearly every day bearing fresh-baked cookies and departmental gossip. Ross had agreed to step in to handle the fallout from the news story that one of the school's tenured professors had plagiarized a student's work and then killed her to keep her quiet. Dottie worked full-time through the intersession with him, answering emails, writing press releases, arranging interviews. For a while it looked like the publicity would destroy the college. If Chad and Marie Dawson had chosen to sue it might well have, but instead, just before the spring term began, they issued a statement that they were satisfied that their daughter's killer had been brought to justice by another Acheron English professor, Leia's favorite teacher, Nan Lewis.

"You're a hero, Nan," Dottie told me, her sewing needle flashing over a square of bright blue cloth.

"You're the hero," I countered. "If you hadn't called Joe . . ."

When I had left the chapel Dottie had sat there thinking about the first line I had read of Leia's story. "I knew it sounded familiar," she told me later. She opened the copy of *The Sentences*, which she'd looked at before the reading began, and read the first chapter. She said she heard Leia's voice behind the words as she sat in the chapel reading it.

"I just knew Leia had written it. She talked to me about that quilting circle all the time. I recognized things she had said to me about it and I heard her love and passion in it. I knew Cressida didn't have that kind of love for her students."

She called Joe right away and told him her suspicions. He was driving back from Poughkeepsie, the anonymous lead having dissolved into thin air, and gunned it back to my house. When he saw I wasn't there he went straight to Cressida's house. He'd walked around the dark and empty house, frantic, a bad feeling rising in him. Then, as he stood on the hill overlooking the river, he heard a voice in the distance say his name. He recognized it as my voice.

"At first I thought I was going crazy. It was like that part in *Jane Eyre* when Jane hears Rochester calling her name—"

"You've read *Jane Eyre*?" I interrupted.

He looked at me like I was crazy. "I read it in your class. Don't you remember? You said it was your favorite book, so . . ."

I told him then that I loved him.

"Because I've read *Jane Eyre*?" he asked incredulously. "Not because I realized the voice really was yours and ran down the hill to find you?"

"Both," I told him. "But mostly because of *Jane Eyre*."

Hearing me say his name hadn't been the only bit of luck he'd run into that night. He'd almost collided with Troy Van Donk Sr., out on his snowmobile, still looking for his son. Van took him to the boathouse and was able to get Troy out of the river while Joe resuscitated me.

"If Van hadn't been there with the snowmobile I don't know how I'd have gotten you up to the road and to the hospital in time."

"Remind me to thank Van," I'd said.

But it was Van who spent the rest of the winter thanking me. After Troy told his father that I'd stepped in front of a bullet meant for him, my driveway was miraculously plowed after every snowfall. When I brought my car in for its inspection (late, since I'd been in the hospital when it expired), it came back with a new bumper to replace the one dented by the deer. More than free plowing and auto care, Van spread the word throughout the village that I had saved his son's life. It turned out that Van's word in the community was stronger than any internet gossip. By the time I was released from the hospital my reputation was rehabilitated. The checker at the supermarket smiled at me and double-bagged my groceries, the proprietor of the Acheron Baking Company gave me free pie whenever I had lunch there, and when I ordered a latte at the café it was delivered with a heart inscribed in the foam. When I went to my first AA meeting in the basement of the Lutheran church, people came up to me and squeezed my hand. "Maybe they always do that at AA meetings," I told Joe afterward.

"Nah," he replied, "you're a local hero."

But I still wasn't sure about going back to the college. As hard as it had been to stand up in front of a group of strangers and tell them I was an alcoholic it seemed even harder to stand in front of a classroom of students knowing that the events that had led to Leia's death had at least partly come out of my writing class. Truthfully, I didn't even know if I believed in teaching writing anymore.

Can you even teach writing? My stepbrother-in-law Cooper liked to hector me over holiday dinners with that old chestnut.

I'd always thought it was a stupid question. No one asked if you could teach the violin or how to play basketball. But now I found myself asking another question: *Should I teach writing when I haven't written a word of my own work for years?* Writing hadn't pulled me out of the pit. The people who loved me—Joe, Dottie, Anat, the Van Donks—had. Could I really stand in front of a class of twenty students and tell them writing could save their lives?

I was no closer to an answer the first week of the spring term when Ross came to my house to plead with me to take my creative writing section along with Cressida's and her memoir workshop. "We're a teacher short," he told me. "We can't afford to lose you. Abbie has ordered a review of your tenure decision next year on the grounds that your leading detractor tried to kill you. I'm sure it will go better this time. Please, Nan, those students are lining up to get into your classes."

I suspected that most of those students had been drawn by morbid curiosity—Come see the professor who stopped a speeding bullet!—but I gave in to Ross's request, if only because Dottie said she didn't know how they would manage the schedule if I didn't.

"I'll teach this semester," I told him, "but I can't promise anything after that."

So I dove into teaching a full load—two creative writing workshops, Cressida's memoir class, and an advanced fiction seminar. After a week of silly questions—*Did you really say a writer should experience everything? Have you sold the movie rights to your story yet?*—we settled into learning the craft of writing by example and practice. We read Chekhov and Carver, Hemingway and Junot Díaz. We talked about voice, characterization, dialogue, exposition, chronology, narrative arc, and revision. My students wrote stories about their childhood pets, their parents' divorces and deaths, their bad breakups, their fears and hopes for the future. One young man wrote a story set in the Middle Ages about a blacksmith's son who is blinded when he witnesses his sister being killed by a wandering apprentice. An exchange student wrote a funny, irreverent piece about growing up Mormon in Scotland. One girl wrote a story about a boy who returns to the site of his twin's drowning in the Colorado desert that took my breath away with its mastery of setting and mature vision. I was so busy and engrossed with my students' work that I didn't think I could add one more thing to my schedule, but then in March Dottie handed me a phone message from Cressida's editor.

"What could she be calling me about? Do you think they blame the department for Cressida's plagiarism? Shouldn't Ross handle this?"

"She especially asked for you," Dottie told me.

I waited two days and then called her after classes on a Friday. She told me that the publisher had, of course, pulled Cressida's book.

"Such a shame," she said. "It was a beautiful book."

"Yeah, well," I said, "*Leia* was a good writer."

"Yes, that's what I wanted to talk to you about." She'd heard that the police had found Leia's original journal and she wondered if it wasn't possible to sort out what was Leia's from Cressida's and do something with *that*.

"I suppose . . ." I began.

"The thing is, I need someone with a sensitive touch, a good sense of narrative—I loved your first book, by the way . . ."

When I realized she was asking me to edit Leia's work I told her I couldn't possibly. We'd have to talk to her parents—

But she'd already spoken with the Dawsons, who had agreed on two conditions—that half the proceeds of the book go to a drug prevention program and that I be the editor.

"They say that Leia trusted you."

I got off quickly, saying I'd think about it. I told Joe that night that I planned to say no. "Yeah, I can see that . . . but Leia's journal's been released to the Dawsons and they said they planned to send it all to you."

The next day I got a package from the Dawsons. It contained a black-and-white marbled composition book that Leia had kept as her journal while teaching at the prison. I stuck it on my desk, where it was soon buried under a stack of student papers. While I was straightening up over spring break, though, I noticed it and felt a pang of guilt. I should at least read through the journal and write back to the Dawsons.

I sat down at my desk one rainy morning and started reading and kept reading all day. I could hear Leia's voice as I read—funny and posturing at times as she took in the experiences of teaching at the prison, and vulnerable and scared at others. *A woman told me today that if only she'd gone to school instead of ditching the day the police raided her boyfriend's apartment she'd be in college now instead of prison. It made me wonder how many mistakes I'll make along the way and what price I'll pay for them.*

I looked up from the notebook into my own reflection in the darkened glass. I wanted to tell Leia that she'd paid too high a price for the mistake she'd made—and because I'd been hearing her voice in my head all day long I thought I heard her say: *So did you.*

I called up the editor the next day and told her I'd help her edit Leia's journal. "Great!" she said. "Have your agent get in touch with me and we'll work out a deal. Can you have it for me by June? And can I get you to write a foreword?"

I told her I'd have it for her by the end of my summer break. Then she asked me a question that I had been asking myself for the last few months. "What do you think Cressida was *thinking* when she was copying her student's writing into her own book? I mean, did she think Leia wouldn't recognize her own work and complain?"

"I don't know," I admitted. "I read *The Sentences* last night. It's not *all* Leia's work but bits of Leia's writing are all over it. Maybe it really was unconscious borrowing—or maybe Cressida thought she could bully Leia into keeping quiet about it by giving her a good recommendation for grad school. I don't suppose we'll ever really know for sure."

I put aside Leia's journal, telling myself that I didn't have time to work on it before summer break. Besides classwork I was helping Dottie arrange a dedication ceremony in the Peace Garden. At first I'd been leery of yet another memorial, but Dottie had coaxed me by explaining that it wasn't a memorial exactly. The Friends of the Peace Garden had received a grant to restore one of the original statues. When Dottie showed me a picture of the statue I said I would help.

Dottie fretted over the weather forecast for the day of the dedication ceremony. It said rain. "We can set up refreshments on the chapel porch," I reminded her. "And the garden will still be beautiful in the rain. The flowers this year are spectacular."

They were. Perhaps it was because I'd shut myself inside during the last weeks of the spring semester for the last seven years—or maybe it was because I'd stopped drinking that my senses had become sharper. The orchards were thick with heavy pink blooms, River Road was edged with drifts of white hawthorn and wild violets, the beds in the Peace Garden were a patchwork of perennials. I often ate my lunch in it and I held my last class there. I'd read up on the history of the garden and so I was able to tell my students that Amos Blackwell had commissioned the garden as a memorial for his drowned daughter.

"I always thought it had been named the Peace Garden by some hippies in the sixties," I told them. "But it's the name Amos gave the garden. He meant it to be a place of quiet contemplation for him and his wife after they lost their daughter."

"I guess it didn't work for the wife," one of my students pointed out. "Doesn't the story go that she drowned herself and still haunts the place?"

"Well, that's the thing about stories," I told them. "They're always changing, growing from one teller to the next, morphing to fit the time and needs of each new reader. Charlotte Blackwell did grieve for her daughter but according to her husband's diary she fell through the ice because she was chasing after her dog."

"Maybe he wrote that because he didn't want anyone to know she'd offed herself," another student said.

"I like the version where she kills herself better," another chimed in.

"See," I told them, "that's what I meant. You hear the story you want to hear." *And maybe the one you need to hear*, I thought.

The morning of the dedication ceremony was overcast but dry, ink-blue clouds massing over the mountains in the west. I drove to campus with my car windows open, inhaling the scent of hawthorn and apple blossom. The threat of rain seemed to bring out the color and scent of the flowers. When I walked into the garden I felt intoxicated for a moment with the heady mix of perfumes, as if I'd already had one of the plastic tumblers of pink champagne lined up on the refreshment table on the chapel porch. A little crowd was gathered around the new statue in the center of the garden. I saw Joe and Dottie, Ross and Abbie, John Abbot and his wife, Roisin. My mother was there too, with my niece Amanda, who was running around the garden with Aleesha's daughter, Isabel, and a dozen of my students were there, including Troy, Aleesha, and Kelsey Manning typing on her phone. I started walking toward Joe but he tilted his chin in the direction of a lone man standing on the edge of the group, looking over the balustrade at the river. I smiled at Joe and held up my hand to tell him I'd be with him in a minute and he nodded back. I walked over to the lone man standing at the parapet.

"I didn't know if you'd come."

Evan turned around. I was startled to see gray in his hair and lines around his eyes. "I wasn't sure if I would. I swore to myself I'd never set foot in this place again." He looked around the garden. "But then I remembered how much Emmy loved it. Do you remember how we had a picnic here that time and she jumped in the fountain?"

"And we had to rush home because she was soaking and you drew her a picture of Emmy the Mermaid of the Fountain—yes, I remember," I ended breathlessly.

He looked away, toward the river, his eyes reflecting the storm-gray in the approaching clouds. "I just couldn't bear to stay here with all those memories."

"I know," I said. I also knew that it wasn't just the place. When he looked at me he saw Emmy. I knew that because looking at him I saw her too. That day when I found him standing in the kitchen holding the Scuffy the Tugboat mug I hadn't just known he was leaving. I wanted him to leave. It was too painful seeing Emmy in him. But now, seeing the storm-gray of his eyes, the shape of his ears, the way he moved— for a fleeting moment I felt her here, riding a gust of moist air that smelled like the sea and ruffled the summer dresses of the women, that caught in the happy laughter of Amanda and Isabel and snatched the pink paper napkins from the refreshment table and sent them spinning around the garden like apple blossoms. Evan took a deep breath and turned back to me, braced, and then something eased in his face. As if the breeze had stroked away some of the pain there. At least for the moment. I was finding that since I'd stopped drinking the pain came in waves. I still wanted a drink when it did. But if I rode that wave instead I would come out into these brief recesses that felt like stepping onto a clean, windswept beach at dawn. As if I'd ridden the pain to someplace worth being. I could only hope that those brief moments would become longer—for him and for me.

"So what's this statue?" he asked.

I led him over to the statue standing in the middle of the garden. As if by prior agreement, the others drifted away from it as we approached so we stood in front of it alone. It was a sculpture of a cloaked and veiled woman.

"It looks like a Saint-Gaudens."

"The original was. Amos Blackwell commissioned it for his daughter. It came to be called *Grief* but it was originally called *Compassion*, modeled after a painting of the Buddha of Compassion. There's something about it—" I stared at the marble veil rippling over the woman's face, not sure why I was so drawn to it or if Evan would see what I saw.

"It's the way grief feels, isn't it?" he said. "As if a pall were hanging between you and the rest of the world."

"Yes," I said, relieved he saw it too and glad now that he'd come. "The veil separates her but it also protects her, doesn't it?"

As if in answer another gust blew through the garden, strong enough that it might have tugged that marble veil away. It brought with it a curtain of rain that sent everyone scurrying, clutching their rain-sodden pink napkins to their plastic tumblers, laughing and crowding onto the porch. Ross gave a little speech about the garden and his hope that it would be a place where anyone could find peace and hear the voices of those they had lost. Then he said Leia's name and turned to Aleesha, who said Shawna's name, and she turned to someone else, who said "Nana Marcowitz," and then my mother, who said my father's name, and so on, each of us saying the name of someone we'd lost, all those names swept up in the rain and carried out onto the river and down to the sea. I looked for Evan when I said Emmy's name and we said her name together.

The next time I saw him he was talking to Aleesha and I guessed she was thanking him for the college fund I'd transferred into Isabel's name. I'd been nervous when I called him to ask if it was all right but from the look on his face when Aleesha hugged him, I was guessing it was.

I lost track of him after that, busy helping Dottie replenish champagne and strawberry tarts and then talking to Ross and Abbie about Leia's book and then Joe came over to tell me he had to go back to the station and he'd see me later at the house. He kissed me and told me to be careful driving home in the rain. I told him I hadn't had any champagne and that besides, the rain had stopped.

A sliver of sunlight appeared between the mountains and the rain

clouds. It lit up the river and the garden and the face of the statue, turning her marble veil into a wave of gold light. It lit up the trees on River
Road, turning the canopy of new leaves into a tangle of copper and the
stone walls into amber lozenges. Mist rose from the fields, like a veil
cloaking the apple trees. I was driving a bit too fast because I wanted
to get home and get in a little writing before dinner. Although I hadn't
told anyone, I'd gone ahead and written the foreword to Leia's book,
and the day after I finished that I'd turned the page in my notebook and
written: "She came out of nowhere." It took me a day to write the next
sentence and a week to write the one after that but now the sentences
were coming quicker and quicker. I wasn't sure where the story was
going, but for now I was content to follow where the sentences were
taking me.

I came around the curve before Orchard Drive a bit too fast and
there she was. Luckily, Van had just fixed my brakes. The car screeched
to a halt three feet away from her. She stood, regarding me, her breath
misting the air, brown eyes solemn and unafraid, as if she had been
waiting for me. As she turned her long neck I followed her gaze and
noticed a long white scar along her flank . . . and then I saw the fawn following her. I waited while she led her fawn across the road and nudged
her over a bit of broken wall into the orchard. I watched them until they
vanished into the mist and then I drove home.

ACKNOWLEDGMENTS

I would like to thank the friends and family who listened to my first ideas for this book and read early drafts: Sarah Alpert, Nathaniel Bellows, Mike Kelly, Alisa Kwitney, Wendy Gold Rossi, Lee Slonimsky, Nora Slonimsky, and Maggie Vicknair.

Sergeant Patrick Hildenbrand of the Red Hook Police Department was generous and insightful in answering my questions. Any errors of police procedure are solely my responsibility.

Thanks to my editor, Sally Kim, for giving *River Road* and me a new home at Touchstone and thanks to my marvelous agent, Robin Rue, and the wonderful Beth Miller for finding that home.

Finally, I would like to thank my students and colleagues at SUNY New Paltz. Teaching writing, reading my students' work, and listening to my students bravely and generously share their stories has been both an inspiration and a bulwark against the dark. I would especially like to thank Ethel Wesdorp, Secretary of the English Department, who has all of Dottie's goodness but none of her flaws, for being a good friend throughout the writing of this book.

ABOUT THE AUTHOR

Carol Goodman is the critically acclaimed author of fourteen novels, including *The Lake of Dead Languages* and *The Seduction of Water*, which won the 2003 Hammett Prize. Her novel *Blythewood* was named a best young adult novel by the American Library Association. Her books have been translated into sixteen languages. She lives in the Hudson Valley with her family, and teaches creative writing at The New School and SUNY New Paltz.

RIVER ROAD

Nan Lewis's life has been on a downward spiral ever since her daughter, Emmy, was killed in a hit-and-run drunk driving accident on River Road six years ago. She's recently been denied tenure at the upstate New York university where she teaches creative writing. Then Nan accidentally hits a deer while driving home on River Road from a faculty holiday party. Or was it a deer? The next morning she learns that one of her favorite students, Leia Dawson, was killed in a hit-and-run on the same road, and Nan's car has significant damage. As her community turns against her, Nan must uncover who exactly killed Leia and how she's connected to this tragic event.

FOR DISCUSSION

1. Early in the novel Nan says *"That kind of woman* would have a drink right now after the ordeal of that interrogation in the police station, but I *never* drank in the daytime and *never* before class." How does Nan's denial factor into her day-to-day life? In what ways does it affect how the community treats her after Leia Dawson's death?

2. The Greek goddess of the hunt, Artemis, is traditionally associated with deer. Discuss the symbolism of Nan hitting a deer on her way home from the faculty holiday party.

3. Like Nan, Sue Bennet lost a child to a drunk driving accident and, consequentially, believes that drivers who've had DUIs "should be registered like sex offenders." Discuss Sue's belief. Do you agree with her, or no? How does grief change our view of the world?

4. Nan blames herself for Emmy's death because at the time she was too busy writing and punishes herself by not writing anymore, yet she teaches her students the Alice Walker quote "writing is a very sturdy ladder out of the pit." To what degree is Nan

culpable for her daughter's death? Do you believe that writing is a path toward emotional healing?

5. In many ways Hannah Mulder is Nan's foil and her mirror image. Compare and contrast how the two women handle trauma and grief.

6. Sergeant McAffrey observes, "a person takes a child's life, they've destroyed their own life. They'll never be free of that." Can there be personal and public absolution for someone who accidentally kills a child? Should there be? Examine the ways Nan goes from victim to publicly accused criminal.

7. All the characters in *River Road* are playing a role to a certain extent: Ross in front of his students during his lectures, Nan hiding her drinking from her co-workers, Leia in her social life. What *is* authenticity? Do you every find yourself playing a role in your own life?

8. Acheron College is named for the mythological river Acheron, which was one of the tributary rivers to the Underworld in Greek mythology, and River Road is the location where both Emmy and Leia, along with numerous other victims, have been killed in car accidents. Discuss other mythological parallels you see in *River Road*. What sort of influence does a place's name have?

9. The college legend says Charlotte Blackwell killed herself out of grief, but at the end of the book we learn, according to her husband's diary, that she died chasing after her dog on the ice. Which version resonates with you more? Why do you think the legendary version was constructed?

ENHANCE YOUR BOOK CLUB

1. Greek mythology plays a significant part in Nan's creative writing class and in *River Road* as a whole. Have each member of your group write a short modern-day version of their favorite Greek myth and take turns workshopping your pieces.

2. Consider reading *The Opposite of Loneliness* by Marina Keegan, a girl who, like Leia, was killed in a car accident right after her college graduation, as a companion book. How do you think the book Leia's family creates compares to Marina's book? How does reading a book published after the author's death change your understanding of it?

3. At the end of the book the town rededicates the Peace Garden in memory of their loved ones, and to "hear the voices of those they had lost." Create your own Peace Garden by going around and sharing stories about loved ones who have passed away too soon.

A CONVERSATION WITH
CAROL GOODMAN

Where did the idea for *River Road* originate?

In January 2013 I was driving home from a weekend trip to Boston with my husband when I hit a deer. It was dusk, the end of a long day, and the deer came out of nowhere. I pulled to the side of the road, crying, so upset my husband was more alarmed by my reaction than by my hitting the deer. We got out to look for the deer but couldn't find it. My husband reassured me that the deer was probably all right. I tried to believe him. But for the next days the feeling of that impact, that awful *thump*, stayed with me. I told people the story and wrote about it, even writing a poem for a class I was teaching, trying to exorcise the experience.

Then a week or two afterward something truly tragic happened. Two young girls, college students at Bard College, were killed in a hit-and-run. My daughter, who was going to Bard at the time, emailed me early the next morning so I'd know she was all right. The incident happened just a few miles from my house, to girls the same age as my daughter and who attended my daughter's college. Like everyone in the college and town community, I was struck by the tragedy. I read the emails from the college president, the police report, watched video of the suspect (who was caught a mile down the road buying beer, one of the girl's phones stuck in her car's bumper) walking into court. I heard people talking about the incident in the supermarket, the café where one of the girls worked, and among my daughter's friends. I was, of course, devastated for the girls and their parents most of all, but I also found myself thinking about the woman who had committed the hit-and-run. What terrible place had her life gotten to that she would do something like this? How could a person live with knowing they had taken two young lives?

It didn't at first occur to me to write about the incident, but in the next few months I kept thinking about the hit-and-run and reliving that moment of hitting the deer. I thought about it as I drove on River Road, a beautiful road a few miles from my house, and as I taught my classes at SUNY New Paltz. Eventually the character of Nan Lewis emerged in my head, a woman who had already had the worst thing that could happen to a person happen, who while driving home from a faculty party after one or two glasses of wine hits a deer and is then accused of hitting one of her students.

Early in the book you quote Margaret Atwood: "All writing is motivated deep down by a desire to make the risky trip to the Underworld, and to bring someone or something back from the dead." In what way was *River Road* a trip to the Underworld for you?

Whenever I write a book I feel that I end up taking the journey of the narrator I've chosen. I knew right away that following Nan would take me to a dark place. She's already in a low place in her life and then she does something that could potentially ruin her life forever. It felt scary to explore that and yet I was somehow compelled to. Through her own recklessness Nan has done something that neither she nor the community she lives with would ever forgive her for. I didn't know until I'd written the first chapter that Nan had lost a child herself. I've actually never written about a character who had lost a child because, as a mother, it is such a deep-seated fear. When I began the book I literally could not imagine how anyone lived through that. Writing this book was my own way of imagining how someone might.

That Margaret Atwood quote has always resonated with me. I believe that one of the main reasons we write is to bring back to life the people we've lost—or parts of our past and self that we've lost—even if doing that means traveling to a dark place.

Who or what were your inspirations for the Blackwell family and the ice hag?
There are some wonderful old mansions along the Hudson River near where I live. They have some spooky stories associated with them that I've borrowed from. The Blackwell machine factory is actually taken from an abandoned factory, called Sedgwick Machine Works, that I can see from the train window just south of Poughkeepsie. As for the ice hag, well, I wrote *River Road* during an extremely snowy winter. It was easy to imagine that the ice and snow was a malevolent force!

As a creative writing teacher at SUNY New Paltz, how much of your own teaching experience did you incorporate into *River Road*?
Lots! I'm continually amazed by the stories my students write in my classes. Around the time I started thinking of *River Road* I taught a class in which some of my students asked if they could write memoir pieces instead of fiction. They'd tell me something that was going on in their lives and say, I just need to write about that. So of course I said, yes, you do. I was impressed by their honesty and bravery in writing about painful events in their lives and touched by their own accounts of how writing about those events helped them understand them. I wanted to honor that in *River Road* while also depicting a teacher who is evading her own pain by immersing herself in her work. Teaching is a very demanding and all-encompassing activity. You can easily lose yourself in it. I think that in the end, though, it's part of what leads Nan out of her darkness.

Near the end of *River Road*, Nan expresses doubt about whether writing can save someone's life: "writing hadn't pulled me out of the pit. The people who loved me—Joe, Dottie, Anat, the van Donks—had." Which side of the argument do you fall on?

I'm not sure it's an argument. I think ultimately writing comes from life, from the people we know and love (and even the ones we dislike), and that you can't have one without the other. I think writing is a way of understanding life and people better, so if writing is saving your life, well, it's really the people in your life that have given you that.

You also write books for young adults. Is your writing process different when writing adult versus YA books?

Not really. I always start with a character who's in a difficult situation and explore what happens to her next. In my Blythewood books I wrote about a sixteen-year-old girl who has lost her mother and has to make her way in the world—and then happens to end up at a magical school. I wrote it the same way I write all my books, the narrator just happened to be sixteen years old. But because she's sixteen years old her voice is different—she's more emotional than, say, Nan Lewis. She notices different things.

Nan follows in a long and great tradition of unreliable female narrators. Why do you think readers respond to these anti-heroes?

I think because we don't know whom to trust. When someone tells us a story, do we believe them? Do we even completely understand our own actions? Are we completely honest with ourselves? The present popularity of the unreliable narrator I think comes from the possibilities of surprise and suspense inherent in believing the wrong person.

River Road deals a lot with the transformative power of writing on both the reader and the writer. How do you think being a writer has affected your life?

I literally can't imagine my life without writing. I began writing when I was nine years old. I wrote a story about a girl named Carol who goes to live with a wild herd of horses. No mention is ever made of Carol's human family. So very early I was using writing as an imaginative escape. I continue to use writing to think through and deal with what happens to me and what I see around me, trying to make some narrative sense out of the chaos of life. Writing has also compelled me to look at all sides of a question, to always consider what an experience looks like from the point of view of someone else. And it's made me a much nosier person than I am by nature. I'm always listening to other people's conversations and asking questions. There's a great line in the HBO show *Girls* when Hannah, following suspicious sounds to her friend's bedroom, says something like "Everything is my business." Being a writer makes me feel as if the whole world is my business.

What are you working on next?

I am working on a middle-grade novel called *The Metropolitans*. It's about a group of young kids who, on the eve of World War II, have to find a magical book at the Metropolitan Museum of Art in order to stop a sabotage attack on New York City. It's a nice break from traveling to the Underworld!